P9-DEA-355

Buddy Berlin

LUCIA BERLIN (1936–2004) worked brilliantly but sporadically throughout the 1960s, 1970s, and 1980s. Her stories are inspired by her early childhood in Western mining towns; her glamorous teenage years in Santiago, Chile; three failed marriages; a lifelong problem with alcoholism; her years spent in Berkeley, New Mexico, and Mexico City; and the various jobs she later held to support her writing and her four sons. Sober and writing steadily by the 1990s, she took a visiting writer's post at the University of Colorado Boulder in 1994 and was soon promoted to associate professor. In 2001, in failing health, she moved to Southern California to be near her sons. She died in 2004 in Marina del Rey.

ALSO BY LUCIA BERLIN

A Manual for Cleaning Ladies

Legacy

Angels Laundromat

Phantom Pain

Safe & Sound

Homesick: New and Selected Stories

So Long: Stories 1987–1992

Where I Live Now: Stories 1993–1998

Additional Praise for *A Manual for Cleaning Women*

"This new selection of short stories establishes [Lucia Berlin] as a singular, remarkable writer worthy of a wide audience."
　　　　　　　　　　　　　　　　　　　　—*The New Yorker*

"[Lucia Berlin] might be the most interesting person you've never met. . . . Every detox ward, dingy Laundromat, and sunbaked Mexican palapa spills across the page in sentences so bright and fierce and full of wild color that you'll want to turn each one over just to see how she does it. And then go back and read them all again."
　　　　　　　　　　　　　　　—*Entertainment Weekly* (Grade: A)

"This revelatory collection [introduces Berlin] as an uncompromising and largehearted observer of life whose sympathies favor smart, mouthy women struggling to get by. . . . With their maximalist emotions and sparse, unadorned language, Berlin's stories are the kind a woman in a Tom Waits song might tell a man she's just met during a long humid night."
　　　　　　　　　　　　　—*The New York Times Book Review*

"[Berlin is] the literary godmother, it seems to me, of tough women writers like Jennifer Egan and Rachel Kushner. . . . Berlin had been around the block a few too many times to sugarcoat things. But her hard-earned, one-of-a-kind voice and vision make these stories well worth the pain."　　　—Maureen Corrigan, NPR's *Fresh Air*

"Lucia Berlin's electrifying posthumous collection *A Manual for Cleaning Women* is a miracle of storytelling economy, showcasing this largely unheard-of writer's genius for streetwise erudition and sudden, soul-baring epiphanies."　　　　　　　　　　—*Elle*

"[These stories] showcase a singular if unsung American voice."
—*Vogue*

"Marvelous . . . Berlin's beautiful, rangy prose builds into unpredictable shapes that speak of the sprawling rural and urban western and South American landscapes that fueled her imagination."
—Laird Hunt, *The Washington Post*

"[Berlin's stories] alternate between light and dark so seamlessly and suddenly that a certain emotion barely fades before you feel something abruptly different. The bleakness of some of her subjects—alcoholism, suicide, sickness—belies her wonderful gift for coaxing humor from the most improbable material. The comic moments, in turn, shade into deep poignancy. The result is a fictional world of wide-ranging impact, a powerful chiaroscuro that manages to encompass the full spectrum of human experience."
—*The Boston Globe*

"A writer's writer whose posthumous, highly semiautobiographical collection will catapult her into a household name. Women who behave badly oscillate beautifully between funny–ha-ha and funny-sad, in these perfectly clipped, nuanced stories."
—*Marie Claire*

"The brilliant, iconoclastic Lucia Berlin (1936–2004), whose surreally vivid life may out-blaze Frida Kahlo's, should have been honored as a national treasure while she lived. . . . Berlin's prose—raw, jangly, wide-open, nervy, compassionate—is like no one else's, leading us through exploding-kaleidoscope ordeals, by turns funny, tragic and filled with strange grace."
—*San Francisco Chronicle*

"This writing affirms . . . Berlin's rightful place in the canon of American short fiction." —*The New Republic*

"The reemergence of Ms. Berlin's work a little more than a decade after her death feels less like an archaeological discovery than a spotlight belatedly sweeping onto a contemporary. Her stories speak in a voice at once direct and off-kilter, sincere and wry. They are singular, but also immediately accessible to anyone raised on the comic searching of Lorrie Moore or the offbeat irony of George Saunders." —John Williams, *The New York Times*

"In sensibility and tone and grace, *A Manual* reminds me of the stories of Chekhov and Eudora Welty and Barry Hannah . . . but in other respects it reminds me of no one else at all. It's as if Berlin had looked around and seen an empty space in fiction that no one else had noticed, so she decided to fill it with as much life as it could hold—and it turned out it could hold all of it." —*Chicago Tribune*

"The vivacity, humor, sorrow, pragmatism, and sheer literary star power that fill the forty-three stories collected in *A Manual* hit with such immediacy and vigor that it seems unbelievable that their author, Lucia Berlin, died in 2004, at the age of 68, before most of us ever knew about her. . . . Anyone who loves the stories of Grace Paley and Lorrie Moore will find another master of the form here." —*Newsday*

"Those unfamiliar with Berlin's fiction are advised to read *A Manual for Cleaning Women* at least twice, for essentially this is a memoir of the author's life related in installments and fragments that fit together upon a second reading and generate a consider-

able emotional power. It is an achievement greater than the sum of its heterogeneous parts."
—Joyce Carol Oates, *The New York Review of Books*

"Sometimes compared to Raymond Carver or the Denis Johnson of *Jesus' Son*, I like her better. If this sounds crazy, read the book."
—Thomas McGuane, *Publishers Weekly*
("Top Authors Pick Their Favorite Books of the Year")

A Manual for Cleaning Women

SELECTED STORIES

Lucia Berlin

Edited and with an Introduction by Stephen Emerson
Foreword by Lydia Davis

Picador   Farrar, Straus and Giroux   New York

This is a work of fiction. All of the characters, organizations, and events portrayed in this novel are either products of the author's imagination or are used fictitiously.

A MANUAL FOR CLEANING WOMEN. Copyright © 1977, 1983, 1984, 1988, 1990, 1993, 1999 by Lucia Berlin. Copyright © 2015 by the Literary Estate of Lucia Berlin LP. Foreword copyright © 2015 by Lydia Davis. Introduction copyright © 2015 by Stephen Emerson. All rights reserved. Printed in the United States of America. For information, address Picador, 175 Fifth Avenue, New York, N.Y. 10010.

picadorusa.com • picadorbookroom.tumblr.com
twitter.com/picadorusa • facebook.com/picadorusa

Picador® is a U.S. registered trademark and is used by Farrar, Straus and Giroux under license from Pan Books Limited.

For book club information, please visit facebook.com/picadorbookclub or e-mail marketing@picadorusa.com.

Most of these stories have previously appeared in the collections *Angels Laundromat* (Turtle Island, 1981), *Phantom Pain* (Tombouctou, 1984), *Safe & Sound* (Poltroon, 1988), *Homesick* (Black Sparrow Press, 1991), *So Long* (Black Sparrow Press, 1993), and *Where I Live Now* (Black Sparrow Press, 1999). Stories from *So Long* and *Where I Live Now* are preprinted by permission of David R. Godine. The story "B.F. and Me" appeared, in slightly different form, in *The Paris Review*.

The Library of Congress has cataloged the Farrar, Straus and Giroux edition as follows:

Berlin, Lucia.
  [Short stories. Selections]
  A manual for cleaning women : selected stories / Lucia Berlin ; edited by Stephen Emerson.—First edition.
    p. cm.
  ISBN 978-0-374-20239-2 (hardcover)
  ISBN 978-0-374-71286-0 (e-book)
  I. Emerson, Stephen, editor. II. Title.
  PS3552.E72485 A6 2015
  813'.54—dc23   2014047119

Picador Paperback ISBN 978-1-250-09473-5

Our books may be purchased in bulk for promotional, educational, or business use. Please contact your local bookseller or the Macmillan Corporate and Premium Sales Department at 1-800-221-7945, extension 5442, or by e-mail at MacmillanSpecialMarkets @macmillan.com.

First published by Farrar, Straus and Giroux

First Picador Edition: August 2016

10 9

Contents

Foreword: "The Story Is the Thing"

Lydia Davis

Lucia Berlin's stories are electric, they buzz and crackle as the live wires touch. And in response, the reader's mind, too, beguiled, enraptured, comes alive, all synapses firing. This is the way we like to be, when we're reading—using our brains, feeling our hearts beat.

Part of the vibrancy of Lucia Berlin's prose is in the pacing—sometimes fluent and calm, balanced, ambling and easy; and sometimes staccato, notational, speedy. Part of it is in her specific naming of things: Piggly Wiggly (a supermarket), Beenie-Weenie Wonder (a strange culinary creation), Big Mama panty hose (a way to tell us how large the narrator is). It is in the dialogue. What is that exclamation? "Jesus wept." "Well, I'm blamed!" The characterization: The boss of the switchboard operators says she can tell when it's close to quitting time by the behavior of Thelma: "Your wig gets crooked and you start talking dirty."

And there is the language itself, word by word. Lucia Berlin is always listening, hearing. Her sensitivity to the sounds of the language is always there, and we, too, savor the rhythms of the syllables, or the perfect coincidence of sound and sense. An angry switchboard operator moves "with much slamming and slapping of her things." In another story, Berlin evokes the cries of the "gawky raucous crows." In a letter she wrote to me from Colorado in 2000, "Branches heavy with snow break and crack against my roof and the wind shakes the walls. Snug though, like being in a good sturdy boat, a scow or a tug." (Hear those monosyllables, and that rhyme.)

Her stories are also full of surprises: unexpected phrases, insights, turns of events, humor, as in "So Long," whose narrator is living in Mexico and speaking mostly Spanish, and comments a little sadly: "Of course I have a self here, and a new family, new cats, new jokes. But I keep trying to remember who I was in English."

In "Panteón de Dolores," the narrator, as child, is contending with a difficult mother—as she will in several more stories:

> One night after he had gone home she came in, to the bedroom where I slept with her. She kept on drinking and crying and scribbling, literally scribbling, in her diary.
>
> "Are you okay?" I finally asked her, and she slapped me.

In "Dear Conchi," the narrator is a wry, smart college student:

> Ella, my roommate . . . I wish we got along better. Her mother mails her her Kotex from Oklahoma every month. She's a drama major. God, how can she ever play Lady Macbeth if she can't relax about a little blood?

Or the surprise can come in a simile—and her stories are rich in similes:

In "A Manual for Cleaning Women," she writes, "Once he told me he loved me because I was like San Pablo Avenue."

She goes right on to another, even more surprising comparison: "He was like the Berkeley dump."

And she is just as lyrical describing a dump (whether in Berkeley or in Chile) as she is describing a field of wildflowers:

> I wish there was a bus to the dump. We went there when we got homesick for New Mexico. It was stark and windy and gulls soared like

nighthawks in the desert. You can see the sky all around you and above you. Garbage trucks thunder through dust-billowing roads. Gray dinosaurs.

Always embedding the stories in a real physical world is just this kind of concrete physical imagery: the trucks "thunder," the dust "billows." Sometimes the imagery is beautiful, at other times it is not beautiful but intensely palpable: we experience each story not only with our intellects and our hearts, but also through our senses. The smell of the history teacher, her sweat and mildewed clothing, in "Good and Bad." Or, in another story, "the sinking soft tarmac . . . the dust and sage." The cranes flying up "with the sound of shuffling cards." The "Caliche dust and oleander." The "wild sunflowers and purple weed" in yet another story; and crowds of poplars, planted years before in better times, thriving in a slum. She was always watching, even if only out the window (when it became hard for her to move): in that same letter of 2000 to me, magpies "dive-bomb" for the apple pulp—"quick flashes of aqua and black against the snow."

A description can start out romantic—"the parroquia in Veracruz, palm trees, lanterns in the moonlight"—but the romanticism is cut, as in real life, by the realistic Flaubertian detail, so sharply observed by her: "dogs and cats among the dancers' polished shoes." A writer's embrace of the world is all the more evident when she sees the ordinary along with the extraordinary, the commonplace or the ugly along with the beautiful.

She credits her mother, or one of her narrators does, with teaching her that observant eye:

We have remembered your way of looking, never missing a thing. You gave us that. Looking.

Not listening though. You'd give us maybe five minutes, to tell you about something, and then you'd say, "Enough."

The mother stayed in her bedroom drinking. The grandfather stayed in his bedroom drinking. The girl heard the separate gurgling of their bottles from the porch where she slept. In a story, but maybe also in reality—or the story is an exaggeration of the reality, so acutely witnessed, so funny, that even as we feel the pain of it, we have that paradoxical pleasure in the way it is told, and the pleasure is greater than the pain.

Lucia Berlin based many of her stories on events in her own life. One of her sons said, after her death, "Ma wrote true stories, not necessarily autobiographical, but close enough for horseshoes."

Although people talk, as though it were a new thing, about the form of fiction known in France as *auto-fiction* ("self-fiction"), the narration of one's own life, lifted almost unchanged from the reality, selected and judiciously, artfully told, Lucia Berlin has been doing this, or a version of this, as far as I can see, from the beginning, back in the 1960s. Her son went on to say, "Our family stories and memories have been slowly reshaped, embellished and edited to the extent that I'm not sure what really happened all the time. Lucia said this didn't matter: the story is the thing."

Of course, for the sake of balance, or color, she changed whatever she had to, in shaping her stories—details of events and descriptions, chronology. She admitted to exaggerating. One of her narrators says, "I exaggerate a lot and I get fiction and reality mixed up, but I don't actually ever lie."

Certainly she invented. For example, Alastair Johnston, the publisher of one of her early collections, reports this conversation: "I love that description of your aunt at the airport," he said to her, "how you sank into her great body like a chaise." Her answer was: "The truth is . . . no one met me. I thought of that image the other day and as I was writing that story just worked it in." In fact, some of her stories were entirely made up, as she explains in an inter-

view. A person could not think he knew her just because he had
read her stories.

Her life was rich and full of incident, and the material she took
from it for her stories was colorful, dramatic, and wide-ranging.
The places she and her family lived in her childhood and youth
were determined by her father—where he worked in her early
years, then his going off to serve in WWII, and then his job when
he returned from the war. Thus, she was born in Alaska and grew
up first in mining camps in the west of the U.S.; then lived with
her mother's family in El Paso while her father was gone; then was
transplanted south into a very different life in Chile, one of wealth
and privilege, which is portrayed in her stories about a teenage
girl in Santiago, about Catholic school there, about political turbu-
lence, yacht clubs, dressmakers, slums, revolution. As an adult she
continued to lead a restless life, geographically, living in Mexico,
Arizona, New Mexico, New York City; one of her sons remembers
moving about every nine months as a child. Later in her life she
taught in Boulder, Colorado, and at the very end of it she moved
closer to her sons, to Los Angeles.

She writes about her sons—she had four—and the jobs she
worked to support them, often on her own. Or, we should say, she
writes about a woman with four sons, jobs like her jobs—cleaning
woman, ER nurse, hospital ward clerk, hospital switchboard operator, teacher.

She lived in so many places, experienced so much—it was
enough to fill several lives. We have, most of us, known at least
some part of what she went through: children in trouble, or early
molestation, or a rapturous love affair, struggles with addiction, a
difficult illness or disability, an unexpected bond with a sibling, or
a tedious job, difficult fellow workers, a demanding boss, or a de-
ceitful friend, not to speak of awe in the presence of the natural

world—Hereford cattle knee deep in Indian paintbrush, a field of bluebonnets, a pink rocket flower growing in the alley behind a hospital. Because we have known some part of it, or something like it, we are right there with her as she takes us through it.

Things actually happen in the stories—a whole mouthful of teeth gets pulled at once; a little girl gets expelled from school for striking a nun; an old man dies in a mountaintop cabin, his goats and his dog in bed with him; the history teacher with her mildewed sweater is dismissed for being a Communist—"That's all it took. Three words to my father. She was fired sometime that weekend and we never saw her again."

Is this why it is almost impossible to stop reading a story of Lucia Berlin's once you begin? Is it because things keep happening? Is it also the narrating voice, so engaging, so companionable? Along with the economy, the pacing, the imagery, the clarity? These stories make you forget what you were doing, where you are, even who you are.

"Wait," begins one story. "Let me explain . . ." It is a voice close to Lucia's own, though never identical. Her wit and her irony flow through the stories and overflow in her letters, too: "She is taking her medication," she told me once, in 2002, about a friend, "which makes a big difference! What did people do before Prozac? Beat up horses I guess."

Beat up horses. Where did that come from? The past was maybe as alive in her mind as were other cultures, other languages, politics, human foibles; the range of her reference so rich and even exotic that switchboard operators lean into their boards like milkmaids leaning into their cows; or a friend comes to the door, "Her black hair . . . up in tin rollers, like a kabuki headdress."

The past—I read this passage from "So Long" a few times, with relish, with wonder, before I realized what she was doing:

> One night it was bitterly cold, Ben and Keith were sleeping with me, in
> snowsuits. The shutters banged in the wind, shutters as old as Herman
> Melville. It was Sunday so there were no cars. Below in the streets the
> sailmaker passed, in a horse-drawn cart. Clop clop. Sleet hissed cold
> against the windows and Max called. Hello, he said. I'm right around
> the corner in a phone booth.
>
> He came with roses, a bottle of brandy and four tickets to Aca-
> pulco. I woke up the boys and we left.

They were living in lower Manhattan, at a time when the heat
would be turned off at the end of the working day if you lived in
a loft. Maybe the shutters really were as old as Herman Melville,
since in some parts of Manhattan buildings did date from the
1860s, back then, more of them than now, though now, too. Though
it could be that she is exaggerating again—a beautiful exaggeration, if so, a beautiful flourish. She goes on: "It was Sunday so
there were no cars." That sounded realistic, so, then, I was fooled
by the sailmaker and the horse-drawn cart, which came next—I
believed it and accepted it, and only realized after another reading
that she must have jumped back effortlessly into Melville's time
again. The "Clop clop," too, is something she likes to do—waste
no words, add a detail in note form. The "sleet hissing" took me in
there, within those walls, and then the action accelerated and we
were suddenly on our way to Acapulco.

This is exhilarating writing.

Another story begins with a typically straightforward and
informative statement that I can easily believe is drawn directly
from Berlin's own life: "I've worked in hospitals for years now and
if there's one thing I've learned it's that the sicker the patients are
the less noise they make. That's why I ignore the patient intercom." Reading that, I'm reminded of the stories of William Carlos
Williams when he wrote as the family doctor he was—his direct-
ness, his frank and knowledgeable details of medical conditions

and treatment, his objective reporting. Even more than Williams, she also saw Chekhov (another doctor) as a model and teacher. In fact, she says in a letter to Stephen Emerson that what gives life to their work is their physician's detachment, combined with compassion. She goes on to mention their use of specific detail and their economy—"No words are written that aren't necessary." Detachment, compassion, specific detail, and economy—and we are well on the way to identifying some of the most important things in good writing. But there is always a little more to say.

How does she do it? It's that we never know quite what is going to come next. Nothing is predictable. And yet everything is also natural, true to life, true to our expectations of psychology and emotion.

At the end of "Dr. H. A. Moynihan," the mother seems to soften a bit toward her drunk and mean, bigoted old father: "'He did a good job,' my mother said." This is the tail end of the story, and so we think—having been trained by all our years of reading stories—that now the mother will relent, people in troubled families can be reconciled, at least for a while. But when the daughter asks, "'You don't still hate him, do you Mama?'" the answer, brutally honest, and in some way satisfying, is: "'Oh yes . . . Yes I do.'"

Berlin is unflinching, pulls no punches, and yet the brutality of life is always tempered by her compassion for human frailty, the wit and intelligence of that narrating voice, and her gentle humor.

In a story called "Silence," the narrator says: "I don't mind telling people awful things if I can make them funny." (Though some things, she adds, just weren't funny.)

Sometimes the comedy is broad, as in "Sex Appeal," where the pretty cousin Bella Lynn sets off in an airplane toward what she hopes will be a Hollywood career, her bust enhanced by an inflatable bra—but when the airplane reaches cruising altitude, the bra explodes.

Usually the humor is more understated, a natural part of the narrative conversation—for instance, about the difficulty of buying alcoholic beverages in Boulder: "The liquor stores are gigantic Target-size nightmares. You could die from DTs just trying to find the Jim Beam aisle." She goes on to inform us that "the best town is Albuquerque where the liquor stores have drive-through windows, so you don't even have to get out of your pajamas."

As in life, comedy can occur in the midst of tragedy: the younger sister, dying of cancer, wails, "I'll never see donkeys again!" and both sisters eventually laugh and laugh, but the poignant exclamation stays with you. Death has become so immediate—no more donkeys, no more of so many things.

Did she learn her fantastic ability to tell a story from the storytellers she grew up with? Or was she always attracted to storytellers, did she seek them out, learn from them? Both, no doubt. She had a natural feel for the form, the structure of a story. Natural? What I mean is that a story of hers has a balanced, solid structure and yet moves with such an illusion of naturalness from one subject to another, or, in some stories, from present into past—even within a sentence, as in the following:

"I worked mechanically at my desk, answering phones, calling for oxygen and lab techs, drifting away into warm waves of pussy-willows and sweet peas and trout pools. The pulleys and riggings of the mine at night, after the first snow. Queen Anne's lace against the starry sky."

About the way a story develops, Alastair Johnston has this insight: "Her writing was cathartic but instead of building to an epiphany, she would evoke the climax more circumspectly, let the reader sense it. As Gloria Frym said in the *American Book Review*, she would 'underplay it, surround it and let the moment reveal itself.'"

And then, her endings. In so many stories, Wham! comes the end, at once surprising and yet inevitable, resulting organically from the material of the story. In "Mama," the younger sister finds a way to sympathize, finally, with the difficult mother, but the last few words of the older sister, the narrator—talking to herself, now, or to us—take us by surprise: "Me . . . I have no mercy."

How did a story come into being, for Lucia Berlin? Johnston has a possible answer: "She would start with something as simple as the line of a jaw, or a yellow mimosa." She herself goes on to say: "But the image has to connect to a specific intense experience." Elsewhere, in a letter to August Kleinzahler, she describes how she goes forward: "I *get* started, & then it's just like writing this to you, only more legible . . ." Some part of her mind, at the same time, must always have been in control of the shape and sequence of the story, and the end of it.

She said the story had to be real—whatever that meant for her. I think it meant not contrived, not incidental or gratuitous: it had to be deeply felt, emotionally important. She told a student of hers that the story he had written was too clever—don't try to be clever, she said. She typeset one of her own stories in hot metal on a Linotype machine, and after three days of work threw all the slugs back into the melting pot, because, she said, the story was "false."

What about the difficulty of the (real) material?

"Silence" is a story she tells about some of the same real events she also mentions more briefly to Kleinzahler, in a kind of pained shorthand: "Fight with Hope devastating." In the story, the narrator's uncle John, who is an alcoholic, is driving drunk with his little niece in the truck. He hits a boy and a dog, injuring both, the dog badly, and doesn't stop. Lucia Berlin says, of the incident, to Kleinzahler: "The disillusion when he hit the kid and the dog was Awful for me." The story, when she turns it into fiction, has the same incident, and the same pain, but there is a resolution of sorts. The narrator knows Uncle John later in his life, when, in a happy marriage, he is mild, gentle, and no longer drinking. Her last words, in the story, are: "Of course by this time I had realized all the reasons why he couldn't stop the truck, because by this time I was an alcoholic."

About handling the difficult material, she comments: "Somehow there must occur the most imperceptible alteration of reality. A transformation, not a distortion of the truth. The story itself becomes the truth, not just for the writer but for the reader. In any good piece of writing it is not an identification with a situation, but this recognition of truth that is thrilling."

A transformation, not a distortion of the truth.

I have known Lucia Berlin's work for more than thirty years—ever since I acquired the slim beige 1981 Turtle Island paperback called *Angels Laundromat*. By the time of her third collection, I had come to know her personally, from a distance, though I can't remember how. There on the flyleaf of the beautiful *Safe & Sound* (Poltroon Press, 1988) is her inscription. We never did meet face-to-face.

Her publications eventually moved out of the small-press world and into the medium-press world of Black Sparrow and then, later, of Godine. One of her collections won the American Book Award. But even with that recognition, she had not yet found the wide readership she should have had by then.

I had always thought another story of hers included a mother and her children out picking the first wild asparagus of early spring, but I have found it only, so far, in another letter she wrote to me in

2000. I had sent her a description of asparagus by Proust. She replied:

> Only ones I ever saw growing were the thin crayon-green wild ones. In New Mexico, where we lived outside of Albuquerque, by the river. One day in spring they'd be up beneath the cotton woods. About six inches tall, just right to snap off. My four sons and I would gather dozens, while down the river would be Granma Price and her boys, up river all of the Waggoners. No one ever seemed to see them as one or two inch high, only at the perfect height. One of the boys would run in and shout "Asparagus!" just as somebody was doing the same at the Prices' and Waggoners'.

I have always had faith that the best writers will rise to the top, like cream, sooner or later, and will become exactly as well known as they should be—their work talked about, quoted, taught, performed, filmed, set to music, anthologized. Perhaps, with the present collection, Lucia Berlin will begin to gain the attention she deserves.

I could quote almost any part of any story by Lucia Berlin, for contemplation, for enjoyment, but here is one last favorite:

> So what is marriage anyway? I never figured it out. And now it is death I don't understand.

Introduction

Stephen Emerson

Birds ate all the hollyhock and larkspur seeds I planted . . . sitting together
all in a row like at a cafeteria. —Letter to me, May 21, 1995

Lucia Berlin was as close a friend as I've ever had. She was also one of the most signal writers I've ever encountered.

The latter fact is what I want to write about here. Her extraordinary life—its color, its afflictions, and the heroism she showed especially in the fight against a brutal drinking habit—is evoked in the biographical note at the back.

Lucia's writing has got snap. When I think of it, I sometimes imagine a master drummer in motion behind a large trap set, striking ambidextrously at an array of snares, tom-toms, and ride cymbals while working pedals with both feet.

It isn't that the work is percussive, it's that there's so much going on.

The prose claws its way off the page. It has vitality. It reveals.

An odd little electric car, circa 1950: "It looked like any other car except that it was very tall and short, like a car in a cartoon that had run into a wall. A car with its hair standing on end."

The car was tall *and* short. Elsewhere, outside Angel's Laundromat, where the travelers go:

> Dirty mattresses, rusty high chairs tied to the roofs of dented old Buicks. Leaky oil pans, leaky canvas water bags. Leaky washing machines. The men sit in the cars, shirtless.

And the mother (ah, the mother):

> You always dressed carefully . . . Stockings with seams. A peach satin slip you let show a little on purpose, just so those peasants would know you wore one. A chiffon dress with shoulder pads, a brooch with tiny diamonds. And your coat. I was five years old and even then knew that it was a ratty old coat. Maroon, the pockets stained and frayed, the cuffs stringy.

What her work has, is joy. A precious commodity, not encountered all that often. Balzac, Isaac Babel, García Márquez come to mind.

When prose fiction is as expansive as hers, the result is that the world gets celebrated. Out through the work, a joy radiating off the world. It is writing continuous with the irrepressibility of—humanity, place, food, smells, color, language. The world seen in all its perpetual motion, its penchant to surprise and even delight.

It has nothing to do with whether the author is pessimistic or not, whether the events or feelings evoked are cheerful. The palpability of what we're shown is affirmative:

> People in cars around us were eating sloppy things. Watermelons, pomegranates, bruised bananas. Bottles of beer spurted on ceilings, suds cascaded on the sides of cars . . . I'm hungry, I whined. Mrs. Snowden had foreseen that. Her gloved hand passed me fig newtons wrapped in talcumy Kleenex. The cookie expanded in my mouth like Japanese flowers.

About this "joy": no, it is not omnipresent. Yes, there are stories of unalloyed bleakness. What I have in mind is the overriding effect.

Consider "Strays." Its ending is as poignant as a Janis Joplin ballad. The addict-girl, ratted out by a ne'er-do-well lover who's a cook and trustee, has stuck to the program, gone to group, and been good. And then she flees. In a truck, alongside an old gaffer from a TV production crew, she heads toward the city:

> We got to the rise, with the wide valley and the Rio Grande below us, the Sandia Mountains lovely above.
>
> "Mister, what I need is money for a ticket home to Baton Rouge. Can you spare it, about sixty dollars?"
>
> "Easy. You need a ticket. I need a drink. It will all work out."

Also like a Janis Joplin ballad, that ending has *lilt*.

Of course, at the same time, a riotous humor animates Lucia's work. To the topic of joy, it is germane.

Example: the humor of "502," which is an account of drunk driving that occurs—with no one behind the wheel. (The driver is asleep upstairs, drunk, as the parked car rolls down the hill.) Fellow drunk Mo says, "Thank the Lord you wasn't in it, sister . . . First thing I did, I opened the door and said, 'Where she be?'"

In another story, the mother: "'She hated children. I met her once at an airport when all four of my kids were little. She yelled "Call them off!" as if they were a pack of Dobermans.'"

Unsurprisingly, readers of Lucia's work have sometimes used the term "black humor." I don't see it that way. Her humor was too funny, and it had no axe to grind. Céline and Nathanael West, Kafka—theirs is a different territory. Besides, Lucia's humor is bouncy.

But if her writing has a secret ingredient, it is suddenness. In the prose itself, shift and surprise produce a liveliness that is a mark of her art.

Her prose syncopates and hops, changes cadences, changes the subject. That's where a lot of its crackle is.

Speed in prose is not something you hear much about. Certainly not enough.

Lucia's "Panteón de Dolores" is a wide-ranging story with great emotional depth. But it also has her alacrity. Read the passage that begins "Not listening though" and continues through "because of the pollution level."*

Or this: "Mama, you saw ugliness and evil everywhere, in everyone, in each place. Were you crazy or a seer?"

The last story Lucia wrote, "B.F. and Me," is a small one. It has no wallop or big themes, no infanticides, no smuggling, no mother-daughter or reconciliation. In a way, that's why its art is so remarkable. It's gentle; but it's fast.

She introduces the creaky old handyman who comes to work on her trailer, as follows:

[B.F. was] gasping and coughing after he climbed the three steps. He was an enormous man, tall, very fat and very old. Even when he was still outside catching his breath, I could smell him. Tobacco and dirty wool, rank alcoholic sweat. He had bloodshot baby-blue eyes that smiled. I liked him right away.

---

* In Lucia's prose, punctuation is often unorthodox and sometimes inconsistent. Speed is one of the reasons. She abhors the comma that results in a pause that would not be heard in speech, or that produces an undesired slowing of any kind. In other cases, the eschewal of a comma will result in a certain hectic quality that promotes momentum. For the most part, we have avoided sanitizing her punctuation. The same goes for a few grammatical quirks rooted in vernacular and a characteristic hurry-up shorthand.

That "I liked him right away." It's nearly a non sequitur. And in the near non sequitur lies the speed. And the wit. (Just look what it tells us about "I.")

With a writer of this caliber, you can often recognize the work in one sentence. Here is a sentence from that same, final story, still on B.F. and his aroma:

Bad smells can be nice.

It is pure Lucia Berlin. It's so corny ("nice"), so close to being just dumb. But it's true, and it's deep. Beyond that, set off against her generally urbane voice, the sentence is almost disingenuous. Which is part of why it's fast. The shift in tone, and even voice, sends us, just like that, into new terrain.

Too, the sentence is dry. (How could a bad smell really be "nice.") Dryness, it so happens—where things are more, and other, than they seem—is fast.

It's five words, all monosyllables.

Of B.F.'s stench—no, she can't call it a stench. Reek? No. She has to reach over to British slang to find a term that's strong enough but still has neutrality, still makes no judgment.

"Pong." His pong. Which brings us to—Proust.

"The pong of him was madeleine-like for me."

Who but Lucia Berlin would write that? The pong was madeleine-like.

Compiling the stories for this book has been a joy in countless ways. One was discovering that in the years since her last book and her death, the work had *grown* in stature.

Black Sparrow and her earlier publishers gave her a good run, and certainly she's had one or two thousand dedicated readers. But that is far too few. The work will reward the most acute of readers, but there is nothing rarefied about it. On the contrary, it is inviting.

Still, the constraints of a small-press audience may, at the time, have been inevitable. After all, Lucia's whole existence occurred, pretty much, *outside*.

West Coast bohemia, clerical and blue-collar work, laundromats, "meetings," stores that sell "one-shoes," and dwellings like that trailer were the backdrop of much of her adult life (throughout which, her genteel demeanor never flagged).

And it was, in fact, "outside" that gave her work its special strength.

From Boulder, she wrote to me (and here she alludes to her constant later companion, the oxygen tank):

> Bay Area, New York and Mexico City [were the] only places I didn't feel
> I was an other. I just got back from shopping and everybody kept on
> saying have a great day now and smiling at my oxygen tank as if it were
> a poodle or a child.

Myself, I can't imagine anyone who wouldn't want to read her.

A Manual for
Cleaning Women

Angel's Laundromat

A tall old Indian in faded Levi's and a fine Zuni belt. His hair white and long, knotted with raspberry yarn at his neck. The strange thing was that for a year or so we were always at Angel's at the same time. But not at the same times. I mean some days I'd go at seven on a Monday or maybe at six thirty on a Friday evening and he would already be there.

Mrs. Armitage had been different, although she was old too. That was in New York at the San Juan Laundry on Fifteenth Street. Puerto Ricans. Suds overflowing onto the floor. I was a young mother then and washed diapers on Thursday mornings. She lived above me, in 4-C. One morning at the laundry she gave me a key and I took it. She said that if I didn't see her on Thursdays it meant she was dead and would I please go find her body. That was a terrible thing to ask of someone; also then I had to do my laundry on Thursdays.

She died on a Monday and I never went back to the San Juan. The super found her. I don't know how.

For months, at Angel's, the Indian and I did not speak to each other, but we sat next to each other in connected yellow plastic chairs, like at airports. They skidded in the ripped linoleum and the sound hurt your teeth.

He used to sit there sipping Jim Beam, looking at my hands. Not directly, but into the mirror across from us, above the Speed

Queen washers. At first it didn't bother me. An old Indian staring
at my hands through the dirty mirror, between yellowing IRONING
$1.50 A DUZ and orange Day-Glo serenity prayers. GOD GRANT ME
THE SERENITY TO ACCEPT THE THINGS I CANNOT CHANGE. But
then I began to wonder if he had something about hands. It made
me nervous, him watching me smoke and blow my nose, leaf
through magazines years old. Lady Bird Johnson going down the
rapids.

Finally he got me staring at my hands. I saw him almost grin
because he caught me staring at my own hands. For the first
time our eyes met in the mirror, beneath DON'T OVERLOAD THE
MACHINES.

There was panic in my eyes. I looked into my own eyes and
back down at my hands. Horrid age spots, two scars. Un-Indian,
nervous, lonely hands. I could see children and men and gardens
in my hands.

His hands that day (the day I noticed mine) were on each taut
blue thigh. Most of the time they shook badly and he just let them
shake in his lap, but that day he was holding them still. The effort
to keep them from shaking turned his adobe knuckles white.

The only time I had spoken with Mrs. Armitage outside of the
laundry was when her toilet had overflowed and was pouring down
through the chandelier on my floor of the building. The lights were
still burning while the water splashed rainbows through them. She
gripped my arm with her cold dying hand and said, "It's a miracle,
isn't it?"

His name was Tony. He was a Jicarilla Apache from up north.
One day I hadn't seen him but I knew it was his fine hand on my
shoulder. He gave me three dimes. I didn't understand, almost said
thanks, but then I saw that he was shaky-sick and couldn't work
the dryers. Sober, it's hard. You have to turn the arrow with one
hand, put the dime in with the other, push down the plunger,
then turn the arrow back for the next dime.

He came back later, drunk, just as his clothes were starting to fall limp and dry. He couldn't get the door open, passed out in the yellow chair. My clothes were dry, I was folding.

Angel and I got Tony back onto the floor of the pressing room. Hot. Angel is responsible for all the AA prayers and mottoes. DON'T THINK AND DON'T DRINK. Angel put a cold wet one-sock on Tony's head and knelt beside him.

"Brother, believe me . . . I've been there . . . right down there in the gutter where you are. I know just how you feel."

Tony didn't open his eyes. Anybody says he knows just how someone else feels is a fool.

Angel's Laundromat is in Albuquerque, New Mexico. Fourth Street. Shabby shops and junkyards, secondhand stores with army cots, boxes of one-socks, 1940 editions of *Good Hygiene*. Grain stores and motels for lovers and drunks and old women with hennaed hair who do their laundry at Angel's. Teenage Chicana brides go to Angel's. Towels, pink shortie nighties, bikini underpants that say *Thursday*. Their husbands wear blue overalls with names in script on the pockets. I like to wait and see the names appear in the mirror vision of the dryers. *Tina, Corky, Junior.*

Traveling people go to Angel's. Dirty mattresses, rusty high chairs tied to the roofs of dented old Buicks. Leaky oil pans, leaky canvas water bags. Leaky washing machines. The men sit in the cars, shirtless, crush Hamm's cans when they're empty.

But it's Indians who go to Angel's mostly. Pueblo Indians from San Felipe and Laguna and Sandia. Tony was the only Apache I ever met, at the laundry or anywhere else. I like to sort of cross my eyes and watch the dryers full of Indian clothes blurring the brilliant swirling purples and oranges and reds and pinks.

I go to Angel's. I'm not sure why, it's not just the Indians. It's across town from me. Only a block away is the Campus, air-conditioned, soft rock on the Muzak. *New Yorker, Ms.,* and *Cosmopolitan.* Wives of graduate assistants go there and buy their kids

Zero bars and Cokes. The Campus laundry has a sign, like most laundries do, POSITIVELY NO DYEING. I drove all over town with a green bedspread until I came to Angel's with his yellow sign, YOU CAN DIE HERE ANYTIME.

I could see it wasn't turning deep purple but a darker muddy green, but I wanted to come back anyway. I liked the Indians and their laundry. The broken Coke machine and the flooded floor reminded me of New York. Puerto Ricans mopping, mopping. Their pay phone was always out of order, like Angel's. Would I have gone to find Mrs. Armitage's body on a Thursday?

"I am chief of my tribe," the Indian said. He had just been sitting there, sipping port, looking at my hands.

He told me that his wife worked cleaning houses. They had had four sons. The youngest one had committed suicide, the oldest had died in Vietnam. The other two were school bus drivers.

"You know why I like you?" he asked.

"No, why?"

"Because you are a redskin." He pointed to my face in the mirror. I do have red skin, and no, I never had seen a red-skinned Indian.

He liked my name, pronounced it in Italian. *Lu-chee-a.* He had been in Italy in World War II. Sure enough there was a dog tag with his beautiful silver and turquoise necklaces. It had a big dent in it. "A bullet?" No, he used to chew it when he got scared or horny.

Once he suggested that we go lie down in his camper and rest together.

"Eskimos say laugh together." I pointed to the lime-green Day-Glo sign, NEVER LEAVE THE MACHINES UNATTENDED. We both giggled, laughing together on our connected plastic chairs. Then we sat, quiet. No sound but the sloshy water, rhythmic as ocean waves. His Buddha hand held mine.

A train passed. He nudged me: "Great big iron horse!" and we started giggling all over again.

I have a lot of unfounded generalizations about people, like all blacks are bound to like Charlie Parker. Germans are horrible, all Indians have a weird sense of humor like my mother's. One favorite of hers is when this guy is bending down tying his shoe and another comes along and beats him up and says, "You're always tying your shoe!" The other one is when a waiter is serving and he spills beans in somebody's lap and says, "Oh, oh, I spilled the beans." Tony used to repeat these to me on slow days at the laundry.

Once he was very drunk, mean drunk, got into a fight with some Okies in the parking lot. They busted his Jim Beam bottle. Angel said he'd buy him a half-pint if he would listen to him in the pressing room. I moved my clothes from the washer to the dryer while Angel talked to Tony about One Day at a Time.

When Tony came out he shoved his dimes into my hand. I put his clothes into a dryer while he struggled with the Jim Beam bottle cap. Before I could sit down he hollered at me.

"I am a chief! I am a chief of the Apache tribe! Shit!"

"Shit yourself, Chief." He was just sitting there, drinking, looking at my hands in the mirror.

"How come you do the Apache laundry?"

I don't know why I said that. It was a horrible thing to say. Maybe I thought he would laugh. He did, anyway.

"What tribe are you, redskin?" he said, watching my hands take out a cigarette. "You know my first cigarette was lit by a prince? Do you believe that?"

"Sure I believe it. Want a light?" He lit my cigarette and we smiled at each other. We were very close and then he passed out and I was alone in the mirror.

There was a young girl, not in the mirror but sitting by the window. Her hair curled in the mist, wispy Botticelli. I read all the signs. GOD GIVE ME THE COURAGE. NEW CRIB NEVER USED— BABY DIED.

The girl put her clothes into a turquoise basket and she left. I moved my clothes to the table, checked Tony's, and put in another dime. I was alone in Angel's with Tony. I looked at my hands and eyes in the mirror. Pretty blue eyes.

Once I was on a yacht off Viña del Mar. I borrowed my first cigarette and asked Prince Aly Khan for a light. "Enchanté," he said. He didn't have a match, actually.

I folded my laundry, and when Angel came back I went home.

I can't remember when it was that I realized I never did see that old Indian again.

Dr. H. A. Moynihan

I hated St. Joseph's. Terrified by the nuns, I struck Sister Cecilia one hot Texas day and was expelled. As punishment, I had to work every day of summer vacation in Grandpa's dental office. I knew the real reason was they didn't want me to play with the neighborhood children. Mexicans and Syrians. No Negroes, but that was only a matter of time, my mother said.

I'm sure they also wanted to spare me Mamie's dying, her moaning, her friends' praying, the stench and the flies. At night, with the help of morphine, she would doze off and my mother and Grandpa would each drink alone in their separate rooms. I could hear the separate gurgles of bourbon from the porch where I slept.

Grandpa barely spoke to me all summer. I sterilized and laid out his instruments, tied towels around the patients' necks, held the Stom Aseptine mouthwash cup and told them to spit. When there weren't any patients, he went into his workshop to make teeth or into his office to paste. I wasn't allowed in either room. He pasted Ernie Pyle and FDR; had different scrapbooks for the Japanese and German wars. He had scrapbooks for Crime and Texas and Freak Accidents: Man gets mad and throws a watermelon out of a second-story window. It hits his wife on the head and kills her, bounces off, hits the baby in the buggy, kills it too, and doesn't even break.

Everybody hated Grandpa but Mamie, and me, I guess. Every night he got drunk and mean. He was cruel and bigoted and proud. He had shot my uncle John's eye out during a quarrel and had shamed and humiliated my mother all her life. She wouldn't speak to him, wouldn't even get near him because he was so filthy, slopping food and spitting, leaving wet cigarettes everywhere. Plaster from teeth molds covered him with white specks, like he was a painter or a statue.

He was the best dentist in West Texas, maybe in all of Texas. Many people said so, and I believed it. It wasn't true that his patients were all old winos or Mamie's friends, my mother said that. Distinguished men came even from Dallas or Houston because he made such wonderful false teeth. His false teeth never slipped or whistled, and they looked completely real. He had invented a secret formula to color them right, sometimes even made them chipped or yellowed, with fillings and caps on them.

He wouldn't let anyone in his workshop—just the firemen, that once. It hadn't been cleaned in forty years. I went in when he went to the bathroom. The windows were caked black with dirt and plaster and wax. The only light came from two flickering blue Bunsen burners. Huge sacks of plaster stacked against the walls, sifted over onto a floor lumpy with chunks of broken tooth molds, and jars of various single teeth. Thick pink and white globs of wax hung on the walls, trailing cobwebs. Shelves were crammed with rusty tools and rows of dentures, grinning, or upside down, frowning, like theater masks. He chanted while he worked, his half-smoked cigarettes often igniting gobs of wax or candy bar wrappers. He threw coffee on the fires, staining the plaster-soft floor a deep cave brown.

The workshop opened into a small office with a rolltop desk where he pasted in scrapbooks and wrote checks. After he signed his name, he always flicked the pen, splashing black across his signature, sometimes obliterating the amount so that the bank would have to call to verify it.

There was no door between the room where he worked on patients and the waiting room. While he worked, he would turn around to talk to people in the waiting room, waving his drill. The extraction patients would recover on a chaise longue; the rest sat on windowsills or radiators. Sometimes someone sat in the phone booth, a big wooden booth with a pay phone, a fan, and a sign, "I never met a man I didn't like."

There weren't any magazines. If someone brought one and left it there, Grandpa would throw it away. He just did this to be contrary, my mother said. He said it was because it drove him crazy, people sitting there turning the pages.

When his patients weren't sitting, they wandered around the room fooling with things on the two safes. Buddhas, skulls with false teeth wired to open and close, snakes that bit you if you pulled their tails, domes you turned over and it snowed. On the ceiling was a sign, WHAT THE HELL YOU LOOKING UP HERE FOR? The safes contained gold and silver for fillings, stacks of money, and bottles of Jack Daniel's.

On all the windows, facing the main street of El Paso, were large gold letters that read, "Dr. H. A. Moynihan. I Don't Work for Negroes." The signs were reflected in the mirrors that hung on the remaining three walls. The slogan was written on the door to the hall. I never sat facing the door because I was afraid Negroes would come and look in over the sign. I never saw a Negro in the Caples Building though, except for Jim, the elevator man.

When people called for appointments, Grandpa had me tell them he was no longer taking patients, so as summer went on, there was less and less to do. Finally, just before Mamie died, there were no patients at all. Grandpa just stayed locked in his workshop or office. I used to go up on the roof sometimes. You could see Juárez and all of downtown El Paso from there. I would pick out one person in the crowd and follow him with my eyes until he disappeared. But mostly I just sat inside on the radiator, looking down at Yandell Drive. I spent hours decoding letters from Captain

Marvel Pen Pals, although that was really boring; the code was just A for Z, B for Y, etc.

Nights were long and hot. Mamie's friends stayed even when she slept, reading from the Bible, singing sometimes. Grandpa went out, to the Elks, or to Juárez. The 8-5 cabdriver helped him up the stairs. My mother went out to play bridge, she said, but she came home drunk, too. The Mexican kids played outside until very late. I watched the girls from the porch. They played jacks, squatting on the concrete under the streetlight. I ached to play with them. The sound of the jacks was magical to me, the toss of the jacks like brushes on a drum or like rain, when a gust of wind shimmers it against the windowpane.

One morning when it was still dark, Grandpa woke me up. It was Sunday. I dressed while he called the cab. To call a cab he asked the operator for 8-5 and when they answered, he said, "How about a little transportation?" He didn't answer when the cabdriver asked why we were going to the office on Sunday. It was dark and scary in the lobby. Cockroaches clattered across the tiles and magazines grinned at us behind bars of grating. He drove the elevator, maniacally crashing up and then down and up again until we finally stopped above the fifth floor and jumped down. It was very quiet after we stopped. All you heard were church bells and the Juárez trolley.

At first I was too frightened to follow him into the workshop, but he pulled me in. It was dark, like in a movie theater. He lit the gasping Bunsen burners. I still couldn't see, couldn't see what he wanted me to. He took a set of false teeth down from a shelf and moved them close to the flame on the marble block. I shook my head.

"Keep lookin' at them." Grandpa opened his mouth wide and I looked back and forth between his own teeth and the false ones.

"They're yours!" I said.

The false teeth were a perfect replica of the teeth in Grandpa's mouth, even the gums were an ugly, sick pale pink. The teeth were filled and cracked, some were chipped or worn away. He had changed only one tooth, one in front that he had put a gold cap on. That's what made it a work of art, he said.

"How did you get all those colors?"

"Pretty dang good, eh? Well . . . is it my masterpiece?"

"Yes." I shook his hand. I was very happy to be there.

"How do you fit them?" I asked. "Will they fit?"

Usually he pulled out all the teeth, let the gums heal, then made an impression of the bare gum.

"Some of the new guys are doing it this way. You take the impression before you pull the teeth, make the dentures and put them in before the gums have a chance to shrink."

"When are you getting your teeth pulled?"

"Right now. We're going to do it. Go get things ready."

I plugged in the rusty sterilizer. The cord was frayed; it sparked. He started toward it. "Never mind the—" but I stopped him. "No. They have to be sterile," and he laughed. He put his whiskey bottle and cigarettes on the tray, lit a cigarette, and poured a paper cup full of Jack Daniel's. He sat down in the chair. I fixed the reflector, tied a bib on him, and pumped the chair up and back.

"Boy, I'll bet a lot of your patients would like to be in my shoes."

"That thing boiling yet?"

"No." I filled some paper cups with Stom Aseptine and got out a jar of smelling salts.

"What if you pass out?" I asked.

"Good. Then you can pull them. Grab them as close as you can, twist and pull at the same time. Gimme a drink." I handed him a cup of Stom Aseptine. "Wise guy." I poured him whiskey.

"None of your patients get a drink."

"They're my patients, not yours."

"Okay, it's boiling." I drained the sterilizer into the spitting bowl, laid out a towel. Using another one, I placed the instruments in an arc on the tray above his chest.

"Hold the little mirror for me," he said and took the pliers.

I stood on the footrest between his knees, to hold the mirror close. The first three teeth came out easy. He handed them to me and I tossed them into the barrel by the wall. The incisors were harder, one in particular. He gagged and stopped, the root still stuck in his gum. He made a funny noise and shoved the pliers into my hand. "Take it!" I pulled at it. "Scissors, you fool!" I sat down on the metal plate between his feet. "Just a minute, Grandpa."

He reached over above me for the bottle, drank, then took a different tool from the tray. He began to pull the rest of his bottom teeth without a mirror. The sound was the sound of roots being ripped out, like trees being torn from winter ground. Blood dripped onto the tray, plop, plop, onto the metal where I sat.

He started laughing so hard I thought he had gone mad. He fell over on top of me. Frightened, I leaped up so hard I pushed him back into the tilted chair. "Pull them!" he gasped. I was afraid, wondered quickly if it would be murder if I pulled them and he died.

"Pull them!" He spat a thin red waterfall down his chin.

I pumped the chair way back. He was limp, did not seem to feel me twist the back top teeth sideways and out. He fainted, his lips closing like gray clamshells. I opened his mouth and shoved a paper towel into one side so I could get the three back teeth that remained.

The teeth were all out. I tried to bring the chair down with the foot pedal, but hit the wrong lever, spinning him around, spattering circles of blood on the floor. I left him, the chair creaking slowly to a stop. I wanted some tea bags, he had people bite down on them to stop the bleeding. I dumped Mamie's drawers out: talcum, prayer cards, thank you for the flowers. The tea bags were in a canister behind the hot plate.

The towel in his mouth was soaked crimson now. I dropped it on the floor, shoved a handful of tea bags into his mouth and held his jaws closed. I screamed. Without any teeth, his face was like a skull, white bones above the vivid bloody throat. Scary monster, a teapot

come alive, yellow and black Lipton tags dangling like parade decorations. I ran to phone my mother. No nickel. I couldn't move him
to get to his pockets. He had wet his pants; urine dripped onto the
floor. A bubble of blood kept appearing and bursting in his nostril.

The phone rang. It was my mother. She was crying. The pot
roast, a nice Sunday dinner. Even cucumbers and onions, just like
Mamie. "Help! Grandpa!" I said and hung up.

He had vomited. Oh good, I thought, and then giggled because
it was a silly thing to think oh good about. I dropped the tea bags
into the mess on the floor, wet some towels and washed his face. I
opened the smelling salts under his nose, smelled them myself,
shuddered.

"My teeth!" he yelled.

"They're gone!" I called, like to a child. "All gone!"

"The new ones, fool!"

I went to get them. I knew them now, they were exactly like
his mouth had been inside.

He reached for them, like a Juárez beggar, but his hands shook
too badly.

"I'll put them in. Rinse first." I handed him the mouthwash.
He rinsed and spat without lifting his head. I poured peroxide
over the teeth and put them in his mouth. "Hey, look!" I held up
Mamie's ivory mirror.

"Well, dad gum!" He was laughing.

"A masterpiece, Grandpa!" I laughed too, kissed his sweaty
head.

"Oh my God." My mother shrieked, came toward me with her
arms outstretched. She slipped in the blood, and slid into the teeth
barrels. She held on to get her balance.

"Look at his teeth, Mama."

She didn't even notice. Couldn't tell the difference. He poured
her some Jack Daniel's. She took it, toasted him distractedly, and
drank.

"You're crazy, Daddy. He's crazy. Where did all the tea bags come from?"

His shirt made a tearing sound coming unstuck from his skin. I helped him wash his chest and wrinkled belly. I washed myself, too, and put on a coral sweater of Mamie's. The two of them drank, silent, while we waited for the 8-5 cab. I drove the elevator down, landed it pretty close to the bottom. When we got home, the driver helped Grandpa up the stairs. He stopped at Mamie's door, but she was asleep.

In bed, Grandpa slept too, his teeth bared in a Bela Lugosi grin. They must have hurt.

"He did a good job," my mother said.

"You don't still hate him, do you Mama?"

"Oh, yes," she said. "Yes I do."

Stars and Saints

Wait. Let me explain . . .

My whole life I've run into these situations, like that morning with the psychiatrist. He was staying in the cottage behind my house while his new house was being remodeled. He looked really nice, handsome too, and of course I wanted to make a good impression, would have taken over brownies but didn't want him to think I was aggressive. One morning, just at dawn, as usual, I was drinking coffee and looking out the window at my garden, which was wonderful then, the sweet peas and delphiniums and cosmos. I felt, well, I felt full of joy . . . Why do I hesitate to tell you this? I don't want you to think I'm sappy, I want to make a good impression. Anyway I was happy, and I tossed a handful of birdseed out onto the deck, sat there smiling to myself as dozens of mourning doves and finches flew down to eat the seeds. Then flash, two big cats leaped onto the deck and began chomping away on birds, feathers flying, just at the very moment the psychiatrist came out his door. He looked at me, aghast, said "How terrible!" and fled. He avoided me completely after that morning, and it wasn't my imagination. There was no way I could explain that it had all happened so fast, that I wasn't smiling away at the cats chewing the birds. It was that my happiness about the sweet peas and the finches hadn't had time to fade.

As far back as I can remember I have made a very bad first impression. That time in Montana when all I was trying to do was get Kent Shreve's socks off so we could go barefoot but they were pinned to his drawers. But what I really want to talk about is St. Joseph's School. Now, psychiatrists (please don't get the wrong idea, I'm not obsessed by psychiatrists or anything)—it seems to me psychiatrists concentrate entirely too much upon the primal scene and preoedipal deprivation and they ignore the trauma of grade school and other children, who are cruel and ruthless.

I won't even go into what happened at Vilas, the first school I went to in El Paso. A big misunderstanding all around. So two months into the year, of third grade, there I was in the playground outside of St. Joseph's. My new school. Absolutely terrified. I had thought that wearing a uniform would help. But I had this heavy metal brace on my back, for what was called the curvature, let's face it, a hunchback, so I had to get the white blouse and plaid skirt way too big to go over it, and of course my mother didn't think to at least hem up the skirt.

Another big misunderstanding. Months later, Sister Mercedes was hall monitor. She was the young sweet one who must have had a tragic love affair. He probably died in the war, a bombardier. As we filed past her, two in a row, she touched my hunchback and whispered, "Dear child, you have a cross to bear." Now how was she to know that I had become a religious fanatic by that time, that those innocent words of hers would only convince me of my predestined link to Our Savior?

(Oh, and mothers. Just the other day, on the bus, a mother got on with her little boy. She was obviously a working mother, had picked him up at nursery school, was tired but glad to see him, asked him about his day. He told her all these things he had done. "You're so special!" she said as she hugged him. "Special means I'm retarded!" the kid said. He had big tears in his eyes and sat there scared to death while his mother went on smiling away just like me with the birds.)

That day on the playground I knew that never in my life was I going to get in. Not just fit in, get in. In one corner two girls were twirling a heavy rope and one by one beautiful rosy-cheeked girls would spring from line to jump under the rope, jump, jump and out again just in time and back in line. Whap, whap, no one missed a beat. In the middle of the playground was a round swing, with a circular seat that spun dizzily merrily around and never stopped but laughing children leaped on and off it without a . . . not even without falling, without a change of pace. Everywhere around me on the playground was symmetry, synchronicity. Two nuns, their beads clicking in unison, their clean faces nodding as one to the children. Jacks. The ball bouncing with a clean crack on the cement, the dozen jacks flying into the air and caught all at once with the spin of a tiny wrist. Slap slap slap, other girls played intricate complicated hand-clapping games. There was a tiny little dutchman. Slap slap. I wandered around not only unable to get in but seemingly invisible, which was a mixed blessing. I fled around the corner of the building where I could hear noises and laughter from the school kitchen. I was hidden there from the playground; the friendly noises inside were reassuring to me. I couldn't go in there either though. But then there were shriekings and hollerings and a nun was saying, oh I can't I simply can't, and I knew then it was okay for me to go in because what she couldn't do was take the dead mice out of the traps. "I'll do that," I said. And the nuns were so pleased they didn't say anything about me being in the kitchen, except one of them did whisper "Protestant" to another one.

And that's how it started. Also they gave me a biscuit, hot and delicious, with butter. Of course I had had breakfast but it was so good I wolfed it down and they gave me another. Every day then in exchange for emptying and resetting two or three traps I not only got biscuits but a St. Christopher medal that I used later for a lunch token. This saved me the embarrassment before class started of lining up to exchange dimes for the medals we used for lunch.

Because of my back I was allowed to stay in the classroom during gym and recess. It was just the mornings that were hard, because the bus got there before the school was unlocked. I forced myself to try to make friends, to talk to girls from my class, but it was hopeless. They were all Catholic and had been together since kindergarten. To be fair, they were nice, normal children. I had been skipped in school, so was much younger, and had only lived in remote mining camps before the war. I didn't know how to say things like "Do you enjoy studying the Belgian Congo?" or "What are your hobbies?" I would lurch up to them and blurt out "My uncle has a glass eye." Or "I found a dead Kodiak bear with his face full of maggots." They would ignore me, or giggle or say "Liar, liar, pants on fire!"

So for a while I had someplace to go before school. I felt useful and appreciated. But then I heard the girls whispering "Charity case" along with "Protestant" and then they started calling me "Rat trap" and "Minnie Mouse." I pretended I didn't care and besides I loved the kitchen, the soft laughter and murmurs of the nun-cooks, who wore homespun nightgown-looking habits in the kitchen.

I had of course decided to become a nun by then, because they never looked nervous but mostly because of the black habits and the white coifs, the headdresses like giant starched white fleur-de-lis. I'll bet the Catholic church lost out on a lot of would-be nuns when they started dressing like ordinary meter maids. Then my mother visited the school to see how I was getting along. They said my classwork was excellent and my deportment perfect. Sister Cecilia told her how much they appreciated me in the kitchen and how they saw to it that I had a good breakfast. My mother, the snob, with her ratty old coat with the ratty fox collar the beady eyes had fallen out of. She was mortified, disgusted about the mice and really furious about the St. Christopher medal, because I had gone on getting my dime every morning and spending it on candy after school. Devious little thief. Whap. Whap. Mortified!

So that ended that, and it was a big misunderstanding all around. The nuns apparently thought I had been hanging around the kitchen because I was this poor hungry waif, and just gave me the mousetrap job out of charity, not because they really needed me at all. The problem is I still don't see how the false impression could have been avoided. Perhaps if I had turned down the biscuit?

That's how I ended up hanging out in church before school and really decided to become a nun, or a saint. The first mystery was that the rows of candles under each of the statues of Jesus and Mary and Joseph were all flickering and trembling as if there were gusts of wind when in fact the vast church was shut tight and none of the heavy doors were open. I believed that the spirit of God in the statues was so strong it made the candles flutter and hiss, tremulous with suffering. Each tiny burst of light lit up the caked blood on Jesus's bony white feet and it looked wet.

At first I stayed way in the back, giddy, drunk with the smell of incense. I knelt, praying. Kneeling was very painful, because of my back, and the brace dug into my spine. I was sure this made me holy and was penance for my sins but it hurt too bad so I finally stopped, just sat there in the dark church until the bell rang for class. Usually there was no one in the church but me, except for Thursday when Father Anselmo would go shut himself in the confessional. A few old women, girls from the upper school, once in a while a grade school pupil would make their way, stopping to kneel to the altar and cross themselves, kneeling and crossing again before they entered the other side of the confessional. What was puzzling was the varying time they took to pray when they left. I would have given anything in the whole wide world to know what went on in there. I'm not sure how long it was before I found myself inside, my heart pounding. It was more exquisite inside than I could have imagined. Smoky with myrrh, a velvet cushion to kneel on, a blessed virgin looking down upon me with infinite pity and compassion. Through the carved screen was Father Anselmo, who was ordinarily a preoccupied little man. But he was silhouetted, like the man on Mamie's wall in the top hat. He could be anybody . . . Tyrone Power, my father, God. His voice was not like Father Anselmo at all but deep and softly echoing. He asked me to say a prayer I didn't know, so he said the lines and I repeated them, grievously sorry for having offended thee. Then he asked about my sins. I wasn't lying. I really and truly had no sins to confess. Not a one. I was so ashamed, surely I could think of something. Search deep into your heart, my child . . . Nothing. Desperate, wanting so badly to please I made one up. I had hit my sister on the head with a hairbrush. Do you envy your sister? Oh, yes, Father. Envy is a sin, my child, pray to have it removed from you. Three Hail Marys. As I prayed, kneeling, I realized that this was a short penance, next time I could do better. But there would be no next time. That day Sister Cecilia kept me after class. What made it worse was that she was so kind. She understood how I would want to experience the church's sacraments and mysteries. Mysteries, yes! But I was a Protestant and I wasn't baptized or confirmed. I was allowed to come to their school, and she was glad, because I was a good obedient pupil, but I couldn't take part in their church. I was to stay on the playground with the other children.

I had a terrible thought, pulled from my pocket my four Saint cards. Every time we got a perfect score in reading or arithmetic we got a star. On Fridays the pupil with the most stars was given a Saint card, similar to a baseball card except the halo had glitter on it. May I keep my Saints? I asked her, sick at heart.

"Of course you may, and I hope that you will be earning many more." She smiled at me and did me another favor. "You can still pray, dear, for guidance. Let us say a Hail Mary together." I closed my eyes and prayed fervently to our Mother, who will always have Sister Cecilia's face.

Whenever a siren sounded outside in the streets, near or far, Sister Cecilia had us stop whatever we were doing, lay our heads down on our desks, and say a Hail Mary. I still do that. Say a Hail Mary, I mean. Well, also I lay my head down on wooden desks, to listen to them, because they do make sounds, like branches in the wind, as if they were still trees. A lot of things were really bothering me in those days, like what gave life to the candles and where the sound came from in the desks. If everything in God's world has a soul, even the desks, since they have a voice, there must be a heaven. I couldn't go to heaven because I was Protestant. I'd have to go to limbo. I would rather have gone to hell than limbo, what an ugly word, like dumbo, or mumbo jumbo, a place without any dignity at all.

I told my mother I wanted to become a Catholic. She and my grandpa had a fit. He wanted to put me back in Vilas school but she said no, it was full of Mexicans and juvenile delinquents. I told her there were lots of Mexicans at St. Joseph's but she said they came from nice families. Were we a nice family? I didn't know. What I still do is look in picture windows where families are sitting around and wonder what they do, how do they talk to one another?

Sister Cecilia and another nun came to our house one afternoon. I don't know why they came and they didn't get a chance to say. Everything was a mess. My mother crying and Mamie, my grandma, crying, Grandpa was drunk and went lunging at them calling them crows. The next day I was afraid Sister Cecilia would be mad at me and not say "Good-bye, dear" when she left me alone in the room at recess. But before she left she handed me a book called *Understood Betsy* and said she thought I would like it. It was the first real book I ever read, the first book I fell in love with.

She praised my work in class, and commented to the other students every time I got a star, or on Fridays when I was given a Saint

card. I did everything to please her, carefully scrolling A.M.D.G. at
the top of every paper, rushing to erase the board. My prayers
were the loudest, my hand the first to go up when she asked a
question. She continued to give me books to read and once she
gave me a paper bookmark that said "Pray for us sinners now and
at the hour of our death." I showed it to Melissa Barnes in the
cafeteria. I had foolishly believed that since Sister Cecilia liked
me the girls would begin to like me too. But now instead of laughing at me they hated me. When I stood up to answer in class they
would whisper Pet, pet, pet. Sister Cecilia chose me to collect the
dimes and pass out the medals for lunch and when each girl took
her medal she whispered Pet.

Then one day out of the clear blue sky my mother got mad at
me because my father wrote me more than he did her. It's because
I write to him more. No, you're his pet. One day I got home late. I
had missed the bus from the plaza. She stood at the top of the
stairs with a blue airmail letter from my father in one hand. With
the other she lit a kitchen match on her thumbnail and burned
the letter as I raced up the stairs. That always scared me. When I
was little I didn't see the match, thought she lit her cigarettes with
a flaming thumb.

I stopped talking. I didn't say, Well now I'm not going to talk
anymore, I just gradually stopped and when the sirens passed I
laid my head down on the desk and whispered the prayer to myself. When Sister Cecilia called on me I shook my head and sat
back down. I stopped getting Saints and stars. It was too late.
Now they called me dumb-dumb. She stayed in the classroom
after they had left for gym. "What is wrong, dear? May I help you?
Please talk to me." I locked my jaws and refused to look at her.
She left and I sat there in the hot semidarkness of the classroom.
She came back, later, with a copy of *Black Beauty* that she placed
before me. "This is a lovely book, only it's very sad. Tell me, are
you sad about something?"

I ran away from her and the book into the cloakroom. Of
course there were no cloaks since it was so hot in Texas, but boxes
of dusty textbooks. Easter decorations. Christmas decorations.
Sister Cecilia followed me into the tiny room. She spun me around
and forced me to my knees. "Let us pray," she said.

Hail Mary, full of grace, the Lord is with thee. Blessed is the
fruit of thy womb, Jesus . . . Her eyes were filled with tears. I
could not bear their tenderness. I wrenched away from her grasp,
accidentally knocking her down. Her headdress caught in a coat
hook and was yanked off. Her head wasn't shaved like the girls
said. She cried out and ran from the room.

I was sent home that same day, expelled from St. Joseph's for
striking a nun. I don't know how she could have thought that I
would hit her. It wasn't like that at all.

A Manual for Cleaning Women

42–PIEDMONT. Slow bus to Jack London Square. Maids and old ladies. I sat next to an old blind woman who was reading Braille, her finger gliding across the page, slow and quiet, line after line. It was soothing to watch, reading over her shoulder. The woman got off at Twenty-ninth, where all the letters have fallen from the sign NATIONAL PRODUCTS BY THE BLIND except for BLIND.

Twenty-ninth is my stop too, but I have to go all the way downtown to cash Mrs. Jessel's check. If she pays me with a check one more time I'll quit. Besides she never has any change for carfare. Last week I went all the way to the bank with my own quarter and she had forgotten to sign the check.

She forgets everything, even her ailments. As I dust I collect them and put them on her desk. 10 AM. NAUSEEA (sp) on a piece of paper on the mantel. DIARREEA on the drainboard. DIZZY POOR MEMORY on the kitchen stove. Mostly she forgets if she took her phenobarbital or not, or that she has already called me twice at home to ask if she did, where her ruby ring is, etc.

She follows me from room to room, saying the same things over and over. I'm going as cuckoo as she is. I keep saying I'll quit but I feel sorry for her. I'm the only person she has to talk to. Her husband is a lawyer, plays golf and has a mistress. I don't think Mrs. Jessel knows this, or remembers. Cleaning women know everything.

Cleaning women do steal. Not the things the people we work for are so nervous about. It is the superfluity that finally gets to you. We don't want the change in the little ashtrays.

Some lady at a bridge party somewhere started the rumor that to test the honesty of a cleaning woman you leave little rosebud ashtrays around with loose change in them, here and there. My solution to this is to always add a few pennies, even a dime.

The minute I get to work I first check out where the watches are, the rings, the gold lamé evening purses. Later when they come running in all puffy and red-faced I just coolly say, "Under your pillow, behind the avocado toilet." All I really steal is sleeping pills, saving up for a rainy day.

Today I stole a bottle of Spice Islands sesame seeds. Mrs. Jessel rarely cooks. When she does she makes Sesame Chicken. The recipe is pasted inside the spice cupboard. Another copy is in the stamp and string drawer and another in her address book. Whenever she orders chicken, soy sauce, and sherry she orders another bottle of sesame seeds. She has fifteen bottles of sesame seeds. Fourteen now.

At the bus stop I sat on the curb. Three other maids, black in white uniforms, stood above me. They are old friends, have worked on Country Club Road for years. At first we were all mad . . . the bus was two minutes early and we missed it. Damn. He knows the maids are always there, that the 42–PIEDMONT only runs once an hour.

I smoked while they compared booty. Things they took . . . nail polish, perfume, toilet paper. Things they were given . . . one-earrings, twenty hangers, torn bras.

(Advice to cleaning women: Take everything that your lady gives you and say Thank you. You can leave it on the bus, in the crack.)

To get into the conversation I showed them my bottle of sesame seeds. They roared with laughter. "Oh, child! Sesame seeds?" They asked me how come I've worked for Mrs. Jessel so long. Most women can't handle her for more than three times. They asked if it is true she has one hundred and forty pairs of shoes. Yes, but the bad part is that most of them are identical.

The hour passed pleasantly. We talked about all the ladies we each work for. We laughed, not without bitterness.

I'm not easily accepted by most old-time cleaning women. Hard to get cleaning jobs too, because I'm "educated." Sure as hell can't find any other jobs right now. Learned to tell the ladies right away that my alcoholic husband just died, leaving me and the four kids. I had never worked before, raising the children and all.

43–SHATTUCK–BERKELEY. The benches that say SATURATION ADVERTISING are soaking wet every morning. I asked a man for a match and he gave me the pack. SUICIDE PREVENTION. They were the dumb kind with the striker on the back. Better safe than sorry.

Across the street the woman at SPOTLESS CLEANERS was sweeping her sidewalk. The sidewalks on either side of her fluttered with litter and leaves. It is autumn now, in Oakland.

Later that afternoon, back from cleaning at Horwitz's, the SPOTLESS sidewalk was covered with leaves and garbage again. I dropped my transfer on it. I always get a transfer. Sometimes I give them away, usually I just hold them.

Ter used to tease me about how I was always holding things all the time.

"Say, Maggie May, ain't nothing in this world you can hang on to. 'Cept me, maybe."

One night on Telegraph I woke up to feel him closing a Coors fliptop into my palm. He was smiling down at me. Terry was a young cowboy, from Nebraska. He wouldn't go to foreign movies. I just realized it's because he couldn't read fast enough.

Whenever Ter read a book, rarely—he would rip each page off and throw it away. I would come home, to where the windows were always open or broken and the whole room would be swirling with pages, like Safeway lot pigeons.

33—BERKELEY EXPRESS. The 33 got lost! The driver overshot the turn at SEARS for the freeway. Everybody was ringing the bell as, blushing, he made a left on Twenty-seventh. We ended up stuck in a dead end. People came to their windows to see the bus. Four men got out to help him back out between the parked cars on the narrow street. Once on the freeway he drove about eighty. It was scary. We all talked together, pleased by the event.

Linda's today.

(Cleaning women: As a rule, never work for friends. Sooner or later they resent you because you know so much about them. Or else you'll no longer like them, because you do.)

But Linda and Bob are good, old friends. I feel their warmth even though they aren't there. Come and blueberry jelly on the sheets. Racing forms and cigarette butts in the bathroom. Notes from Bob to Linda: "Buy some smokes and take the car . . . dooh-dah dooh-dah." Drawings by Andrea with Love to Mom. Pizza crusts. I clean their coke mirror with Windex.

It is the only place I work that isn't spotless to begin with. It's filthy in fact. Every Wednesday I climb the stairs like Sisyphus into their living room where it always looks like they are in the middle of moving.

I don't make much money with them because I don't charge by the hour, no carfare. No lunch for sure. I really work hard. But I sit around a lot, stay very late. I smoke and read *The New York Times*, porno books, *How to Build a Patio Roof*. Mostly I just look out the window at the house next door, where we used to live. 2129½ Russell Street. I look at the tree that grows wooden pears Ter used to shoot at. The wooden fence glistens with BBs. The BEKINS sign that lit our bed at night. I miss Ter and I smoke. You can't hear the trains during the day.

40—TELEGRAPH. MILLHAVEN CONVALESCENT HOME. Four old women in wheelchairs staring filmily out into the street. Behind them, at the nurses' station, a beautiful black girl dances to "I

Shot the Sheriff." The music is loud, even to me, but the old women can't hear it at all. Beneath them, on the sidewalk, is a crude sign: TUMOR INSTITUTE 1:30.

The bus is late. Cars drive by. Rich people in cars never look at people on the street, at all. Poor ones always do . . . in fact it sometimes seems they're just driving around, looking at people on the street. I've done that. Poor people wait a lot. Welfare, unemployment lines, laundromats, phone booths, emergency rooms, jails, etc.

As everyone waited for the 40 we looked into the window of MILL AND ADDIE'S LAUNDRY. Mill was born in a mill in Georgia. He was lying down across five washing machines, installing a huge TV set above them. Addie made silly pantomimes for us, how the TV would never hold up. Passersby stopped to join us watching Mill. All of us were reflected in the television, like a Man on the Street show.

Down the street is a big black funeral at FOUCHÉ's. I used to think the neon sign said "Touché," and would always imagine death in a mask, his point at my heart.

I have thirty pills now, from Jessel, Burns, Mcintyre, Horwitz, and Blum. These people I work for each have enough uppers or downers to put a Hell's Angel away for twenty years.

18–PARK–MONTCLAIR. Downtown Oakland. A drunken Indian knows me by now, always says, "That's the way the ball bounces, sugar."

At Park Boulevard a blue County Sheriff's bus with the windows boarded up. Inside are about twenty prisoners on their way to arraignment. The men, chained together, move sort of like a crew team in their orange jumpsuits. With the same camaraderie, actually. It is dark inside the bus. Reflected in the window is the traffic light. Yellow WAIT WAIT. Red STOP STOP.

A long sleepy hour up into the affluent foggy Montclair hills. Just maids on the bus. Beneath Zion Lutheran church is a big black-and-white sign that says WATCH OUT FOR FALLING ROCKS. Every time I see it I laugh out loud. The other maids and the driver turn around and stare at me. It is a ritual by now. There was a time when I used to automatically cross myself when I passed a Catholic church. Maybe I stopped because people in buses always turned around and stared. I still automatically say a Hail Mary, silently, whenever I hear a siren. This is a nuisance because I live on Pill Hill in Oakland, next to three hospitals.

At the foot of the Montclair hills women in Toyotas wait for their maids to get off the bus. I always get a ride up Snake Road with Mamie and her lady who says, "My don't we look pretty in that frosted wig, Mamie, and me in my tacky paint clothes." Mamie and I smoke.

Women's voices always rise two octaves when they talk to cleaning women or cats.

(Cleaning women: As for cats . . . never make friends with cats, don't let them play with the mop, the rags. The ladies will get jealous. Never, however, knock cats off of chairs. On the other hand, always make friends with dogs, spend five or ten minutes scratching Cherokee or Smiley when you first arrive. Remember to close the toilet seats. Furry, jowly drips.)

The Blums. This is the weirdest place I work, the only beautiful house. They are both psychiatrists. They are marriage counselors with two adopted "preschoolers."

(Never work in a house with "preschoolers." Babies are great. You can spend hours looking at them, holding them. But the older ones . . . you get shrieks, dried Cheerios, accidents hardened and walked on in the Snoopy pajama foot.)

(Never work for psychiatrists, either. You'll go crazy. I could tell *them* a thing or two . . . Elevator shoes?)

Dr. Blum, the male one, is home sick again. He has asthma, for crissake. He stands around in his bathrobe, scratching a pale hairy leg with his slipper.

Oh ho ho ho, Mrs. Robinson. He has over two thousand dollars' worth of stereo equipment and five records. Simon and Garfunkel, Joni Mitchell, and three Beatles.

He stands in the doorway to the kitchen, scratching the other leg now. I make sultry Mr. Clean mop-swirls away from him into the breakfast nook while he asks me why I chose this particular line of work.

"I figure it's either guilt or anger," I drawl.

"When the floor dries may I make myself a cup of tea?"

"Oh, look, just go sit down. I'll bring you some tea. Sugar or honey?"

"Honey. If it isn't too much trouble. And lemon if it . . ."

"Go sit down." I take him tea.

Once I brought Natasha, four years old, a black sequined blouse. For dress-up. Ms. Dr. Blum got furious and hollered that it was sexist. For a minute I thought she was accusing me of trying to seduce Natasha. She threw the blouse into the garbage. I retrieved it later and wear it now, sometimes, for dress-up.

(Cleaning women: You will get a lot of liberated women. First stage is a CR group; second stage is a cleaning woman; third, divorce.)

The Blums have a lot of pills, a plethora of pills. She has uppers, he has downers. Mr. Dr. Blum has belladonna pills. I don't know what they do but I wish it was my name.

One morning I heard him say to her, in the breakfast nook, "Let's do something spontaneous today, take the kids to go fly a kite!"

My heart went out to him. Part of me wanted to rush in like the maid in the back of *Saturday Evening Post*. I make great kites, know good places in Tilden for wind. There is no wind in Montclair. The other part of me turned on the vacuum so I couldn't hear her reply. It was pouring rain outside.

The playroom was a wreck. I asked Natasha if she and Todd actually played with all those toys. She told me when it was Monday she and Todd got up and dumped them, because I was coming. "Go get your brother," I said.

I had them working away when Ms. Dr. Blum came in. She lectured me about interference and how she refused to "lay any guilt or duty trips" on her children. I listened, sullen. As an after-thought she told me to defrost the refrigerator and clean it with ammonia and vanilla.

Ammonia and vanilla? It made me stop hating her. Such a simple thing. I could see she really did want a homey home, didn't want guilt or duty trips laid on her children. Later on that day I had a glass of milk and it tasted like ammonia and vanilla.

40—TELEGRAPH—BERKELEY. MILL AND ADDIE'S LAUNDRY. Addie is alone in the laundromat, washing the huge plate glass window. Behind her, on top of a washer is an enormous fish head in a plastic bag. Lazy blind eyes. A friend, Mr. Walker, brings them fish heads for soup. Addie makes immense circles of flurry white on the glass. Across the street, at St. Luke's nursery, a child thinks she is waving at him. He waves back, making the same swooping circles. Addie stops, smiles, waves back for real. My bus comes. Up Telegraph toward Berkeley. In the window of the MAGIC WAND BEAUTY PARLOR there is an aluminum foil star connected to a fly-swatter. Next door is an orthopedic shop with two supplicating hands and a leg.

Ter refused to ride buses. The people depressed him, sitting there. He liked Greyhound stations though. We used to go to the ones in San Francisco and Oakland. Mostly Oakland, on San Pablo Avenue. Once he told me he loved me because I was like San Pablo Avenue.

He was like the Berkeley dump. I wish there was a bus to the dump. We went there when we got homesick for New Mexico. It is stark and windy and gulls soar like nighthawks in the desert. You can see the sky all around you and above you. Garbage trucks thunder through dust-billowing roads. Gray dinosaurs.

I can't handle you being dead, Ter. But you know that.

It's like the time at the airport, when you were about to get on the caterpillar ramp for Albuquerque.

"Oh, shit. I can't go. You'll never find the car."

"Watcha gonna do when I'm gone, Maggie?" you kept asking over and over, the other time, when you were going to London.

"I'll do macramé, punk."

"Whatcha gonna do when I'm gone, Maggie?"

"You really think I need you that bad?"

"Yes," you said. A simple Nebraska statement.

My friends say I am wallowing in self-pity and remorse. Said I don't see anybody anymore. When I smile, my hand goes involuntarily to my mouth.

I collect sleeping pills. Once we made a pact . . . if things weren't okay by 1976 we were going to have a shoot-out at the end of the Marina. You didn't trust me, said I would shoot you first and run, or shoot myself first, whatever. I'm tired of the bargain, Ter.

58–COLLEGE–ALAMEDA. Old Oakland ladies all go to Hink's department store in Berkeley. Old Berkeley ladies go to Capwell's department store in Oakland. Everyone on this bus is young and black or old and white, including the drivers. The old white drivers are mean and nervous, especially around Oakland Tech High School. They're always jolting the bus to a stop, hollering about smoking and radios. They lurch and stop with a bang, knocking the old white ladies into posts. The old ladies' arms bruise, instantly.

The young black drivers go fast, sailing through yellow lights at Pleasant Valley Road. Their buses are loud and smoky but they don't lurch.

Mrs. Burke's house today. Have to quit her, too. Nothing ever changes. Nothing is ever dirty. I can't understand why I am there at all. Today I felt better. At least I understood about the thirty Lancers Rosé Wine bottles. There were thirty-one. Apparently yesterday was their anniversary. There were two cigarette butts in his ashtray (not just his one), one wineglass (she doesn't drink), and my new rosé bottle. The bowling trophies had been moved, slightly. Our life together.

She taught me a lot about housekeeping. Put the toilet paper in so it comes out from under. Only open the Comet tab to three holes instead of six. Waste not, want not. Once, in a fit of rebellion, I ripped the tab completely off and accidentally spilled Comet all down the inside of the stove. A mess.

(Cleaning women: Let them know you are thorough. The first day put all the furniture back wrong . . . five to ten inches off, or facing the wrong way. When you dust, reverse the Siamese cats, put the creamer to the left of the sugar. Change the toothbrushes all around.)

My masterpiece in this area was when I cleaned the top of Mrs. Burke's refrigerator. She sees everything, but if I hadn't left the flashlight on she would have missed the fact that I scoured and re-oiled the waffle iron, mended the geisha girl, and washed the flashlight as well.

Doing everything wrong not only reassures them you are thorough, it gives them a chance to be assertive and a "boss." Most American women are very uncomfortable about having servants. They don't know what to do while you are there. Mrs. Burke does things like recheck her Christmas card list and iron last year's wrapping paper. In August.

Try to work for Jews or blacks. You get lunch. But mostly Jewish and black women respect work, the work you do, and also they are not at all ashamed of spending the entire day doing absolutely nothing. They are paying *you*, right?

The Christian Eastern Stars are another story. So they won't feel guilty always try to be doing something they never would do. Stand on the stove to clean an exploded Coca-Cola off the ceiling. Shut yourself inside the glass shower. Shove all the furniture, including the piano, against the door. They would never do that, besides, they can't get in.

Thank God they always have at least one TV show that they are addicted to. I flip the vacuum on for half an hour (a soothing sound), lie down under the piano with an Endust rag clutched in my hand, just in case. I just lie there and hum and think. I refused to identify your body, Ter, which caused a lot of hassle. I was afraid I would hit you for what you did. Died.

Burke's piano is what I do last before I leave. Bad part about that is the only music on it is "The Marine Hymn." I always end up marching to the bus stop "From the Halls of Monte-zu-u-ma . . ."

58–COLLEGE–BERKELEY. A mean old white driver. It's raining, late, crowded, cold. Christmas is a bad time for buses. A stoned hippy girl shouted, "Let me off this fuckin' bus!" "Wait for the designated stop!" the driver shouted back. A fat woman, a cleaning woman, vomited down the front seat onto people's galoshes and my boot. The smell was foul and several people got off at the next stop, when she did. The driver stopped at the Arco station on Alcatraz, got a hose to clean it up but of course just ran it all into the back and made things wetter. He was red-faced and furious, ran the next light, endangering us all, the man next to me said.

At Oakland Tech about twenty students with radios waited behind a badly crippled man. Welfare is next door to Tech. As the man got on the bus, with much difficulty, the driver said, "OH JESUS *CHRIST*" and the man looked surprised.

Burke's again. No changes. They have ten digital clocks and they all have the same right time. The day I quit I'll pull all the plugs.

I finally did quit Mrs. Jessel. She kept on paying me with a check and once she called me four times in one night. I called her husband and told him I had mononucleosis. She forgot I quit, called me last night to ask if she had looked a little paler to me. I miss her.

A new lady today. A real lady.

(I never think of myself as a cleaning lady, although that's what they call you, their lady or their girl.)

Mrs. Johansen. She is Swedish and speaks English with a great deal of slang, like Filipinos.

The first thing she said to me, when she opened the door, was "HOLY MOSES!"

"Oh. Am I too early?"

"Not at all, my dear."

She took the stage. An eighty-year-old Glenda Jackson. I was bowled over. (See, I'm talking like her already.) Bowled over in the foyer.

In the foyer, before I even took off my coat, Ter's coat, she explained to me the event of her life.

Her husband, John, died six months ago. She had found it hard, most of all, to sleep. She started putting together picture puzzles. (She gestured toward the card table in the living room, where Jefferson's Monticello was almost finished, a gaping protozoan hole, top right.)

One night she got so stuck with her puzzle she didn't go to sleep at all. She forgot, actually forgot to sleep! Or eat to boot, matter of fact. She had supper at eight in the morning. She took a nap then, woke up at two, had breakfast at two in the afternoon and went out and bought another puzzle.

When John was alive it was Breakfast 6, Lunch 12, Dinner 6. I'll tell the cockeyed world times have changed.

"No, dear, you're not too early," she said. "I might just pop off to bed at any moment."

I was still standing there, hot, gazing into my new lady's radiant sleepy eyes, waiting for talk of ravens.

All I had to do was wash windows and vacuum the carpet. But, before vacuuming the carpet, to find a puzzle piece. Sky with a little bit of maple. I know it is missing.

It was nice on the balcony, washing windows. Cold, but the sun was on my back. Inside she sat at her puzzle. Enraptured, but striking a pose nevertheless. She must have been very lovely.

After the windows came the task of looking for the puzzle piece. Inch by inch in the green shag carpet, cracker crumbs, rubber bands from the *Chronicle*. I was delighted, this was the best job I ever had. She didn't "give a hoot" if I smoked or not so I just crawled around on the floor and smoked, sliding my ashtray with me.

I found the piece, way across the room from the puzzle table. It was sky, with a little bit of maple.

"I found it!" she cried, "I knew it was missing!"

"*I* found it!" I cried.

Then I could vacuum, which I did as she finished the puzzle with a sigh. As I was leaving I asked her when she thought she might need me again.

"Who knows?" she said.

"Well . . . anything goes," I said, and we both laughed.

Ter, I don't want to die at all, actually.

40—TELEGRAPH. Bus stop outside the laundry. MILL AND ADDIE'S is crowded with people waiting for machines, but festive, like waiting for a table. They stand, chatting at the window drinking green cans of Sprite. Mill and Addie mingle like genial hosts, making change. On the TV the Ohio State band plays the national anthem. Snow flurries in Michigan.

It is a cold, clear January day. Four sideburned cyclists turn up at the corner at Twenty-ninth like a kite string. A Harley idles at the bus stop and some kids wave at the rasty rider from the bed of a '50 Dodge pickup truck. I finally weep.

My Jockey

I like working in Emergency—you meet men there, anyway. Real men, heroes. Firemen and jockeys. They're always coming into emergency rooms. Jockeys have wonderful X-rays. They break bones all the time but just tape themselves up and ride the next race. Their skeletons look like trees, like reconstructed brontosaurs. St. Sebastian's X-rays.

I get the jockeys because I speak Spanish and most are Mexican. The first jockey I met was Muñoz. God. I undress people all the time and it's no big deal, takes a few seconds, Muñoz lay there, unconscious, a miniature Aztec god. Because his clothes were so complicated it was as if I were performing an elaborate ritual. Unnerving, because it took so long, like in Mishima where it takes three pages to take off the lady's kimono. His magenta satin shirt had many buttons along the shoulder and at each tiny wrist; his pants were fastened with intricate lacings, pre-Columbian knots. His boots smelled of manure and sweat, but were as soft and dainty as Cinderella's. He slept on, an enchanted prince.

He began to call for his mother even before he woke. He didn't just hold my hand, like some patients do, but clung to my neck, sobbing, *Mamacita! Mamacita!* The only way he would let Dr. Johnson examine him was if I held him cradled like a baby. He was as tiny as a child but strong, muscular. A man in my lap. A dream man? A dream baby?

Dr. Johnson sponged my forehead while I translated. For sure he had a broken collarbone, at least three broken ribs, probably a concussion. No, Muñoz said. He had to ride in tomorrow's races. Get him to X-ray, Dr. Johnson said. Since he wouldn't lie down on the gurney I carried him down the corridor, like King Kong. He was weeping, terrified, his tears soaked my breast.

We waited in the dark room for the X-ray tech. I soothed him just as I would a horse. *Cálmate, lindo, cálmate. Despacio . . . despacio.* Slowly . . . slowly. He quieted in my arms, blew and snorted softly. I stroked his fine back. It shuddered and shimmered like that of a splendid young colt. It was marvelous.

El Tim

A nun stood in each classroom door, black robes floating into the hall with the wind. The voices of the first grade, praying, *Hail Mary, full of grace, the Lord is with Thee*. From across the hall, the second grade began, clear, *Hail Mary, full of grace*. I stopped in the center of the building, and waited for the triumphant voices of the third grade, their voices joined by the first grade, *Our Father, Who art in Heaven*, by the fourth grade, then, deep, *Hail Mary, full of grace*.

As the children grew older they prayed more quickly, so that gradually the voices began to blend, to merge into one sudden joyful chant . . . *In the name of the Father and of the Son and of the Holy Ghost. Amen*.

I taught Spanish in the new junior high, which lay at the opposite end of the playground like a child's colored toy. Every morning, before class, I went through the grade school, to hear the prayers, but also simply to go into the building, as one would go in a church. The school had been a mission, built in 1700 by the Spaniards, built to stand in the desert for a long time. It was different from other old schools, whose stillness and solidity is still a shell for the children who pass through them. It had kept the peace of a mission, of a sanctuary.

The nuns laughed in the grade school, and the children laughed. The nuns were all old, not like tired old women who clutch their bags at a bus stop, but proud, loved by their God and by their children. They responded to love with tenderness, with soft laughter that was contained, guarded, behind the heavy wooden doors.

Several junior high nuns swept through the playground, checking for cigarette smoke. These nuns were young and nervous. They taught "underprivileged children," "borderline delinquents," and their thin faces were tired, sick of a blank stare. They could not use awe or love like the grade school nuns. Their recourse was impregnability, indifference to the students who were their duty and their life.

The rows of windows in the ninth grade flashed as Sister Lourdes opened them, as usual, seven minutes before the bell. I stood outside the initialed orange doors, watching my ninth-grade students as they paced back and forth in front of the wire fence, their bodies loose and supple, necks bobbing as they walked, arms and legs swaying to a beat, to a trumpet that no one else could hear.

They leaned against the wire fence, speaking in English-Spanish-Hipster dialect, laughing soundlessly. The girls wore the navy-blue uniforms of the school. Like muted birds they flirted with the boys, who cocked their plumed heads, who were brilliant in orange or yellow or turquoise pegged pants. They wore open black shirts or V-neck sweaters with nothing under them, so that their crucifixes gleamed against their smooth brown chests . . . the crucifix of the pachuco, which was also tattooed on the back of their hand.

"Good morning, dear."

"Good morning, Sister." Sister Lourdes had come outside to see if the seventh grade was in line.

Sister Lourdes was the principal. She had hired me, reluctantly having to pay someone to teach, since none of the nuns spoke Spanish.

"So, as a lay teacher," she had said, "the first one at San Marco, it may be hard for you to control the students, especially since many of them are almost as old as you. You must not make the mistake that many of my young nuns do. Do not try to be their friend. These students think in terms of power and weakness. You must keep your power . . . through aloofness, discipline, punishment, control. Spanish is an elective, give as many Fs as you like. During the first three weeks you may transfer any of your pupils to my Latin class. I have had no volunteers," she smiled. "You will find this a great help."

The first month had gone well. The threat of the Latin class was an advantage; by the end of the second week I had eliminated seven students. It was a luxury to teach such a relatively small class, and a class with the lower quarter removed. My native Spanish helped a great deal. It was a surprise to them that a "gringa" could speak as well as their parents, better even than they. They were impressed that I recognized their obscene words, their slang for marijuana and police. They worked hard. Spanish was close, important to them. They behaved well, but their sullen obedience and their automatic response were an affront to me.

They mocked words and expressions that I used and began to use them as much as I. "La Piña," they jeered, because of my hair, and soon the girls cut their hair like mine. "The idiot can't write," they whispered, when I printed on the blackboard, but they began to print all of their papers.

These were not yet the pachucos, the hoods that they tried hard to be, flipping a switchblade into a desk, blushing when it slipped and fell. They were not yet saying: "You can't show me nothing." They waited, with a shrug, to be shown. So what could I show them? The world I knew was no better than the one they had the courage to defy.

I watched Sister Lourdes whose strength was not, as mine, a front for their respect. The students saw her faith in the God, in the life that she had chosen; they honored it, never letting her know their tolerance for the harshness she used for control.

She couldn't laugh with them either. They laughed only in derision, only when someone revealed himself with a question, with a smile, a mistake, a fart. Always, as I silenced their mirthless laughter, I thought of the giggles, the shouts, the grade school counterpoint of joy.

Once a week I laughed with the ninth grade. On Mondays, when suddenly there would be a banging on the flimsy metal door, an imperious BOOM BOOM BOOM that rattled the windows and echoed through the building. Always at the tremendous noise I would jump, and the class would laugh at me.

"Come in!" I called, and the knocking would stop, and we laughed, when it was only a tiny first grader. He would pad in sneakers to my desk. "Good morning," he whispered, "may I have the cafeteria list?" Then he would tiptoe away and slam the door, which was funny, too.

"Mrs. Lawrence, would you come inside for a minute?" I followed Sister Lourdes into her office and waited while she rang the bell.

"Timothy Sanchez is coming back to school." She paused, as if I should react. "He has been in the detention home, one of many times—for theft and narcotics. They feel that he should finish school as quickly as possible. He is much older than his class, and according to their tests he is an exceptionally bright boy. It says here that he should be 'encouraged and challenged.'"

"Is there any particular thing you want me to do?"

"No, in fact, I can't advise you at all . . . he is quite a different problem. I thought I should mention it. His parole officer will be checking on his progress."

The next morning was Halloween, and the grade school had come in costume. I lingered to watch the witches, the hundreds of devils who trembled their morning prayers. The bell had rung when I got to the door of the ninth grade. "Sacred Heart of Mary, pray for us," they said. I stood at the door while Sister Lourdes took the roll. They rose as I entered the room, "Good morning." Their chairs scraped as they sat down.

The room became still. "El Tim!" someone whispered.

He stood in the door, silhouetted like Sister Lourdes from the skylight in the hall. He was dressed in black, his shirt open to the waist, his pants low and tight on lean hips. A gold crucifix glittered from a heavy chain. He was half-smiling, looking down at Sister Lourdes, his eyelashes creating jagged shadows down his gaunt cheeks. His black hair was long and straight. He smoothed it back with long slender fingers, quick, like a bird.

I watched the awe of the class. I looked at the young girls, the pretty young girls who whispered in the restroom not of dates or love but of marriage and abortion. They were tensed, watching him, flushed and alive.

Sister Lourdes stepped into the room. "Sit here, Tim." She motioned to a seat in front of my desk. He moved across the room, his broad back stooped, neck forward, tssch-tssch, tssch-tssch, the pachuco beat. "Dig the crazy nun!" he grinned, looking at me. The class laughed. "Silence!" Sister Lourdes said. She stood beside him. "This is Mrs. Lawrence. Here is your Spanish book." He seemed not to hear her. Her beads rattled nervously.

"Button your shirt," she said. "Button your shirt!"

He moved his hands to his chest, began with one to move the button in the light, with the other to inspect the buttonhole. The nun shoved his hands away, fumbled with his shirt until it was buttoned.

"Don't know how I ever got along without you, Sister," he drawled. She left the room.

It was Tuesday, dictation. "Take out a paper and pencil." The class complied automatically. "You too, Tim."

"Paper," he commanded quietly. Sheets of paper fought for his desk.

"*Llegó el hijo,*" I dictated. Tim stood up and started toward the back of the room. "Pencil's broken," he said. His voice was deep and hoarse, like the hoarseness people have when they are about to cry. He sharpened his pencil slowly, turning the sharpener so that it sounded like brushes on a drum.

"*No tenían fé.*" Tim stopped to put his hand on a girl's hair.

"Sit down," I said.

"Cool it," he muttered. The class laughed.

He handed in a blank paper, the name "EL TIM" across the top.

From that day everything revolved around El Tim. He caught up quickly with the rest of the class. His test papers and his written exercises were always excellent. But the students responded only to his sullen insolence in class, to his silent, unpunishable denial. Reading aloud, conjugating on the board, discussions, all of the things that had been almost fun were now almost impossible. The boys were flippant, ashamed to get things right; the girls embarrassed, awkward in front of him.

I began to give mostly written work, private work that I could check from desk to desk. I assigned many compositions and essays, even though this was not supposed to be done in ninth-grade Spanish. It was the only thing Tim liked to do, that he worked on intently, erasing and recopying, thumbing the pages of a Spanish dictionary on his desk. His compositions were imaginative, perfect in grammar, always of impersonal things . . . a street, a tree. I wrote comments and praise on them. Sometimes I read his papers to the class, hoping that they would be impressed, encouraged by his work. Too late I realized that it only confused them for him to be praised, that he triumphed anyway with a sneer . . . "*Pues, la tengo . . .*" I've got her pegged.

Emiterio Perez repeated everything that Tim said. Emiterio was retarded, being kept in the ninth grade until he was old enough to quit school. He passed out papers, opened windows. I had him do everything the other students did. Chuckling, he wrote endless pages of neat formless scribbles that I graded and handed back. Sometimes I would give him a B and he would be very happy. Now even he would not work. *"Para qué, hombre?"* Tim whispered to him. Emiterio would become confused, looking from Tim to me. Sometimes he would cry.

Helplessly, I watched the growing confusion of the class, the confusion that even Sister Lourdes could no longer control. There was not silence now when she entered the room, but unrest . . . a brushing of a hand over a face, an eraser tapping, flipping pages. The class waited. Always, slow and deep, would come Tim's voice. "It's cold in here, Sister, don't you think?" "Sister, I got something the matter with my eye, come see." We did not move as each time, every day, automatically the nun buttoned Tim's shirt. "Everything all right?" she would ask me and leave the room.

One Monday, I glanced up and saw a small child coming toward me. I glanced at the child, and then, smiling, I glanced at Tim.

"They're getting littler every time . . . have you noticed?" he said, so only I could hear. He smiled at me. I smiled back, weak with joy. Then with a harsh scrape he shoved back his chair and walked toward the back of the room. Halfway, he paused in front of Dolores, an ugly, shy little girl. Slowly he rubbed his hands over her breasts. She moaned and ran crying from the room.

"Come here!" I shouted to him. His teeth flashed.

"Make me," he said. I leaned against the desk, dizzy.

"Get out of here, go home. Don't ever come back to my class."

"Sure," he grinned. He walked past me to the door, fingers snapping as he moved . . . tsch-tsch, tsch-tsch. The class was silent.

As I was leaving to find Dolores, a rock smashed through the window, landing with shattered glass on my desk.

"What is going on!" Sister Lourdes was at the door. I couldn't get past her.

"I sent Tim home."

She was white, her bonnet shaking.

"Mrs. Lawrence, it is your duty to handle him in the classroom."

"I'm sorry, Sister, I can't do it."

"I will speak to the Mother Superior," she said. "Come to my office in the morning. Get in your seat!" she shouted at Dolores, who had come in the back door. The nun left.

"Turn to page ninety-three," I said. "Eddie, read and translate the first paragraph."

I didn't go to the grade school the next morning. Sister Lourdes was waiting, sitting behind her desk. Outside the glass doors of the office, Tim leaned against the wall, his hands hooked in his belt.

Briefly, I told the nun what had happened the day before. Her head was bowed as I spoke.

"I hope you will find it possible to regain the respect of this boy," she said.

"I'm not going to have him in my class," I said. I stood in front of her desk, gripping the wooden edge.

"Mrs. Lawrence, we were told that this boy needed special attention, that he needed 'encouragement and challenge.'"

"Not in junior high. He is too old and too intelligent to be here."

"Well, you are going to have to learn to deal with this problem."

"Sister Lourdes, if you put Tim in my Spanish class, I will go to the Mother Superior, to his parole officer. I'll tell them what happened. I'll show them the work that my pupils did before he came and the work they have done since. I will show them Tim's work, it doesn't belong in the ninth grade."

She spoke quietly, dryly. "Mrs. Lawrence, this boy is our responsibility. The parole board turned him over to us. He is going to remain in your class." She leaned toward me, pale. "It is our duty as teachers to control such problems, to teach in spite of them."

"Well, I can't do it."

"You are weak!" she hissed.

"Yes, I am. He has won. I can't stand what he does to the class and to me. If he comes back I resign."

She slumped back in her chair. Tired, she spoke. "Give him another chance. A week. Then you can do as you please."

"All right."

She rose and opened the door for Tim. He sat on the edge of her desk.

"Tim," she began softly, "will you prove to me, to Mrs. Lawrence, and to the class that you are sorry?" He didn't answer.

"I don't want to send you back to the detention home."

"Why not?"

"Because you are a bright boy. I want to see you learn something here, to graduate from San Marco's. I want to see you go on to high school, to . . ."

"Come on, Sister," Tim drawled. "You just want to button my shirt."

"Shut up!" I hit him across the mouth. My hand remained white in his dark skin. He did not move. I wanted to be sick. Sister Lourdes left the room. Tim and I stood, facing each other, listening as she started the ninth-grade prayers . . . *Blessed art Thou amongst women, Blessed is the fruit of thy womb, Jesus* . . .

"How come you hit me?" Tim asked softly.

I started to answer him, to say, "Because you were insolent and unkind," but I saw his smile of contempt as he waited for me to say just that.

"I hit you because I was angry. About Dolores and the rock. Because I felt hurt and foolish."

His dark eyes searched my face. For an instant the veil was gone.

"I guess we're even then," he said.

"Yes," I said, "let's go to class."

I walked with Tim down the hall, avoiding the beat of his walk.

Point of View

Imagine Chekhov's story "Grief" in the first person. An old man telling us his son has just died. We would feel embarrassed, uncomfortable, even bored, reacting precisely as the cabman's fares in the story did. But Chekhov's impartial voice imbues the man with dignity. We absorb the author's compassion for him and are deeply moved, if not by the son's death, by the old man talking to his horse.

I think it's because we are all pretty insecure.

I mean if I just presented to you this woman I'm writing about now . . .

"I'm a single woman in her late fifties. I work in a doctor's office. I ride home on the bus. Every Saturday I do my laundry and then I shop at Lucky's and buy the Sunday *Chronicle* and go home." You'd say, Give me a break.

But my story opens with "Every Saturday, after the laundromat and the grocery store, she bought the Sunday *Chronicle*." You'll listen to all the compulsive, obsessive boring little details of this woman's, Henrietta's, life only because it is written in the third person. You'll feel, hell if the narrator thinks there is something in this dreary creature worth writing about there must be. I'll read on and see what happens.

Nothing happens, actually. In fact the story isn't even written yet. What I hope to do is, by the use of intricate detail, to make this woman so believable you can't help but feel for her.

Most writers use props and scenery from their own lives. For example, my Henrietta eats her meager little dinner every night on a blue place mat, using exquisite heavy Italian stainless cutlery. An odd detail, inconsistent, it may seem, with this woman who cuts out coupons for Brawny towels, but it engages the reader's curiosity. At least I hope it will.

I don't think I'll give any explanation in the story. I myself eat with such elegant cutlery. Last year I ordered six place settings from the Museum of Modern Art Christmas catalog. Very expensive, a hundred dollars, but worth it, it seemed. I have six plates and six chairs. Maybe I'll give a dinner party, I thought at the time. It turned out to be, however, a hundred for six pieces. Two forks, two knives, two spoons. One place setting. I was embarrassed to send them back, figured well maybe next year I'd order another one.

Henrietta eats with her pretty cutlery and drinks Calistoga from a goblet. She has salad in a wooden bowl and a Lean Cuisine on a dinner plate. While she eats she reads the *This World* section where all the articles seem to have been written by the same first person.

Henrietta can't wait for Monday. She is in love with Dr. B., the nephrologist. Many nurse/secretaries are in love with "their" doctors. Sort of a Della Street syndrome.

Dr. B. is based upon the nephrologist I used to work for. I certainly wasn't in love with him. I'd joke sometimes and say we had a love/hate relationship. He was so hateful it must have reminded me of how love affairs get, sometimes.

Shirley, my predecessor, was in love with him, though. She pointed out all the birthday presents she had given him. The planter with the ivy and the little brass bicycle. The mirror with the frosted koala bear. The pen set. She said he just loved all his presents except for the furry sheepskin bicycle seat. She had to exchange it for biking gloves.

In my story Dr. B. laughs at Henrietta about the seat, is really mocking and cruel, as he most certainly could be. This will actually be the climax of the story, when she realizes the disdain he feels for her, how pitiful her love is.

The day I started working there I ordered paper gowns. Shirley used cotton ones: "Blue plaid for boys, pink roses for girls." (Most of our patients were so old they used walkers.) Every weekend she'd lug the laundry home on the bus and not only wash it but starch and iron it. I have my Henrietta doing this too . . . ironing on Sunday, after she cleans her apartment.

Of course a lot of my story is about Henrietta's habits. Habits. Not even that they are so bad in themselves, but they go on for so long. Every Saturday, year after year.

Every Sunday Henrietta reads the pink section. The horoscope first, always on page 16, the paper's habit. Usually the stars have racy things to say about Henrietta. "Full moon, sexy Scorp, and you know what that means! Get set to sizzle!"

On Sundays, after cleaning and ironing, Henrietta makes something special for dinner. A Cornish game hen. Stove Top stuffing and cranberry sauce. Creamed peas. A Forever Yours for dessert.

After she washes the dishes she watches *60 Minutes*. It's not that she is particularly interested in the program. She likes the staff. Diane Sawyer so well-bred and pretty and the men are all solid and reliable and concerned. She likes it when they look worried and shake their heads or when it's a funny story they smile and shake their heads. Most of all she likes the shots of the big watch. The minute hand and the click click click of the time.

Then she watches *Murder, She Wrote*, which she doesn't like but there is nothing else on.

I'm having a hard time writing about Sunday. Getting the long hollow feeling of Sundays. No mail and faraway lawn mowers, the hopelessness.

Or how to describe Henrietta's eagerness for Monday morning. The tick tick of his bicycle pedals and the click when he locks his door to change into his blue suit.

"Have a nice weekend?" she asks. He never answers. He never says hello or good-bye.

At night she holds the door open for him, as he is walking out with his bike.

"Good-bye! Have a good one!" she smiles.

"A good *what*? For Christ's sake, stop saying that."

But no matter how nasty he is to her Henrietta believes there is a bond between them. He has a clubfoot, a severe limp, whereas she has scoliosis, a curvature. A hunchback, in fact. She is self-conscious and shy but understands how he can be so caustic. Once he told her she had the two qualifications for being a nurse . . . "stupid and servile."

After *Murder, She Wrote*, Henrietta takes a bath, pampering herself with floral-scented bath beads.

She watches the news then as she smoothes lotion on her face and hands. She has put water on for tea. She likes the weather report. The little suns above Nebraska and North Dakota. Rain clouds over Florida and Louisiana.

She lies in bed, sipping Sleepytime tea. She wishes she had her old electric blanket with the switch LO-MED-HOT. The new blanket was advertised as the Intelligent Electric Blanket. The blanket knows it isn't cold so it doesn't get hot. She wishes it would get hot, comforting. It's too smart for its own good! She laughs out loud. The sound is startling in the little room.

She turns off the TV and sips her tea, listening to cars pulling in and out of the Arco station across the street. Sometimes a car stops with a screech at the telephone booth. A car door slams and soon the car speeds away.

She hears someone drive up slowly to the phones. Loud jazz music comes from the car. Henrietta turns off the light, raises the blind by her bed, just a little. The window is steamed. The car radio plays Lester Young. The man talking on the phone holds it with his chin. He wipes his forehead with a handkerchief. I lean against the cool windowsill and watch him. I listen to the sweet saxophone play "Polka Dots and Moonbeams." In the steam of the glass I write a word. What? My name? A man's name? Henrietta? Love? Whatever it is I erase it quickly before anyone can see.

Her First Detox

Carlotta woke, during the fourth week of steady October rain, in the County detox ward. I'm in a hospital, she thought, and walked shakily down the hall. There were two men in a large room that would have been sunny if it weren't raining. The men were ugly, wore black-and-white denim. They were bruised, had bloody bandages. These men are here from a prison but then she saw that she was wearing black-and-white denim, that she was bruised and bloody too. She remembered handcuffs, a straitjacket.

It was Halloween. The volunteer AA lady taught them how to make pumpkins. You blow up the balloon, she knots it. Then you stick gooey paper strips all around it. The next night, when your balloon is dry, you paint it orange. The lady cuts out the eyes and the nose and the mouth. You get to choose whether you want a smile or a frown on yours. You don't get scissors.

There was much childlike laughter, because of the slippery balloons, their shaky hands. It was hard, making the pumpkins. If they had been allowed to cut out the eyes and nose and mouth they would have been given those dull dumb scissors. Whenever they wanted to write they were given fat pencils, like first grade.

Carlotta had a good time in the detox ward. The men were awkwardly gallant toward her. She was the only woman, she was pretty, didn't "look like a lush." Her gray eyes were clear, her laughter easy. She had transformed her black-and-white pajamas with a brilliant magenta scarf.

Most of the men were street winos. The police brought them in or they simply checked in when their SSI money ran out, when there was no port, no shelter. County was a great place to dry out, they told her. They give you Valium, Thorazine, Dilantin if you seize. Big yellow-jacket Nembutals at night. This wouldn't be so for much longer, soon there would be only "social model" detoxes, with no drugs at all. "Shit—why come?" Pepe asked.

The food is good, but cold. You have to get your own tray off the cart and carry it to the table. Most people can't do that at first, or they drop it. Some of the men shook so bad they had to be fed, or they just bent down and lapped up their food, like cats.

The patients were given Antabuse after the third day. If you drink alcohol within seventy-two hours after taking Antabuse you will be deathly ill. Convulsions, chest pains, shock, often death. The patients saw the Antabuse movie every morning at nine thirty, before Group Therapy. Later, in the sunroom, the men figured out how soon they could drink again. They wrote on napkins, with fat pencils. Carlotta alone said she wouldn't drink again.

"Wha' you drink, woman?" Willie asked.

"Jim Beam."

"Jim Beam?" The men all laughed.

"Shee-ut . . . you ain' no alkie. Us alkies drink sweet wine."

"Oo-wee how sweet it is!"

"Wha' the fuck you doin' here anyhows?"

"You mean what's a nice girl like me . . . ?" What was she doing here, anyway? She hadn't thought about it yet.

"Jim Beam. You don' need detox . . ."

"She sure as hell did. She was a crazy woman when they brought her in, beatin' on that chink cop. Wong. Then later she seized bad, 'bout three minutes bangin' around like a wrung-neck chicken."

Carlotta remembered nothing. The nurse told her she had wrecked her car into a wall. The police had brought her here instead of to jail when they found out she was a teacher, had four kids, no husband. No priors, whatever they were.

"You get DTs?" Pepe asked.

"Yes," she lied. God, just listen to me . . . please accept me you guys, please like me you runny-eyed bums.

I don't know what DTs are. The doctor asked me that too. I said yes and he wrote it down. I think I've had them all my life, if, in fact, they are visions of demons.

They all laughed, plastering sticky paper on their balloons. How Joe had been eighty-sixed out of the Adam and Eve, figured he could find a better bar. Climbed into a taxi hollering, "To the Shalimar!" but the taxi was a squad car and they brought him here. The difference between a connoisseur and a wino? The connoisseur takes it out of the paper bag. Mac, on the virtues of Thunderbird wine: "Dumb dagos fergot to take their socks off."

At night after the balloons and the last Valium came the AA people. Half of the patients nodded out through the whole meeting, listening to them tell how they used to be at the bottom too. One AA woman told how she used to chew garlic all day so nobody would smell liquor on her breath. Carlotta chewed cloves. Her mother had breathed fingerfuls of Vicks salve. Uncle John always had bits of Sen-Sen stuck in his teeth, so he looked like one of their pumpkins, smiling.

Carlotta liked it best at the end, when they all held hands and she said the Lord's Prayer. They would have to wake their buddies up, prop them up like dead soldiers in *Beau Geste*. She felt a closeness with the men as they prayed for sobriety, forever and ever.

After the AA people left the patients got milk and cookies and Nembutal. Almost everyone went to sleep, including the nurses. Carlotta played poker with Mac and Joe and Pepe until three in the morning. Nothing wild.

She called home every day. Her older sons, Ben and Keith, were taking care of Joel and Nathan. Everything was fine, they said. There was not much she could say.

She stayed in the hospital seven days. On the morning she left there was a sign in the rainy dark dayroom. "Lotsa Luck Lottie." The police had left her car in the parking lot. One big dent, a broken mirror.

Carlotta drove to Redwood Park. She turned the radio up loud, sat on the dented car hood in the rain. Below her glinted the golden Mormon Temple. Fog covered the bay. It was good to be outside, to hear music. She smoked, planned what to do in classes the next week, wrote down lesson plans, library books she would need.

(Excuses had been made at school. An ovarian cyst . . . Benign, fortunately.)

Grocery list. Make lasagna tonight—her sons' favorite. Tomato paste, veal, beef. Salad and garlic bread. Soap and toilet paper, probably. Pick up a carrot cake for dessert. Her lists reassured her, held everything back together again.

Her sons and Myra, her principal, were the only ones who knew where she had been. They had been supportive. Don't worry. Everything will be okay.

Everything was somehow always okay. She was a good teacher and a good mother really. At home the small house overflowed with projects, books, arguments, laughter. Everyone met their obligations.

In the evenings, after dishes and laundry, correcting papers, there was TV or Scrabble, problems, cards, or silly conversations. Good night, guys! A silence then that she celebrated by doubling her drinks, no manic ice cubes now.

If they awakened, her sons would stumble upon her madness which, then, only occasionally spilled over into morning. But for as far back as she could remember, late at night, she would hear

Keith checking ashtrays, the fireplace. Turning out lights, locking doors.

This had been her first experience with the police, even though she didn't remember it. She had never driven drunk before, never missed more than a day at work, never . . . She had no idea of what was yet to come.

Flour. Milk. Ajax. She only had wine vinegar at home, which, with Antabuse, could throw her into convulsions. She wrote cider vinegar on the list.

Phantom Pain

I was five then, at the Deuces Wild mine in Montana. Every few months, before it snowed, my father and I would climb into the mountains, following blazes old Hancock had made back in the 1890s. My father carried a duffel bag filled with coffee, cornmeal, jerky, things like that. I carried a stack of *Saturday Evening Posts*, most of the way, anyway. Hancock's cabin was at the edge of a crater-shaped meadow on the very top of the mountain. Blue sky over it, all around it. His dog was named Blue. Grass grew on the roof, down in a rakish fringe over the porch where they drank coffee and talked, passing chunks of ore, squinting through cigarette smoke. I played with Blue and the goats or pasted pages of the *Post* on cabin walls already thickly layered with past issues. Evenly in neat rectangles one on top of another all around the small room. Snowed-in in the long winter Hancock would read his walls, page by page. If he found the end of a story he'd try to make up what came before, or piece it together with other pages around the cabin. When he had read the whole room he'd paste for days and days and then start all over. I hadn't gone up with my father the first trip that spring, when he found the old man dead. The goats and the dog too, all in his bed. "When I get cold I just pull me up another goat," he used to say.

"Come on, Lu, just take me up there and leave me." That's what my father kept begging me to do when I first put him in the nursing home. That's all he talked about then, different mines, different mountains. Idaho, Arizona, Colorado, Bolivia, Chile. His mind was starting to go then. He wouldn't just remember those places, but would actually think he was there, in that time. He would think I was a child, would talk to me as if I were the age I had been in different places. He'd tell the nurses things like, "Little Lu can read all of *Our Friendly Helpers* and she's only four years old." Or, "Help the lady take out the dishes. That's a good girl."

I'd bring him café con leche every morning. I'd shave him and comb him, walk him up and down, up and down the rank-smelling halls. Most of the other patients were still in bed, calling, rattling their bars, ringing their bells. Senile old ladies play with themselves. After walking with him I'd tie him in his wheelchair, so he wouldn't try to run away and fall down. And I'd do it too. I mean I wouldn't pretend or just humor him—I'd actually go with him someplace. To the Trench mine in the mountains above Patagonia, Arizona: I was eight years old, purple with gentian violet for ringworm. In the evening we would all go out to the cliff to dump cans and burn the garbage. Deer and antelope, the puma, sometimes, would come close, not afraid of our dogs. Nighthawks darted against the sheer rock face of the cliffs beyond us, deeper red in the sunset.

The only time my father said he loved me was just before I came back to the States for college. We were on the beach in Tierra del Fuego. Antarctic cold. "We've tramped through this whole continent together . . . the same mountains, the same ocean, from top to bottom." I was born in Alaska, but I don't remember it. He kept thinking I should, in the nursing home, so finally I did pretend to know Gabe Carter, to remember Nome, the bear in the camp.

In the beginning he kept asking about my mother, where was she, when was she coming. Or he would think she was there, would talk to her, make me feed her a bite for every bite he took. I stalled him. She was packing, she was coming. When he was better we would all live together in a big house in Berkeley. He would nod, reassured, except for one day when he said, "You're lying through your teeth." And then went on talking about something else.

One day he just killed her off. When I arrived he was lying in bed, weeping, curled up like a baby. He told the story as if in shock, with irrelevant details, like someone who has witnessed a horrible accident. They were on a Mississippi steamboat; my mother was gambling belowdecks. Colored people were allowed on now and Florida (his nurse) had won every cent of their money. My mother had bet the whole thing, their life savings, in one last hand of five-card draw. One-eyed jacks wild. "I should have known," he said, "when I saw that hussy laughing away with her gold teeth, counting all that money. She gave John here at least four thousand."

"Dry up, you snob," John said from the bed next to my father's. He took a Hershey bar from the back of his Bible. He wasn't allowed sweets, it was the one I'd brought my father the day before. My father's reading glasses showed from under John's pillow. I got them. John began to moan and cry: "My legs! My legs hurt!" He didn't have any legs. He was a diabetic and they had been amputated above the knees.

On the steamboat my father had been in the bar with Bruce Sasse (a diamond driller from Bisbee). They had heard the shot and then a long time later the splash. "I didn't have change for a tip but I didn't want to leave a dollar." "Cheap snob! Typical! Typical!" John said from his bed. My father and Bruce Sasse rushed around to the starboard side just as my mother was floating away. Blood in the wake of the boat.

He grieved for her only that one day, but for weeks he talked about her funeral. Thousands of people had been there. None of my sons had worn a suit, but I looked lovely and was gracious. Ed Titman came, the ambassador to Peru, Domingo the butler, even

Charlie Bloom the old Swede from Mullan, Idaho. Charlie once told me he always put sugar on his oatmeal. What if you don't have any? I asked, smart aleck. I puts it on yust the same.

The day my father killed off my mother was the day he stopped knowing me. After that he ordered me around like a secretary or a servant. One day I finally asked him where I was. I had run off. Bad blood, a Moynihan just like my mother and Uncle John. I had just taken off one afternoon, right outside the nursing home, up Ashby Avenue with a good-for-nothing greaser in a four-holed Buick. The man he described was, in fact, a dark sleazy type I find attractive.

He began hallucinating most of the time then. Wastebaskets turned into dogs that talked, leaf shadows on the walls became marching soldiers, the hefty nurses were now transvestite spies. He talked incessantly about Eddie and Little Joe; neither seemed to be anyone he might have known. Every night they had some wild free-wheeling adventure on an ammunition ship outside Nagasaki, in helicopters above Bolivia. My father would laugh, loose and easy as I had never known him.

It got so I would pray for him to be this way, but more and more he was becoming rational, "oriented as to time and place." He talked about money. Money he had made, money he had lost, money he would make. He saw me then as a broker, maybe, would drone on and on about options and percentages, scrawling figures all over the Kleenex box. Margins and options, T-notes and stocks and bonds and mergers. He would bitterly denounce his daughter (me) for murdering his wife and locking him up, just to get his money. Florida was the only black nurse in the hospital who would work with him. He accused them all of stealing, called them pickaninnies or whores. He'd use the urinal to call the police. Florida and John had stolen all his money. John would ignore him, reading his Bible or just lying in his bed, writhing, screaming, "My legs! Lord Jesus stop the pain in my legs!"

"Hush John," Florida said. "That's only phantom pain."

"Is it real?" I asked her.

She shrugged. "All pain is real."

He talked to Florida about me. She laughed, winking at me, agreeing, "She's rotten to the *core*." He told us all the ways I had been a disappointment to him, from the spelling bee to my failed marriages.

"It's getting to you," Florida said. "You've stopped ironing his shirts—pretty soon you won't come no more."

But there was a new bond I felt. I had never seen him bitter or bigoted or money-conscious. This was the man whose idols had been Thoreau and Jefferson and Thomas Paine. I wasn't disillusioned. The fear and awe I had felt toward him were beginning to disappear.

The other thing I liked was that I could touch him now. Hug him and bathe him, cut his toenails and hold his hand. I didn't really listen to anything he said anymore. I'd hold him, listening to Florida and the other nurses singing and laughing, *Days of Our Lives* blaring from the dayroom. I'd feed him Jell-O and listen to John read from Deuteronomy. I've never understood how so many barely literate people read the Bible so much. It's hard. In the same way it surprises me that uneducated seamstresses all over the world can figure out how to put in sleeves and zippers.

He ate in his room and wouldn't associate with the other patients at all. I would, just for a break or to keep from crying. On the bulletin board was a big sign that said, Today is ———. The weather is ———. The next meal is ———. The next holiday is ———. For two months it was a rainy Tuesday before lunch and Easter, but after that the spaces were always blank.

A volunteer named Ada read the paper every morning. Turning and turning pages, avoiding crime and violence. Most days all she ended up with were bus crashes in Pakistan, Dennis the Menace, and the horoscope. Hurricanes in Galveston. (I also can't understand how people have stayed in Galveston after all these years.) I came to enjoy the other patients. Most of them were even more senile than my father, but they were glad to see me, clawed at me with tiny fingers. They all recognized me, called me different names.

I kept going to visit him. Maybe out of guilt, as Florida said, but with hope too. I kept waiting for him to praise me, forgive me. Please know me, Daddy, say you love me. He never did, and I only go now to take shaving things or pajamas or candy. He can't walk anymore. He gets violent, so they have him in a Posey day and night.

The last real time I was with him was on the picnic to Lake Merritt. Ten patients went. Ada, Florida, Sam, and I. Sam is the janitor. (Chimp, my father called him.) It took an hour to load them into the van, wheelchairs up a whining lift. It was very hot, the day after Memorial Day. Most of them had peed even before we got moving; windows steamed up. The old people laughed and were excited, but frightened too, flinching when buses passed us, sirens, motorcycles. My father looked nice in a seersucker suit, but then the front turned blue with Parkinson's drool and dark blue all down one leg.

I had imagined that we would be under the trees, by the water, but Ada had us set up the wheelchairs in a semicircle facing the street, by the duck pond. I also imagined the winos would leave, but they just stayed on the benches in front of the old people. Some of the patients smelled cigarettes and asked for them. One of the winos gave John one, but Ada took it away and stomped it out. Exhaust fumes, and radios from the pimpmobiles and low-riders and motorcycles. The ground vibrated with joggers who bunched up when they got to us, running in place as they tried to get around. We were passing food, feeding the "feeders." Potato salad and fried chicken. Pickled beets and Kool-Aid. Florida and I served plates to the four winos on the bench, and Ada got furious.

There was way too much food, though. Neapolitan ice cream melted onto bibs. Lula and Mae just mashed the bars, played with them in their laps. My father was very neat when he ate, had always been meticulous. I washed each of his fingers. He has beautiful hands. I don't know why they pluck at their clothes and blankets. It's called "floccillation."

After lunch a big woman in a park ranger uniform brought out a baby raccoon and passed it around. It was soft and smelled sweet and everyone liked it, loved it, really, holding him and stroking him, but Lula squeezed him so hard he clawed at her face. "Rabid!" my father said. "My legs!" John cried. The man gave John another cigarette. Ada didn't notice, was putting the food trays into the van. The ranger gave the raccoon to the winos. The little animal obviously knew them, curled around their necks, calm. Ada said we had twenty minutes to give people rides around the duck pond and the birdcages, up the hill for a view of the lake.

My father had always loved birds. I parked him in front of the ratty horned owls, talking to him about different birds we had seen. The porcupine with green hair. The pileated woodpecker against the white aspen. A frigate bird off Antofagasta. Road-runners mating, majestic. My father just sat there, his eyes glazed. The owls slept or were stuffed. I wheeled the chair away. All the others were festive, hollered and waved to us. John was really having a good time. Florida had made friends with a jogger who loaned her his tape recorder. Lula held it and sang while they fed the ducks.

It was hard to push the chair up the hill. Hot and loud with the cars and radios and interminable thud thud of the runners. It was so smoggy we could barely see the other shore. Memorial Day litter and debris. Paper cups floated in the foamy brown lake serene as swans. At the top of the hill I put on his brakes and lit a cigarette. He was laughing, an ugly laugh.

"It's awful, isn't it, Daddy?"

"It sure is, Lu."

He loosened his brakes and the chair started down the brick path. I hesitated, just stood there watching it, but then I threw away my cigarette and caught his chair just as it was picking up speed.

Tiger Bites

The train slowed down outside of El Paso. I didn't wake my baby, Ben, but carried him out to the vestibule so I could look out. And smell it, the desert. Caliche, sage, sulphur from the smelter, wood fires from Mexican shacks by the Rio Grande. The Holy Land. When I first went there, to live with Mamie and Grandpa during the war, that's when I first heard about Jesus and Mary and the Bible and sin, so Jerusalem got all mixed up with El Paso's jagged mountains and deserts. Rushes by the river and huge crucifixes everywhere. Figs and pomegranates. Dark-shawled women with infants and poor gaunt men with sufferer's, savior's eyes. And the stars at night were big and bright like in the song, so insistently dazzling it made sense that wise men couldn't help but follow any one of them and find their way.

My uncle Tyler had cooked up a family reunion for Christmas. For one thing he was hoping my folks and I would make up. I dreaded seeing my parents . . . they were furious because my husband, Joe, had left me. They had almost died when I got married at seventeen, so my divorce was the last straw. But I couldn't wait to see my cousin Bella Lynn and my uncle John, who was coming from L.A.

And there was Bella Lynn! In the train depot parking lot. Standing up and waving from a powder-blue Cadillac convertible, wearing a fringed suede cowgirl outfit. She was probably the most beautiful woman in West Texas, she must have won a million beauty contests. Long pale blond hair and yellow-brown eyes. Her smile, though, no, it was her laugh, a dusky, deep cascading laughter that caught the joy, implied and mocked the sorrow in every joy.

She tossed our bags and Ben's little bed in the backseat. All of us Moynihans are strong, physically anyway. She kissed and hugged us both over and over. We got in and headed for the A & W across town. It was cold but the air was clean and dry, she kept the top down and the heater blasting, talked nonstop as she drove, one-handed since she waved at just about everybody we passed.

"First off I should tell you we're short on yuletide joy out at our place. Uncle John gets here day after tomorrow, Christmas Eve, praise the Lord. Mary, your mama and my mama started drinking and fighting right off the bat. Mama went up on the garage roof and won't come down. Your mother slit her wrists."

"Oh, God."

"Well you know, not bad or anything. She wrote a suicide note about how you had always ruined her life. Signed it Bloody Mary! She's in Saint Joseph's psych ward on a seventy-two-hour hold. At least your father isn't coming, he's furious about your D.I.V.O.R.C.E. My crazy grandma is there. Looney Tunes! And a passel of horrid relatives from Lubbock and Sweetwater. Daddy has them all put up at a motel and they drive over and eat all day and watch TV. They're all born again so think you and me are just rotten to the core. Rex Kipp is here! He and Daddy are buying presents and stuff for poor people all day and hanging out in Daddy's shop. So boy am I ever glad to see you . . ."

At the drive-in we ordered Papa burgers and fries and malts, like always. I told her Ben could have some of mine. He was just ten months old. But she ordered him a Papa burger and a banana split. Our whole family is extravagant. Well, no, my father isn't like this at all. He is from New England, is thrifty and responsible. I turned out a Moynihan.

After Bella had filled me in on the reunion situation she told me about Cletis, her husband of only two months. Her folks had been as mad when she got married as mine had been with me. Cletis was a construction worker, rodeo rider, roughneck. Tears rolled down Bella's lovely cheeks as she told me what happened.

"Lou, we were happy as clams. I swear nobody ever had such a sweet tender love. Why in heaven's name are clams happy? We had a dear little trailer in the south valley, by the river. Our little blue heaven. I cleaned house and washed dishes! I cooked, made pineapple upside-down cake and macaroni, all kinds of things, and he was proud of me, and me of him. First bad thing that happened was Daddy forgave me for marrying him and he bought us a house. On Rim Road, you know, a mansion, columns on the porch, but we didn't want his house so Cletis and Daddy had an awful fight. I tried to explain to Daddy we didn't need his ol' house, how I'd be happy living with Cletis on the back of a flatbed truck. And I had to explain it over and over to Cletis too, because even though I refused to move he took to sulking. Then one day I went to the Popular Dry Goods and bought some clothes and towels, just a few things, on my old charge account I've had my entire life long. Cletis had a fit, said I had spent more money in two hours than he made in six months. So I just took it all outside and poured kerosene on it, set fire to everything, and we kissed and made up. Oh, Little Lou, I love him so bad, so bad! Next darn fool thing I did and why I did it I'll never know. Mama had come to call. I guess I was just feeling like a married lady, you know? A grown-up. I made coffee and served Oreos on a little dish. Blabbed my big mouth about S.E.X. I suppose I felt I was big enough to talk to her now about S.E.X. Oh God, well, and I didn't *know*, either, so I asked her if I could get pregnant if I swallowed Cletis's come. She tore out of the trailer and ran home to Daddy. All hell broke loose. That night Daddy and Rex came and beat the living daylights out of Cletis. Put him in the hospital with a broken collarbone and two broken ribs. Talking about he was a pervert, and putting him in jail for sodomy and annulling the marriage. Can you imagine, going down on your own lawful wedded husband is against the *law*? Anyways I wouldn't go home with Daddy and just stayed at Cletis's bedside until I could bring him home. And we were fine, happy as those old clams again, even though Cletis took to drinking a lot, account of he couldn't go back to work for a while. Then last week I look out and see this brand-new Cadillac in our driveway, with a huge stuffed Santa sitting in it, and satin ribbons all around it. I laughed, you know, 'cause it was funny, but Cletis said, 'Happy, huh? Well, I ain't never going to make you happy like your precious Daddy does.' And he left. I figured he'd just gone off on a tear and he'd be back. Oh, Lou. He's not coming back. He's *gone*! He went to work on an oil rig off Louisiana. He didn't even call. His trashy mother told me when she came to get his clothes and his saddle."

Little Ben had actually eaten all that burger and most of the banana split. He threw up all over himself and Bella Lynn's jacket. She tossed the jacket in the backseat, washed him off with napkins dipped in water while I got him out some clean clothes and a diaper. He didn't cry once though. He loved the rock and roll music and the hillbilly music, and Bella Lynn's voice or her hair, never took his eyes off her.

I envied Bella and Cletis, being so in love. I had adored Joe, but had always been afraid of him, trying to please him. I don't think he ever even liked me much. I was miserable not so much because I missed him but for the whole failure of things and how it all seemed like my fault.

I told her my short sad story. How Joe was a wonderful sculptor. He had been given a Guggenheim, got a patron and a villa and foundry in Italy, and he left. "Art is his life." (I had taken to saying that, to everybody, dramatically.) No, no child support. I didn't even know his address.

Bella Lynn and I hugged and cried for a while and then she sighed. "Well, at least you have his baby."

"Babies."

"What?"

"I'm almost four months pregnant. That was the last straw for Joe, me having another baby."

"It's the last darn straw for you, little fool! What are you going to do? No way those folks of yours are going to help. Your ma will just kill herself all over again when she hears *this* news."

"I don't know what to do. Another really dumb problem . . . I wanted to come so bad but they wouldn't even give me Christmas Eve off at the escrow company. So I just quit, and came. Now I'm going to have to look for a job pregnant."

"You need an abortion, Lou. That's all there is to it."

"Where would I do that? Anyway . . . it will be as easy to have two babies alone as one."

"As *hard*. Besides, that's not true. Reason Ben here is so sweet is because you were with him as a baby. He's old enough now to go to somebody while you work although it's a crying shame to leave him. But you can't go leaving a newborn infant."

"Well that's the situation."

"You're talking like your father. The situation is that you're nineteen and you're pretty. You have to find yourself a good strong decent man who will be willing to love little Ben as his own. But you'll have a hell of a time finding somebody who'd take on two of them. He'd have to be some kind of rescuer do-gooder saint type you'd marry out of gratitude and then you'd feel guilty and hate him so you'd fall madly in love with some fly-by-night saxophone player . . . Oh it would be tragic, tragic, Lou. Let's think. This is serious. Just you listen to me now and let me take care of you. Haven't I always had you do what's best?"

Well, far from it, as a matter of fact, but I was so confused I didn't say anything. I wished I hadn't told her. I had wanted just to come to the reunion and be happy, forget all about my troubles. Now they were worse, with my mother killing herself again, and Daddy not even coming.

"You wait right here. Order us coffee while I make some phone calls." She smiled and waved to people, men mostly, who called to her from other cars at the drive-in as she made her way to the phone booth. She was in there a long time, came out twice, once to borrow a sweater and get some coffee and later to get more dimes. Ben played with the radio knobs for a while and turned the windshield wipers on and off. The carhop warmed a bottle for me; Ben drank it and fell asleep in my lap.

Bella put the top up when she got back, flashed me a smile and took off down Mesa toward the Plaza. "South of the border . . . down Mexico way!" she was singing.

"Okay, Lou. It's all settled. I've been through this myself. It's horrible, but it is safe and the place is clean. You'll go in this afternoon at four and be out by ten in the morning. They'll give you antibiotics and painkillers to bring home, but it doesn't hurt real bad, it's like having a period. I called home and told them we were going shopping in Juárez, were spending the night at the Camino Real. That's where little Ben and I will be, getting to know each other, and you can come the minute it's all over."

"Wait a minute, Bella. I haven't thought this out."

"I know you haven't. That's why I'm doing all the thinking."

"What if something goes wrong?"

"We'll get you to a doctor here. They can save your life and everything in Texas. They just can't do abortions."

"What if I die? Who will care for Ben?"

"Well, I will! And I'll be a darn good mother too."

I had to laugh then. She made sense. In fact a big load was off my mind. Not worrying about a little infant in addition to Ben.

God, what a relief. She was right. An abortion was the best thing to do. I closed my eyes and leaned back against the leather seat.

"I don't have any money! What does it cost?"

"Five hundred. Cash. Which I happen to have in my hot little hand. I have money to burn. Every time I go near Mama or Daddy—sometimes I just want a hug or to tell 'em I miss Cletis or ask maybe should I go to secretarial school—they shove money at me, go get yourself something pretty."

"I know," I said. I knew what that was like. Or did, before my folks disowned me. "I used to think if a big old tiger bit off my hand and I went running up to my mother she'd just slap some money on the stump. Or make a joke . . . 'What's that, the sound of one hand clapping?'"

We came to the bridge and the smell of Mexico. Smoke and chili and beer. Carnations and candles and kerosene. Oranges and Delicados and urine. I buzzed the window down and hung my head out, glad to be home. Church bells, ranchera music, bebop jazz, mambos. Christmas carols from the tourist shops. Rattling exhaust pipes, honkings, drunken American soldiers from Fort Bliss. El Paso matrons, serious shoppers, carrying piñatas and jugs of rum. There were new shopping areas and a luxurious new hotel, where one gracious young man took the car, another the bags, and still another gathered Ben into his arms without waking him. Our room was elegant, with fine weavings and rugs, good fake antiquities and bright folk art. The shuttered windows opened onto a patio with a tiled fountain, lush gardens, a steaming swimming pool beyond. Bella tipped everyone and got on the phone to room service. Jug of coffee, rum, Coke, pastries, fruit. I had formula and cereal and plenty of clean bottles for Ben, begged her not to feed him candy and ice cream.

"Flan?" she asked. I nodded. "Flan," she told the phone. Bella called the gift shop and ordered a size 8 bathing suit, crayons, any toys they had, and fashion magazines. "Maybe we should stay here the whole time! Plumb forget Christmas!" she said.

We walked around the grounds with Ben between us. I was so relaxed and happy I was surprised when Bella Lynn said, "Okay, hon, it's time for you to go."

She gave me the five hundred dollars. Told me to take a cab back to the hotel and have her come down and pay it. "You can't take any other money or identification with you. You can give them my name, and this number."

She and Ben waved good-bye to me after she had put me in a cab, paid for it and told him where to go.

The taxi took me to the Nueva Poblana Restaurant, to the back entrance of the parking lot, where I would wait for two men dressed in black, wearing dark glasses.

I was only there for two or three minutes before they appeared behind me. Quickly and silently an old sedan pulled up. One of the men opened the door and beckoned to me to get in, the other ran around to the other side. The driver, a young boy, looked around, nodded and took off. The back windows were curtained, the seat so low I couldn't see out; it seemed we were driving in circles at first and then the whap whap whap of a stretch of highway, more circles, a stop. The creaking of heavy wooden gates. We drove a few yards and stopped, the gate closed behind us.

I had a glimpse of the courtyard as I was led inside by an old woman in black. She didn't exactly look at me with scorn but her failure to speak or greet me was so devoid of usual Mexican warmth and graciousness it felt like an insult.

The building was yellow brick, maybe an old factory, the ground was entirely cemented, but there were still canaries, pots of four o'clocks and portulacas. Bolero music, laughter, and the clatter of dishes from across the yard. Chicken cooking, a smell of onions and garlic, epazote.

A businesslike woman nodded to me from her desk, and when I sat down she shook my hand but did not give her name. She asked for my name and the five hundred dollars, please. The name and number of someone to call in case of an emergency. That was all she asked, and I signed nothing. She spoke little English but I didn't speak Spanish to her, or to any of them; it would have seemed too familiar a thing to do.

"At five o'clock the doctor will come. You will have exam, catheter placed in utero. During the night cause contractions but sleeping medicine, you don't feel bad. No food, water after dinner. Early morning spontaneous abortion most usually. Six o'clock you go to operating room, go to sleep, get D and C. Wake up in your bed. We give you ampicillin against infection, codeine for pain. At ten car will take you to Juárez or to El Paso Airport or bus."

The old woman took me to my bed, which was in a dark room with six other beds. She held up her hand to show five o'clock, then pointed to the bed, then gestured toward a sitting room across the hall.

There had been so little sound that I was surprised to find twenty women in the room, all Americans. Three of them were girls, almost children, with their mothers. The others were emphatically alone, reading magazines, sitting. Four of the women were in their forties, perhaps even fifties . . . change-of-life pregnancies, I imagined, which proved to be true. The rest of the women seemed to be in their late teens or early twenties. Every one of them looked frightened, embarrassed, but most of all, intensely ashamed. That they had done something terrible. Shame. There appeared to be no bond of sympathy between any of them; my entrance was scarcely noticed. A pregnant Mexican woman swirled a dirty damp mop around, staring at us all with undisguised curiosity and contempt. I felt an unreasonable fury toward her. What do you tell your priest, bitch? You have no husband and seven children . . . you have to work in this wicked place or starve? Oh, God, that was probably true. I felt a tiredness, an immense sadness, for her, for all of us in the room.

We were, each of us, alone. The young girls perhaps most of all, for even though two of them were crying, their mothers also seemed distant from them, staring out into the room, isolated in their own shame and anger. Alone. Tears started to come to my eyes, because Joe was gone, because my mother wasn't there, ever.

I didn't want to have an abortion. I didn't need an abortion. The scenarios I imagined for all the other women in the room were all awful, painful stories, impossible situations. Rape, incest, all kinds of serious things. I could take care of this baby. We would be a family. It and Ben and me. A real family. Maybe I'm crazy. At least this is my own decision. Bella Lynn is always telling me what to do.

I went out into the hall. I wanted to call Bella Lynn, to leave. All the other doors were locked, except for the kitchen, where the cooks shooed me away.

A door slammed. The doctor had arrived. There was no question that he was the doctor, although he looked like an Argentine movie star or a Las Vegas nightclub singer. The old woman helped him off with his camel's hair coat and scarf. An expensive silk suit, a Rolex watch. It was his arrogance and authority that labeled him as doctor. He was dark, liquidly sexy, he walked softly, like a thief.

The doctor took my arm. "Back with the other girls, dear, time for your exam."

"I changed my mind. I want to leave."

"Go to your room, sweetie. Some change their mind a dozen times in an hour. We'll talk later . . . Go on. *Ándale!*"

I found my bed. The other women were sitting on the edge of theirs. Two of the young girls. The old woman had us strip, put on gowns. The really young girl was trembling, near hysterical with fear. He began with her first, and I must say, was patient and reassuring but she slapped out at him, kicked her mother away. He gave her an injection, covered her with a blanket.

"I'll be back. Just relax," he told the mother.

The other young girl got a sedative too, before he began a perfunctory exam. He asked a brief history, listened to the heart through a stethoscope, took a temperature and blood pressure. No urine or blood samples had been taken from us. He did a quick pelvic exam on each woman, nodded, and then the old woman started packing each woman's uterus with a ten-foot length of IV tubing, shoving it in, slowly, like stuffing a turkey. She wore no gloves, moved from one patient on to the next. Some of them cried out, as if in terrible pain.

"This will cause some discomfort," he said to us all. "It will also induce contractions and a healthy, natural rejection of the fetus."

He was examining the older woman next to me. When he asked when her last period had been she said she didn't know . . . had stopped having periods. He took a long time on her exam.

"I'm sorry," he said. "You are over five months along. I can't take the risk."

He gave her a sedative too. She was staring up at the ceiling, wretched. Oh, Jesus Christ. Christ.

"Look who's here. Our little runaway." He put the thermometer in my mouth and the cuff around my arm, pinning my other arm. When he let go to listen to my heart I took out the thermometer.

"I want to leave. I have changed my mind."

He couldn't hear, the stethoscope was in his ears. He cupped my breast, insolently smiling at me while he listened to my lungs. I recoiled, furious. In Spanish he said to the old woman, "Little tart acts like nobody touched her tit before." I spoke then in Spanish, roughly translated I said, "*You* don't touch it, asshole scum."

He laughed. "How rude of you, to allow me to stumble along in English!" Then he apologized and went on about how cynical and bitter one became after fifteen, twenty cases a day. A tragic but so necessary an occupation. Etc. By the time he was through I was sorry for *him* and, Lord forgive me, was gazing back into his big brown swimmy eyes while he stroked my arm.

Back to business. "Look, Doctor, I don't want to do this and I would like to leave now."

"You realize that the money you paid is nonrefundable?"

"That's okay. I still don't want to do it."

"*Muy bien.* I'm afraid that it will still be necessary for you to spend the night. We are far from town and our drivers won't return until morning. I will give you a sedative for sleep. You will be gone by ten tomorrow. Are you sure, m'ija, that this is what you want to do? Last chance."

I nodded. He was holding my hand. It felt like comfort, I was dying to cry, be held. Oh, what we won't do for just a little comfort.

"You could really help me," he said. "The child in the corner is very traumatized. Her mother is in bad shape and no support. I suspect the father, or some particularly bad situation. She really should have this abortion. Will you help me with her? Soothe her a little tonight?"

I went with him to the girl's bed, introduced myself. He had me tell her what he was going to do, what to expect, to explain that it was safe and easy and everything would be fine. Now he is going to listen to your heart and your lungs . . . Now the doctor needs to feel up inside you . . . (He said it wouldn't hurt. I told her it would hurt.) He has to do this to make sure everything will be okay.

She still resisted. "*A fuerzas!*" he said. By force. The old woman and I held her. The doctor and I held her then, talking to her, trying to calm her, while the old woman packed her tiny body with the tubing, foot after foot. I hugged her when it was over; she clung to me, sobbing. Her mother sat stone-faced in the chair at the foot of the bed.

"Is she in shock?" I asked the doctor. "No. She's dead drunk." On cue, she toppled to the floor; we lifted her to the bed next to her daughter's.

He and the old woman left then to go to two other rooms full of patients. Two young Indian girls came in bringing dinner trays.

"Do you want me to have my dinner here with you?" I asked the girl. She nodded. Her name was Sally; she was from Missouri. That's about all she said, but she ate, ravenously. She had never had tortillas before, wished there was some plain ol' bread. What's this stuff? Avocado. It's good. Put some with your meat on the tortilla. Like this, roll it up.

"Will your mama be all right?" I asked.

"She'll be sick in the morning." Sally lifted the mattress. There was a half-pint of Jim Beam. "If I'm not here and you are, this is for her. She needs it so she don't be sick."

"Yes. My mother drinks too," I said.

They took away the trays then and the old woman came with big Seconals for us to take. The young girls were given injections. The old woman hesitated by Sally's mother, then gave the sleeping woman a shot of barbiturate too.

I lay in bed. The sheets were rough, smelled of being dried in the sun, good, and the rough Mexican blanket smelled of raw wool. I remembered summers in Nacogdoches.

The doctor hadn't even said good-bye. Maybe Joe would come home. Oh, I had no sense at all. Maybe I should have the abortion. Not fit to raise one child, much less two. Dear God . . . what should I . . . ? I fell asleep.

There was a ghastly sobbing from somewhere. The room was dark, but from the dim hall light I could see that Sally's bed was empty. I ran out into the hall. At first I couldn't budge the bathroom door. She was lying against it, unconscious, dead white.

Blood was everywhere. She was hemorrhaging badly, tangled up
in coils and coils of tubing like a berserk Laocoön. The tubing had
clots of bloody matter sticking to it. It arched and buckled, slithering around her as if it were alive. She had a pulse but I couldn't
rouse her.

I ran down the hall, banging on doors until I woke the old
woman. She was still dressed in her white uniform; she put on her
shoes and ran to the bathroom. She took one quick look and ran to
the office and the phone. I waited outside, listening. She kicked
the door shut.

I went back to Sally, washed her face and arms off.

"Doctor is coming. Go to your room," the old woman said. The
Indian girls were behind her. They grabbed me and put me in my
bed; the woman gave me an injection.

I woke in a room filled with sunlight. There were six empty
beds, neatly made, with bright pink bedspreads. Canaries and
finches sang outside and magenta bougainvillea rustled against
the opened shutters in the breeze. My clothes were on the foot of
my bed. I took them to the bathroom, spotless now. I washed and
dressed, combed my hair. I was staggering, still sedated. When I
got back to the room the other women began to be wheeled in on
gurneys to their beds. The woman who didn't have an abortion
was sitting on a chair, looking out the window. The Indian girls
came in with trays of café con leche, pan dulce, slices of orange
and watermelon. Some of the women had breakfast, others retched
into a basin or went stumbling toward the bathroom. Everyone
moved in slow motion.

"*Buenos días.*" The doctor was in a long green gown, his mask
under his chin, his long black hair tousled. He smiled.

"I hope you slept well," he said. "You will leave in the first car,
in a few minutes."

"Where is Sally? Where is her mother?" My tongue was thick.
Hard to get out the words.

"Sally needed blood transfusions."

"Is she here?" Alive? The word wouldn't come out.

He grabbed my wrist. "Sally is fine. Do you have everything? The car is leaving now."

Five of us were hurried down the hall, outside and into the car. We took off and heard the gates close behind us. "Who goes to the El Paso airport?" All of the other women were going to the airport.

"Leave me at the bridge, on the Juárez side," I said. We drove along. None of us spoke. I was dying to say something stupid, like "Isn't it a lovely day?" It was a lovely day, matter of fact, crisp and clear, the sky a gaudy Mexican blue.

But the silence in the car was impenetrable, heavy with shame, with pain. Only the fear was gone.

The din and the smells of downtown Juárez were the same as when I was a little girl. I felt little and like I wanted to just wander around, but I waved for a cab. The hotel turned out to be only a few blocks away. The doorman paid the cab. Bella Lynn had taken care of it. They were in the room, he said.

The room was a complete wreck. Ben and Bella were in the middle of the bed, laughing, ripping up magazines and tossing the pages into the air.

"This is his favorite game. He's going to be a critic when he grows up?"

She got up and hugged me, looked into my eyes.

"Judas Priest. You didn't do it. You little fool! Fool!"

"No, I didn't!" I was holding Ben to me, oh I loved his smell, his bony little self. He was babbling away. I could tell they had had a great time.

"No, I didn't do it. I still had to pay, but I'll get you the money back. Just don't go lecturing me. Bella, there was this girl, Sally . . ."

People say Bella Lynn is spoiled and flighty. Not a care in the world. But nobody understands things like she does . . . She just knew everything. I didn't have to say a word, although of course I did anyway, later. I just cried and so did she and Ben.

We Moynihans, though, we cry or get mad and then that's that. Ben got tired of it first, started jumping on the bed.

"Look, Lou, of course I'm not going to lecture you. Anything you ever do would be okay with me. All I want to know is what do we do now? Tequila sunrise? Lunch? Shopping? I'm starved, myself."

"Me too. Let's go eat. And I want to get something for your grandma and Rex Kipp."

"Well, Ben, does that settle that, or what? Can you say 'Shopping'? We got to teach this kid values. Shopping!"

Room service came with her fringed jacket. We both changed and put on makeup, dressed Ben. I had thought he had a rash, it was only her lipsticked kisses all over his face.

We had lunch in the beautiful dining room. We were gay, not a care in the world. Young and pretty and free, with our future stretching out before us. We gossiped and laughed and figured out everybody in the dining room's whole life story.

"Well, we'd better get on home to this reunion sometime," I finally said, over our third coffee and Kahlua.

We bought presents and a straw basket to put everything in, including all the toys in the room. Bella Lynn sighed as we left. "Hotels are so homey, I always hate to leave . . ."

Inside the massive front door of Uncle Tyler's country house Roy Rogers and Dale Evans were belting out Christmas carols. A bubble machine was rigged up inside the door too so your first view of the gigantic Christmas tree was through a soapy blur of prisms.

"Judas Priest, it's like going through a car wash! And look at the rug." Bella Lynn unplugged the machine, turned off the music.

We went down the flagstone steps into the mammoth living room. Logs, whole trees, burning in the fireplace. Aunt Tiny's relatives were all slouching around on leather couches and Barca-loungers watching football on TV. Ben sat right down; he had never seen television. Sweet little baby, never been away from home; he was taking everything in stride.

Bella Lynn introduced us all, but most of them just nodded, barely took their eyes from their plates or the game. They were all dressed up, like for a funeral or a wedding, but still looked like a bunch of sharecroppers or tornado victims.

We went back up the stairs. "I can't wait to see them at Daddy's party tomorrow. In the morning we pick up Uncle John, then go spring your ma. Then there's a huge open house. Eligible bachelors, mostly, so we won't like any of them. But lots of old friends too, who want to see you and the baby."

"Jesus, our Blessit Redeemer!" It was old Mrs. Veeder, Tiny's mother. She had swooped Ben up in her arms, dropping her cane, teetering around with him in the dining room. He laughed, thought it was a game, the two of them crashing against sideboards and china closets, crystal shattering. One of my mother's favorite expressions is "Life is fraught with peril." Mrs. Veeder staggered off with him to her room, where there was another TV, tuned to soap operas, and enough junk on her bed to amuse him for months. Outhouse saltshakers from Texarkana, poodle toilet paper covers, felt sachet bags, bracelets with stones missing. All grimy, in the process of being recycled as Christmas presents. Mrs. Veeder and Ben fell together onto the bed. Ben stayed in there with her for hours, chewing on Jesus statues that glowed in the dark while she wrapped presents with wrinkled paper scraps and tangled ribbon. Singing away, "Jesus loves me, yes I know! Cuz the Bible tells me so!"

The dining room table resembled the ads for smorgasbords on cruise ships. I stood staring at the array of meat platters, salads, barbecued ribs, aspics, shrimp, cheeses, cakes, pies, wondering where it would all go, when it began disappearing before my eyes as Tiny's relatives darted in, one at a time, making furtive forays and dashing back down to the football game.

Esther was in the kitchen, in a black uniform, stooped over a huge washtub of masa for tamales. Mince pies were baking in the oven. Bella Lynn hugged Esther as if she'd been gone for months.

"Did he call?"

"Course not, honey. He ain't gonna call." Esther held her, rocking her. She had taken care of Bella Lynn since she was a baby. Didn't spoil her though, like everybody else. I used to think she was mean. Well, she is, matter of fact. She greeted me with "Looka here . . . another empty-headed girl!" She held me too. She was a tiny fine-boned woman, but she enveloped you.

"Where's that poor baby?" She went in to see Ben, came back and hugged me again. "Blessed love. He's a blessed child. Are you grateful, girl?" I nodded, smiling.

"We can help you make tamales," I said. "I just want to say hello to Tyler and Rex. And Aunt Tiny. Is she . . . ?"

"She's not coming down. She has an electric blanket, a radio, and liquor. No, she's up there for a while."

"Praise the Lord," Bella said.

"Go fix some food for those men-children out in the shop. Plenty of shrimp for Rex."

Tyler's "shop" was really an old adobe house, with a big den and guest room, a gigantic room full of guns, new ones and antique ones. The den had a big fireplace, animal trophies all over the walls and bearskins on the tile floor. The bathroom was a carpet of breasts, rubber breasts of all colors and sizes. The carpet had been a present to Tyler from Barry Goldwater, who once ran for president of the USA.

It was dark now, cold and clear. I followed Bella Lynn down the walk.

"Hussies! White trash!"

I gasped, startled. Bella laughed.

"That's just Mama, on the roof."

Rex and Uncle Tyler were glad to see me. They said when Joe set foot on American soil again to let them know, they'd tear him limb from limb. They were drinking bourbon and making lists. The room was stacked with shopping bags. Every year they took presents to old folks' homes and children's hospitals and orphanages. Thousands and thousands, they spent. Only they didn't just write out checks. The fun was picking out everything and then going to the places with food and Santa Clauses.

This year they had a new scheme, because Rex had a plane now. A Piper Cub he landed in Tyler's south pasture. On Christmas Eve they were going to air-drop bags of toys and food over Juárez shantytown. The two men were laughing and carrying on about their plans.

"But Daddy," Bella said, "what will we do about Mama? And Aunt Mary? What about Lou and me here? Tigers went and knocked her up, ran off with my husband."

"Hope you two have knockout outfits for tomorrow's party. Caterers are coming, but Esther will still need some help. Rex, how many candy canes you figure for them crippled children?"

Emergency Room Notebook, 1977

You never hear sirens in the emergency room—the drivers turn them off on Webster Street. I see the red backup lights of ACE or United Ambulance out of the corner of my eye. Usually we are expecting them, alerted by the MED NET radio, just like on TV. "City One: This is ACE, Code Two. Forty-two-year-old male, head injury, BP 190 over 110. Conscious. ETA three minutes." "City One . . . 76542 Clear."

If it is Code Three, where life is in critical danger, the doctor and nurses wait outside, chatting in anticipation. Inside, in room 6, the trauma room, is the Code Blue team. EKG, X-ray technicians, respiratory therapists, cardiac nurses. In most Code Blues, though, the EMT drivers or firemen are too busy to call in. Piedmont Fire Department never does, and they have the worst. Rich massive coronaries, matronly phenobarbital suicides, children in swimming pools.

All day long the heavy hearselike Cadillacs of Care Ambulance back up just to the left of emergency parking. All day long, just outside my window, their gurneys sail past to cobalt, radiation therapy. The ambulances are gray, the drivers wear gray, the blankets are gray, the patients are yellow-gray except where the doctors have marked their skulls or throats with a dazzling red Magic Marker X.

They asked me to work over there. No thanks. I hate lingering good-byes. Why do I still make tasteless jokes about death? I take it very seriously now. Study it. Not directly, just sniffing around. I see death as a person . . . sometimes many people, saying hello. Blind Mrs. Diane Adderly, Mr. Gionotti, Madame Y, my grandma.

Madame Y is the most beautiful woman I have ever seen. She looks dead, actually, her skin translucent blue-white, her exquisitely boned Oriental face serene and ageless. She wears black slacks and boots, mandarin-collared jackets cut and trimmed in Asia? France? The Vatican, maybe—they have the weight of a bishop's cassock—or an X-ray robe. The piping has been done by hand in rich fuchsias, magentas, oranges.

Her Bentley drives up at nine, driven by a flippant Filipino who chain-smokes Shermans in the parking lot. Her two sons, tall, in suits made in Hong Kong, escort her from the car to the entrance of radiation therapy. It is a long walk from there, down a corridor. She is the only person who walks it alone. At the entrance she turns to her sons, smiles, and bows. They bow back to her and watch until she has reached the end of the hall. When she disappears they go for coffee and talk on the telephone.

An hour and a half later everyone reappears at once. She, with two flushed spots of mauve on her cheekbones, her sons, the Bentley with the Filipino, and they all glide away. Glisten and sheen of the silver car, her black hair, her silk jacket. The entire ritual as silent and flowing as blood.

She is dead now. Not sure when it happened, on one of my days off. She always seemed dead anyway, but nicely so, like an illustration or advertisement.

I like my job in Emergency. Blood, bones, tendons seem like affirmations to me. I am awed by the human body, by its endurance. Thank God—because it'll be hours before X-ray or Demerol. Maybe I'm morbid. I am fascinated by two fingers in a baggie, a glittering switchblade all the way out of a lean pimp's back. I like the fact that, in Emergency, everything is reparable, or not.

Code Blues. Well, everybody loves Code Blues. That's when somebody dies—their heart stops beating, they stop breathing— but the Emergency team can, and often does, bring them back to life. Even if the patient is a tired eighty-year-old you can't help but get caught up in the drama of resuscitation, if only for a while. Many lives, young fruitful ones, are saved.

The pace and excitement of ten or fifteen people, performers . . . it's like opening night at the theater. The patients, if they are conscious, take part too, if just by looking interested in all the goings-on. They never look afraid.

If the family is with the patient it is my job to get information from them, to keep them informed about what's going on. Reassure them, mostly.

While the staff members think in terms of good or bad codes— how well everyone did what they were supposed to do, whether the patient responded or not—I think in terms of good or bad deaths.

Bad deaths are ones with the manager of a hotel as next of kin, or the cleaning woman who found the stroke victim two weeks later, dying of dehydration. Really bad deaths are when there are several children and in-laws I have called in from somewhere inconvenient and none of them seem to know each other or the dying parent at all. There is nothing to say. They keep talking about making arrangements, about having to make arrangements, about who will make arrangements.

Gypsies are good deaths. I think so . . . the nurses don't and security guards don't. There are always dozens of them, demanding to be with the dying person, to kiss them and hug them, unplugging and screwing up the TVs and monitors and assorted apparatus. The best thing about Gypsy deaths is they never make their kids keep quiet. The adults wail and cry and sob but all the children continue to run around, playing and laughing, without being told they should be sad or respectful.

Good deaths seem to be coincidentally good Codes—the patient responds miraculously to all this life-giving treatment and then just quietly passes away.

Mr. Gionotti's death was good . . . The family respected the staff's request that they stay outside, but one by one they went in and made their presence known to Mr. Gionotti and came out to reassure the others that everything was being done. There were a lot of them, sitting, standing, touching, smoking, laughing sometimes. I felt I was present at a celebration, a family reunion.

One thing I do know about death. The "better" the person, the more loving and happy and caring, the less of a gap that person's death makes.

When Mr. Gionotti died, well, he was dead, and Mrs. Gionotti wept, they all did, but they all went weeping off together, and with him, really.

I saw blind Mr. Adderly on the 51 bus the other night. His wife, Diane Adderly, came in DOA a few months ago. He had found her body at the foot of the stairs, with his cane. Ratshit Nurse McCoy kept telling him to stop crying.

"It simply won't help the situation, Mr. Adderly."

"Nothing will help. It's all I can do. Let me alone."

When he heard McCoy had left, to make arrangements, he told me that he had never cried before. It scared him, because of his eyes.

I put her wedding band on his little finger. Over a thousand dollars in grimy cash had been in her bra, and I put it in his wallet. I told him that the denominations were fifties, twenties, and hundreds and he would need to find somebody to sort it all out.

When I saw him later on a bus he must have remembered my walk or smell. I didn't see him at all—just climbed on the bus and slumped into the nearest seat. He even got up from the front seat near the driver to sit by me.

"Hello, Lucia," he said.

He was very funny, describing his new, messy roommate at the Hilltop House for the Blind. I couldn't imagine how he could know his roommate was messy, but then I could and told him my Marx Brothers idea of two blind roommates—shaving cream on the spaghetti, slipping on spilled stuffaroni, etc. We laughed and were silent, holding hands . . . from Pleasant Valley to Alcatraz Avenue. He cried, softly. My tears were for my own loneliness, my own blindness.

The first night I worked in Emergency, an ACE ambulance brought in a Jane Doe. Staff was short that night so the ambulance drivers and I undressed her, pulled the shredded panty hose off of varicose veins, toenails curling like parrots'. We unstuck her papers, not from her gray flesh-colored bra but from her clammy breasts. A picture of a young man in a marine uniform: George 1944. Three wet coupons for Purina cat chow and a blurred red, white, and blue Medicare card. Her name was Jane. Jane Daugherty. We tried the phone book. No Jane, no George.

If their purses haven't already been stolen old women never seem to have anything in them but bottom dentures, a 51 bus schedule, and an address book with no last names.

The drivers and I worked together with pieces of information, calling the California Hotel for Annie, underlined, the Five-Spot cleaners. Sometimes we just have to wait until a relative calls, looking for them. Emergency phones ring all day long. "Have you seen a ———?" Old people. I get mixed up about old people. It seems a shame to do a total hip replacement or a coronary bypass on some ninety-five-year-old who whispers, "Please let me go."

It doesn't seem old people should fall down so much, take so many baths. But maybe it's important for them to walk alone, stand on their own two feet. Sometimes it seems they fall on purpose, like the woman who ate all those Ex-Lax—to get away from the nursing home.

There is a great deal of flirty banter among the nurses and the ambulance crews. "So long—seizure later." It used to shock me, all the jokes while they're in the middle of a tracheotomy or shaving a patient for monitors. An eighty-year-old woman, fractured pelvis, sobbing, "Hold my hand! Please hold my hand!" Ambulance drivers rattling on about the Oakland Stompers.

"Hold her bloody *hand*, man!" He looked at me like I was crazy. I don't hold many hands anymore and I joke a lot, too, if not around patients. There is a great deal of tension and pressure. It's draining—being involved in life-and-death situations all the time.

Even more draining, and the real cause of tension and cynicism, is that so many of the patients we get in Emergency are not only not emergencies, there is nothing the matter with them at all. It gets so you yearn for a good cut-and-dried stabbing or a gunshot wound. All day long, all night long, people come in because they don't have much appetite, have irregular BMs, stiff necks, red or green urine (which invariably means they had beets or spinach for lunch).

Can you hear all those sirens in the background, in the middle of the night? More than one of them is going to pick up some old guy who ran out of Gallo port.

Chart after chart. Anxiety reaction. Tension headaches. Hyperventilation. Intoxication. Depression. (These are the diagnoses—the patients' complaints are cancer, heart attack, blood clots, suffocation.) Each of these patients costs hundreds of dollars including ambulance, X-ray, lab work, EKG. The ambulances get a Medi-Cal sticker, we get a Medi-Cal sticker, the doctor gets a Medi-Cal sticker, and the patient dozes off for a while until a taxi comes to take him home, paid for with a voucher. God, have I become as inhuman as Nurse McCoy? Fear, poverty, alcoholism, loneliness are terminal illnesses. Emergencies, in fact.

We do get critical trauma or cardiac patients, and they are treated and stabilized with awesome skill and efficiency in a matter of minutes and rushed to surgery or ICU, CCU.

Drunks and suicides take hours of time holding up needed rooms and nurses. Four or five people waiting at my desk to sign in. Ankle fractures, strep throat, whiplash, etc.

Maude, beery, bleary, is sprawled on a gurney, kneading my arm like a neurotic cat.

"You're so kind . . . so charming . . . it's this vertigo, dear."

"What is your last name and your address? What happened to your Medi-Cal card?"

"Gone, everything is gone . . . I'm so miserable and so alone. Will they keep me here? There must be something the matter with my inner ear. My son Willie never calls. Of course, it's Daly City and a toll call. Do you have children?"

"Sign here."

I have found a minimum of information among the rest of the mess in her purse. She uses Zig-Zag papers to blot her lipstick. Big smeary kisses, billowing like popcorn all over her purse.

"What's Willie's last name and phone number?"

She begins to cry, reaching both arms for my neck.

"Don't call him. He says I'm disgusting. You think I'm disgusting. Hold me!"

"I'll see you later, Maude. Let go of my neck and sign this paper. Let go."

Drunks are invariably alone. Suicides come in with at least one other person, usually many more. Which is probably the general idea. At least two Oakland police officers. I have finally understood why suicide is considered a crime.

Overdoses are the worst. Time again. Nurses usually too busy. They give them some medication but then the patient has to drink ten glasses of water. (These are not the stomach-pump critical overdoses.) I'm tempted to stick my finger down their throat. Hiccups and tears. "Here, one more cup."

There are "good" suicides. "Good reasons" many times like terminal illness, pain. But I'm more impressed with good technique. Bullets through the brain, properly slashed wrists, decent barbiturates. Such people, even if they don't succeed, seem to emanate a peace, a strength, which may have come from having made a thoughtful decision.

It's the repeats that get to me—the forty penicillin capsules, the twenty Valium and a bottle of Dristan. Yes, I am aware that, statistically, people who threaten or attempt suicide eventually succeed. I am convinced that this is always an accident. John, usually home by five, had a flat tire and could not rescue his wife in time. I suspect a form of manslaughter sometimes, the husband or some other regular rescuer having at last finally tired of showing up just in the guilty nick of time.

"Where's Marvin? Must be worried sick."

"He's phoning."

I hate to tell her he's in the cafeteria, has gotten to like their Reuben sandwiches.

Exam week at Cal. Many suicides, some succeeding, mostly Oriental. Dumbest suicide of the week was Otis.

Otis's wife, Lou-Bertha, had left him for another man. Otis took two bottles of Sominex, but was wide awake. Peppy, even.

"Get Lou-Bertha before it's too late!"

He kept hollering instructions to me from the trauma room. "My mother . . . Mary Brochard 849-0917 . . . Try the Adam and Eve Bar for Lou-Bertha."

Lou-Bertha has just left the Adam and Eve for the Shalimar. It was busy for a long time, then an answer, and Stevie Wonder for a whole record of "Don't You Worry 'Bout a Thing."

"Run that by me one more time, honey . . . He OD'd on *what*?"

I told her.

"Shit. You go tell that toothless worthless nigger he better be taking a lot more of something a lot stronger if'n he expects to get me outta *here*."

I went in to tell him . . . what? She was glad he was okay,
maybe. But he was on the telephone in room 6. Had his pants on,
still wore a polka-dot gown on top. He had located the half-pint of
Royal Gate in his jacket pocket. Was just sort of lounging around,
like an executive.

"Johnnie? Yeah. Otis here. I'm up here at City Emergency
Room. You know, off Broadway. What's happening? Fine, fine.
That bitch Lou-Bertha messing 'round with Darryl . . . [Silence.]
No shit."

The charge nurse came in. "He still here? Get him *out*! We
have four Codes coming in. Auto accident, all Code Three, ETA
ten minutes."

I try to sign as many patients as possible before the ambulances arrive. The people will just have to wait later, about half of
them will leave, but meanwhile all are restless and angry.

Oh, hell . . . there were three here before this one but better
just sign her in. It's Marlene the Migraine, an Emergency habi-
tuée. She is so beautiful, young. She stops talking with two Laney
College basketball players, one with an injured right knee, and
stumbles to my desk to go into her act.

Her howls are like Ornette Coleman in early "Lonely Woman"
days. Mostly what she does is first, bang her head against the wall
near my desk, dump everything off my desk with a swoop.

Then she starts her cries. Whooping, anguished yelps, remi-
niscent of Mexican corridas, Texan love songs, "Aiee, Vi, Yi!"

"Ah-hah, San Antone!"

She has slumped to the floor and all I can see is an elegantly
manicured hand, extending her Medi-Cal card above the desk.

"Can't you see I'm dying? I'm going blind, for crissakes!"

"Come on, Marlene—how'd you get those false eyelashes on?"

"Nasty whore."

"Marlene, sit up and sign in. Ambulances are coming, so you'll
have to wait. Sit up!"

She sits up, starts to light a Kool. "Don't light that, sign here," I say. She signs and Zeff comes to put her into a room.

"Well, well, if it isn't our old angry pal, Marlene."

"Don't you humor me, you dumb nurse."

The ambulances arrive, and for sure they are emergencies. Two die. For an hour all the nurses, doctors, on-call doctors, surgeons, *everybody* is tied up in room 6 with the two surviving young patients.

One of Marlene's hands is struggling into a velvet coat sleeve, the other is applying magenta lipstick.

"Holy Christ—I can't hang around *this* joint all night, right? Seeya, honey!"

"See ya, Marlene."

Temps Perdu

I've worked in hospitals for years now and if there's one thing I've learned it's that the sicker the patients are the less noise they make. That's why I ignore the patient intercom. I'm a ward clerk, my priorities are ordering meds and IVs, getting patients to surgery or X-ray. Of course I answer the calls eventually, usually tell them, "Your nurse will be there soon!" Because sooner or later she'll show up. My attitude toward nurses has changed a lot. I used to think they were rigid and heartless. But it's sickness that's what's wrong. I see now that nurses' indifference is a weapon against disease. Fight it, stamp it out. Ignore it, if you will. Catering to a patient's every whim just encourages him to like being sick and that's the truth.

At first, when a voice on the intercom would say, "Nurse! Quick!" I'd ask, "What's the matter?" That took too much time; besides, nine times out of ten it's just that the color's off on the TV.

The only ones I pay attention to are the ones who can't talk. The light comes on and I push down the button. Silence. Obviously they have something to say. Usually something is the matter, like a full colostomy bag. That's one of the only other things I know for sure now. People are fascinated by their colostomy bags. Not just the demented or senile patients who actually play with them but everyone who has one is inevitably awed by the visibility

of the process. What if our bodies were transparent, like a washing machine window? How wondrous to watch ourselves. Joggers
would jog even harder, blood pumping away. Lovers would love
more. God damn! Look at that old semen go! Diets would improve—
kiwi fruit and strawberries, borscht with sour cream.

Anyway, when 4420, Bed Two's light came on I went into his
room. Mr. Brugger, an old diabetic who had had a massive stroke.
I saw the full bag first, just as I figured. "I'll tell your nurse," I said
and smiled into his eyes. My God, the shock that hit me, like falling on a bicycle bar, a Vinteuil sonata right there on Four East.
Little beady black eyes laughing from epicanthic gray-white folds.
Eyes just past Buddha eyes . . . sloe eyes, slow eyes, near-Mongoloid
eyes. Kentshereve's eyes, laughing into mine . . . I was engulfed
with the memory of love, no with love itself. Mr. Brugger felt this
no doubt, since now he rings his ever-loving bell all night long.

He shook his head, mocking me for thinking it was his colostomy bag. I looked around. *The Odd Couple* was spinning dizzily
up on the screen. I adjusted the set and left, hurrying back to my
desk, to soft billows of memory.

Mullan, Idaho, 1940, at the Morning Glory mine. I was five
years old, making shadows from the early spring sun with my big
toe. I heard him first. The sound of apples. Celery? No, it was
Kentshereve, under my window, eating hyacinth bulbs. Dirt in the
corners of his mouth, purple liver lips, wet like Mr. Brugger's.

I flew to him (Kentshereve), no looking back, no hesitation. At
least the next thing I remember is biting into the crisp cold bursting bulbs myself. He grinned at me, raisin eyes glinting through
doughy slits, encouraging me to savor. He didn't use that word—
my first husband did showing me the subtleties of leeks and shal-
lots (in our adobe kitchen in Santa Fe, vigas and Mexican tile).
We vomited, later (Kentshereve and I).

I worked mechanically at my desk, answering phones, calling
for oxygen and lab techs, drifting away into warm waves of

pussywillows and sweet peas and trout pools. The pulleys and riggings of the mine at night, after the first snow. Queen Anne's lace against the starry sky.

"He knew every inch of my body." Did I read that somewhere? Surely no one would ever say such a thing. Later that spring, naked in the woods, we counted every single mole each other had, marking where we left off each day with India ink. Kentshereve pointed out that the ink dabber was just like a cat's pecker.

Kentshereve could read. His name was Kent Shreve, but when he told me I thought it was his first name and that first night said it over and over, sang it over and over to myself as I have done with Jeremys and Christophers ever since. Kentshereve Kentshereve. He could even read the Wanted posters at the post office. He said that when we grew up he'd probably read a poster about me. Of course I'd be using an alias but he would know it was me because it would say large mole on ball of left foot, blaze on right knee, mole in the crack of the ass. Maybe somebody will read this who was once my lover. Bet you didn't remember those things. Kentshereve would. My third son was born with the same mole, just at the crack of his buttocks. The day he was born I kissed him there, pleased that probably one day another woman would kiss him there, or count it. Kentshereve took longer to document than I did since he had freckles as well and there was a fine line. He didn't trust me when I got to his back, accused me of exaggerating.

I was annoyed when we got two post-op patients—pages of orders, just as I was having all these insights. That blast of love I got from room 4420, Bed Two, it was indistinguishable from all the others. Kentshereve, my palimpsest. An older intellectual with a sardonic wit, obsessed with food and sex. He started a lifetime of cookouts that ranged from Zihuatanejo to upstate New York. Hamburgers on top of a Zuni grave with Harrison, that fraud.

None so delicious and scary. Since he was able to read he could tell that the fire we built could mean a thousand-dollar fine or imprisonment. Not for us, for our parents, he chuckled, tossing more pine cones onto the blaze. Massé nipple cream, heat lamps to the perineum, Americaine spray for hemorrhoids, sitz baths TID. I flew through the orders so I could get back to smelling pine, to tasting his chipped beef on white bread. The sauce was a bottle of Jergen's hand lotion—honey and almonds—and no sweet-and-sour sauce since has rivaled it. He could make pancakes in the shape of Texas and Idaho and California. His teeth were black until Wednesday from Saturday's licorice, blueberry blue all summer long.

We tried to duplicate the sexual act but gave up and concentrated on hitting targets with our pee. Of course, he was better, but it's no mean trick for a girl to aim. He gave me my due, with a nod, a glint from the slits of his eyes.

He took me to my first trout pool. Only trout pool. Empty pool, I mean, at the hatchery. Only a few times a year would they drain these shallow pools, but he knew just when to go. He saw everything even though his eyes looked closed, like wooden Eskimo sunglasses. The trick was to get there on a warm day before they cleaned out the empty pond. There was about three inches of gelatinous mucusy trout-come slime lining the pools. I'd give him the first push, shooting him off to the end when he'd ricochet back into me, a jet-propelled toad, and off we'd go careening from the walls like greased pneumatic tubes, shimmering with trout scales.

We'd wash our hair in tomato juice to get the smell out but it didn't. Days later, when he'd be at school and I'd be lying there making toe shadows on the wall I'd get a whiff of dead fish and I would long for him, for the moment when I could hear him coming up the hill, his lunch pail banging against his leg.

We hid in the shed back of J.R.'s kitchen, watching him and his skinny wife doing it, an act so monumentally hilarious it has since ruined many a blissful moment of my life with a giggle fit. They would sit at the oilcloth table, glum, smoking and drinking away, just smoking and drinking, silent, and then he would rip off his miner's hat with the lamp, holler "Doggie style!" and flip her over the kitchen stool.

Most of the miners were Finns and when they got off work they would shower and sauna. There was a wooden pen outside the sauna and in winter they would run out and jump into the snow. Big men, little men, fat men, skinny men, all pink men, rolling over and over in the snow. At first watching from our hole in the fence, we giggled at all the blue peckers and balls but then we would just laugh too as they did with the joy of it, with the snow and the blue blue sky.

The night quieted down at work. Wendy, the charge nurse, and her best friend Sandy doodled at the desk near me. Really doodled, practicing writing 1982 and their names if they married whoever it is they are going out with now. Grown women, in this day and age. I felt pity for them, these lovely young nurses, who had not yet known romance.

"What are *you* daydreaming about?" Wendy asked.

"An old love," I sighed.

"That's neat—that you still think of love at your age."

I didn't even react. Poor fool had no idea of the passion that had just occurred between me and 4420, Bed Two.

His bell had, in fact, been ringing away. I answered it. "Your nurse will be in soon." I told Sandy that he wanted to get back into bed. Because I knew him by now, just by letting in those Kentshereve eyes. Sandy had me page the orderly to help her. Dead weight.

I've always been a good listener. That's it, my best quality. Kentshereve had all the ideas maybe but I was the one who heard them. We were a classic couple, like Zelda and Scott, Paul et Virginie. We made the Wallace, Idaho, weekly paper three times. Once when we got lost. We weren't lost at all, just out in the woods after curfew but they drained the ditches anyway. Then we found the dead hobo in the woods. Heard his death first, from way down in the clearing, the flies buzzing. The last time was when the ladder fell over Sextus. At least the paper appreciated it, our folks didn't at all. Kentshereve had to babysit Sextus (the sixth child, only a month old). Just a soggy little bundle and he slept all the time so it didn't seem to matter if we took him out to the shed. We decided to swing from the rafters, left the little bundle on the floor and climbed the ladder. Kentshereve never once blamed me for kicking over the ladder. He took such things as they came. What came was that the ladder fell over the baby, the rungs just missing him on all four sides and he didn't wake up. A miracle, but I don't think we knew that word yet. There we were, for hours, on the narrow two-by-four, far above the ground, hanging from it by our knees as it was too scary to sit up. Blood-red faces, talking funny upside down. No one heard us holler. Both our families had gone to Spokane and no other cabins were near. It got darker and darker. We figured out how to sit up and inch our way to the edge, took turns leaning against the wall. We played owl and spat, aiming at things. I wet my pants. Sextus woke up and began to wail and wail. Loud, above the baby, we listed all the things we wanted to eat. Bread and butter with sugar on it. Kentshereve ate those all day long. I know he's a diabetic by now, sneaking Jergen's lotion and going into shock. He always exhaled, his plaid shirts sparkled with sugar in the sun.

He had to pee, got the idea that if he aimed just next to Sextus it would warm him and cheer him up. That's what he was doing when my father came in and screamed. I got so scared I fell off the rafter. That's how I broke my arm the first time. Then Red, Kentshereve's father, came in and grabbed up the baby. Nobody got Kentshereve down or even noticed the miracle of the ladder missing the baby on all four sides. From the car, shivering with pain, I saw Red beating up Kentshereve. He didn't cry. He nodded at me across the yard and his eyes told me it had been worth it.

I spent one night with him, the night my baby sister had her tonsils out. Red sent me and my blankets up the ladder to the loft where the five older children slept on straw. There was no window, just an opening in the eaves covered with black oilcloth. Kentshereve poked a hole in it with an ice pick and there was a jet of air like on airplanes only icy cold. If you put your ear to it you could hear icicles in the pines, chandeliers, the creaking of the mine shaft, ore cars. It smelled of cold and wood smoke. When I put my one eye to the tiny hole I saw the stars as if for the first time, magnified, the sky, dazzling and vast. If I so much as blinked my eye it all disappeared.

We stayed awake waiting to hear his parents doing it but they never did. I asked him what he thought it was like. He held his hand up to mine so our fingers were all touching, had me run my thumb and forefinger over our touching ones. You can't tell which is which. Must be something like that he said.

I didn't go to the cafeteria on my break, but went outside the fourth floor onto the terrace. Cold January night, but already there were Japanese plum blossoms lit by the streetlamps. Californians defend their seasons by saying they are subtle. Who wants a subtle spring? Give me an Idaho thaw any old day with Kentshereve and me sliding down muddy hills on a flattened cardboard box. Give me the blatant blast of lilac, of a surviving hyacinth. I smoked on the terrace, the metal chair making cold stripes on my thighs. I yearned for love, for whispers on a clear winter night.

We fought only at the movies, on Saturdays in Wallace. He could read the credits but wouldn't tell me what they said. I was jealous, as I was to be later of one husband's music, another's drugs. The lady in the lake. When the first title appeared he would whisper, "Now! Quiet!" The writing slipped up the screen as he squinted, nodding. Sometimes he'd shake his head or chuckle or say, "Hmmph!" I know now that the hardest thing the titles ever say is cinematographic but I'm still sure I'm missing something. Then I would writhe, frantic, shaking his arm. Come on. What's it say? Hush! He'd fling my arm away and lean forward in his seat, covering his ears, his lips moving as he read. I longed to go to school, for second grade to hurry up and come. (He said first was a waste of time.) Nothing then, between us, would not be shared.

4420, Bed Two's bell rang. I went into his room. His roommate's visitors had accidentally moved the curtain over his TV as they left. I pulled it back and he nodded at me. Anything else? I asked and he shook his head. The credits for *Dallas* were floating up the screen.

"You know, I finally learned to read, you dirty rat," I said and his BB eyes glittered as he laughed. You couldn't tell really—it was just a wheezing rusty pipe sound that shook his zigzag bed, but I'd know that laugh anywhere.

Carpe Diem

Most of the time I feel all right about getting old. Some things give me a pang, like skaters. How free they seem, long legs gliding, hair streaming back. Other things throw me into a panic, like BART doors. A long wait before the doors open, after the train comes to a stop. Not very long, but it's too long. There's no time.

And laundromats. But they were a problem even when I was young. Just too long, even the Speed Queens. Your entire life has time to flash before your eyes while you sit there, a drowner. Of course if I had a car I could go to the hardware store or the post office and then come back and put things into the dryer.

The laundries with no attendants are even worse. Then it seems I'm always the only person there at all. But all of the washers and dryers are going . . . everybody is at the hardware store.

So many laundromat attendants I have known, the hovering Charons, making change or who never have change. Now it is fat Ophelia who pronounces No Sweat as No Thwet. Her top plate broke on beef jerky. Her breasts are so huge she has to turn sideways and then kitty-corner to get through doors, like moving a kitchen table. When she comes down the aisle with a mop everybody moves and moves the baskets too. She is a channel hopper. Just when we've settled in to watch *The Newlywed Game* she'll flick it to *Ryan's Hope*.

Once, to be polite, I told her I got hot flashes too, so that's what she associates me with . . . The Change. "How ya coming with the change?" she says, loud, instead of hello. Which only makes it worse, sitting there, reflecting, aging. My sons have all grown now, so I'm down from five washers to one, but one takes just as long.

I moved last week, maybe for the two hundredth time. I took in all my sheets and curtains and towels, my shopping cart piled high. The laundromat was very crowded; there weren't any washers together. I put all my things into three machines, went to get change from Ophelia. I came back, put the money and the soap in, and started them. Only I had started up three wrong washers. Three that had just finished this man's clothes.

I was backed into the machines. Ophelia and the man loomed before me. I'm a tall woman, wear Big Mama panty-hose now, but they were both huge people. Ophelia had a prewash spray bottle in her hand. The man wore cutoffs, his massive thighs were matted with red hair. His thick beard wasn't like hair at all but a red padded bumper. He wore a baseball hat with a gorilla on it. The hat wasn't too small but his hair was so bushy it shoved the hat high up on his head making him about seven feet tall. He was slapping a heavy fist into his other red palm. "Goddamn. I'll be god-damned!" Ophelia wasn't menacing; she was protecting me, ready to come between him and me, or him and the machines. She's always saying there's nothing at the laundry she can't handle.

"Mister, you may's well sit down and relax. No way to stop them machines once they've started. Watch a little TV, have yourself a Pepsi."

I put quarters in the right machines and started them. Then I remembered that I was broke, no more soap and those quarters had been for dryers. I began to cry.

"What the fuck is *she* crying about? What do you think this does to my Saturday, you dumb slob? Jesus wept."

I offered to put his clothes into the dryers for him, in case he wanted to go somewhere.

"I wouldn't let you near my clothes. Like stay away from my clothes, you dig?" There was no place for him to sit except next to me. We looked at the machines. I wished he would go outside, but he just sat there, next to me. His big right leg vibrated like a spinning washer. Six little red lights glowed at us.

"You always fuck things up?" he asked.

"Look, I'm sorry. I was tired. I was in a hurry." I began to giggle, nervously.

"Believe it or not, I am in a hurry. I drive a tow. Six days a week. Twelve hours a day. This is it. My day off."

"What were you in a hurry for?" I meant this nicely, but he thought I was being sarcastic.

"You stupid broad. If you were a dude I'd wash you. Put your empty head in the dryer and turn it to cook."

"I said I was sorry."

"Damn right you're sorry. You're one big sorry excuse for a chick. I had you spotted for a loser before you did that to my clothes. I don't believe this. She's crying again. Jesus wept."

Ophelia stood above him.

"Don't you be bothering her, you hear? I happens to know she's going through a hard time."

How did she know that? I was amazed. She knows everything, this giant black Sybil, this Sphinx. Oh, she must mean The Change.

"I'll fold your clothes if you'd like," I said to him.

"Hush, girl," Ophelia said. "Point is, what's the big deal? In a hunnert years from now just who is gonna care?"

"A hunnert years," he whispered. "A hunnert years."

And I was thinking that too. A hundred years. Our machines were shimmying away, and all the little red spin lights were on.

"At least yours are clean. I used up all my soap."

"I'll buy you some soap for crissake."

"It's too late. Thanks anyway."

"She didn't ruin my day. She's ruined my whole fuckin' week. No soap."

Ophelia came back, stooped down to whisper to me.

"I been spottin' some. Doctor says it don't quit I'll need a D and C. You been spottin'?"

I shook my head.

"You will. Women's troubles just go on and on. A whole life-time of troubles. I'm bloated. You bloated?"

"Her head is bloated," the man said. "Look, I'm going out to the car, get a beer. I want you to promise not to go near my machines. Yours are thirty-four, thirty-nine, forty-three. Got that?"

"Yeah. Thirty-two, forty, forty-two." He didn't think it was funny.

The clothes were in the final spin. I'd have to hang mine up to dry on the fence. When I got paid I'd come back with soap.

"Jackie Onassis changes her sheets every single day," Ophelia said. "Now that is sick, you ask me."

"Sick," I agreed.

I let the man put his clothes in a basket and go to the dryers before I took mine out. Some people were grinning but I just ig-nored them. I filled my cart with soggy sheets and towels. It was almost too heavy to push and, wet, not everything fit. I slung the hot-pink curtains over my shoulder. Across the room the man started to say something, then looked away.

It took a long time to get home. Even longer to hang every-thing, although I did find a rope. Fog was rolling in.

I poured some coffee and sat on the back steps. I was happy. I felt calm, unhurried. Next time I am on BART, I won't even think about getting off until the train stops. When it does, I'll make it out just in time.

Toda Luna, Todo Año

Toda luna, todo año
Todo día, todo viento
Camina, y pasa también.
También, toda sangre llega
Al lugar de su quietud.

(Books of Chilam-Balam)

Automatically, Eloise Gore began to translate the poem in her head. *Each moon, each year.* No. *Every moon, every year* gets the fricative sound. *Camina? Walks.* Shame that doesn't work in English. Clocks walk in Spanish, don't run. *Goes along, and passes away.*

She snapped the book shut. You don't read at a resort. She sipped her margarita, made herself take in the view from the restaurant terrace. The dappled coral clouds had turned a fluorescent pewter, crests of waves shattered silver on the gray-white beach below. All down the beach, from the town of Zihuatanejo, was a faint dazzle and dance of tiny green light. Fireflies, neon lime-green. Village girls placed them in their hair when they walked at dusk, strolling in groups of twos or threes. Some of the girls scattered the insects through their hair, others arranged them into emerald tiaras.

This was her first night here and she was alone in the dining room. Waiters in white coats stood near the steps to the pool and bar where most of the guests still danced and drank. *Mambo! Que rico el Mambo!* Ice cubes and maracas. Busboys lit flickering candles. There was no moon; it seemed the stars gave the metallic sheen to the sea.

Sunburned wildly dressed people began to come into the dining room. Texans or Californians she thought, looser, breezier than anyone from Colorado. They called across the tables to each other: "Go for it, Willy!" "Far fuckin' out!"

What am I doing here? This was her first trip anywhere since her husband's death three years before. Both Spanish teachers, they had traveled every summer in Mexico and Latin America. After he died she had not wanted to go anywhere without him, had signed up each June to teach summer school. This year she had been too tired to teach. In the travel office they had asked her when she needed to return. She had paused, chilled. She didn't need to return, didn't need to teach at all anymore. There was no place she had to be, no one to account to.

She ate her ceviche now, feeling painfully conspicuous. Her gray seersucker suit, appropriate in class, in Mexico City . . . it was dowdy, ludicrously the wrong thing. Stockings were tacky, and hot. There would probably even be a wet spot when she stood up.

She forced herself to relax, to enjoy langostinos broiled in garlic. Mariachis were strolling from table to table, passed hers by when they saw her frozen expression. *Sabor a tí.* The taste of you. Imagine an American song about how somebody tasted? Everything in Mexico tasted. Vivid garlic, cilantro, lime. The smells were vivid. Not the flowers, they didn't smell at all. But the sea, the pleasant smell of decaying jungle. Rancid odor of the pigskin chairs, kerosene-waxed tiles, candles.

It was dark on the beach and fireflies played in the misty green swirls, on their own now. Out in the bay were red flares for luring fish.

"*Pues, cómo estuvo?*" the waiter asked.

"*Esquisito, gracias.*"

The hotel boutique was still open. She found two simple hand-woven dresses, one white and one rose. The dresses were soft and loose, unlike anything she had ever worn. She bought a straw bag and several combs with jade fireflies on them, for prizes for her students.

A nightcap? the manager suggested as she crossed the lobby. Well, why not? she thought and entered the now empty bar by the pool. She ordered Madero brandy with Kahlua, Mel's favorite drink. She missed him acutely, wanted his hand on her hair. She closed her eyes to the sound of palms rippling, ice shaking in the mixer, the creak of oars.

In her room she looked at the poem again. *Thus all life arrives / at the place of its quietude.* No. And not *life*, anyway, the word is *sangre*, blood, all that pulsates and flows. The lamp was too dim, bugs clattered into the shade. As she shut off her light the music began again in the bar. Insistent thud of the bass. Her heart beat, was beating. *Sangre.*

She missed her own firm bed, the efficient lull of cars on the distant freeway. What I really miss is my morning crossword puzzle. Oh, Mel, what am I going to do? Quit teaching? Travel? Get a doctorate? Commit suicide? Where did that thought come from? But teaching is my whole life. And that's pitiful. Miss Gore is a Bore. Every year a new student invented that, gleeful. Eloise was a good teacher, dry, dispassionate, the kind that years later the students liked.

Cuando calienta el sol, aquí en la playa. At any lull in the music sounds from nearby rooms came through the shutters. Laughter, lovemaking.

"Mr. World Traveler! Mr. Know-it-all! World Traveler!"

"Honey, I do! (ah dew)," the Texan drawled. A crash then and a silence. He must have fallen, passed out. The woman laughed throatily. "Praise the Lord!"

Eloise wished she had a mystery book. She got up and went to the bathroom, cockroaches and land crabs clattering out of her way. She showered with coconut soap, dried with damp towels. She wiped the mirror so she could look at herself. Mediocre and grim, she thought. Not mediocre, her face, with wide gray eyes, fine nose and smile, but it was grim. A good body, but so long disregarded it seemed grim too.

The band stopped playing at two thirty. Footsteps and whispers, a glass shattering. *Say you dig it, baby, say it!* A moan. Snores.

Eloise woke at six, as usual. She opened the shutters, watched the sky turn from milky silver to lavender gray. Palm branches slipped in the breeze like shuffled cards. She put on her bathing suit and her new rose dress. No one was up, not even in the kitchen. Roosters crowed and zopilotes flapped around the garbage. Four pigs. In the back of the garden Indian busboys and gardeners slept, uncovered, curled on the bricks.

She stayed on the jungle path away from the beach. Dark dripping silence. Orchids. A flock of green parrots. An iguana arched on a rock, waiting for her to pass. Branches slapped sticky warm into her face.

The sun had risen when she climbed a hill, down then to a rise above a white beach. From where she stood she could see onto the calm cove of Las Gatas. Underwater was a stone wall built by Terascans to protect the cove from sharks. A school of sardines swirled through the transparent water, disappeared like a tornado out to sea. Clusters of palapa huts stretched down the beach. Smoke drifted from the farthest one but there was no one to be seen. A sign said BERNARDO'S SCUBA DIVING.

She dropped her dress and bag on the sand, swam with a sure crawl far out to the stone wall. Back then, floating and swimming. She treaded water and laughed out loud, finally lay in the water near the shore rocking in the waves and silence, her eyes open to the startling blue sky.

She walked past Bernardo's, down the beach toward the smoke. An open thatch-roofed room with a raked sand floor. A large wooden table, benches. Beyond that room was a long row of bamboo alcoves, each with a hammock and mosquito netting. In the primitive kitchen a child washed dishes at the pila; an old woman fanned the fire. Chickens darted around them, pecking in the sand.

"Good morning," Eloise said. "Is it always so quiet here?"

"The divers are out. You want breakfast?"

"Please." Eloise reached out her hand. "My name is Eloise Gore." But the old woman just nodded. "*Siéntese.*"

Eloise ate beans, fish, tortillas, gazing across the water to the misted hills. Her hotel looked blowsy and jaded to her, askew on the hillside. Bougainvillea spilled over its walls like a drunken woman's shawls.

"Could I stay here?" she asked the woman.

"We're not a hotel. Fishermen live here."

But when she came back with hot coffee she said, "There is one room. Foreign divers stay here sometimes."

It was an open hut behind the clearing. A bed and a table with a candle on it. A mildewed mattress, clean sheets, a mosquito netting. "No scorpions," the woman said. The price she asked for room and board was absurdly low. Breakfast and dinner at four when the divers got back.

It was hot as Eloise went back through the jungle but she found herself skipping along, like a child, talking to Mel in her head. She tried to remember when she had last felt happy. Once, soon after he died, she had watched the Marx Brothers on television. *A Night at the Opera.* She had had to turn it off, could not bear to laugh alone.

The hotel manager was amused that she was going to Las Gatas. "*Muy típico.*" Local color: a euphemism for primitive or dirty. He arranged for a canoe to take her and her things across the bay that afternoon.

She was dismayed when they neared her peaceful beach. A large wooden boat, *La Ida*, was anchored in front of the palapa. Multicolored canoes and motored pangas from town slipped in and out, loading from it. Lobsters, fish, eels, octopus, bags of clams. A dozen men were on the shore or taking air tanks and regulators off the boat, laughing and shouting. A young boy tied a mammoth green turtle to the anchor line.

Eloise put her things in her room, wanted to lie down but there was no privacy at all. From her bed she could see out into the kitchen, through it to the divers at the table, out to the blue green sea.

"Time to eat," the woman called to her. She and the child were taking dishes to the table.

"May I help you?" Eloise asked.

"*Siéntese.*"

Eloise hesitated at the table. One of the men stood and shook her hand. Squat, massive, like an Olmec statue. He was a deep brown color, with heavy-lidded eyes and a sensuous mouth.

"*Soy César. El maestro.*"

He made a place for her to sit, introduced her to the other divers, who nodded to her and continued to eat. Three very old men. Flaco, Ramón, and Raúl. César's sons, Luis and Cheyo. Madaleno, the boatboy. Beto, "a new diver—the best." Beto's wife, Carmen, sat back from the table nursing their child.

Steaming bowls of clams. The men were talking about El Peine. Old Flaco had finally seen it, after diving all his life. The comb? Later, with a dictionary, she found out that they were talking about a giant sawfish.

"*Gigante.* Big as a whale. Bigger!"

"*Mentira!* You were hallucinating. High on air."

"Just wait. When the Italians come with their cameras, I'll take them, not any of you."

"Bet you can't remember where he was."

Flaco laughed. "*Pues* . . . not exactly."

Lobster, grilled red snapper, octopus. Rice and beans and tortillas. The child put a dish of honey on a far table to distract the flies. A long loud meal. When it was over everyone except César and Eloise went to hammocks to sleep. Beto and Carmen's room had a curtain, the others were open.

"*Acércate a mí,*" César said to Eloise. She moved closer to him. The woman brought them papaya and coffee. She was César's sister, Isabel; Flora was her daughter. They had come two years before when César's wife had died. Yes, Eloise was widowed too. Three years.

"What do you want from Las Gatas?" he asked.

She didn't know. "Quiet," she said. He laughed.

"But you're always quiet, no? You can dive with us, there's no noise down there. Go rest now."

It was dusk when she awoke. A lantern glowed in the dining room. César and the three old men were playing dominos. The old men were his mother and father, César told her. His own parents had died when he was five and they had taken him in, taken him underwater his first day. The three men had been the only divers then, free divers for oysters and clams, years before tanks or spearguns.

At the far end of the palapa Beto and Carmen talked, her tiny foot pushing their hammock. Cheyo and Juan sharpened speargun points. Away from the others Luis listened to a transistor radio. Rock and roll. You can teach me English! He invited Eloise to sit by him. The words to songs weren't what he had imagined at all. Can't get no satisfaction.

Beto's baby lay naked on the table, his head cradled in César's free hand. The baby peed and César swept the urine off the table, dried his hand in his hair.

Fog. Two white cranes. Rippling of the turtle tied near the boat. The wind flickered the lantern, lightning illuminated the pale green sea. The cranes left and it began to rain.

A young long-haired American stumbled in from the wet, shivering, out of breath. Oh God Oh God. He kept laughing. No one moved. He laid his pack and a soggy sketch pad on the table, continued to laugh.

"*Drogas?*" Flaco asked. César shrugged and left, came back with towels and cotton clothes. The young man stood, docile, while César stripped and dried him, dressed him. Madaleno brought him soup and tortillas; when he had finished César led him to a hammock and covered him. The young man fell asleep, rocking.

The compressor for air tanks was banging and clattering long before dawn. Roosters crowed, the parrot squawked on the outside pila, vultures flapped at the edge of the clearing. César and Raúl filled tanks; Madaleno raked the sand floor. Eloise washed at the pila, combed her hair in the reflection of the water, silver now. The only mirror was a broken piece nailed to a palm tree where Luis was shaving, singing to his smile. Guantanamera! He waved to Eloise. "Good morning, teasher!"

"Good morning. *Dí* 'teacher,'" she smiled.

"Teacher."

In her room she started to put her rose shift on over her suit.

"No, don't dress—we're going for clams."

César carried the heavy tanks and weights. She had the masks and flippers, a string bag.

"I've never been diving before."

"You can swim, can't you?"

"I'm a good swimmer."

"You're strong," he said, looking at her body. She flushed. Strong. Her students called her mean and cold. He strapped the weights around her waist, the tank onto her back. She reddened again as he brushed her breasts, fastening the clasp. He told her the basic rules, how to come up slow, how to turn on the reserve tank. He showed her how to clean her mask with spit, adjust the regulator. The tank on her back was unbearably heavy.

"Stop, I can't carry this."

"You will," he said. He put her mouthpiece in her mouth and drew her underwater.

The weight vanished. Not just the tank's weight but her own. She was invisible. She flippered, using fins for the first time, soaring through the water. Because of the mouthpiece she couldn't laugh out loud or shout. Mel, this is wonderful! She flew on, with César next to her.

The sun came up through the frosted glass surface of the water, a pale metallic glow. Slowly then, like stage lighting, the world underwater came into being. Fuchsia anemones, schools of blue angelfish, blue and red neons, a stingray. César showed her how to relieve the pressure as they went deeper, farther out. Near the Terascan wall he swam down to the sunny bottom where he began to jab a spike into the sand again and again. When a bubble appeared he dug out a clam and put it into the bag. She motioned for the spike, swam along poking as he gathered clams until the bag was filled. They swam back toward shore through myriads of fish and plants. Absolutely everything was new to Eloise, each creature, each sensation. A school of sardines splintered into her like crisp jets of water. Suddenly she had no air; she forgot about the reserve tank, panicked, thrashing. César caught her, held her head, pulled her air cord with the other hand.

They surfaced. The green water showed nothing of what was beneath it. By the sun she realized that they had not even been down for an hour. With no weight you lose your self as a point of reference, lose your place in time.

"Thank you," she said.

"Thank you—we got a lot of clams."

"What do you charge for lessons?"

"I'm not a diving teacher."

She nodded toward Bernardo's sign. "Lessons 500 pesos."

"You're not at Bernardo's. You showed up to us."

And that's it, she thought later, at the breakfast table. The acceptance she felt from them wasn't because they liked her or because she fit in. She had simply shown up, like the young man, who had since disappeared. Maybe it was because the divers were so much underwater, among such vastness. Anything was expected, of equal unimportance.

Yellow air tanks rolled and clanked in the bottom of the boat. *La Ida*. Not a name but *The Going*, the going out.

The fishermen were laughing, knotting and reknotting the rubbers of their spearguns, strapping knives onto scarred brown legs. Hiss of the tanks as César checked each one for air.

They told stories. The Peine. The killer whale. The Italian diver and the sharks. When Mario drowned, when César's air hose broke. Even Eloise was to hear them again and again, the litany before each dive.

A manta ray played with the big boat. Madaleno veered sharply, keeping just out of its path. It flopped over high into the sky, white belly glistening. Parasite fish exploded away from it, ricocheting into the boat. Out to sea a pair of deep green turtles were mating in the waves. They stayed locked, rocked dreamily on and on, blinking sometimes in the glare.

Madaleno anchored in the north part of the bay, away from the rocks. Fins, masks, weights, tanks on. They sat in a circle on the rim of the boat. Flaco and Ramón went back first. They just fell back and disappeared. Then Raúl and Cheyo, Beto and Luis. César saw that Eloise was afraid. The waves were high, navy blue. With a grin he shoved her off the boat. Cold. A flash of blue sky and then a whole new translucent sky. Reality of the boat and anchor line. Deeper, colder. Go slow, he motioned.

A suspension of time. A multiplicity of time because of the gradations of light and dark, of cold and warm. Down past layers, strata, each with a distinct hierarchy of coexisting plants and fish. Nights and days, winters and summers. Near the bottom it is warm, sunny, a Montana meadow years ago. Moray eels bared their fangs. Flaco showed her what to look for. The glimpse of a blue lobster feeler. Wait—watch for the morays. The divers floated in and out of the crevasses like dancers in a dream. Eloise waved to the closest men when she spotted a lobster. Occasionally a huge lora or pargo would glide past and one of the divers would shoot it. A flash of blood. Shimmer of silver as it slid onto the rope line.

The next dive was out in the open sea. Eloise waited in the boat with Madaleno. He sang, she watched the frigate birds, dozed, lying against the slippery fish. Her dreams dissolved with shatters of spray, a yell from a diver, surfacing with his catch.

The men were jubilant on the way back, except for Luis. Sure it was a good catch, but they needed catches like that twice a day if they were going to keep *La Ida*. They were behind two payments, still owed 20,000 pesos. Their old boat had carried only four divers, tanks enough for only one dive. *La Ida* was a good idea, he said, if his father would let go of the three old men. The viejos catch two fish for every ten of ours. With three good divers we'd pay off the boat in months.

"Luis really wants to buy a speedboat," César said, "to take gringas waterskiing. *Que se vaya a Acapulco.* I would never tell them they couldn't dive. And don't you ever tell me."

Eloise went every morning with César for clams and on the first dive every day. They still didn't take her down on the deep second dive of the day, although she was becoming surer and stronger, beginning to shoot her own good portion of fish. In the evenings she sat with the old men. Luis and César went over accounts, argued. Sometimes the sons went into town. There were consultations between Luis and Eloise about his clothes. Believe me, the white cotton pants are nicer than those green dacron ones. Of course leave the shark's teeth around your neck.

One night César cut everyone's hair. Even hers. She longed for a mirror, but it felt good, light, curling.

"Berry pretty," Luis said. *Very*, she corrected him but knew he had discovered the charm of an accent.

Usually they sat silent as the sunset came, night fell. She listened to the click click of dominos, the creaking of the anchor rope. A few times she tried to read or work on the poem, but gave it up. I may never read again. What would she do when she got home? Who knows—maybe Denver will be entirely underwater. She laughed out loud at the thought.

"*Estás contenta,*" César said.

She shouted to him above the generator the next day.

"Can I go on a deep dive before I leave?"

"You need a bad dive first."

"How do I get one?"

"You will. Maybe today. It's rough. Rained all night."

The first dive was in a rocky spot, with many sea urchins and moray eels. The water was murky; cold strong currents made it hard to see or to swim. A needlefish jabbed her in the arm. Ramón and Raúl surfaced with her, binding the cut tight with rags to keep blood from attracting sharks. Underwater again she lost sight of them; she hadn't seen César at all. I hope this qualifies for a bad dive, she joked to herself, but she was terrified. She couldn't see anyone, anything. She treaded water, like being lost in the woods. Her air ran out. She pulled the reserve cord but nothing happened. Don't panic. Surface slow. Slow. But she was panicked, her lungs bursting. She surfaced slowly, jerking frantically on the cord. No air. César was there in front of her. She grabbed his mouthpiece away from him and put it into her own mouth.

She gulped air with a sob of relief. He waited, then calmly took the mouthpiece back, breathed himself. He led her to the surface, passing the air hose back and forth between them.

They broke water. Air, light. She was shaking; Madaleno helped her into the boat.

"I'm so ashamed. Please forgive me."

César held her head in his hands. "I tied your reserve tank shut. You did exactly what you were supposed to do."

The divers teased her on the way back but all agreed she could go to Los Morros the next day. "*Pues, es brava,*" Raúl said. "*Sí.*" César grinned. "*Ella podría ir sola.*" She could go alone. He must think her one of those aggressive competent American women. I am competent, she thought, her head lying on the edge of the boat, tears swept away by the high waves. She closed her eyes and thought about the poem, knew how to end it. *And thus all blood arrives / to its own quiet place.*

The next day was dazzling clear. Los Morros was a stark monolith far out to sea, almost out of sight of land. White with guano, the island palpitated dizzily with a million birds. *La Ida* anchored far off but even above the shattering waves, the shrieking of the birds, was the ghostly flap and flutter of wings. The stench of urine and guano was nauseating, as intoxicating as ether.

Deep descent. Fifty feet, seventy-five, a hundred, a hundred and twenty. It was as if the mountains of Colorado were underwater. Crags and ravines, gulleys and valleys. Fish and plants that Eloise had never seen; the fish she knew were huge here, bold. She aimed at a garlopa, missed, aimed again and shot it just right. It was so big Juan helped her load it onto her stringer; the rope burned out through her fingers. Frenzied loading and shooting all around her. Loras, pargos, medregals. *Sangre.* She hit a mero and another garlopa, pleased because she hadn't seen César, was on her own. Frightened then, but spotted him far away, flew fast down the jagged cliffs toward him. He flippered, waiting for her in the dark, then drew her to him. They embraced, their regulators clanking. She realized then that his penis was inside her; she twined her legs around him as they spun and undulated in the dark sea. When he left her his sperm drifted up between them like pale octopus ink.

When Eloise was to think of this later it was not as one remembers a person or a sexual act but as if it were an occurrence of nature, a slight earthquake, a gust of wind on a summer day.

He handed her his rope of fish when he saw a mammoth pintillo, shot it, strung it on the line. There was a pargo above them, far, and she raced after him toward it, met him at the mouth of a dark cave. The pargo had gone. César motioned to her to wait, held her back in the cold darkness. Particles of gold dust filtered in the murky purple. A blue parrot fish. Silence. Then they came. A school of barracuda. There was nothing else in the sea. Endless, subliminal, hundreds of them. The dim light turned their quick slickness into molten silver. César shot, shattering them into a spill of mercury that flowed quickly back together and disappeared.

La Ida lay low in the water, soaked in spray. The divers sprawled exhausted on the still-pulsating bodies of the fish. Beto had caught a turtle and the men dug inside her for her eggs, eating them with lime and salt. Eloise refused at first, self-righteous, turtle were out of season, but then, hungry, she ate them too. The boat was circling and recircling Los Morros. No one had said anything; at first Eloise didn't notice that Flaco hadn't surfaced, didn't sense any fear until it was at least an hour after he should have been sighted. Even as the sun went down no one said he must be drowned, be dead. César finally told Madaleno to head for shore.

They ate by the light of the one lantern. No one spoke. When they finished, César, Raúl, and Ramón went back out to sea with lanterns and a bottle of raicilla.

"But they can't hope to find him in the dark."

"No," Luis said.

She went to her room to pack, hang up her seersucker suit. She was leaving in the morning, a panga had been sent for. She lay awake in the damp bed, watching the pewter moonlit night through the mosquito netting. César came into her bed, held her, caressed her with his strong scarred hands. His mouth and body tasted of salt. Their bodies were land-heavy, hot, rocking. Beat of the sea. They smiled in the pale light and fell asleep, locked like turtles.

When she awoke he was sitting on her bed, dressed in trunks and a shirt.

"Eloisa, can you give me the twenty thousand for the boat?"

She hesitated. In pesos it sounded like a lot. It was a lot. "Yes," she said. "Can you take a check?" He nodded. She wrote the check and he put it in his pocket. *Gracias*, he said and he kissed her eyelids and left.

The sun was up. César was at the generator, black oil dripped down his arm. Eloise put on lipstick at the broken mirror. Pigs and chickens scavenged in the yard, scattering zopilotes. Madaleno raked the sand. Isabel came out of the kitchen.

"Pues ya se va?" Eloise nodded, started to shake Isabel's hand to say good-bye but the old woman threw her arms around her. The two women swayed, embracing; Isabel's soapy hands were wet, warm on Eloise's back.

The motorboat was coming in just as *La Ida* passed the Terascan wall, out to sea. The men waved across the water to Eloise, briefly. They were checking their regulators, strapping on their weights and knives. César checked the tanks for air.

Good and Bad

Nuns tried hard to teach me to be good. In high school it was Miss Dawson. Santiago College, 1952. Six of us in the school were going on to American colleges; we had to take American History and Civics from the new teacher, Ethel Dawson. She was the only American teacher, the others were Chilean or European.

We were all bad to her. I was the worst. If there was to be a test and none of us had studied I could distract her with questions about the Gadsden Purchase for the whole period, or get her started on segregation or American imperialism if we were really in trouble.

We mocked her, imitated her nasal Boston whine. She had a tall lift on one shoe because of polio, wore thick wire-rimmed glasses. Splayed gap teeth, a horrible voice. It seemed she deliberately made herself look worse by wearing mannish, mismatched colors, wrinkled, soup-spotted slacks, garish scarves on her badly cut hair. She got very red-faced when she lectured and she smelled of sweat. It was not simply that she flaunted poverty . . . Madame Tournier wore the same shabby black skirt and blouse day after day, but the skirt was cut on the bias; the black blouse, green and frayed with age, was of fine silk. Style, cachet were all-important to us then.

She showed us movies and slides about the condition of the Chilean miners and dock workers, all of it the USA's fault. The ambassador's daughter was in the class, a few admirals' daughters. My father was a mining engineer, worked with the CIA. I knew he truly believed Chile needed the United States. Miss Dawson thought that she was reaching impressionable young minds, whereas she was talking to spoiled American brats. Each one of us had a rich, handsome, powerful American daddy. Girls feel about their fathers at that age like they do about horses. It is a passion. She implied that they were villains.

Because I did most of the talking I was the one she zeroed in on, keeping me after class, and one day even walked with me in the rose garden, complaining about the elitism of the school. I lost patience with her.

"What are you doing here then? Why don't you go teach the poor if you're so worried about them? Why have anything to do with us snobs at all?"

She told me that this was where she was given work, because she taught American history. She didn't speak Spanish yet, but all her spare time was spent working with the poor and volunteering in revolutionary groups. She said it wasn't a waste of time working with us . . . if she could change the thinking of one mind it would be worthwhile.

"Perhaps you are that one mind," she said. We sat on a stone bench. Recess was almost over. Scent of roses and the mildew of her sweater.

"Tell me, what do you do with your weekends?" she asked.

It wasn't hard to sound utterly frivolous, but I exaggerated it anyway. Hairdresser, manicurist, dressmaker. Lunch at the Charles. Polo, rugby or cricket, *thés dansants*, dinners, parties until dawn. Mass at El Bosque at seven on Sunday morning, still wearing evening clothes. The country club then for breakfast, golf or swimming, or maybe the day in Algarrobo at the sea, skiing in winter. Movies of course, but mostly we danced all night.

"And this life is satisfying to you?" she asked.

"Yes it is."

"What if I asked you to give me your Saturdays, for one month, would you do it? See a part of Santiago that you don't know."

"Why do you want me?"

"Because, basically, I think you are a good person. I think you could learn from it." She clasped both my hands. "Give it a try."

Good person. But she had caught me earlier, with the word *revolutionary*. I did want to meet revolutionaries, because they were bad.

Everyone seemed a lot more upset than necessary about my Saturdays with Miss Dawson, which then made me really want to do it. I told my mother I was going to help the poor. She was disgusted, afraid of disease, toilet seats. I even knew that the poor in Chile had no toilet seats. My friends were shocked that I was going with Miss Dawson at all. They said she was a loony, a fanatic, and a lesbian, was I crazy or what?

The first day I spent with her was ghastly, but I stuck with it out of bravado.

Every Saturday morning we went to the city dump, in a pickup truck filled with huge pots of food. Beans, porridge, biscuits, milk. We set up a big table in a field next to miles of shacks made from flattened tin cans. A bent water faucet about three blocks away served the entire shack community. There were open fires in front of the squalid lean-tos, burning scraps of wood, cardboard, shoes, to cook on.

At first the place seemed to be deserted, miles and miles of dunes. Dunes of stinking, smoldering garbage. After a while, through the dust and smoke, you could see that there were people all over the dunes. But they were the color of the dung, their rags just like the refuse they crawled in. No one stood up, they scurried on all fours like wet rats, tossing things into burlap bags that gave them humped animal backs, circling on, darting, meeting each other, touching noses, slithering away, disappearing like iguanas over the ridges of the dunes. But once the food was set up scores of women and children appeared, sooty and wet, smelling of decay and rotted food. They were glad for the breakfast, squatted, eating with bony elbows out like praying mantises on the garbage hills. After they had eaten, the children crowded around me, still crawling or sprawled in the dirt, they patted my shoes, ran their hands up and down my stockings.

"See, they like you," Miss Dawson said. "Doesn't that make you feel good?"

I knew that they liked my shoes and stockings, my red Chanel jacket.

Miss Dawson and her friends were exhilarated as we drove away, chatting happily. I was sickened and depressed.

"What good does it do to feed them once a week? It doesn't make a dent in their lives. They need more than biscuits once a week, for Lord's sake."

Right. But until the revolution came and everything was shared you had to do whatever helped at all.

"They need to know somebody realizes they live out here. We tell them that soon things will change. Hope. It's about hope," Miss Dawson said.

We had lunch in a tenement in the south of the city, six flights up. One window that looked onto an air shaft. A hot plate, no running water. Any water they used had to be carried up those stairs. The table was set with four bowls and four spoons, a pile of bread in the center. There were many people, talking in small groups. I spoke Spanish, but they spoke in a heavy *caló* with almost no consonants, and were hard for me to understand. They ignored us, looked at us with amused tolerance or complete disdain. I didn't hear revolutionary talk, but talk about work, money, filthy jokes. We all took turns eating lentils, drinking *chicha*, a raw wine, using the same bowls and glass as the person before.

"Nice you don't seem to mind about dirt," beamed Miss Dawson.

"I grew up in mining towns. Lots of dirt." But the cabins of Finnish and Basque miners were pretty, with flowers and candles, sweet-faced Virgins. This was an ugly, filthy place with misspelled slogans on the walls, Communist pamphlets stuck up with chewing gum. There was a newspaper photograph of my father and the minister of mines, splattered with blood.

"Hey!" I said. Miss Dawson took my hand, stroked it. "Sh," she said in English. "We're on a first-name basis here. Don't for heaven's sake say who you are. Now, Adele, don't be uncomfortable. To grow up you need to face all the realities of your father's personae."

"Not with blood on them."

"Precisely that way. It is a strong possibility and you should be aware of it." She squeezed both my hands then.

After lunch she took me to El Niño Perdido, an orphanage in an old stone ivy-covered building in the foothills of the Andes. It was run by French nuns, lovely old nuns, with fleur-de-lis coifs and blue-gray habits. They floated through the dark rooms, above the stone floors, flew down the passages by the flowered courtyard, popped open wooden shutters, calling out in birdlike voices. They brushed away insane children who were biting their legs, dragging them by their little feet. They washed ten faces in a row, all the eyes blind. They fed six mongoloid giants, reaching up with spoons of oatmeal.

These orphans all had something the matter. Some were insane, others had no legs or were mute, some had been burned over their entire bodies. No noses or ears. Syphilitic babies and mongoloids in their teens. The assorted afflictions spilled together from room to room, out into the courtyard into the lovely unkempt garden.

"There are many things that need doing," Miss Dawson said. "I like feeding and changing babies. You might read to the blind children . . . they all seem particularly intelligent and bored."

There were few books. La Fontaine in Spanish. They sat in a circle, staring at me, really blankly. Nervous, I began a game, a clapping and stomping kind of game like musical chairs. They liked that and so did some other children.

I hated the dump on Saturdays but I liked going to the orphanage. I even liked Miss Dawson when we were there. She spent her time bathing and rocking babies and singing to them, while I made up games for the older children. Some things worked and others didn't. Relay races didn't because nobody would let go of the stick. Jump rope was great because two boys with Down's syndrome would turn the rope for hours on end without stopping, while everybody, especially the blind girls, took turns. Even nuns jumped, jump jump they hovered blue in the air. Farmer in the Dell. Button Button. Hide-and-go-seek didn't work because nobody came home. The orphans were glad to see me, I loved going there, not because I was good, but because I liked to play.

Saturday nights we went to revolutionary theater or poetry readings. We heard the greatest Latin American poets of our century. These were poets whose work I would later love, whom I would study and teach. But then I did not listen. I suffered an agony of self-consciousness and confusion. We were the only Americans there, all I heard were the attacks against the United States. Many people asked questions about American policy that I couldn't answer, I referred them to Miss Dawson and translated her answers, ashamed and baffled by what I told them, about segregation, Anaconda. She didn't realize how much the people scorned us, how they mocked her banal Communist clichés about their reality. They laughed at me with my Josef haircut and nails, my expensive casual clothes. At one theater group they put me onstage and the director hollered, "Okay, *gringa*, tell me why you are in my country!" I froze and sat down, to hooting and laughter. Finally I told Miss Dawson I couldn't go out on Saturday nights anymore.

Dinner and dancing at Marcelo Errazuriz's. Martinis consommé in little cups on the terrace, fragrant gardens beyond us. A six-course dinner that began at eleven. Everyone teased me about my days with Miss Dawson, begged me to tell them where I went. I couldn't talk about it, not with my friends nor my parents. I remember someone making a joke about me and my *rotos*, "broken" meant poor people then. I felt ashamed, aware that there were almost as many servants in the room as guests.

I joined Miss Dawson in a workers' protest outside the United States Embassy. I had only walked about a block when a friend of my father's, Frank Wise, grabbed me out of the crowd, took me to the Crillon Hotel.

He was furious. "What in God's name do you think you are doing?" He soon understood what Miss Dawson didn't . . . that I had not the faintest idea of politics, of what any of this was about. He told me that it would be terrible for my father if the press found out what I was doing. I understood that.

On another Saturday afternoon I agreed to stand downtown and collect money for the orphanage. I stood on one corner and Miss Dawson on another. In only a few minutes dozens of people had insulted and cursed me. I didn't understand, shifted my sign for "Give to El Niño Perdido," and rattled the cup. Tito and Pepe, two friends, were on their way to the Waldorf for coffee. They whisked me away, forced me to go with them to coffee.

"This is *not* done here. Poor people beg. You are insulting the poor. For a woman to solicit anything gives a shocking image. You will destroy your reputation. Also no one would believe you are not keeping the money. A girl simply can't stand on the street unescorted. You can go to charity balls or luncheons, but physical contact with other classes is simply vulgar, and patronizing to them. Also you absolutely cannot afford to be seen with someone of her sexual persuasion in public. My dear, you are too young, you don't understand . . ."

We drank Jamaican coffee and I listened to them. I told them I saw what they were saying but I couldn't just leave Miss Dawson alone on the corner. They said they would speak to her. The three of us went down Ahumada to where she stood, proudly, while passersby muttered *"Gringa loca"* or *"Puta coja,"* crippled whore, at her.

"It is not appropriate, in Santiago, for a young girl to do this, and we are taking her home" was all Tito said to her. She looked at him with disdain, and later that week, in the hallway at school, she told me it was wrong to let men dictate my actions. I told her that I felt everybody dictated my actions, that I had gone with her on Saturdays a month longer than I had first promised. That I wasn't going anymore.

"It is wrong for you to return to a totally selfish existence. To fight for a better world is the only reason for living. Have you learned nothing?"

"I learned a lot. I see that many things need to change. But it's their struggle, not mine."

"I can't believe you can say that. Don't you see, that's what is wrong with the world, that attitude."

She limped crying to the bathroom, was late to class, where she told us we were excused for the day. The six of us went out and lay on the grass in the gardens, away from the windows so no one could see that we weren't in class. The girls teased me, said that I was breaking Miss Dawson's heart. She was obviously in love with me. Did she try to kiss me? This really made me confused and mad. In spite of everything I was beginning to like her, her dogged naive commitment, her hopefulness. She was like a little kid, like one of the blind children when they gasped with pleasure, playing in the water sprinkler. Miss Dawson never flirted with me or tried to touch me all the time like boys did. But she wanted me to do things I didn't want to do and I felt like a bad person for not wanting to, for not caring more about the injustice in the world. The girls got mad at me because I wouldn't talk about her. They called me Miss Dawson's mistress. There was nobody I could talk to about any of this, nobody to ask what was right or wrong, so I just felt wrong.

It was windy my last day at the dump. Sand sifted into the porridge in glistening waves. When the figures rose on the hills it was with a swirl of dirt so they looked like silver ghosts, dervishes. None of them had shoes and their feet crept silently over the soggy mounds. They didn't speak, or shout to each other, like most people do who work together, and they never spoke to us. Beyond the steaming dung hills was the city and above us all the white Andes. They ate. Miss Dawson didn't say a word, gathering up the pots and utensils in the sigh of wind.

We had agreed to go to a farm workers' rally outside of town that afternoon. We ate *churrascos* on the street, stopped by her apartment for her to change.

Her apartment was dingy and airless. The fact that her hot plate for cooking was on the toilet tank made me feel ill, as did the odor of old wool and sweat and hair. She changed in front of me, which I found shocking and frightening, her naked, distorted blue-white body. She put on a sleeveless sundress with no brassiere.

"Miss Dawson, that would be all right at night, in someone's home, or at the beach, but you just can't go around bare like that in Chile."

"I pity you. All your life you are going to be paralyzed by What Is Done, by what people tell you you should think or do. I do not dress to please others. It is a very hot day, and I feel comfortable in this dress."

"Well . . . it makes me not comfortable. People will say rude things to us. It is different here, from the United States . . ."

"The best thing that could happen to you would be for you to be uncomfortable once in a while."

We took several crowded buses to get to the *fundo* where the rally was, waiting in the hot sun and standing on the buses. We got down and walked down a beautiful lane lined with eucalyptus, stopped to cool off in the stream by the lane.

We had arrived too late for the speeches. There was an empty platform, a banner with "Land Back to the People" hanging askew behind the mike. There was a small group of men in suits, obviously the organizers, but most of the people were farm laborers. Guitars were playing and there was a crowd around a couple dancing La Cueca in a desultory fashion, languidly waving handkerchiefs as they circled one another. People were pouring wine from huge vats or standing in line for spit-roasted beef and beans. Miss Dawson told me to find us a place at one of the tables, that she would bring our food.

I squeezed into a spot at the end of a table crowded with families. Nobody was talking politics, it seemed that these were just country people who had come to a free barbeque. Everyone was very, very drunk. I could see Miss Dawson, chattering away in line. She was drinking wine too, gesticulating and talking very loud so people would understand her.

"Isn't this great?" she asked, bringing two huge plates of food. "Let's introduce ourselves. Try to talk to the people more, that's how you learn, and help."

The two farmworkers we sat by decided with gales of laughter that we were from another planet. As I had feared, they were amazed by her bare shoulders and visible nipples, couldn't figure out what she was. I realized that not only did she not speak Spanish, she was nearly blind. She would squint through her inch-thick glasses, smiling, but she couldn't see that these men were laughing at us, didn't like us, whatever we were. What were we doing here? She tried to explain that she was in the Communist party, but instead of *partido* she kept toasting the "*fiesta,*" which is a festive party, so they kept toasting her back, "*La Fiesta!*"

"We've got to leave," I said, but she only looked at me, slack-jawed and drunk. The man next to me was halfheartedly flirting with me, but I was more worried about the big drunk man next to Miss Dawson. He was stroking her shoulders with one hand while he ate a rib with the other. She was laughing away until he started grabbing her and kissing her, then she began to scream.

Miss Dawson ended up on the ground, sobbing uncontrollably. Everyone had rushed over at first, but they soon left, muttering, "Nothing but some drunken *gringa*." The men we had sat by now ignored us totally. She got up and began to run toward the road; I followed her. When she got to the stream she tried to wash herself off, her mouth and her chest. She just got muddy and wet. She sat on the bank, crying, her nose running. I gave her my handkerchief.

"Miss Perfect! An ironed linen handkerchief!" she sneered.

"Yes," I said, fed up with her and only concerned now with getting home. Still crying, she staggered down the path toward the main road, where she started to hail down cars. I pulled her back into the trees.

"Look, Miss Dawson. You can't hitchhike here. They don't understand . . . it could get us in trouble, two women hitchhiking. Listen to me!"

But a farmer in an old truck had stopped, the engine ticking on the dusty road. I offered him money to take us to the outskirts of town. He was going all the way to downtown, could take us all the way to her house easy for twenty pesos. We climbed into the bed of the truck.

She put her arms around me in the wind. I could feel her wet dress, her sticky armpit hairs as she clung to me.

"You can't go back to your frivolous life! Don't leave! Don't leave me," she kept saying until at last we got to her block.

"Good-bye," I said. "Thanks for everything," or something dumb like that. I left her on the curb, blinking at my cab until it turned the corner.

The maids were leaning on the gate talking to the neighborhood *carabinero*, so I didn't think anyone was home. But my father was there, changing to go play golf.

"You're back early. Where have you been?" he asked.

"To a picnic, with my history teacher."

"Oh, yes. What is she like?"

"Okay. She's a Communist."

I just blurted that out. It had been a miserable day. I was fed up with Miss Dawson. But that's all it took. Three words to my father. She was fired sometime that weekend and we never saw her again.

No one else knew what had happened. The other girls were happy she was gone. We had a free period now, even though we would have to make up American history when we got to college. There was nobody to speak to. To say I was sorry.

Melina

In Albuquerque, in the evening, my husband Rex would go to class at the university or to his sculpture studio. I took Ben, the baby, for long walks in his stroller. Up the hill, on a street leafy with elm trees was Clyde Tingley's house. We always went past that house. Clyde Tingley was a millionaire who gave all his money to children's hospitals in the state. We went by his house because not just at Christmas but all the time he had Christmas tree lights strung up, all over the porch and on all the trees. He would turn them on just as it was dusk, as we were on the way home. Sometimes he would be in his wheelchair on the porch, a skinny old man who would holler "Hello" and "Lovely evening" to us as we passed. One night though he yelled at me, "Stop! Stop! Something wrong with that there child's feet! Need to be seen to."

I looked down at Ben's feet, which were fine.

"No, it's because he's too big for the stroller now. He's just holding them up funny so they won't drag on the ground."

Ben was so smart. He didn't even talk yet but he seemed to understand. He set his feet squarely on the ground, as if to show the old man they were okay.

"Mothers never want to admit there's any problem. You take him to a doctor now."

Just then a man dressed all in black walked up. Even then you rarely saw people out walking so he was a surprise. He was squatting on the sidewalk holding Ben's feet in his hands. A saxophone strap dangled from his neck and Ben grabbed at it.

"No, sir. Nothing wrong with this boy's feet," he said.

"Well, I'm glad to hear it," Clyde Tingley called.

"Thanks, anyway," I said.

The man and I stood there talking, and then he walked us home. This happened in 1956. He was the first beatnik I ever met. There hadn't been anyone like him that I had seen in Albuquerque. Jewish, with a Brooklyn accent. Long hair and a beard, dark glasses. But he didn't seem sinister. Ben liked him right away. His name was Beau. He was a poet and a musician, played saxophone. It was later I found out that it was a saxophone strap hanging from his neck.

We became friends right away. He played with the baby while I made iced tea. After I put Ben to bed we sat outside on the porch steps talking until Rex came home. The two men were polite to each other but didn't get along too well, I could see that right away. Rex was a graduate student. We were really poor then, but Rex seemed like someone older and powerful. An air of success, maybe a little conceit. Beau acted like he didn't much care about anything, which I already knew wasn't true. After he left, Rex said he didn't like the idea of me dragging home stray hepcats.

Beau was hitchhiking his way home to New York . . . the Apple . . . after six months in San Francisco. He was staying with friends, but they worked all day, so he came to see me and Ben every day, the four days he was there.

Beau really needed to talk. It was wonderful for me to hear somebody talk, besides Ben's few words, so I was glad to see him. Besides, he talked about romance. He had fallen in love. Now I knew that Rex loved me, and we were happy, would have a happy life together, but he wasn't madly in love with me the way Beau was with Melina.

Beau had been a sandwich man in San Francisco. He had a little cart with sweet rolls and coffee, soft drinks and sandwiches. He pushed it up and down the floors of a gigantic office building. One day he had pulled his cart into an insurance office and he saw her. Melina. She was filing, but not really filing, looking out the window with a dreamy smile on her face. She had long dyed blond hair and wore a black dress. She was very tiny and thin. But it was her skin, he said. It was like she wasn't a person at all but some creature made of white silk, of milk glass.

Beau didn't know what came over him. He left the cart and his customers, went through a little gate over to where she stood. He told her he loved her. I want you, he said. I'll get the bathroom key. Come on. It will just take five minutes. Melina looked at him and said, I'll be right there.

I was pretty young then. This was the most romantic thing I had ever heard.

Melina was married and had a baby girl about a year old. Ben's age. Her husband was a trumpet player. He was on the road for the two months Beau knew Melina. They had a passionate affair and when her husband was coming home she said to Beau, "Time to hit the road." So he did.

Beau said you had to do anything she said, that she cast a spell on him, on her husband, on any man who knew her. You couldn't get jealous, he said, because it seemed perfectly natural that any other man would love her.

For example . . . the baby wasn't even her husband's. For a while they had been living in El Paso. Melina worked at Piggly Wiggly packing meat and chickens and sealing them in plastic. Behind a glass window, in a funny paper hat. But still this Mexican bullfighter who was buying steaks saw her. He banged on the counter and rang a bell, insisted to the butcher that he see the wrapping woman. He made her leave work. That's how she affected you, Beau said. You had to be near her immediately.

A few months later Melina realized she was pregnant. She was really happy, and told her husband. He was furious. You can't be, he said, I had a vasectomy. What? Melina was indignant. And you married me without telling me this? She kicked him out of the house, changed the locks. He sent flowers, wrote her passionate letters. He camped out outside the door until at last she forgave him for what he did.

She sewed all their clothes. She had covered all the rooms in the apartment with fabric. There were mattresses and pillows on the floors so you crawled, like a baby, from tent to tent. In candle-light day and night you never knew what time it was.

Beau told me everything about Melina. About her childhood in foster homes, how she ran away at thirteen. She was a B-girl in a bar (I'm not sure what that is) and her husband had rescued her from a very ugly situation. She's tough, Beau said, she talks nasty. But her eyes, her touch, they are like an angel child's. She was this angel that just came into my life and ruined it forever . . . He did get dramatic about her, and even cried and cried sometimes, but I loved hearing all about her, wished I could be like her. Tough, mysterious, beautiful.

I was sorry when Beau left. He was like an angel in my life, too. When he was gone I realized how little Rex ever talked to me or Ben. I felt so lonely I even thought about turning our rooms into tents.

A few years later I was married to a different man, a jazz piano player named David. He was a good man but he was quiet too. I don't know why I married those quiet guys, when the thing I like best in the world to do is to talk. We had a lot of friends though.

Musicians coming into town would stay with us and while the men played we women cooked and talked and lay around on the grass playing with the kids.

It was like pulling teeth to get David to tell me what he was like in first grade, or about his first girlfriend, anything. I knew he had lived with a woman, a beautiful painter, for five years, but he didn't want to talk about her. Hey, I said, I've told you my whole life story, tell me something about you, tell me when you first fell in love . . . He laughed then, but he actually told me. That's easy, he said.

It was a woman who was living with his best friend, a bass player, Ernie Jones. Down in the south valley, by the irrigation ditch. Once he had gone to see Ernie and when he wasn't home he went down to the ditch.

She was sunbathing, naked and white against the green grass. For sunglasses she wore those paper lace doilies they put under ice cream.

"So. That's it?" I prodded.

"Well, yeah. That's it. I fell in love."

"But what was she like?"

"She wasn't like anyone in this world. Once, Ernie and I were lying around by the ditch, talking, smoking weed. We were real blue because we were both out of work. She was supporting us both, working as a waitress. One day she worked a noon banquet and she brought all the flowers home, a whole roomful. But what she did was carry them all upstream and dump them in the ditch. So Ernie and I were sitting there, gloomy, on the bank, staring at the muddy water and then a billion flowers floated by. She had taken food and wine, even silver and tablecloths that she set up on the grass."

"So, did you make love with her?"

"No. I never even talked to her, alone anyway. I just remember her—in the grass."

"Hm," I said, pleased by all that information and by the sort of sappy look on his face. I loved romance in any form.

We moved to Santa Fe, where David played piano at Claude's. A lot of good musicians passed through town in those years and would sit in with David's trio for one or two nights. Once a really good trumpet player came, Paco Duran. David liked playing with him, and asked if it was okay with me if Paco and his wife and child stayed with us for a week. Sure, I said, it will be nice.

It was. Paco played great. He and David played all night at work and together all day at home. Paco's wife, Melina, was exotic and fun. They talked and acted like L.A. jazz musicians. Called our house a pad and said "you dig?" and "outta sight." Their little girl and Ben got along great but were both at the age where they got into everything. We tried putting them both in a playpen but neither one of them would go for it. Melina got the idea that we should just let them carry on and she and I should get inside the playpen with our coffee and ashtrays safe. So there we were, sitting in there while the kids took books out of the bookcase. She was telling me about Las Vegas, making it sound like another planet. I realized, listening to her, not just looking at her but being surrounded by her otherworldly beauty, that this was Beau's Melina.

Somehow I couldn't say anything about it. I couldn't say, Hey, you are so beautiful and weird you must be Beau's romance. But I thought of Beau and missed him, hoped he was doing fine.

She and I cooked dinner and the men went off to work. We bathed the children and went out on the back porch, smoked and drank coffee, talked about shoes. We talked about all the important shoes in our lives. The first penny loafers, first high heels. Silver platforms. Boots we had known. Perfect pumps. Handmade sandals. Huaraches. Spike heels. While we talked our bare feet wriggled in the damp green grass by the porch. Her toenails were painted black.

She asked me what my sign was. Usually this annoyed me but I let her tell me everything about my Scorpio self and I believed every word. I told her I read palms, a little, and looked at her hands. It was too dark so I went in and got a kerosene lantern, set it on the steps between us. I held her two white hands by lantern and moonlight, and remembered what Beau had said about her skin. It was like holding cool glass, silver.

I know Cheiro's palmistry book by heart. I have read hundreds of palms. I'm telling you this so you'll know I did tell her things that I saw in the lines and mounds of her hands. But mostly I told her everything Beau had told me about her.

I'm ashamed of why I did this. I was jealous of her. She was so dazzling. She didn't really do anything special, her *being* dazzled. I wanted to impress her.

I told her her life story. I told her about the horrible foster parents, how Paco protected her. Said things like, "I see a man. Handsome man. Danger. You are not in danger. He is in danger. A race driver, bullfighter maybe?" Fuck, she said, nobody knew about the bullfighter.

Beau had told me that once he put his hand on her head and said, "It will all be all right . . ." and she had wept. I told her that she never ever cried, not when she was sad or mad. But that if someone was really kind and just put their hand on her head and said not to worry, that might make her cry . . .

I won't tell you any more. I'm too ashamed. But it had exactly the effect I had intended. She sat there staring at her beautiful hands and she whispered, "You are a witch. You are magic."

We had a wonderful week. We all went to Indian dances and climbed in Bandolier monument and Acoma pueblo. We sat in the cave where Sandia man had lived. We soaked in hot springs near Taos and went to the church of the Santo Nino. Two nights we even got a babysitter so Melina and I could go to the club. The music was great. "I have had a wonderful time this week," I said. She smiled. "I always have a wonderful time," she said, simply.

The house was very quiet when they had gone. I woke up, as usual, when David came home. I think I wanted to confess to him about the palm reading, but I'm glad I didn't. We were lying in bed together in the dark when he said to me,

"That was her."

"That was who?"

"Melina. She was the woman in the grass."

Friends

Loretta met Anna and Sam the day she saved Sam's life.

Anna and Sam were old. She was eighty and he was eighty-nine. Loretta would see Anna from time to time when she went to swim at her neighbor Elaine's pool. One day she stopped by as the two women were convincing the old guy to take a swim. He finally got in, was dog-paddling along with a big grin on his face when he had a seizure. The other two women were in the shallow end and didn't notice. Loretta jumped in, shoes and all, pulled him to the steps and up out of the pool. He didn't need resuscitation but he was disoriented and frightened. He had some medicine to take, for epilepsy, and they helped him dry off and dress. They all sat around for a while until they were sure he was fine and could walk to their house, just down the block. Anna and Sam kept thanking Loretta for saving his life, and insisted that she go to lunch at their house the next day.

It happened that she wasn't working for the next few days. She had taken three days off without pay because she had a lot of things that needed doing. Lunch with them would mean going all the way back to Berkeley from the city, and not finishing everything in one day, as she had planned.

She often felt helpless in situations like this. The kind where you say to yourself, Gosh, it's the least I can do, they are so nice. If you don't do it you feel guilty and if you do you feel like a wimp.

She stopped being in a bad mood the minute she was inside their apartment. It was sunny and open, like an old house in Mexico, where they had lived most of their lives. Anna had been an archaeologist and Sam an engineer. They had worked together every day at Teotihuacan and other sites. Their apartment was filled with fine pottery and photographs, a wonderful library. Downstairs, in the backyard was a large vegetable garden, many fruit trees, berries. Loretta was amazed that the two birdlike, frail people did all the work themselves. Both of them used canes, and walked with much difficulty.

Lunch was toasted cheese sandwiches, chayote soup, and a salad from their garden. Anna and Sam prepared the lunch together, set the table and served the lunch together.

They had done everything together for fifty years. Like twins, they each echoed the other or finished sentences the other had started. Lunch passed pleasantly as they told her, in stereo, some of their experiences working on the pyramid in Mexico, and about other excavations they had worked on. Loretta was impressed by these two old people, by their shared love of music and gardening, by their enjoyment of each other. She was amazed at how involved they were in local and national politics, going to marches and protests, writing congressmen and editors, making phone calls. They read three or four papers every day, read novels or history to each other at night.

While Sam was clearing the table with shaking hands, Loretta said to Anna how enviable it was to have such a close lifetime companion. Yes, Anna said, but soon one of us will be gone . . .

Loretta was to remember that statement much later, and wonder if Anna had begun to cultivate a friendship with her as a sort of insurance policy against the time when one of them would die. But, no, she thought, it was simpler than that. The two of them had been so self-sufficient, so enough for each other all their lives, but now Sam was becoming dreamy and often incoherent.

He repeated the same stories over and over, and although Anna was always patient with him, Loretta felt that she was glad to have someone else to talk to.

Whatever the reason, she found herself more and more involved in Sam and Anna's life. They didn't drive anymore. Often Anna would call Loretta at work and ask her to pick up peat moss when she got off, or take Sam to the eye doctor. Sometimes both of them felt too bad to go to the store, so Loretta would pick things up for them. She liked them both, admired them. Since they seemed so much to want company, she found herself at dinner with them once a week, every two weeks at the most. A few times she asked them to her house for dinner, but there were so many steps to climb and the two arrived so exhausted that she stopped. So then she would take fish or chicken or a pasta dish to their house. They would make a salad, serve berries from the garden for dessert.

After dinner, over cups of mint or Jamaica tea they would sit around the table while Sam told stories. About the time Anna got polio, at a dig deep in the jungle in the Yucatán, how they got her to a hospital, how kind people were. Many stories about the house they built in Xalapa. The mayor's wife, the time she broke her leg climbing out of a window to avoid a visitor. Sam's stories always began, "That reminds me of the time . . ."

Little by little Loretta learned the details of their life story. Their courtship on Mount Tam. Their romance in New York while they were Communists. Living in sin. They had never married, still took satisfaction in this unconventionality. They had two children; both lived in distant cities. There were stories about the ranch near Big Sur, when the children were little. As a story was ending Loretta would say, "I hate to leave, but I have to get to work very early tomorrow." Often she would leave then. Usually though, Sam would say, "Just let me tell you what happened to the wind-up phonograph." Hours later, exhausted, she would drive home to her house in Oakland, saying to herself that she couldn't keep on doing this. Or that she would keep going, but set a definite time limit.

It was not that they were ever boring or uninteresting. On the contrary, the couple had lived a rich, full life, were involved and perceptive. They were intensely interested in the world, in their own past. They had such a good time, adding to the other's remarks, arguing about dates or details, that Loretta didn't have the heart to interrupt them and leave. And it did make her feel good to go there, because the two people were so glad to see her. But sometimes she felt like not going over at all, when she was too tired or had something else to do. Finally she did say that she couldn't stay so late, that it was hard to get up the next morning. Come for Sunday brunch, Anna said.

When the weather was fair they ate on a table on their porch, surrounded by flowers and plants. Hundreds of birds came to the feeders right by them. As it grew colder they ate inside by a cast-iron stove. Sam tended it with logs he had split himself. They had waffles or Sam's special omelette, sometimes Loretta brought bagels and lox. Hours went by, the day went by as Sam told his stories, with Anna correcting them and adding comments. Sometimes, in the sun on the porch or by the heat of the fire, it was hard to stay awake.

Their house in Mexico had been made of concrete block, but the beams and counters and cupboards had been made of cedar-wood. First the big room—the kitchen and living room—was built. They had planted trees, of course, even before they started building the house. Bananas and plums, jacarandas. The next year they added a bedroom, several years later another bedroom and a studio for Anna. The beds, the workbenches and tables were made of cedar. They got home to their little house after working in the field, in another state in Mexico. The house was always cool and smelled of cedar, like a big cedar chest.

Anna got pneumonia and had to go to the hospital. As sick as she was, all she could think of was Sam, how he would get along without her. Loretta promised her she would go by before work, see that he took his medication and had breakfast, that she would cook him dinner after work, take him to the hospital to see her.

The terrible part was that Sam didn't talk. He would sit shivering on the side of the bed as Loretta helped him dress. Mechanically he took his pills and drank pineapple juice, carefully wiped his chin after he ate breakfast. In the evening when she arrived he would be standing on the porch waiting for her. He wanted to go see Anna first, and then have dinner. When they got to the hospital, Anna lay pale, her long white braids hanging down like a little girl's. She had an IV, a catheter, oxygen. She didn't speak, but smiled and held Sam's hand while he told her how he had done a load of wash, watered the tomatoes, mulched the beans, washed dishes, made lemonade. He talked on to her, breathless, told her every hour of his day. When they left, Loretta had to hold him tight, he stumbled and wavered as he walked. In the car going home he cried, he was so worried. But Anna came home and was fine, except that there was so much to be done in the garden. The next Sunday, after brunch, Loretta helped weed the garden, cut back blackberry vines. Loretta was worried then, what if Anna got really sick? What was she in for with this friendship? The couple's dependence upon each other, their vulnerability, saddened and moved her. Those thoughts passed through her head as she worked, but it was nice, the cool black dirt, the sun on her back. Sam, telling his stories as he weeded the adjacent row.

The next Sunday that Loretta went to their house she was late. She had been up early, there had been many things to do. She really wanted to stay home, but didn't have the heart to call and cancel.

The front door was not unlatched, as usual, so she went to the garden, to go up the back steps. She walked into the garden to look around, it was lush with tomatoes, squash, snow peas. Drowsy bees. Anna and Sam were outside on the porch upstairs. Loretta was going to call to them but they were talking very intently.

"She's never been late before. Maybe she won't come."

"Oh, she'll come . . . these mornings mean so much to her."

"Poor thing. She is so lonely. She needs us. We're really her only family."

"She sure enjoys my stories. Dang. I can't think of a single one to tell her today."

"Something will come to you . . ."

"Hello!" Loretta called. "Anybody home?"

Unmanageable

In the deep dark night of the soul the liquor stores and bars are closed. She reached under the mattress; the pint bottle of vodka was empty. She got out of bed, stood up. She was shaking so badly that she sat down on the floor. She was hyperventilating. If she didn't get a drink she would go into DTs or have a seizure.

Trick is to slow down your breathing and your pulse. Stay as calm as you can until you can get a bottle. Sugar. Tea with sugar, that's what they gave you in detox. But she was shaking too hard to stand. She lay on the floor breathing deep yoga breaths. Don't think, God don't think about the state you're in or you will die, of shame, a stroke. Her breath slowed down. She started to read titles of books in the bookcase. Concentrate, read them out loud. Edward Abbey, Chinua Achebe, Sherwood Anderson, Jane Austen, Paul Auster, don't skip, slow down. By the time she had read the whole wall of books she was better. She pulled herself up. Holding on to the wall, shaking so badly she could barely move each foot, she made it to the kitchen. No vanilla. Lemon extract. It seared her throat and she retched, held her mouth shut to reswallow it. She made some tea, thick with honey, sipped it slowly in the dark. At six, in two hours, the Uptown Liquor Store in Oakland would sell her some vodka. In Berkeley you had to wait until seven. Oh, God, did she have any money? She crept back to her room to check in her purse on the desk. Her son Nick must have taken her wallet and car keys. She couldn't look for them in her sons' room without waking them.

There was a dollar and thirty cents in a change jar on her desk. She looked through several purses in the closet, in the coat pockets, a kitchen drawer, until she got together the four dollars that bloody wog charged for a half-pint at that hour. All the sick drunks paid him. Although most of them bought sweet wine, it worked quicker.

It was far to walk. It would take her three quarters of an hour; she would have to run home to be there before the kids woke up. Could she make it? She could hardly walk from one room to the other. Just pray a patrol car didn't pass. She wished she had a dog to walk. I know, she laughed, I'll ask the neighbors if I can borrow their dog. Sure. None of the neighbors spoke to her anymore.

It kept her steady to concentrate on the cracks in the sidewalk to count them one two three. Pulling herself along on bushes, tree trunks, like climbing a mountain sideways. Crossing the streets was terrifying, they were so wide, with their lights blinking red red, yellow yellow. An occasional *Examiner* truck, an empty taxi. A police car going fast, without lights. They didn't see her. Cold sweat ran down her back, her teeth chattered loudly in the still dark morning.

She was panting and faint by the time she got to the Uptown on Shattuck. It wasn't open yet. Seven black men, all old except for one young boy, stood outside on the curb. The Indian man sat oblivious to them inside the window, sipping coffee. On the sidewalk two men were sharing a bottle of NyQuil cough syrup. Blue death, you could buy that all night long.

An old man they called Champ smiled at her. "Say, mama, you be sick? Your hair hurt?" She nodded. That's how it felt, your hair, your eyeballs, your bones. "Here," Champ said, "you better eat some of these." He was eating saltines, passed her two. "Gotta make yourself eat." "Say Champ, lemme have a few," the young boy said.

They let her go to the counter first. She asked for vodka and poured her pile of coins onto the counter.

"It's all there," she said.

He smiled. "Count it for me."

"Come on. Shit," the boy said as she counted out the coins with violently shaking hands. She put the bottle into her purse, stumbled toward the door. Outside she held on to a telephone pole, afraid to cross the street.

Champ was drinking from his bottle of Night Train.

"You too much a lady to drink on the street?" She shook her head. "I'm afraid I'll drop the bottle."

"Here," he said. "Open your mouth. You need something or you'll never get home." He poured wine into her mouth. It coursed through her, warm. "Thank you," she said.

She quickly crossed the street, jogged clumsily down the streets toward her house, ninety, ninety-one, counting the cracks. It was still pitch dark when she got to her door.

Gasping for air. Without turning on the light she poured some cranberry juice into a glass and a third of the bottle. She sat down at the table and sipped the drink slowly, the relief of the alcohol seeping throughout her body. She was crying, with relief that she had not died. She poured another third from the bottle and some juice, rested her head on the table between sips.

When she had finished that drink she felt better, and she went into the laundry room and started a load of wash. Taking the bottle with her, she went to the bathroom then. She showered and combed her hair, put on clean clothes. Ten more minutes. She checked to see if the door was locked, sat on the toilet and finished the vodka. This last drink didn't just get her well but got her slightly drunk.

She moved the laundry from the washer to the dryer. She was mixing orange juice from frozen concentrate when Joel came into the kitchen, rubbing his eyes. "No socks, no shirt."

"Hi, honey. Have some cereal. Your clothes will be dry by the time you finish breakfast and shower." She poured him some juice, another glass for Nicholas who stood silent in the doorway.

"How in the hell did you get a drink?" He pushed past her and poured himself some cereal. Thirteen. He was taller than she.

"Could I have my wallet and keys?" she asked.

"You can have your wallet. I'll give you the keys when I know you're okay."

"I'm okay. I'll be back at work tomorrow."

"You can't stop anymore without a hospital, Ma."

"I'll be fine. Please don't worry. I'll have all day to get well." She went to check the clothes in the dryer.

"The shirts are dry," she told Joel. "The socks need about ten more minutes."

"Can't wait. I'll wear them wet."

Her sons got their books and backpacks, kissed her good-bye and went out the door. She stood in the window and watched them go down the street to the bus stop. She waited until the bus picked them up and headed up Telegraph Avenue. She left then, for the liquor store on the corner. It was open now.

Electric Car, El Paso

Mrs. Snowden waited for my grandmother and me to get into her electric car. It looked like any other car except that it was very tall and short, like a car in a cartoon that had run into a wall. A car with its hair standing on end. Mamie got in front and I got into the back.

It was the zone where nails scrape on a blackboard. The windows were covered with a film of yellow dust. The walls and seats were mildewed dusty velvet. Taupe. I bit my nails a lot then and the touch of the moldy dusty velvet on the raw ends of my fingers, on my scratched elbows and knees . . . it was anguish. My teeth ached, my hair hurt. I shuddered as if I had touched a matted dead cat, accidentally. Crouching, I reached up and hung on to the carved gold flowerpots above the dirty windows. The straps for holding on were rotted and stringy, dangled beneath the flowerpots like old wigs. Hanging on this way I was suspended high in the air, swayed above the backseats of other cars where I could see bags of groceries, babies playing in ashtrays, Kleenex boxes.

The car made such a faint whirring sound it didn't seem as if we were moving. Were we? Mrs. Snowden wouldn't, or she couldn't, go over 15 miles an hour. So slow we went that I saw things in a way I never had before. Through time, like watching someone sleep, all night. A man on the sidewalk deciding to go

into a café, he changed his mind, walked to the corner, turned
back again and went in, put the napkin in his lap and looked ex-
pectant before we were even at the end of the block.

If I ducked my head, like a swing seat beneath my dangling
arms, when I looked up all I could see of tiny Mamie and
Mrs. Snowden was their straw hats, as if they were just two straw
hats perched on the dashboard. I giggled hysterically every time I
did this. Mamie turned around to smile as if she didn't notice. We
weren't even downtown yet, not even at the Plaza.

She and Mrs. Snowden talked about friends who had died or
were sick or who had lost a husband. They ended everything they
said with a quote from the Bible.

"Well, I think she was *very* unwise to . . ."

"Oh mercy yes. 'Yet count on him not as an enemy but admon-
ish him as a brother.'"

"Thessalonians Three!" Mamie said. This was sort of a game.

Finally I couldn't hang on to the flowerpots any longer. I lay
down on the floor. Mildewed rubber. Dust. Mamie turned around
to smile. Mercy! Mrs. Snowden pulled over to the side of the road.
They thought I had fallen out. Much later, hours later, I had to
go to the bathroom. All the clean restrooms were on the other
side of the road, on the left side. Mrs. Snowden couldn't make
left turns. It took us about ten blocks of right turns and one-way
streets before we got to a restroom. I had already wet my pants
by then but didn't tell them, drank from the cool cool Texaco
faucet. It took even longer to get back on the right side again
because we had to go all the way back to the overpass on Wyo-
ming Avenue.

It was dry at the airport, cars grinding in and out on the gravel.
Tumbleweeds caught in the fence. Asphalt, metal, a haze of dusty
dancing atoms that reflected dazzling from the wings and windows of the airplanes. People in cars around us were eating sloppy
things. Watermelons, pomegranates, bruised bananas. Bottles of

beer spurted on ceilings, suds cascaded on the sides of cars. I
wanted to suck on an orange. I'm hungry, I whined.

Mrs. Snowden had foreseen that. Her gloved hand passed me
fig newtons wrapped in talcumy Kleenex. The cookie expanded in
my mouth like Japanese flowers, like a burst pillow. I gagged and
wept. Mamie smiled and passed me a sachet-dusted handkerchief,
whispered to Mrs. Snowden, who was shaking her head.

"Don't pay her no mind . . . just showing off."

"For whom the Lord loveth He chasteneth."

"John?"

"Hebrews, Eleven."

A few planes took off and one landed. Well, best we be getting
back home. She didn't see so well at night, the lights and all, so
she slowed down on the way home, drove far from the parked cars
at the curbs. All the Sunday drivers were honking at us. I stood up
on the seat, propped myself away from the velvet with my hands
against the rear window, watching the necklace of headlights
stuck behind us all the way back to the airport.

"Cops!" I hollered. A red light, a siren. Mrs. Snowden signaled,
pulled slowly over to let him pass, but he stopped next to us. She
buzzed her window halfway down to listen to him.

"Lady, the lights are geared for forty miles an hour. Also, you
are driving in the middle of the road."

"Forty is much too fast."

"Speed up or I'll have to give you a ticket."

"They can simply go around me."

"Sweetie, they wouldn't dare!"

"Well!"

She buzzed the electric window up in his face. He banged on
it with his fist, red-faced. Horns were bleating behind us and the
people just in back of us were laughing. Furious, the policeman
stomped around and got into the patrol car, gunned his engine,
and roared off, sirens wailing right through a red light, crash into

the tan end of an Oldsmobile and then crash again, into the front end of a pickup truck. Glass tinkled. Mrs. Snowden buzzed down her window. She drove carefully past the back of the wrecked truck.

"Let he who think he standeth take heed lest he fall."

"Corinthians!" Mamie said.

Sex Appeal

Bella Lynn was my cousin, and just about the prettiest girl in West Texas. She had been a drum majorette at El Paso High and Miss Sun Bowl in 1946 and 1947. Later she went to Hollywood to become a starlet. That didn't work out. The trip started off badly because of her brassiere. It didn't have falsies in it, but you blew it up, like a balloon. Two balloons.

Uncle Tyler, Aunt Tiny and I went to see her off. In a twin-engine DC-6. None of us had ever been in an airplane before. She said that she was a nervous wreck, but she didn't look it. She looked just lovely in a pink angora sweater. Her breasts were very big.

The three of us watched her plane, waving at it, until it was way off toward California and Hollywood and then it disappeared. Apparently at about that time it also reached a certain altitude, and because of the pressure in the cabin Bella Lynn's brassiere blew up. Exploded, I mean. Fortunately, no one in El Paso heard about it. She didn't even tell me about it for twenty years. But I don't think that's why she never became a starlet.

Her picture was always coming out in the El Paso paper. Once it was in it every day for a week . . . when she was dating Rickie Evers. Rickie Evers had just divorced a famous movie star. His daddy was a millionaire hotel owner and lived on top of the Hotel del Norte in El Paso.

Rickie Evers was in town for the National Golf Open, and Bella Lynn was bound and determined to go out with him. She made reservations for dinner at the Del Norte. She said I should come along, that eleven years old wasn't too young for me to get some lessons in sex appeal.

I didn't, in fact, know anything about sex appeal. Sex itself seemed to have something to do with being mad. Cats acted pretty mad about the whole thing, and all the movie stars seemed mad. Bette Davis and Barbara Stanwyck were downright mean. Bella Lynn and her friends would slouch in the Court Café under pompadours, blowing smoke from their nostrils like petulant dragons.

They were all excited about the National Golf Open. "A gold mine! An oil well right in our own backyard!"

Wilma, Bella Lynn's best friend, wanted to come with us to the Del Norte Hotel, but Bella Lynn said Nix. A basic principle of sex appeal, she told me, was always work alone. No matter if the other woman was pretty or ugly . . . it simply delayed and complicated any operation.

I dressed up in what I thought was the most wonderful dress I had ever seen. Lavender dotted swiss with puff sleeves and a crinoline. Aunt Tiny did my hair in French braids. I didn't wear lipstick yet, but I put some Merthiolate on my mouth. Aunt Tiny made me wash it right off. She did pinch my cheeks. Bella Lynn wore a mean-looking brown crepe dress with big shoulders, mean dark makeup, and black high heels. We got to the hotel early. She sat in a high-backed chair in the lobby, wearing dark glasses. She crossed her legs. Black silk stockings. I told her that the seams were crooked, but she said slightly crooked seams had sex appeal. She gave me a quarter to go buy a soda, but instead I just went up and down the stairs. A beautiful wide curved staircase carpeted in red velvet, with a curved banister. I'd run to the top and stand beneath the chandelier, smiling regally. Then I'd walk very slowly and graciously to the bottom, my hand lightly brushing the mahogany rail. Then I'd run back up. I did this over and over until finally it seemed that surely it must be time to eat. She said she had postponed the reservation because Evers hadn't shown up yet. I bought an Almond Hershey and sat down a few chairs away. She whispered to stop kicking the seat. She smoked Pall Malls, only she called them Pell Mells.

I recognized the famous Evers and his millionaire father the minute they came in. They went into the dining room with some other men. All in Stetsons and boots, except for Evers, who wore a pinstriped suit and no hat. But I would have known it was them just by how nasty Bella Lynn was looking, using a cigarette holder now. She took off her dark glasses and we went in. Bella Lynn told the head waiter that her escort had been unavoidably detained. That there would only be the two of us to dine.

I wanted chicken fried steak, but she said that was too tacky. She ordered us prime rib. A Manhattan for her and a Shirley Temple for me. Only she ended up with a Shirley Temple too, because she was only eighteen. She told the waiter she must have misplaced her driver's license. How inconvenient.

The men had a bottle of bourbon on the table and except for Rickie Evers, were all smoking cigars.

"So how are you going to meet him?" I asked her.

"I told you. Sex appeal. Just as soon as I catch his eye I'll have him over here and buying us our little old prime rib dinner."

"So far he hasn't even looked this way."

"Yes he has, but he pretended not to . . . that's *his* sex appeal. But he'll look over again, and when he does I'll just look at him as if he was the lowest-down, mangiest old hound dog I ever saw."

Rickie Evers did, then, look over at her, and that's exactly how she looked at him, like how did they ever let *him* in? In two seconds he was standing behind the empty chair.

"May I join you?"

"Well. My escort has been unavoidably detained. Perhaps for a few minutes."

"What are you drinking?" he asked.

"Shirley Temples," I said, but she said Manhattan. He told the waiter to bring me a Shirley Temple. Manhattans for him and the lady. The waiter didn't say anything about her ID.

"I'm Bella Lynn and this is Little Lou, my cousin. Sorry, I didn't catch your name," she said, although she knew perfectly well what it was.

He told her his name and she said, "Your daddy and my daddy play golf together."

"Will you be at the Golf Open tomorrow?" he asked.

"I'm not sure. The crowds are so excruciating. Little Lou has her heart set on it though."

They ended up deciding to go to the golf tournament the next day so I wouldn't be disappointed. It was the last thing I wanted to do, but by tomorrow they had forgotten how much I was supposed to want to go anyway.

They drank their Manhattans and then we had shrimp cocktails before our roast beef. Baked Alaska for dessert, which I thought was amazing.

After dinner they were going nightclubbing in Juárez, and there was the problem, over crème de menthe, of how to get me home. A taxi, Bella Lynn said, but he insisted that they could drop me off before they crossed the border.

Bella Lynn went to powder her nose. I didn't go, didn't know yet that you're always supposed to go, to assess the situation.

When she was gone Rickie Evers dropped his gold cigarette lighter on the floor and when he reached down for it he ran his hand up my leg, stroked the inside of my knee.

I took a bite of the Baked Alaska and said I wondered how they ever managed to do it. He picked his lighter up and told me I had

Baked Alaska on my chin. When he wiped it with the big linen napkin his arm brushed my breast. I was embarrassed, I still didn't even wear a training bra.

Bella Lynn came back from the powder room sauntering in her crooked seams, pretending not to notice all the men staring at her. The whole dining room had been staring at Bella Lynn and Rickie Evers throughout the meal. I think the Mexican busboy saw what Evers did when he dropped his lighter.

I sat between Evers and Bella Lynn in the big black Lincoln. The windows rolled up and down when he pushed a button, even the back ones. There was a cigarette lighter, and he would brush my leg as he pushed it in, and my breasts again as he reached across to light her Pell Mells.

We pulled up in the driveway.

"How about a good-night kiss, Little Lou?" he asked. Bella Lynn laughed. "Why, she's not even sweet sixteen." While she was getting out he bit my neck.

Bella Lynn went in with me to get her wrap and her atomizer of Tabu.

"See what I told you, Lou, about Sex Appeal? Easy as pie!" I went in to listen to *Inner Sanctum* with Uncle Tyler and Aunt Tiny. They were pleased as punch that Bella Lynn was going out with the ex-husband of the most beautiful movie star in the world.

"How did she ever manage that?" Uncle Tyler wondered.

"Why, Tyler . . . you know our Bella Lynn is the prettiest thing west of the Mississippi!"

"No. It was Sex Appeal," I told them.

They glared at me.

"Child, don't you *ever* let me hear you use that word again!" Aunt Tiny said, real mean. She looked just like Mildred Pierce.

Teenage Punk

In the sixties, Jesse used to come over to see Ben. They were young kids then, long hair, strobe lights, weed and acid. Jesse had already dropped out of school, already had a probation officer. The Rolling Stones came to New Mexico. The Doors. Ben and Jesse had wept when Jimi Hendrix died, when Janis Joplin died. That was another year for weather. Snow. Frozen pipes. Everybody cried that year.

We lived in an old farmhouse, down by the river. Marty and I had just divorced, I was in my first year of teaching, my first job. The house was hard to take care of alone. Leaky roof, burned-out pump, but it was big, a beautiful house.

Ben and Jesse played music loud, burned violet incense that smelled of cat pee. My other sons Keith and Nathan couldn't stand Jesse—hippie burnout—but Joel, the baby, adored him, his boots, his guitar, his pellet gun. Beer-can practice in the backyard. Ping.

It was March and cold for sure. The next morning the cranes would be at the clear ditch at dawn. I had learned about them from the new pediatrician. He's a good doctor, and single, but I still miss old Dr. Bass. When Ben was a baby I called him to ask how many diapers I should wash at a time. One, he told me.

None of the kids had wanted to go. I dressed, shivering. Built a piñon fire, poured coffee into a thermos. Fixed batter for pancakes, fed the dogs and cats and Rosie the goat. Did we have a horse then? If so, I forgot to feed him. Jesse came up behind me in the dark, at the barbed wire by the frost-white road.

"I want to see the cranes."

I gave him the flashlight, think I gave him the thermos too. He shined the light everywhere but the road and I kept bugging him about it. Come on. Cut it out.

"You can see. You're walking along. You obviously know the road."

True. The dizzy arcs of light swept into birds' nests in pale winter cottonwoods, pumpkins in Gus's field, prehistoric silhouettes of his Brahmin bulls. Their agate eyes opened to reflect a pinpoint of dazzle, closed again.

We crossed the log above the slow dark irrigation ditch, over to the clear ditch where we lay on our stomachs, silent as guerrillas. I know, I romanticize everything. It is true though that we lay there freezing for a long time in the fog. It wasn't fog. Must have been mist from the ditch or maybe just the steam from our mouths.

After a long time the cranes did come. Hundreds, just as the sky turned blue-gray. They landed in slow motion on brittle legs. Washing, preening on the bank. Everything was suddenly black and white and gray, a movie after the credits, churning.

As the cranes drank upstream the silver water beneath them was shot into dozens of thin streamers. Then very quickly the birds left, in whiteness, with the sound of shuffling cards.

We lay there, drinking coffee, until it was light and the crows came. Gawky raucous crows, defying the cranes' grace. Their blackness zigzagged in the water, cottonwood branches bounced like trampolines. You could feel the sun.

It was light on the road back but he left the flashlight on. Turn it off, will you? He ignored me so I took it from him. We walked in his long strides in the tractor tracks.

"Fuck," he said. "That was scary."

"Really. As terrible as an army with banners. That's from the Bible."

"Oh yeah, teacher?" He already had an attitude, then.

Step

The West Oakland detox used to be a warehouse. It is dark inside and echoes like an underground parking lot. Bedrooms, a kitchen, and the office open off a vast room. In the middle of the room is a pool table and the TV pit. They call it the pit because the walls around it are only five feet high, so the counselors can look down into it.

Most of the residents were in the pit, in blue pajamas, watching *Leave It to Beaver*. Bobo held a cup of tea for Carlotta to drink. The other men were laughing about her running around the train yard, trying to go under the engine. The Amtrak from L.A. had stopped. Carlotta laughed too. All of them running around in pajamas. Not that she didn't care about what she had done. She didn't remember, didn't own the deed at all.

Milton, a counselor, came to the rim of the pit.

"When's the fight?"

"Two hours." Benitez and Sugar Ray Leonard for the welter-weight title.

"Sugar Ray will take it, easy." Milton grinned at Carlotta and the men made comments, jokes. She knew most of the men from other times here, from detoxes in Hayward, Richmond, San Francisco. Bobo she knew from Highland psych ward too.

All twenty of the residents were in the pit now, with pillows and blankets, huddled together like preschool kids at nap time, Henry Moore drawings of people in bomb shelters. On the TV Orson Welles said, "We will sell no wine before its time." Bobo laughed, "It's time, brother, it's time!"

"Stop your shakin', woman, messes the TV."

A man with dreadlocks sat down beside Carlotta, put his hand inside her thigh. Bobo grabbed the man's wrist. "Move it or I'll break it." Old Sam came in wrapped in a blanket. There was no heat and it was bitterly cold.

"Sit there on her feets. You can hold them still."

Cheaper by the Dozen was almost over. Clifton Webb died and Myrna Loy went to college. Willie said he had liked it in Europe because white people were ugly there. Carlotta didn't know what he meant, then realized that the only people solitary drunks ever see are on television. At three in the morning she would wait to see Jack the Ripper for Used Datsuns. Slashin' them prices. Jest a hackin' and a hewin'.

The television was the only light in the detox. It was as if the pit were their own smoky ring, with the boxing ring inside it in color. The announcer's voice was shrill. Tonight's purse is one million dollars! All the men had their money on Sugar Ray, would have had. Bobo told Carlotta some of the men there weren't even alcoholics, had just faked needing detox so they could watch the fight.

Carlotta was for Benitez. You likes them pretty boys, Mama? Benitez was pretty, with fine bones, a dapper mustache. He weighed 144 pounds, had won his first championship at seventeen. Sugar Ray Leonard was scarcely heavier but he seemed to tower, not moving. The men met in the center of the ring. There was no sound. The crowd on TV, the residents in the pit held their breath as the boxers faced each other, circling, sinuous, their eyes locked.

In the third round Leonard's quick hook knocked Benitez to the ground. He was up in a second, with a childlike smile. Embarrassed. I didn't mean for that to happen to me. At that moment the men in the pit began to want him to win.

No one moved, not even during the commercials. Sam rolled cigarettes all through the fight, passed them. Milton came up to the ledge of the pit during the sixth round, just as Benitez took a blow to the forehead, his only mark in the fight. Milton saw the blood reflected in everyone's eyes, in their sweat.

"Figures . . . you'd all be backing a loser," he said.

"Quiet! Round eight."

"Come on, baby, don't you go down."

They weren't asking Benitez to win, just to stay in the fight. He did, he stayed in. He retreated in the ninth behind a jab, then a left hook drove him into the ropes and a right knocked out his mouthpiece.

Round ten, round eleven, round twelve, round thirteen, round fourteen. He stayed in. No one in the pit spoke. Sam had fallen asleep.

The bell rang for the last round. The arena was so quiet you could hear Sugar Ray Leonard whisper. "Oh, my God. He is still standing."

But Benitez's right knee touched the canvas. Briefly, like a Catholic leaving a pew. The slightest deference that meant the fight was over; he had lost. Carlotta whispered,

"God, please help me."

Strays

Got into Albuquerque from Baton Rouge. It was about two in the morning. Whipping wind. That's what the wind does in Albuquerque. I hung out at the Greyhound station until a cabdriver showed up who had so many prison tattoos I figured I could score and he'd tell me where to stay. He turned me on, took me to a pad, a *noria* they call it there, in the south valley. I lucked out meeting him, Noodles. I couldn't have picked a worse place to run to than Albuquerque. Chicanos control the town. *Mayates*, they can't score at all, are lucky not to be killed. Some white guys, with enough long joint time to have been tested. White women, forget it, they don't last. Only way, and Noodles helped me there too, was to get hooked up with a big connection, like I did with Nacho. Then nobody could hurt me. What a pitiful thing I just said. Nacho was a saint, which may seem hard to believe. He did a lot for Brown Berets, for the whole Chicano community, young people, old people. I don't know where he is now. He skipped bail. I mean a huge bail. He shot a narc, Marquez, five times, in the back. The jury didn't think he was a saint, but Robin Hood maybe, because they only gave him manslaughter. I wish I knew where he was. I got busted about the same time, for needle marks.

All this happened many years ago or I couldn't even be talking about it. In those days you could end up with five or ten years for just a roach or marks.

It was when the first methadone rehabilitation programs were starting. I got sent to one of the pilot projects. Six months at La Vida instead of years in "*la pinta*," the state prison in Santa Fe. Twenty other addicts got the same deal. We all arrived in an old yellow school bus at La Vida. A pack of wild dogs met the bus, snarling and baying at us until finally they loped off into the dust.

La Vida was thirty miles out of Albuquerque. In the desert. Nothing around, not a tree, not a bush. Route 66 was too far to walk to. La Vida had been a radar site, a military installation during World War II. It had been abandoned since then. I mean abandoned. We were going to restore it.

We stood around in the wind, in the glare of the sun. Just the gigantic radar disc towering over the whole place, the only shade. Fallen-down barracks. Torn and rusted venetian blinds rattling in the wind. Pinups peeled off the walls. Three- or four-foot sand dunes in every room. Dunes, with waves and patterns like in postcards from the Painted Desert.

A lot of things were going to contribute to our rehabilitation. Number one was removing us from the street environment. Every time a counselor said that we laughed ourselves silly. We couldn't see any roads, much less streets, and the streets in the compound were buried in sand. There were tables in the dining rooms and cots in the barracks but they were buried too. Toilets clogged with dead animals and more sand.

You could only hear the wind and the pack of dogs that kept circling. Sometimes it was nice, the silence, except the radar discs kept turning with a whining petty keening, day and night, day and night. At first it freaked us out, but after a while it grew comforting, like wind chimes. They said it had been used to intercept Japanese kamikaze pilots, but they said a lot of pretty weird things.

Of course, the major part of our rehab was going to be honest work. The satisfaction of a job well done. Learning to interact.

Teamwork. This teamwork started when we lined up for our methadone at six every morning. After breakfast we worked until lunchtime. Group from two until five, more group from seven to ten.

The purpose of these groups was to break us down. Our main problems were anger, arrogance, defiance. We lied and cheated and stole. There were daily "haircuts" where groups screamed at one person all his faults and weaknesses.

We were beaten down until we finally cried uncle. Who the fuck was uncle? See, I'm still angry, arrogant. I was ten minutes late to group and they shaved my eyebrows and cut my eyelashes.

The groups dealt with anger. All day long we dropped slips in a slip box saying who we were angry at and then in group we dealt with it. Mostly we just shouted what losers and fuckups everyone else was. But see, we all did lie and cheat. Half the time none of us was even mad, just shucking and jiving up some anger to play the group game, to stay at La Vida and not go to jail. Most of the slips were at Bobby, the cook, for feeding those wild dogs. Or things like Grenas doesn't weed enough, he just smokes and pushes tumbleweeds around with a rake.

We were mad at those dogs. Lines of us at six a.m. and at one and six outside the dining room. Whipping sand wind. We'd be tired and hungry. Freezing in the morning and hot in the afternoon. Bobby would wait, finally stroll across his floor like a smug bank official to unlock the door for us. And while we waited, a few feet away, at the kitchen door, the dogs would be waiting too, for him to throw them slops. Mangy, motley, ugly dogs people had abandoned out on the mesa. The dogs liked Bobby all right but they hated us, baring their teeth and snarling, day after day, meal after meal.

I got moved from the laundry to the kitchen. Helping cook, dishwashing and mopping up. I felt better about Bobby after a while. I even felt better about the dogs. He named them all. Dumb

names. Duke, Spot, Blackie, Gimp, Shorty. And Liza, his favorite. An old yellow cur, flat-headed, with huge batlike ears and
amber-yellow eyes. After a few months she'd even eat out of his
hand. "Sunshine! Liza, my yellow-eyed sun," he used to croon to
her. Finally she let him scratch behind her ugly ears and just above
the long ratty tail that hung down between her legs. "My sweet
sweet sunshine," he'd say.

Government money kept sending in people to do workshops
with us. A lady who did a workshop about Families. As if any of us
ever had a family. And some guy from Synanon who said our problem was our cool. His favorite expression was "When you think
you're looking good you're looking bad." Every day he had us "blow
our image." Which was just acting like fools.

We got a gym and a pool table, weights and punching bags.
Two color televisions. A basketball court, a bowling alley, and
a tennis court. Framed paintings by Georgia O'Keeffe. Monet's
water lilies. Soon a Hollywood movie company was coming, to
make a science fiction film at the site. We would be able to work
as extras and make some money. The movie was going to center
around the radar disc and what it did to Angie Dickinson. It fell in
love with her and took her soul when she died in a car wreck. It
would take over all these other live souls too, who would be La
Vida residents, us. I've seen it about twenty times, in the middle of
the night, on TV.

All in all the first three months went pretty well. We were
clean and healthy; we worked hard. The site was in great shape.
We got pretty close to one another and we did get angry. But for
those first three months we were in total isolation. Nobody came
in and nobody went out. No phone calls, no newspapers, no mail,
no television. Things started falling apart when that ended. People
went on passes and had dirty urines when they got back, or they
didn't come back at all. New residents kept coming in, but they
didn't have the sense of pride we had about the place.

Every day we had a morning meeting. Part gripe session, part snitch session. We also had to take turns speaking, even if it was just telling a joke or singing a song. But nobody could ever think of anything, so at least twice a week old Lyle Tanner sang, "I thought I saw a whippoorwill." "El Sapo" gave a talk on how to breed chihuahuas, which was gross. Sexy kept on reciting the Twenty-third Psalm. Only the way she caressed words it sounded lewd and everybody laughed, which hurt her feelings.

Sexy's name was a joke. She was an old whore from Mexico. She hadn't come with the first group of us, but later, after five days in solitary with no food. Bobby made her soup and some bacon and eggs. But all she wanted was bread. She sat there and ate three loaves of Wonder Bread, not even chewing it, just swallowing it, famished. Bobby gave the soup and bacon and eggs to Liza.

Sexy kept on eating until finally I took her to our room and she collapsed. Lydia and Sherry were in bed together in the next room. They had been lovers for years. I could tell by their slow laughs that they were high on something, reds or ludes probably. I went back to the kitchen to help Bobby clean up. Gabe, the counselor, came in to get the knives, to lock them up in the safe. He did that every night.

"I'm going to town. You're in charge, Bobby." There never were any staff members at night anymore.

Bobby and I went out to drink coffee under the chinaberry tree. The dogs yelped after something on the mesa.

"I'm glad Sexy came. She's nice."

"She's okay. She won't stay."

"She reminds me of Liza."

"Liza's not that ugly. *Oye*, Tina, be still. It's almost here."

The moon. There's no other moon like one on a clear New Mexico night. It rises over the Sandias and soothes the miles and miles of barren desert with all the quiet whiteness of a first snow. Moonlight in Liza's yellow eyes and the chinaberry tree.

The world just goes along. Nothing much matters, you know? I mean really matters. But then sometimes, just for a second, you get this grace, this belief that it does matter, a whole lot.

He felt that way too. I heard the catch in his throat. Some people may have said a prayer, knelt down, at a moment like that. Sung a hymn. Maybe cavemen would have done a dance. What we did was make love. "El Sapo" busted us. Later, but we were still naked.

So it came out at morning meeting and we had to get a punishment. Three weeks, after cleaning the kitchen, to strip and sand all the paint around the dining room windows. Until one in the morning, every single night. That was bad enough but then Bobby, trying to save his ass, got up and said, "I didn't want to ball Tina. I just want to stay clean, do my time, and go home to my wife Debbi and my baby Debbi-Ann." I could have dropped a slip on those two jive names.

That hurt bad. He had held me and talked to me. He had gone to a lot more trouble making love than most men do and I had been happy with him when the moon came up.

We had to work so hard there wasn't time to talk. I would never have let him know how bad it hurt anyway. We were tired, bone tired every night, all day.

The main thing we hadn't talked about was the dogs. They hadn't shown up for three nights.

Finally I said it. "Where do you think the dogs are?"

He shrugged. "A puma. Kids with guns."

We went back to sanding. It got too late even to go to bed so we made some fresh coffee and sat down under the tree.

I missed Sexy. I forgot to say that she had gone to town to the dentist but had managed to score, got busted and taken back to jail.

"I miss Sexy. Bobby, that was a lie what you said at morning meeting. You did so want to ball *me*."

"Yeah, it was a lie."

We went into the meat locker and held each other again, made love again but not for long because it was freezing cold. We went back outside.

The dogs started coming. Shorty, Blackie, Spot, Duke.

They had gotten into porcupines. Must have been days ago because they were all so infected, septic. Their faces swollen like monster rhinoceros, oozing green pus. Their eyes were bloated shut, quilled shut with tiny arrows. That was the scary part, that none of them could see. Or make a real sound since their throats were engorged too.

Blackie had a seizure. Hurtled up into the air with an eerie gargle. Thrashing, jerking, peeing in the air. High, two, three feet into the air and then he fell wet, dead, into the dust. Liza came in last because she couldn't walk, just crawled until she got to Bobby's feet, writhed there, her paw patting at his boot.

"Get me the goddamn knives."

"Gabe's not back yet." Only counselors could unlock the safe.

Liza pawed at Bobby's foot, gentle, like asking to be petted, for him to throw her a ball.

Bobby went to the locker and brought out a steak. The sky was lavender. It was almost morning.

He had the dogs smell the meat. He called to them, cooed to them to follow him across the road to the machine shop. I stayed under the tree.

When he was in there, when he finally got them all in there, he beat them to death with a sledgehammer. I didn't see it, but I heard it and from where I sat I saw the blood splattering and streaking down the walls. I thought he would say something like "Liza, my sweet sunshine" but he didn't say a word. When he came out he was covered in blood, didn't look at me, went to the barracks.

The nurse drove up with the doses of methadone and everybody started lining up for breakfast. I turned the griddle on and started making batter. Everybody was mad because I took so long with breakfast.

There still wasn't any staff around when the movie trailers started pulling in. They began working right away, checking out locations, casting extras. People were running around with megaphones and walkie-talkies. Somehow nobody went into the machine shop.

They started one scene right away . . . a take of a stuntman who was supposed to be Angie Dickinson driving down from the gym while a helicopter hovered around the radar disc. The car was supposed to crash into the disc and Angie's spirit fly up into it but the car crashed into the chinaberry tree.

Bobby and I made lunch, so tired we were walking in slow motion, just like all the zombie extras were being told to walk. We didn't talk. Once, making tuna salad I said out loud, to myself, "Pickle relish?"

"What did you say?"

"I said pickle relish."

"Christ. Pickle relish!" We laughed, couldn't stop laughing. He touched my cheek, lightly, a bird's wing.

The movie crew thought the radar site was fab, far out. Angie Dickinson liked my eye shadow. I told her it was just chalk, the kind you rub on pool cues. "It's to die for, that blue," she said to me.

After lunch, an old gaffer, whatever that is, came up to me and asked where the nearest bar was. There was a place up the road, toward Gallup, but I told him Albuquerque. I told him I would do anything to get a ride into town.

"Don't worry about that. Hop in my truck and let's go."

Wham, crash, bang.

"Good God, what was that?" he asked.

"A cattle guard."

"Jesus, this sure is one godforsaken place."

We finally hit the highway. It was great, the sound of tires on the cement, the wind blowing in. Semis, bumper stickers, kids fighting in the backseats. Route 66.

We got to the rise, with the wide valley and the Rio Grande below us, the Sandia Mountains lovely above.

"Mister, what I need is money for a ticket home to Baton Rouge. Can you spare it, about sixty dollars?"

"Easy. You need a ticket. I need a drink. It will all work out."

Grief

"Whatever can those two be talking about all the time?" Mrs. Wacher asked her husband at breakfast.

Across the open-air, thatched-roof dining room by the sea the sisters forgot their papaya, their huevos rancheros, talking, talking. Later, as they walked by the edge of the sea, their heads were bent toward each other. Talking, talking. Waves would catch them unawares, soaking them, and they would laugh. The younger one often cried . . . When she cried the older one waited, comforting her, passing her a tissue. When the tears stopped they began talking again. She didn't look hard, the older one, but she never cried.

For the most part the other hotel guests in the dining room and in beach chairs on the sand all sat quietly together, occasionally commenting upon the perfection of the day, the turquoise blue of the sea, telling their children to sit up straight. The honeymoon couple whispered and teased each other, fed one another bites of melon, but most of the time they were silent, gazing into the other's eyes, looking at the other's hands. The older couples drank coffee and read or did crossword puzzles. Their conversations were brief, monosyllabic. The people who were content with each other spoke as little as those who bristled with resentment or boredom; it was the rhythm of their speech that differed, like a lazy tennis ball batted back and forth or the quick swattings of a fly.

In the evening, by lantern light, the German couple, the Wachers, played bridge with another retired couple from Canada, the Lewises. They were all serious players so there was a minimum of conversation. Snap snap of dealt cards, Mr. Wacher's *hmm*s. Two no trump. The sizzle of the surf, ice cubes in their glasses. The women spoke, occasionally, about plans for shopping the next day, a trip to La Isla, the mysterious talking sisters. The older one so elegant and cool. In her fifties but still attractive, vain. The younger one, in her forties, was pretty, but frumpy, self-effacing. There she goes, crying again!

Mrs. Wacher decided to tackle the older sister during her morning swim. Mrs. Lewis would speak to the younger one, who never swam or sat in the sun, but waited for the other, sipping tea, holding an unopened book.

That evening, while Mr. Wacher fetched the score pad and cards and Mr. Lewis ordered drinks and snacks from the bar, the two women pooled their information.

"They talk so much because they haven't seen each other in twenty years! Can you imagine? Sisters? Mine is named Sally, she lives in Mexico City, is married to a Mexican and has three children. We spoke in Spanish, she seems Mexican really. She recently had a mastectomy, which explains why she doesn't swim. She starts cancer therapy next month. That's probably why she's crying all the time. That's all I got, before the sister came up and they went to change."

"No! That's not why she's crying! Their mother has just died! Two weeks ago! Can you imagine . . . they have come to a resort?"

"What else did she say? What is her name?"

"Dolores. She is a nurse from California, with four grown sons. She said that their mother recently died, that she and her sister had a lot to talk about."

The women figured it all out. Sally, the sweet one, must have been taking care of the invalid mother all these years. When the old mother finally died Dolores felt guilty, because of her sister caring for her mother, and she never went to visit them. And then her sister's cancer. Dolores was the one paying for everything, the cabs, the waiters. They saw her buying Sally clothes in the boutiques downtown. That must be it. Guilt. She's sorry she didn't see her mother before she died, wants to be good to her sister before she dies too.

"Or before she dies herself," Mrs. Lewis said. "When your parents are dead your own death faces you."

"Oh, I know what you mean . . . there is no one to protect you against death anymore."

The two women were silent then, pleased with their harmless gossip, their analysis. Thinking of their own deaths to come. Their husbands' deaths to come. But just briefly. Although in their seventies both couples were healthy, active. They lived fully, enjoying each day. When their husbands pulled out their chairs and sat down for the game they entered it with pleasure, forgetting all about the two sisters, who were sitting side by side now on the beach, under the stars.

Sally wasn't crying about their dead mother or her cancer. She was crying because her husband, Alfonso, had left her after twenty years for a young woman. It seemed a brutal thing to do, just after her mastectomy. She was devastated, but no, she wouldn't ever divorce him, even though the woman was pregnant and he wanted to marry her.

"They can just wait until I die. I'll be dead soon, probably next year . . ." Sally wept but the ocean drowned out the sound.

"You're not dying. They said the cancer was gone. The radiation therapy is routine, a precaution. I heard the doctor say that, that they got all the cancer."

"But it will come back. It always does."

"That's not true. Cut it out, Sally."

"You are so cold. Sometimes you are as cruel as Mama."

Dolores said nothing. Her greatest fear, that she was like her mother. Cruel, a drunkard.

"Look, Sally. Just give him a divorce and start taking care of yourself."

"You don't understand! How can you understand how I feel after living with him for twenty years? You've been alone almost that long! For me it has only been Alfonso, since I was seventeen! I love him!"

"I think I can manage to understand," Dolores said, dryly. "Come on, let's go in, it's getting cold."

In the room Dolores's light was on inside her white mosquito net; she was reading before she fell asleep.

"Dolores?"

Sally was crying, again. Christ. Now what.

"Sally, I go crazy if I can't read when I first wake up and before I go to sleep. It's a dumb habit, but there it is. What is it?"

"I have a splinter in my foot."

Dolores got up, went for a needle, some antiseptic, and a Band-Aid, removed the splinter from her sister's foot. Sally cried again, and embraced Dolores.

"Let's always be close now. It's so good to have a sister who takes care of me!"

Dolores smoothed the Band-Aid on Sally's foot, as she had done a dozen times when they were children. "All better," she said, automatically.

"All better!" Sally sighed. She fell asleep soon after. Dolores read for several hours more. Finally she turned out the light, wishing she had a drink.

How could she talk to Sally about her alcoholism? It was not like talking about a death, or losing a husband, losing a breast. People said it was a disease, but nobody made her pick up the drink. I've got a fatal disease. I am terrified, Dolores wanted to say, but she didn't.

The Wachers and the Lewises were always the first people up for breakfast, seated at adjoining tables. The husbands read the paper, the wives chatted with the waiters and each other. After breakfast the four were going out deep-sea fishing.

"Where are the sisters today, I wonder?" Mrs. Lewis said.

"Hollering! When I passed their room they were arguing away. Herman has no compassion, he wouldn't let me eavesdrop. Sally said, No! She didn't want a penny of the old witch's blood money! That when she had been desperate her mother had refused her, cussing away, that meek little thing! *Puta! Desgraciada!* Dolores was hollering at her, 'Can't you understand anything about madness? *You* are the really crazy one . . . because you refuse to see! Mama was crazy!' And then she began yelling at her, 'Take it off! Take it off!'"

"Shh. Here they come now."

Sally was disheveled; she looked, as usual, as if she had been weeping; as usual Dolores was calm and perfectly groomed. She ordered breakfast for the two of them and when it came you could hear her say to her sister,

"Eat. You'll feel better. Drink all the orange juice. It is sweet, delicious."

•

"Take it off!"

Sally cowered, clutching her *huipil* to her body. Dolores tore it away from her, made her stand there, naked, the scars where her breast had been livid red and blue.

Sally cried. "I am hideous! I'm not a woman now! Don't look!"

Dolores gripped her shoulders, shook her. "You want me to be your sister? Let me look! Yes, it is hideous. The scars look brutal, awful. But they are you now. And you're a woman, you silly fool! Without your Alfonso, without your breast, you can be more of a woman than ever, your own woman! For starters you're going swimming today, with that hundred-and-fifty-dollar falsie I brought to pin in your suit."

"I can't."

"Yes you can. Come on, get dressed for breakfast."

"Good morning, ladies!" Mrs. Lewis called to the sisters. "Another splendid day. We're going fishing. What are your plans for the day?"

"We're going for a swim, and then shopping and to the hairdresser."

"Poor Sally," Mrs. Lewis said. "She obviously doesn't want to do any of those things. She's sick, and grieving. That sister of hers is forcing her to be on vacation. Just like my sister Iris. Bossy, bossy! Did you have a big sister?"

"No." Mrs. Wacher laughed. "I was the big sister. Believe me, little sisters have their drawbacks too."

Dolores spread out their towels on the sand.

"Take it off."

She meant the robe her sister had clutched over her bathing suit.

"Take it off," she insisted again. "You look wonderful. Your breast looks real. Your waist is tiny. You have great legs. But then you never, ever, realized how lovely you were."

"No. You were the pretty one. I was the good one."

"That label was hard on me too. Take the hat off. We only have a few days left. You're going back to the city with a tan."

"*Pero . . .*"

"*Cállate.* Keep your mouth shut, so you don't tan with wrinkles."

"The sun feels wonderful," Sally sighed after a while.

"Doesn't your body feel good?"

"I feel so naked. As if everyone could see the scars."

"You know one thing I've learned? Most people don't notice anything at all, or care, if they do."

"You are so cynical."

"Turn over, let me oil your back."

After a while Sally talked to Dolores about the library in the *barrio* where she worked as a volunteer. Heartwarming stories about the children and families who lived in dire poverty. She loved her work there, and they loved her.

"See, Sally, there is so much you can do, that you enjoy."

Dolores couldn't think of any heartwarming stories to tell Sally about her job, at a clinic in East Oakland. Crack babies, abused children, children with brain damage, Down's syndrome, gunshot wounds, malnutrition, AIDS. But she was good at her job, and liked it. Or had—she had finally been fired for drinking, just last month, before their mother died.

"I like my job, too," was all she said. "Come on, let's swim."

"I can't. I'll hurt myself."

"The wounds are healed, Sally. There are only scars. Terrible scars."

"I can't."

"For Christ's sake, get in the water."

Dolores led her sister into the surf and then wrenched her hand away. She watched Sally flounder and fall, swallow water, be

knocked down by a wave. Treading water, she watched as Sally
stood up and dove under the incoming swell, swam on. Dolores
swam after her. Oh Lord, she's crying again, but no, Sally was
laughing out loud.

"It's warm! It's so warm! I'm light as a baby!"

They swam out in the blue water for a long time. At last they
came in to shore. Breathless, laughing, they left the surf. Sally
threw her arms around her sister and the two women held each
other, the foam swirling around their ankles. "*Mariconas!*" mocked
two passing beach boys.

Mrs. Lewis and Mrs. Wacher watched from their beach chairs,
quite moved. "She's not so mean, just firm . . . she knew the sister
would like it once she got in. How happy she looks. Poor thing,
she needed this vacation."

"Yes, it doesn't seem so shocking now, does it? That they should
go on a holiday when their mother died."

"You know . . . it's too bad it isn't a tradition. A post-funeral holiday, like a honeymoon, or a baby shower."

They both laughed. "Herman!" Mrs. Wacher called over to
her husband. "After we two women have died, will you two men
promise to take a vacation together?"

Herman shook his head. "No. You need four for bridge."

When Sally and Dolores got back that evening everyone compli-
mented Sally on how lovely she looked. Rosy from the sun, her
new haircut curling in soft auburn ringlets around her face.

Sally kept shaking her hair, looking in the mirror. Her green
eyes shone like emeralds. She was painting them with Dolores's
makeup.

"Could I borrow your green top?" she asked.

"What? I just bought you three beautiful dresses. Now you want my top? And for that matter you have your own makeup, and your own perfume!"

"See how you resent me! Yes, you give me presents, but you still are selfish, selfish, like her!"

"Selfish!" Dolores took her blouse off. "Here! Take these earrings, too. They go with it."

The sun set as the diners ate their flan. When their coffee came Dolores reached for her sister's hand.

"You realize we're just acting as we did when we were children. It's sort of nice when you think about it. You keep saying that you want us to be real sisters now. We're acting just like real sisters! Fighting!"

Sally smiled. "You're right. I guess I never knew how real families acted. We never had a family vacation, or even a picnic."

"I'm sure that's why I had so many children, why you married into such a huge Mexican family, we wanted a home so badly."

"And that's just why Alfonso leaving me is so hard . . ."

"Don't talk about him anymore."

"What can I talk about then?"

"We need to talk about her. Mama. She's dead now."

"I could have killed her! I'm glad she's dead," Sally said. "It was too awful when Daddy died. I flew to L.A. and took a bus to San Clemente. She wouldn't even let me in the door. I banged on the door and said, 'I need a mother! Let me talk to you!' but she wouldn't let me in. It wasn't fair. I don't care about the money, but that wasn't fair either."

Their mother had never forgiven Sally for marrying a Mexican, had refused to meet her children, left her money to Dolores. Dolores insisted upon dividing the inheritance, but it didn't lessen the insult.

Dolores rocked Sally as they sat on the sand. The sun had set.

"She's gone, Sally. She was sick, afraid. She lashed out, like a wounded . . . hyena. You're lucky you didn't see her. I saw her. I called her to say we were taking Daddy to the hospital by ambulance. You know what she said? 'Could you stop and pick up some bananas?'"

"Today is my last day!" Sally said to Mrs. Wacher. "We're going to the island. Have you ever been?"

"Oh, yes, we went with the Lewises a few days ago. It's perfectly lovely. You're going snorkeling?"

"Scuba," Dolores said. "*Vamos*, Sally, the car is waiting."

"I'm not going scuba diving. That's it," Sally said on the way to Ixtapa.

"You'll see. Wait until you meet César. I lived with him awhile, twenty-five, thirty years ago. He was just a diver then, a fisherman."

He had become famous and rich since then, the Jacques Cousteau of Mexico, with many movies, television programs. This was hard for Dolores to imagine. She remembered his old wooden boat, the sand floor of his palapa, their hammock.

"He was a maestro even then," she said. "Nobody knows the ocean like he does. His press releases call him Neptune, and that sounds pretty corny . . . but it's true. He probably won't remember me, but I still want you to meet him."

He was an old man now, with a long white beard, flowing white hair. Of course he remembered Dolores. Sweet his kiss on her eyelids, his embrace. She remembered his calloused, scarred hands on her skin . . . He led them to a table on the veranda. Two men from the tourist bureau were drinking tequila, fanning themselves with their straw hats, their guayaberas damp and wrinkled.

The vast veranda faced the ocean, but mango and avocado trees totally blocked the ocean from sight.

"How can you cover up such a view of the ocean?" Sally asked. César shrugged. "*Pues*, I've seen it."

He told them all about dives he and Dolores had been on years ago. The time with the sharks, the giant *peine*, the day Flaco drowned. How the divers used to call her "La Brava." But she scarcely heard his praise of her. She heard him say, "When she was young she was a beautiful woman."

"So, have you come to dive with me?" he asked, holding her hands. She longed to dive; she couldn't bear to tell him she was afraid the regulator would break her false teeth.

"No. My back is bad now. I brought my sister to dive with you."

"*Lista?*" he asked Sally. She was drinking tequila, basking in the compliments and flirtations from the men. The men left. César, Sally, and Dolores set out in a canoe to La Isla. Sally gripped the side of the boat, ashen with fear. At one point she leaned over the side, vomiting.

"Are you sure she should dive?" César asked Dolores.

"I'm sure."

They smiled at each other. The years were erased, their communication still there. She had once said wryly that he had been perfect. He couldn't read or write and most of their romance was underwater, where there were no words. There had never been any need for explanations.

Quietly he showed the basics of diving to Sally. At first, out in the shallow water, Sally was still shaking with fear. Dolores sat on the rocks and watched, watched him clean her mask with spit, explain the regulator. He put the tank on her back. Dolores saw Sally stiffen, afraid he would notice her breast, but then she saw Sally unbend, swaying in rhythm before him as he reassured her, fastened her gear and stroked her, soothed her down into the water.

It took four tries. Sally surfaced, choking. No, no it was impossible, she was claustrophobic, couldn't breathe! But he continued to speak softly to her, to coax her, smooth her with his hands. Dolores felt a sick wave of jealousy when he held her sister's head in his hands, smiling into her eyes through their masks. She remembered his smile through the glass.

This was your big idea, she told herself. She tried to be calm, gazing out at the undulating green waves where her sister and César had disappeared. She tried to concentrate upon her sister's pleasure. For she knew it would be pleasure. But all she could feel was regret and remorse, unspeakable loss.

It seemed like hours before they surfaced. Sally was laughing; her laughter was that of a young girl. Impetuously she was kissing and hugging César while he undid her tanks, took off her flippers.

In the diver's hut she embraced Dolores, too. "You knew how great it would be! I flew! The ocean went on forever! Dolores, I felt so alive and strong! I was an Amazon!"

Dolores wanted to point out that Amazons had only one breast, but she bit her tongue. She and César smiled as Sally continued to talk about the beauty of the dive. She'd come back, soon, spend a week diving! Oh, the coral and the anemones, the colors, the brilliant schools of fish.

César asked them to lunch. It was three o'clock. "I'm afraid I need a siesta," Dolores said. Sally was disappointed.

"You'll be back, Sally. I just showed you the way."

"Thank you both," Sally said. Her joy and gratitude were pure, innocent. César and her sister kissed her glowing cheeks.

They were at the cab stand on the beach. César held Dolores's hand tightly. "So, *mi vieja*, will you ever come back?" She shook her head.

"Stay with me tonight."

"*No puedo.*"

César kissed her lips. She tasted the desire and salt of their past. The last night she had spent with him he had bitten all her fingernails to the quick. "Think of me," he said.

Sally talked excitedly all the way into town, an hour's drive. How vital she had felt, how free.

"I knew you would like that part. Your body disappears, because you are so weightless, but at the same time you become intensely aware of it."

"He is wonderful. Wonderful. I can just imagine having a love affair with him! You are so lucky!"

"Can you imagine, Sally. That whole stretch of beach, where the Club Med is? It was pure empty beach. Up in the jungle there was an artesian well. There were deer, almost tame. We spent days there without seeing another soul. And the island. It was just an island, wild jungle. No dive shops or restaurants. Not a single other boat but ours. Can you imagine?"

No. She couldn't.

"It's uncanny," Mrs. Wacher said, as the sisters got down from their cab. "It's as if they have totally reversed roles. Now the younger one is absolutely gorgeous and radiant and the other is haggard and disheveled. Look at her . . . she who never used to have a hair out of place!"

The night was stormy. Black clouds swept across the full moon so that the beach was bright and then dark, like a hotel room with a neon sign blinking outside. Sally's face shone like a child's when the moonlight lit her.

"But did Mama never, ever, speak of me?"

No, matter of fact. Except to mock your sweetness, to say your docility proved that you were a fool.

"Yes, she did, a lot," Dolores lied. "One of her favorite memories of you was how you loved that Dr. Bunny book. You would pretend to read it, turning the pages, real serious. And you got every word perfect, except when Dr. Bunny would say, 'Case dismissed!' you said 'Smith to Smith!'"

"I remember that book! The rabbits were all furry!"

"At first. But you wore the fur out petting them. She liked to remember you and that red wagon, too, when you were around four. You'd put Billy Jameson in the wagon, and all your dolls, and Mabel, the dog, and the two cats, and then you'd say 'All aboard!' but the cats and dog would have gotten out and Billy too, and the dolls fell out. You'd spend all morning packing them up and saying 'All aboard.'"

"I don't remember that at all."

"Oh, I do, it was in the path by Daddy's hyacinths, and the climbing rose by the gate. Can you remember the smell?"

"Yes!"

"She used to ask me if I remembered you in Chile, going off to school on your bicycle. Every single morning you'd look up to the hall window and wave, and your straw hat would fly off."

Sally laughed. "True. I remember. But, Dolores, it was you in the hall window. You I was waving good-bye to."

True. "Well, I guess she used to see you from the window by her bed."

"Silly how good that makes me feel. I mean even if she didn't ever say good-bye. That she even watched me go off to school. I'm so glad you told me about that."

"Good," Dolores whispered, to herself. The sky was black now and huge raindrops were falling cold. The sisters ran together in the rain to their room.

Sally's plane left the next morning; Dolores would leave the following day. At breakfast, before she left, Sally said good-bye to everyone, thanked the waiters, thanked Mrs. Lewis and Mrs. Wacher for being so kind.

"We're glad that you two had such a good visit. What a comfort to have a sister!" Mrs. Lewis said.

"It really is a comfort," Sally said when she kissed Dolores good-bye at the airport.

"We're just beginning to know each other," Dolores said. "We will be there now, always, for each other." Her heart ached to see the sweetness, the trust in her sister's eyes.

On the way back to the hotel she had the cab stop at a liquor store. In her room she drank and she slept and then she sent out for another bottle. In the morning, on the way to her plane for California she bought a half-pint of rum, to cure her shakes and headache. By the time the taxi reached the airport she was, like they say, feeling no pain.

Bluebonnets

"Ma, I can't believe you are doing this. You never even go out with anybody, and here you are spending a week with some stranger. He could be an axe murderer for all you know."

Maria's son Nick was taking her to the Oakland airport. Lord, why hadn't she taken a cab? Her sons, all grown now, could be worse than parents, more judgmental, more old-fashioned when it came to her.

"I haven't met him, but he's not exactly a stranger. He liked my poetry, asked me to translate his book to Spanish. We have written and spoken on the phone for years. We have a lot in common. He raised his four sons alone, too. I garden; he has a farm. I'm flattered that he invited me . . . I don't think he sees many people."

Maria had asked an old friend in Austin about Dixon. A genius. Total eccentric, Ingeborg had said. Never socializes. Instead of a briefcase he has a gunny sack. His students either idolize him or hate him. He's in his late forties, quite attractive. Let me know everything . . .

"That was the weirdest book I ever read," Nick said, "not that I could read it. Admit it . . . could you? Enjoy it, I mean."

"The language was great. Clear and simple. Nice to translate. It is philosophy and linguistics, just very abstract."

"I can't imagine you doing this . . . having some kind of a fling . . . in Texas."

"That's what's bothering you. The idea that your mother might have sex, or that somebody in her fifties might. Anyway he didn't say, 'Let's have a fling.' He said, 'Why not come to my farm for a week? The bluebonnets have just begun to bloom. I can show you notes for my new book. We can fish, go for walks in the woods.' Give me a break, Nick. I work in a county hospital, in Oakland. How do you think a walk in the woods sounds to me? Bluebonnets? I may as well be going to heaven."

They pulled up in front of United and Nick got her bag from the trunk. He hugged her, kissed her cheek. "Sorry I gave you a hard time. Enjoy your trip, Ma. Hey, maybe you can get to a Rangers game."

Snow on the Rocky Mountains. Maria read, listened to music, tried not to think. Of course, in the back of her mind, there was the idea of an affair.

She hadn't taken off her clothes since she had stopped drinking, the idea was terrifying. Well, he sounded pretty stuffy himself, maybe he felt the same way. Take it a day at a time. Practice just being with a man, for Lord's sake, enjoy the visit. You're going to Texas.

The parking lot smelled like Texas. Caliche dust and oleander. He tossed her bag into the bed of an old Dodge pickup truck with dog scratches on the doors. "You know 'Tennessee Border'?" Maria asked. "Sure do." They sang it. ". . . Picked her up in a pickup truck and she broke that heart of mine." Dixon was tall, lean, good laugh lines. Squint lines around open gray eyes. He was entirely at ease, asked her one personal question after another in a nasal drawl just like her uncle John's. How did she know Texas, that old song? Why did she get divorced? What were her sons like? Why didn't she drink? Why was she an alcoholic? Why did she translate other people's work? The questions were embarrassing, buffeting, but soothing, the attention, like a massage.

He stopped at a fish market. Stay here, be right back. Then the freeway and hot gusts of air. Down onto a ribbon of macadam road where they never saw another car. One slow red tractor. Windmills, Hereford cattle knee deep in Indian paintbrush. In the small town of Brewster, Dixon parked across from the town square. Haircut. She followed him past the barber's pole into a one-chair barbershop, sat listening while he and the old man cutting his hair discussed the heat, the rains, fishing, Jesse Jackson running for president, several deaths and a marriage. Dixon had just grinned at her when she asked if her bag would be all right in the back of the truck. She looked out the window at downtown Brewster. It was early afternoon and no one was walking in the streets. Two old men sat on the courthouse steps like extras in a southern movie, chewing tobacco, spitting.

The absence of noise was what was so evocative of her childhood, of another era. No sirens, no traffic, no radios. A horsefly buzzed against the window, snip of scissors, the rhythm of the two men's voices, an electric fan with dirty ribbons flying rustled old magazines. The barber ignored her, not out of rudeness but from courtesy.

Dixon said "much obliged" when he left. As they walked across the square to the grocery store she told him about her Texan grandma, Mamie. Once an old woman had stopped by to visit. Mamie had served tea in a pot with a sugar bowl and creamer, little sandwiches, cookies and cut-up pieces of cake. "Mercy, Mamie, you shouldn't go to so much trouble." "Oh, yes," Mamie had said, "one always should."

They put the groceries in the back of the truck and drove to the feed store, where Dixon got mash and chicken feed, two bales of hay, a dozen baby chicks. He smiled at her when he caught her staring at him and two farmers talking about alfalfa.

"What would you be doing now, in Oakland?" he asked when they got in the truck. Today was pediatric clinic. Crack babies, gunshot wounds, AIDS babies. Hernias and tumors, but mostly wounds of the city's desperate and angry poor.

They were soon out of the town and on a narrow dirt road. The baby chicks chirped in the box on the floor.

"This is what I wanted you to see," he said, "the road to my place this time of year."

They drove along the empty road over gently rolling hills, fragrant and lush with flowers, pink, blue, magenta, red. Bursts of yellow and lavender. The hot, perfumed air enveloped the cab. Huge thunderclouds had formed and the light grew yellow, giving miles of flowers an iridescent luminosity. Larks and meadowlarks, red-winged blackbirds darted above the ditches by the road; the singing of the birds rose above the sound of the truck. Maria leaned out the window, her damp head resting on her arms. It was only April, but the heavy Texan heat suffused her, the perfume of the flowers lulled like a drug.

An old tin-roofed farmhouse with a rocking chair on the porch, a dozen or so kittens of different ages. They put the groceries away in a kitchen with fine Sarouk rugs in front of the sink and stove, another burned by sparks from a woodstove. Two leather chairs. Bookcases lined the walls, with books two-deep. A massive oak table covered with books. Columns of books were stacked on the floor. The old, rippled glass windows looked out onto a field of rich green pasture where kid goats suckled their mothers. Dixon put the food into the refrigerator, put the chicks in a larger box on the floor, with a lightbulb in it, even though it was so warm. His dog had just died, he said. And then for the first time seemed self-conscious. Need to water, he said, and she followed him past the chicken sheds and barns to a large field planted with corn, tomatoes, beans, squash, and other vegetables. She sat on the fence while he opened sluice gates to start the water into the furrows. A chestnut mare and colt galloped in the field of bluebonnets beyond.

It was late afternoon when they fed the animals by the barn, where in a dark corner dripped cloth bags filled with cheese, and more cats scampered along the rafters, indifferent to the birds that flitted in and out of the upper windows by the lofts. An old white mule, Homer, lumbered up when he heard the sound of the bucket. Lie down with me, Dixon said. But they'll step on us. No, just lie down. A circle of goats blocked out the sun, their long-lashed eyes gazing down at her. Nuzzle of Homer's velvety lips on Maria's cheeks. The mare and the colt snorted, spraying hot breaths as they checked her out.

The other rooms in the farmhouse were not like the cluttered kitchen at all. One room with wooden plank floors, nothing in it but a Steinway grand. Dixon's study, which was bare except for four large wooden tables covered with five-by-eight white cards. Each one of them had a paragraph or a sentence on it. She saw that he shuffled them around, the way other people move things in a computer. Don't look at those now, he said.

His living room and bedroom were one large room with tall windows on two sides. Large lush paintings on the other two walls. Maria was surprised that they were done by Dixon. He was so quiet. The paintings were bold, lavish. He had painted a mural on his corduroy couch, figures, sitting there. A brass bed with an old patchwork quilt, exquisite chests and desks and tables, early American antiques that had belonged to his father. The floor in this room was painted glossy white under more priceless Persian rugs. Be sure and take off your shoes, he said.

Her room was a sun porch along the back of the house, with screens on three sides, of a meshed plastic that blurred the pink and green flowers, the new green of the trees, the flash of a cardinal. It was like the basement of L'Orangerie where you sit surrounded by Monet's water lilies. He was filling the bathtub for her in the next room. You'll probably want to lie down awhile. I've got some more chores to do.

Clean, tired, she lay surrounded by the soft colors that blurred when the rain began and the wind swirled the leaves in the trees. Rain on a tin roof. Just as she fell asleep Dixon came and lay down beside her, lay next to her until she woke and they made love, simple as that.

Dixon built a fire in the iron stove and she sat by it while he made crab gumbo. He cooked on a hot plate but had a dishwasher. They ate on the porch by lantern light while the rain abated and when the clouds cleared turned off the lantern to look at the stars.

They fed the animals at the same time each day but the rest of the days and nights got turned around. They stayed in bed all day, had breakfast when it got dark, walked in the woods by the light of the moon. They watched *Mr. Lucky* with Cary Grant at three in the morning. Lazy in the hot sun they rocked in the rowboat on the pond, fishing, reading John Donne, William Blake. They lay in the damp grass, watching the chickens, talking about their childhoods, their children. They watched Nolan Ryan shut out the A's, slept in sleeping bags by a lake hours away through the brush. They made love in the claw-foot tub, in the rowboat, in the woods, but mostly in the shimmering green of the sun porch when it rained.

What was love? Maria asked herself, watching the clean lines of his face as he slept. What's to keep the two of us from doing it, loving.

They both admitted how rarely they spoke with anyone, laughed at themselves for how much they had to say now, how they interrupted each other, yes, but. It was hard when he talked about his new book or referred to Heidegger and Wittgenstein, Derrida, Chomsky and others whose names she didn't even recognize.

"I'm sorry. I'm a poet. I deal with the specific. I am lost with the abstract. I simply don't have the background to discuss this with you."

Dixon was furious. "How the devil did you translate my other book? I know you did a good job by the response it got. Did you read the damn thing?"

"I did do a good job. I didn't distort a word. Someone could translate my poems perfectly but still think they were personal and trivial. I didn't . . . grasp . . . the philosophical implications in the book."

"Then this visit is a farce. My books are everything I am. It is pointless for us to discuss anything at all."

Maria started to feel hurt and angry and to let him go out the door alone. But she followed him, sat down beside him on the porch step. "It's not pointless. And I'm learning about who you are." Dixon held her then, kissed her, gingerly.

While he had been a student he had lived in a cabin a few acres away, in the woods. An old man had lived in this house and Dixon had done errands for him, brought him food and supplies from town. When the old man died he left the house and ten acres to Dixon, the rest of his land to the state for a bird sanctuary. They hiked the next morning to his old cabin. He had even had to carry in his water, he said. It was the best period of his life.

The wooden cabin was in a grove of cottonwood. There had been no path to it, and there seemed to be no landmarks at all in the scrub oak and mesquite. As they got close to it Dixon cried out, as if in pain.

Someone, kids probably, had shot out all the windows of the cabin, hacked up the inside with axes, spray-painted obscenities on the bare pine walls. It was hard to imagine anyone coming so far into the wilderness to do this. It looks like Oakland, Maria said. Dixon glared at her, turned around and started walking back through the trees. She kept him in sight but could not keep up with him. It was eerily quiet. Every once in a while there would be an enormous Brahmin bull in the shade of a tree. Just standing there, unblinking, stolid, silent.

Dixon didn't speak on the drive home. Green grasshoppers clicked against the windshield. "I'm sorry, about what happened to your house," she said and when he didn't answer she said, "I do that too, when I feel pain. Crawl under the house like a sick cat." He still said nothing. When they pulled up outside his house he reached over and opened her door. The engine was still running. "I'm going to go get my mail. Back in a while. Maybe you could read some of my book."

She knew that by book he meant the hundreds of cards on the tables. Why had he asked her to do that now? Maybe it was because he couldn't talk. She did that sometimes. When she wanted to tell someone how she felt it was too hard, so she would show them a poem. Usually they didn't understand what she had intended.

With a sick feeling she went into the house. It would be fine to live where you didn't even close your doors. She started into Dixon's living room to put on some music, but changed her mind, went into the room with the cards. She sat on a stool that she moved from table to table as she read and reread the sentences on the cards.

"You have no idea what they say, do you?" He had come in silently, was standing behind her as she leaned over the table. She had not touched any of the cards.

He began to move them around the table, frantically, like someone playing that game where you line up numbers correctly. Maria left and went out on the porch.

"I asked you not to walk on that floor with shoes on."

"What floor? What are you talking about?"

"The white floor."

"I haven't been near that room. You are crazy."

"Don't lie to me. They are your footprints."

"Oh, sorry. I did start to go in there. I couldn't have taken more than two steps."

"Exactly. Two."

"Thank God I'm going home in the morning. I'm going for a walk right now."

Maria walked down the path toward the pond, got into the green rowboat and shoved herself away from the bank. She laughed at herself when the dragonflies reminded her of Oakland police helicopters.

Dixon strode down the path to the pond, walked out into the water, and pulled himself into the boat. He kissed her, pinned her down into the watery bed of the boat while he entered her. They clashed wildly into each other and the boat bobbed and spun until it finally moored itself in the reeds. They lay there, rocking in the hot sun. She wondered if so much passion had come from simple rage or from a sense of loss. They made love wordlessly most of the night, in the sun porch to the sound of the rain. Before the rain they had heard the cry of a coyote, the squawk of the chickens as they roosted in the trees.

They rode to the airport in silence, past the miles of blue-bonnets and primrose. Just drop me off, she said, not that much time.

Maria took a cab home from the airport to her high-rise apartment in Oakland. Hello to the security guard, check the mail. The elevator was empty, as were the halls during the day. She put down her suitcase inside her door and turned on the air. She took off her shoes, as everyone did when they walked on her carpet. She went into the bedroom and lay down on her own bed.

La Vie en Rose

The two girls lie facedown upon towels that say GRAN HOTEL PUCÓN. The sand is black and fine; the water in the lake is green. Deeper sweet green the pines that edge the lake. Villarica volcano towers white above the lake and the trees, the hotel, the village of Pucón. Spumes of smoke rise from the volcano's cone and vanish into the clear blue of the sky. Blue beach cabanas. Gerda's cap of red hair, a yellow beach ball, the red sashes of *huasos* cantering among the trees.

Once in a while one of Gerda's or Claire's tan legs waves languidly in the air, shaking off sand, a fly. Sometimes their young bodies quiver with the helpless giggle of adolescent girls.

"And the look on Conchi's face! All she could think of to say was '*Ojala.*' What nerve!"

Gerda's laugh is a short Germanic bark. Claire's is high, rippling.

"She won't admit how silly she was either."

Claire sits up to put oil on her face. Her blue eyes scan the beach. *Nada.* The two handsome men haven't reappeared.

"There she is . . . the Anna Karenina woman . . ."

On a red-and-white canvas chair beneath the pines.

The melancholy Russian lady in a panama hat, with a white silk parasol.

Gerda groans. "Oh, she's lovely. Her nose. Gray flannel in summer. And she looks so miserable. She must have a lover."

"I'm going to cut my hair like hers."

"On you it would look like you put a bowl on your head. She
just has style."

"She's the only one here who does. All these tacky Argentines
and Americans. There don't seem to be any Chileans at all, not
even on the staff. The whole village was speaking German."

"When I wake up I think at first that I'm a little girl in Germany or Switzerland. I can hear the maids whispering in the hall,
singing from the kitchen."

"Nobody's smiling but those Americans, not even those children, so serious with their pails."

"Only Americans smile all the time. You're speaking in Spanish but your silly grin gives you away. Your father laughs all the
time too. The bottom just dropped out of the copper market,
ha-ha."

"Your father laughs a lot too."

"Only when something is stupid. Look at him. He must have
swum to that raft a hundred times this morning."

Gerda and Claire always go places with one of their fathers.
To movies and horse races with Mr. Thompson, to the symphony
or to play golf with Herr von Dessaur. In contrast, their Chilean
friends are invariably with mothers and aunts, grandmothers and
sisters.

Gerda's mother was killed in Germany during the war; her
stepmother is a physician, rarely at home. Claire's mother drinks,
is in bed or sanatoriums most of the time. After school the two
friends go home to tea, to read or study. Their friendship began
over books, in their empty houses.

Herr von Dessaur dries himself. He is wet, out of breath. Cool
gray eyes. As a child Claire had felt guilty watching war movies.
She liked the Nazis . . . their overcoats, their cars, cool gray eyes.

"*Ja.* Enough. Go swim. Let me see your crawls, how you are diving now."

"He's being nice, no?" Claire says on the way to the water.

"He's nice when he is not with her."

The girls swim with sure strokes far out into the icy lake, until they hear *Gerdalein!* and see her father waving. They swim to the raft, lie warm against the wood. The white volcano sparkles and smokes high above them. Laughter from a boat far out on the lake, hoofbeats on the dirt road by the shore. No other sound. Lap, lap of the water against the rocking raft.

In the vast high-ceilinged dining room white curtains billow in the breeze from the lake. Palm leaves fan in urns. One waiter in tails ladles the consommé, another breaks eggs, drops one into each pewter bowl. Together the two men bone trout, ignite desserts.

A stooped white-haired gentleman sits down across from the beautiful Anna Karenina.

"Could he be her husband?"

"I hope he isn't Count Vronsky."

"Where did you girls get the idea that they were Russians? I heard them speaking German."

"Really, Papi? What did they say?"

"She said, 'I shouldn't have eaten prunes for breakfast.'"

The girls rent a rowboat, set out for an island. The lake is immense. They take turns, laughing, paddling in circles at first but then gliding smooth. Splash and dip of the oars. They beach the boat in a cove, dive from a rock ledge into the green water that tastes of fish and moss. They swim for a long time and then lie spread-eagled in the sun, their faces buried in wild clover. There is a long slow tremor that rolls and shudders the ground beneath their young bodies. They cling to the clumps of lavender blossoms as the earth undulates below them, away from under them. Their eyes are level with the green rippling of the land. Does it grow dark with smoke from the volcano? The odor of sulfur is intense, terrifying. The temblor stops. For a split second there is no sound and then the birds burst into an alarm of hysterical chatter. Cows low and horses whinny from all around the lake. Dogs are barking, barking. Above the girls the birds whirr and whistle in the branches of the trees. High waves slap against the stones. The girls are silent. Neither can speak about what she feels, something different from fear. Gerda laughs, her bark of a laugh.

"We swam for miles, Papi. Look at our hands, blisters from rowing! Did you feel the tremor?"

He had been playing golf when the temblor came, was on the green. A golfer's nightmare . . . to see your ball coming away from the hole, toward you!

The young men are in the lobby, talking with the desk clerk. Oh, they are handsome. Strong and tanned with white teeth. They are flashily dressed, in their mid-twenties. Claire's, the dark one, has a cleft chin. When he looks down his lashes brush high bronzed cheekbones. Be still, my heart! Claire laughs. Herr von Dessaur says the men are far too old, and vulgar, clearly the worst sort. Farmers, probably. He escorts the girls past them, instructs them to read in their room until dinner.

The dining room is festive. Because of the temblor people nod to the other patrons, speak to the waiters, chat with one another. There are musicians, very old men. Violins play tangos, waltzes. "Frenesi." *La Mer.*

The young men stand in the doorway, framed by potted palms and sconces of wine-colored velvet.

"Papi, they're not farmers. Look!"

They are resplendent in powder-blue uniforms of Chilean aviation cadets. Pale blue trimmed with gold braid. High collars and epaulets, gold buttons. They wear boots with spurs, floor-length woolen capes, swords. They hold their hats and gloves in the crooks of their arms.

"Military! Worse!" Herr von Dessaur laughs. He averts his face, wiping tears of laughter from his eyes.

"Capes on a summer night. Spurs and swords in an airplane? For God's sake, just look at the poor fools!"

Claire and Gerda stare at them with awe. The cadets return their looks with soulful gazes, half-smiles. They sit at a little table by the bandstand, drinking brandy from huge snifters. The blond one has a tortoiseshell cigarette holder which he clamps between his teeth.

"Papi, admit it. His eyes are the very same blue as his cape."

"Yes. Chilean Air Force Blue. The Chilean Air Force does not even have any airplanes!"

It must have been too hot after all. They move to a table by the door to the terrace, drape their capes on their chairs.

The girls plead to be able to stay up longer, to listen to the music, watch the people tango. Sweat curls the hair on the brows of the dancers, whose eyes are locked, hypnotized. Sleepwalking, the dancers twirl and dip to the violins.

The men, Roberto and Andrés, click the heels of their boots. They introduce themselves to Gerda's father, ask for his kind permission to dance with the two young ladies. Herr von Dessaur starts to refuse but still finds the cadets so amusing he says one dance and then it's time for the girls to go to bed.

"La Vie en Rose" the orchestra plays for a very long time as the young people dance around and around on the polished floor. The blue uniforms, the white chiffon dresses reflect in the dark mirrors. People smile, watching the beautiful dancers. Curtains billow like sails. Andrés speaks to Claire in the familiar tense. Roberto suggests that the girls come back downstairs after Herr von Dessaur goes to sleep. The dance is over.

Days go by. The men work on Roberto's fundo, come to the hotel only in the evening. Gerda and Claire swim, climb the volcano.

Hot sun, cool snow. They play golf and croquet with Herr von
Dessaur. They row to their island. They ride horseback with Herr
von Dessaur. Shoulders back, he says. Head up, he says to Claire.
He holds her throat for a long time. Claire swallows. The girls play
canasta with some ladies on the terrace. An Argentine woman
reads their fortunes with cards. A cigarette in her mouth; she
squints through the smoke. Gerda gets a new path and a strange,
mysterious man. Claire gets a new path too and the two of hearts.
A kiss from the gods.

Every night they dance with Roberto and Andrés to "La Vie en
Rose" and finally one night the girls do go back downstairs after
Herr von Dessaur is asleep. A honeymoon couple and some Americans are the only people left in the dining room. Roberto and
Andrés stand and bow. The old men in the orchestra look shocked
but they play "Adiós Muchachos," a mournful, pulsating tango.
The couples dance dreamily out the doors to the terrace, down
the steps to the wet sand. Boots crunch on the sand like on new
snow. They climb into a boat. They sit in the starlit night, holding
hands, listening to the violins. The lights from the hotel and the
white volcano splinter silver in the water. A breeze. It is cool. No,
it is cold. The boat has come unmoored. There are no oars. The
boat is moving fast, gliding like the wind, with the wind, out into
the dark lake. Oh, no! Gerda gasps. The girls are kissed while
there is still a chance. He put his whole tongue in my mouth,
Gerda says, later. Claire is bumped on the forehead. A kiss catches
the corner of her lips, grazes her nose before the girls dive like
mercury into the black water of the lake.

Their shoes are gone. The girls are wet and cold, shivering outside the doorway to the hotel, shuttered now by iron gates. Let's
just wait, Claire says. What, until morning? You must be mad!
Gerda shakes the metal gates until at last lights go on in the hotel.
Gerdalein! her father says from a balcony, but suddenly he is in
front of them, behind the gates. The mayordomo is in a bathrobe,
with keys.

In their room the girls wrap themselves in blankets. Herr von Dessaur is pale. Did he touch you? Gerda shakes her head. No. We danced and then we sat in a boat but then the boat got loose so we . . . Did he kiss you? She doesn't answer. I ask you. Did he kiss you? Gerda nods her head; her father slaps her in the mouth. Slut, he says.

The maid comes in the morning before it is light. She packs their bags. They leave before anyone is awake, wait a long time at the railway station in Temuco. Herr von Dessaur sits across from Claire and Gerda. The girls are reading, silently, the book held between them. *Sonata de Otoño*. The woman dies in his arms, in a distant wing of the castle. He has to carry her body back to her own bed, through the passages. Her long black hair catches on the stones. No candle.

"You will see no one, and especially not Claire, for the rest of the summer."

Finally Herr von Dessaur goes out to smoke and for just a short blessed time the friends can laugh. A joyous splutter of laughter. By the time he returns they are reading quietly.

Macadam

When fresh it looks like caviar, sounds like broken glass, like someone chewing ice.

I'd chew ice when the lemonade was finished, swaying with my grandmother on the porch swing. We gazed down upon the chain gang paving Upson Street. A foreman poured the macadam; the convicts stomped it down with a heavy rhythmic beat. The chains rang; the macadam made the sound of applause.

The three of us said the word often. My mother because she hated where we lived, in squalor, and at least now we would have a macadam street. My grandmother just so wanted things clean—it would hold down the dust. Red Texan dust that blew in with gray tailings from the smelter, sifting into dunes on the polished hall floor, onto her mahogany table.

I used to say *macadam* out loud, to myself, because it sounded like the name for a friend.

Dear Conchi

Dear Conchi,

The University of New Mexico, not how we imagined it at all. Secondary school in Chile was harder than college here. I live in a dorm, hundreds of girls, all outgoing and confident. I still feel strange, ill at ease.

I love the place itself. The campus has many old adobe buildings. The desert is beautiful and there are mountains here. Not like the Andes of course, but big on a different scale. Rugged and rocky. Dumb-dumb . . . that's what they are called, the Rocky Mountains. Clear clean air, cold at night with millions of stars.

My clothes are all wrong. A girl even told me that nobody here "dresses up" like I do. I have to get white sox I guess and huge circular skirts, blue jeans. I mean, the women look really horrible. It's nice on the men, though, casual clothes and boots.

I'll never get used to the food. Cereal for breakfast and coffee as weak as tea. And when I'm ready for tea in the afternoon that's when dinner is served here. When I'm ready for dinner it's lights-out time at the dorm.

I couldn't get a class with Ramon Sender until next semester. I saw him in the hall, though! I told him *Cronica del Alba* was my favorite book. He said, "Yes, but then, you are very young." He is how I imagined him, only real old. Very Spanish and arrogant, dignified . . .

Dear Conchi,

I have a job, can you imagine? Part time, but still. It's proof-reading the college paper, *The Lobo*, which comes out once a week. I work three nights in the journalism building, right next to the dorm. I even have a key to the dorm, since it's locked at ten and I work until eleven. The printer is an old Texan called Jonesy, who works on a linotype machine. A wonderful machine with about a thousand parts and gears. Boiling lead that makes the letters. He puts the words in and they clank and sing and clatter, come out in lines of hot lead. It makes each line seem important.

He teaches me things, about writing headlines, which stories are good, and why. He teases me a lot, plays tricks to keep me on my toes. In the middle of a story about a basketball game he'll slip in something like "Down upon the Swanee River."

Sometimes a man called Joe Sanchez comes in and brings copy and a beer for Jonesy. He's a sports and feature writer. He's a student, but much older than the boys in my classes, because he is a veteran, here on the GI bill. He tells us about Japan, where he was a medic. He looks like an Indian, has shiny black hair, long, combed in a ducktail.

Sorry, I'm already using expressions you've never heard. Most of the boys here wear crew cuts, which is practically shaven heads. Some have longer hair, combed back in what looks like a duck's tail.

I miss you and Quena a lot. I haven't made a friend yet. I am different, coming from Chile. I think people think I'm stuck up because I'm not open. I don't understand the humor yet, get em-barrassed because there's a lot of joking and hinting about sex. Strangers will tell you their whole life story, but they aren't emo-

tional or affectionate like Chileans, so I still don`       `
them.

All those years in South America I wanted to return`    `
country the USA because it was a democracy, not with just `   `
classes like Chile. There are definitely classes here. Girls who
were nice to me in the beginning snub me now because I didn't
go through rush, live in the dorm and not a sorority. And some
sororities are "better" than others. Richer.

I mentioned to my roommate Ella that Joe, the reporter, was
funny and nice and she said, "Yes, but he's Mexican." He's not
from Mexico, that's what they call anybody of Spanish descent
here. There aren't that many Mexicans at the university, when you
consider the population here, and only about ten Negroes.

My journalism classes are going well, great teachers, they even
look like reporters in old movies. I'm starting to get a weird feeling
though. I majored in journalism because I wanted to be a writer,
but the whole point of journalism is to cut out all the good stuff . . .

Dear Conchi,

. . . I have been out several times with Joe Sanchez. He gets
free tickets to events so he'll do stories on them. I like him because he never says things just because they are the right thing to
say. It's very cool to like Dave Brubeck, a jazz musician, but in his
review Joe called him a wimp. People got really mad. And Billy
Graham. Hard to explain to you, being Catholic, what an Evange-
list is. He talks, hollers, about God and sin and tries to get people
to turn their lives over to Jesus. Everybody I know thinks the guy
is crazy, money hungry and hopelessly corny. The column Joe wrote
was about the man's skill and power. It turned into a column about
faith.

We don't go to student hangouts afterward but to little restaurants in the south valley or to Mexican bars or cowboy bars. It's

like being in another country. We drive up into the mountains or out into the desert, walk or climb for miles. He doesn't try to "make out" (*atracar*) like all the other boys do, relentlessly, here. When he says good-bye he just touches my cheek. Once he kissed my hair.

He doesn't talk about things, or events or books. He reminds me of my uncle John. He tells stories, about his brothers, or his grandfather, or geisha girls in Japan.

I like him because he talks to everybody. He really wants to know what everyone is up to.

Dear Conchi,

I'm going out with a really sophisticated man, Bob Dash. We went to a play, *Waiting for Godot,* and to an Italian movie, I forget the title. He looks like a handsome author on a book jacket. A pipe, patches on his elbows. He lives in an adobe house filled with Indian pots and rugs and modern art. We drink gin and tonics with lime in them, listen to music like Bartok's *Sonata for Two Pianos and Percussion.* He talks a lot about books I have never heard of, and has lent me a dozen books . . . Sartre, Keerkegard (sp?), Beckett and T. S. Eliot, many more. I like a poem called "The Hollow Men."

Joe told me it was Dash who was a hollow man. He has been unreasonably upset about me going out with Bob, or even having coffee with him. He says he's not jealous but that he can't bear the idea of me becoming an intellectual. Says I have to listen to Patsy Cline and Charlie Parker as an antidote. Read Walt Whitman and Thomas Wolfe's *Look Homeward, Angel.*

Actually I liked Camus's *The Stranger* better than *Look Homeward, Angel.* But I like Joe because he likes that book. He's not afraid to be corny. He loves America, and New Mexico, the barrio where he lives, the desert. We go for long hikes in the foothills.

Once a huge dust storm came up. Tumbleweeds whipping through the air and blizzards of yellow dust howling. He was dancing around in it. I could barely hear him hollering how wonderful it was, the desert. We saw a coyote, heard it yelping.

He's corny with me, too. He remembers things, and listens to me go on and on. Once I was crying for no reason, just missing you and Quena and home. He didn't try to cheer me up, just held me and let me be sad. We speak Spanish when we're talking about sweet things, or when we're kissing. We've been kissing a lot.

Dear Conchi,

I wrote a short story, "Apples." It's about an old man who rakes apples. Bob Dash red-penciled about a dozen adjectives and said it was "an acceptable little story." Joe said it was precious and false. That I should only write about what I feel, not make up something about an old man I never knew. It doesn't bother me what they said. I read it over and over.

Of course it bothers me.

Ella, my roommate, said she would prefer not to read it. I wish we got along better. Her mother mails her her Kotex from Oklahoma every month. She's a drama major. God, how can she ever play Lady Macbeth if she can't relax about a little blood?

I'm seeing more of Bob Dash. He's like having a personal seminar. Today we went to coffee and talked about *Nausea*. But I'm thinking more about Joe. I see him between classes and when I'm working. He and Jonesy and I laugh a lot, eat pizza and drink beer. Joe has a little room that's sort of his office, that's where we kiss. I don't think about him exactly, but about kissing him. I was thinking about it in Copy Editing I, and even groaned or said something out loud and the professor looked at me and said, "Yes, Miss Gray?"

Dear Conchi,

. . . I'm reading Jane Austen. Her writing is like chamber music, but it's real and funny at the same time. There are a thousand books I want to read, don't know where to start. I'm changing my major to English next semester . . .

Dear Conchi,

An old couple work as janitors in the journalism building. One night they took us up on the roof for a beer after work. The roof is overhung with cottonwood trees and you can just sit under the trees and look at the stars. If you want you can look over and watch the cars on Route 66, or on the other side, into the windows of the dorm where I live. They gave us an extra key to the broom closet, where the ladder to the roof is. Nobody else knows about this place. We go up there between classes and after work. Joe brought a grill and a mattress and candles. It's like our own island or tree house . . .

Dear Conchi,

I am happy. When I wake up in the morning my face is sore from smiling.

When I was little I think I felt peace sometimes, in the woods or a meadow, and in Chile I was always having fun. I felt joy when I skied. But I had never felt happiness like I do with Joe. Never felt that I was me, and loved for that.

I sign out for the weekends to his house, with his father responsible for me. Joe lives with his father, who is very old, a retired schoolteacher. He loves to cook, makes awful greasy food. He drinks beer all day. The only effect it seems to have is to make him sing things like "Minnie the Mermaid" and "Rain on the Roof," over and over while he cooks. He tells stories too, about everybody in Armijo, the neighborhood. He had most of them in school.

Dear Conchi,

Most weekends we go to the Jemez Mountains and climb all day, camp out at night. There are some hot springs up there. So far nobody has been there when we have. Deer and owls, big-horned sheep, blue jays. We lie in the water, talk or read out loud. Joe loves to read Keats.

My classes and job are going fine, but I always can't wait until they are over so I can be with Joe. He's a sports reporter for the *Tribune*, too, so it's hard to find time. We go to track meets and high school basketball games, stock car races. I don't like football, miss soccer and rugby games.

Dear Conchi,

Everyone is unreasonably upset about me and Joe. The house-mother gave me a talk. Bob Dash was horrid, lectured me for about an hour, until I got up and left. Said Joe was vulgar and common, a hedonist with no sense of values and no intellectual scope. Among other things. Mostly people are worried because I'm so young. They think I'm going to throw away my education or career. Or that's what they all say. I think they are jealous because we are so in love. And no matter what their arguments, from ruining my reputation to risk-ing my future, they always bring up the fact that he is Mexican. It never occurs to anybody that coming from Chile I would naturally like a Latin person, someone who feels things. I don't fit in here at all. I wish Joe and I could go home to Santiago . . .

Dear Conchi,

. . . Someone actually wrote to my parents, told them I was having an affair with a man much too old for me.

They called, hysterical, are coming all the way from Chile. They will arrive on New Year's Eve. Apparently my mother started drinking again. My father says it's all my fault.

When I'm with Joe none of this matters. I think he is a reporter because he likes to talk to people. Wherever we go we end
up talking to strangers. And liking them.

I don't think I ever really liked the world until I met him. My
parents don't like the world, or me, or they would trust me.

Dear Conchi,

They arrived on New Year's Eve, but were exhausted from the
trip so we only talked for a little while. They didn't hear that I'm
making straight As, that I love my job, that I was chosen queen of
the Newsprint Ball that night. I have become a fallen woman, a
common tart, etc. "With a greaser," my mother said.

The dance was wonderful. We had dinner with friends from
the department before the dance, laughed a lot. There was a ceremony where I got a newspaper crown and an orchid. For some
reason I had never danced with Joe before. It was wonderful.
Dancing with him.

We had agreed to see my parents the next day, at their motel.
My father said he and Joe could watch the Rose Bowl game, that
it would break the ice.

I am so dumb. I saw that they had been drinking martinis
already, felt they would be more relaxed. Joe was great. At ease,
warm, open. They were like stone.

Daddy relaxed a little when the game came on, both he and
Joe enjoyed it. Mama and I sat there silent. Joe just drinks beer, so
he really loosened up on my father's martinis. Every time there
was a field goal he'd holler "Fuckin' A!" or "*A la verga!*" A few times
he punched Daddy on the shoulder. Mama cringed and drank and
didn't say a word.

After the game Joe invited my parents out to dinner, but my
father said that he and Joe should go get some Chinese food.

While they were gone Mama talked about the shame I had
caused them by being immoral, how disgusted she was.

Conchi, I know we promised to tell the other about sex, the first time either of us made love. It's hard to write about. What is fine about it is that it is between two people, the most naked and close you can get. And each time is different and a surprise. Sometimes we laugh the whole time. Sometimes it makes you cry.

Sex is the most important thing that ever happened to me. I could not understand what my mother was saying, that I was filthy.

Lord knows what Joe and Daddy talked about. They were both pale when they got back. Apparently my father said things like "statutory rape" and Joe said he would marry me tomorrow, which was the worst thing, for my parents, that he could have said.

After we had eaten, Joe said, "Well, we're all pretty tired. I better be going. You coming, Lu?"

"No, she's staying here," my father said.

I stood there, frozen.

"I'm going with Joe," I said. "I'll see you in the morning."

I'm writing you now from the dorm. It's eerily quiet. Most of the girls went home for Christmas.

Except for briefly telling me what my father said, Joe didn't talk while he drove me home. I couldn't talk either. When we kissed good-bye I thought my heart would break.

Dear Conchi,

My parents are taking me out of school at the end of the semester. They'll wait for me in New York. I'm to go there and then we're going to Europe until the fall semester.

I took a taxi to Joe's house. We were going to Sandia Peak to talk, got into the car. I don't know what I thought he would say, what I wanted.

I hoped he'd say he'd wait for me, that he'd still be here when I got back. But he said that if I really loved him I'd marry him right now. I reacted to that. He needs to graduate; he only works

part-time. I didn't say more of the truth which is that I don't want
to leave school. I want to study Shakespeare, the Romantic poets.
He said we could live with his dad until we had enough money.
We were crossing the bridge over the Rio Grande when I said I
didn't want to get married yet.

"You won't know for a long time what it is you're throwing
away."

I said I knew what we had, that it would still be there when I
got back.

"It will, but you won't. No, you'll go on, have 'relationships,'
marry some asshole."

He opened the car door, shoved me out onto the Rio Grande
bridge, the car still moving. He drove away. I walked all the way
across town to the dorm. I kept thinking he'd pull up behind me,
but he never did.

Fool to Cry

Solitude is an Anglo-Saxon concept. In Mexico City, if you're the only person on a bus and someone gets on they'll not only come next to you, they will lean against you.

When my sons were at home, if they came into my room there was usually a specific reason. Have you seen my socks? What's for dinner? Even now, when the bell on my gate rings it will be Hi, Ma! let's go to the A's game, or Can you babysit tonight? But in Mexico, my sister's daughters will come up three flights of stairs and through three doors just because I am there. To lean against me or say, *Qué honda?*

Their mother, Sally, is sleeping soundly. She has taken pain pills and a sleeping pill. She doesn't hear me, in the bed next to hers, turning pages, coughing. When Tino, her fifteen-year-old son, comes home he gives me a kiss, goes to her bed and lies next to her, holds her hand. He kisses her good night and goes to his room.

Mercedes and Victoria live in their own apartment across town, but every night they stop by even though she doesn't wake up. Victoria smooths Sally's brow, arranges her pillows and blankets, draws a star on her bald head with a felt-tip pen. Sally moans in her sleep, wrinkles her brow. Hold still, *Amor*, Victoria says. About four in the morning Mercedes comes to say good night to her mother. She is a set designer for movies. When she's working she works day and night. She too lies against Sally, sings to her, kisses her head. She sees the star and she laughs. Victoria has been here! Tía, are you awake? *Sí. Oye!* Let's go smoke. We go into the kitchen. She is very tired, dirty. Stands staring into the refrigerator, sighs and closes it. We smoke and share an apple, sitting together on the only chair in the kitchen. She is happy. The film they are making is wonderful, the director is the best. She is doing a good job. "They treat me with respect, like a man! Cappelini wants me to work on his next movie!"

In the morning Sally and Tino and I go to La Vega for coffee. Tino carries his cappuccino with him as he goes from table to table, talking with friends, flirting with girls. Mauricio the chauffeur waits outside, to take Tino to school. Sally and I talk and talk, as we have since I arrived from California three days before. She is wearing a curly auburn wig, a green dress that enhances her jade eyes. Everyone stares at her, fascinated. Sally has come to this café for twenty-five years. Everyone knows she is dying, but she has never looked so beautiful or happy.

Now, me . . . if they said I had a year to live, I'll bet I would just swim out to sea, get it over with. But Sally, it is as if the sentence had been a gift. Maybe it's because she fell in love with Xavier the week before she found out. She has come alive. She savors everything. She says whatever she wants, does whatever makes her feel good. She laughs. Her walk is sexy, her voice is sexy. She gets mad and throws things, hollers cusswords. Little Sally, always meek and passive, in my shadow as a girl, in her husband's for most of her life. She is strong, radiant now; her zest is contagious. People stop by the table to greet her, men kiss her hand. The doctor, the architect, the widower.

Mexico City is a huge metropolis but people have titles, like the blacksmith in a village. The medical student; the judge; Victoria, the ballerina; Mercedes, the beauty; Sally's ex-husband, the minister. I am the American sister. Everyone greets me with hugs and cheek kisses.

Sally's ex-husband, Ramon, stops in for an espresso, shadowed by bodyguards. Chairs scrape back all over the café as men stand to shake his hand or give him an *abrazo*. He is a cabinet member now, for the PRI. He kisses Sally and me, asks Tino about his school. Tino hugs his father good-bye and leaves for class. Ramon looks at his watch.

Wait a little bit, Sally says. They want so badly to see you; they are sure to come.

Victoria first, in a low-cut leotard on her way to dance class. Her hair is punk; she has a tattoo on her shoulder. For God's sake, cover yourself! her father says.

"Papi, everybody here is used to me, no, Julian?"

Julian, the waiter, shakes his head. "No, *mi doña*, each day you bring us a new surprise."

He has brought us all what we wanted without taking an order. Tea for Sally, a second latte for me, an espresso, then a latte, for Ramon.

Mercedes arrives, her hair wild, her face heavily made up, on the way to a modeling job before going to the movie set. Everyone in the café has known Victoria and Mercedes since they were babies, but stares at them nonetheless because they are so beautiful, so scandalously dressed.

Ramon starts his usual lecture. Mercedes has appeared in some sexy scenes for Mexican MTV. An embarrassment. He wants Victoria to go to college and get a part-time job. She puts her arms around him.

"Now, Papi, why should I go to school, when all I want to do is dance? And why should I work, when we are so rich?"

Ramon shakes his head, and ends up giving her money for her lessons, more for some shoes, more for a cab, since she's late. She leaves, waving good-byes and blowing kisses to the café.

Ramon groans. "I'm late!" He leaves too, weaving through a gauntlet of handshakes. A black limousine speeds him away, down Insurgentes.

"*Pues*, finally we can eat," Mercedes says. Julian arrives with juice and fruit and chilaquiles. "Mama, could you try something, just a little?" Sally shakes her head. She has chemo later, and it makes her sick.

"I didn't sleep a wink last night!" Sally says. She looks hurt when Mercedes and I laugh, but she laughs too, when we tell her all the people she slept through.

"Tomorrow is Tía's birthday. Basil Day!" Mercedes said. "Mama, were you at the Grange Fête, too?"

"Yes, but I was little, only seven, the time it fell on Carlotta's twelfth birthday, the year she met Basil. Everybody was there . . . grown-ups, children. There was a little English world within the country of Chile. Anglican churches and English manors and cottages. English gardens and dogs. The Prince of Wales Country Club. Rugby and cricket teams. And of course the Grange School. A very good Eton-type boys' school."

"And all the girls at our school were in love with Grange boys . . ."

"The Fête lasted all day. There were soccer and cricket games and cross-country races, shot-put and jumping events. All kinds of games and booths, things to buy and to eat."

"Fortune-tellers," Carlotta said. "She told me I would have many lovers and many troubles."

"I could have told you that. Anyway, it was just like an English country fair."

"What did he look like?"

"Noble and worried. Tall and handsome, except for rather large ears."

"And a lantern jaw . . ."

"Late in the afternoon was prize-giving, and the boys my friends and I had crushes on all won prizes for sports, but Basil kept getting called up to get prizes for physics and chemistry and history, Greek and Latin. Tons more. At first everybody clapped but then it got funny. His face got redder and redder every time he went up to get another prize, a book. About a dozen books. Things like Marcus Aurelius.

"Then it was time for tea, before the dance. Everyone milling around or having tea at little tables. Conchi dared me to ask him to dance, so I did. He was standing with his whole family. A big-eared father, mother and three sisters, all with that same unfortunate jaw. I congratulated him, and asked him to dance. And he fell in love, right before my very eyes.

"He had never danced before, so I showed him how easy it was, just making boxes. To 'Siboney.' 'Long Ago and Far Away.' We danced all night, or made boxes. He came to tea every day for a week. Then it was summer vacation and he went to his family's *fundo*. He wrote to me every day, sent me dozens and dozens of poems."

"Tía, how did he kiss?" Mercedes asked.

"Kiss! He never kissed me, didn't even hold my hand. That would have been very serious, in Chile then. I remember feeling faint when Pirulo Diaz held my hand in the movie *Beau Geste*."

"It was a big deal if a boy should address you as *tú*," Sally said. "This was long, long ago. We rubbed alum rocks under our arms for deodorant. Kotex wasn't even invented; we used rags that maids washed over and over."

"And were you in love with Basil, Tía?"

"No. I was in love with Pirulo Diaz. But for years Basil was always there, at our house, at rugby games, at parties. He came to tea every day. Daddy played golf with him, was always asking him to dinner."

"He was the only suitor Daddy ever approved of."

"The worst thing for romance," Mercedes sighed. "Good men are never sexy."

"My Xavier is good! So good to me! And he's sexy!" Sally said.

"Basil and Daddy were good in a patronizing and judgmental way. I treated Basil horribly, but he kept coming back. Every single year on my birthday he has sent roses or called me. Year after year. For over forty years. He has found me through Conchi, or your mother . . . all kinds of places. Chiapas, New York, Idaho. Once I was even in a lockup psych ward in Oakland."

"So what has he said, in those phone calls all these years?"

"Very little, actually. About his own life I mean. He is president of a grocery chain. Usually asked how I was. Invariably something terrible had just happened . . . our house burned down or a divorce, a car wreck. Each time he calls he says the same thing. Like a rosary. Today, on November 12, he is thinking of the most lovely woman he ever knew. 'Long Ago and Far Away' plays in the background."

"Year after year!"

"And he never wrote to you or saw you?"

"No," Sally said. "When he called last week to ask where Carlotta was I told him she would be in Mexico City, why not have lunch with her. I got the feeling he didn't really want to meet her tomorrow. He said it wouldn't do to tell his wife. I said, why not bring her along, but he said that wouldn't do."

"Here comes Xavier! You are so lucky, Mama. You get no sympathy from us at all. *Pilla envidia!*"

Xavier is at her side, holding both her hands. He is married. Supposedly no one knows about their affair. He has stopped by, as if by chance. How can everyone not feel the electricity? Julian smiles at me.

Xavier has changed too, as much as my sister. He is an aristocrat, a prominent chemist, used to be very serious and reserved. Now he laughs too. He and Sally play and they cry and they fight. They take *danzón* lessons and go to Merida. They dance the *danzón* in the plaza, under the stars, cats and children playing in the bushes, paper lanterns in the trees.

Everything they say, the most trivial thing like "good morning, *mi vida*," or "pass the salt" is charged with such urgency that Mercedes and I giggle. But we are moved, awed, by these two people in a state of grace.

"Tomorrow is Basil Day!" Xavier smiles.

"Victoria and I think she should dress up as a punk, or as an old old lady," Mercedes says.

"Or I could have Sally go in my place!" I say.

"No. Victoria or Mercedes . . . And he'll think you are still back in the forties, almost as he remembers you!"

Xavier and Sally left for her chemo treatment and Mercedes went to work. I spent the day in Coyoacán. In the church the priest was baptizing about fifty babies at once. I knelt at the back, near the bloodiest Christ, and watched the ceremony. The parents and godparents stood in long rows, facing each other in the aisle. The mothers held the babies, dressed in white. Round babies, skinny babies, fat babies, bald babies. The priest walked down the middle of the aisle followed by two altar boys swinging incense censers. The priest prayed in Latin. Wetting his fingers in a chalice he held in his left hand, he made the sign of the cross on each baby's forehead, baptizing them in the name of the Father and the Son and the Holy Ghost. The parents were serious, prayed solemnly. I wished that the priest would bless each mother, too, make some sign, give her some protection.

In Mexican villages, when my sons were infants, Indians would sometimes make the sign of the cross on their brows. *Pobrecito!* they would say. That such a lovely creature should have to suffer this life!

Mark, four years old, in a nursery school on Horatio Street in New York. He was playing pretend house with some other children. He opened a toy refrigerator, poured an imaginary glass of milk and handed it to his friend. The friend smashed the imaginary glass on the floor. Mark's look of pain, the same I have seen later in all my sons during their lives. A wound from an accident, a divorce, a failure. The ferocity of my longing to protect them. My helplessness.

As I leave the church I light a candle beneath the statue of our Blessed Mother Mary. *Pobrecita.*

Sally is in bed, worn out and nauseated. I put cloths cooled in ice water on her head. I tell her about the people in the plaza at Coyoacán, about the baptism. She tells me about the other patients at chemo, about Pedro, her doctor. She tells me the things Xavier said to her, the tenderness of him, and she cries bitter, bitter tears.

When Sally and I first became friends, after we grew up, we spent several years working out our resentments and jealousies. Later, when both of us were in therapy, we spent years venting our rage at our grandfather, our mother. Our cruel mother. Years later still, our rage at our father, the saint, whose cruelty was not so obvious.

But now we speak only in the present tense. In a cenote in the Yucatán, atop Tulum, in the convent in Tepoztlán, in her little room, we laugh with joy at the similarities of our responses, at the stereo of our visions.

The morning of my fifty-fourth birthday we don't stay long at La Vega. Sally wants to rest before her chemo. I need to dress for lunch with Basil. When we get home Mercedes and Victoria are watching a telenovela with Belen and Dolores, the two maids. Belen and Dolores spend most of the day and night watching soap operas. They have both been with Sally for twenty years; they live in a small apartment on the roof. There is not that much for them to do now that Ramon and the daughters are gone, but Sally would never ask them to leave.

Today is a big day on *Los Golpes de la Vida*. Sally dresses in a robe and comes to watch. I have showered and put on makeup, but stay in my robe too, don't want to wrinkle my gray linen.

Adelina is going to have to tell her daughter Conchita that she can't marry Antonio. Has to confess that Antonio is her natural son, Conchita's brother! Adelina had him in a convent twenty-five years ago.

And there they are in Sanborn's but before Adelina can say a word Conchita tells her mother that she and Antonio have been secretly married. And now they are going to have a baby! Close-up of Adelina's grief-stricken face, her mother's face. But she smiles and kisses Conchita. *Mozo*, she says, do bring us some champagne.

Okay, so it's pretty silly. What was really silly was that all six of us women were bawling our eyes out, just sobbing away when the doorbell rang. Mercedes ran to open the door.

Basil stared at Mercedes, aghast. Not just because she was crying, or wearing shorts and a bra-less top. People are always taken aback by the sisters' beauty. After you are around them awhile you get used to it, like a harelip.

Mercedes kissed him on the cheek. "The famous Basil, wearing real English tweeds!"

His face was red. He stared at us, all of us in tears, with such confusion that we got the giggles. Like children do. Serious, punishable giggles. We couldn't stop. I got up, went to give him an *abrazo* too, but again he stiffened, held out his hand for a cool shake.

"Forgive us . . . we're watching a tearjerker of a telenovela." I introduced him to everyone. "Of course you remember Sally?" He looked aghast again. "My wig!" She ran to put on her wig. I went to dress. Mercedes came with me.

"Come on Tía, dress up real whorish and trashy . . . he is so stuffy!"

"There is no place to eat around here, surely," Basil was saying.

"Surely, there is. La Pampa, an Argentinian restaurant, just across from the clock of flowers in the park."

"The clock of flowers?"

"I'll show you," I said. "Let's go."

I followed him down the three flights of stairs, chattering nervously. How good it was to see him, how fit he looked.

In the downstairs foyer he stopped and looked around.

"Ramon is a minister now. Surely he can afford a better place for his family to live?"

"He has a new family now. They live in La Pedregal, a lovely home. But this is a wonderful place, Basil. Sunny and spacious . . . full of antiques and plants and birds."

"The neighborhood?"

"Calle Amores? Sally would never live anyplace else. She knows everybody. I even know everybody."

I was greeting people all the way to his car. He had paid some boys to watch it, keep it safe from bandits.

We buckled up.

"What is the matter with Sally's hair?" he asked.

"She lost it because of chemotherapy. She has cancer."

"How terrible! Is the prognosis good?"

"No. She's dying."

"I'm so sorry. I must say, none of you seem particularly affected by it."

"We're all affected by it. Right now we are happy. Sally is in love. She and I have become close, sisters. That's been like falling in love too. Her children are seeing her, hearing her."

He was silent, hands gripping the wheel.

I directed him to the park on Insurgentes.

"Park anywhere, now. See, there is the clock of flowers!"

"It doesn't look like a clock."

"Of course it does. See the numbers! Well, hell, it looked like a clock the other day. The numbers are marigolds, and they've just grown a little leggy. But everybody knows it's a clock."

We parked a long way from the restaurant. It was hot. I have a bad back, smoke a lot. The smog, my high heels. I was faint with hunger. The restaurant smelled wonderful. Garlic and rosemary, red wine, lamb.

"I don't know," he said, "it's very rowdy. It will be hard to have a proper conversation. It's full of Argentines!"

"Well, yeah, it's an Argentine restaurant."

"Your accent is so American! You say 'yeah' all the time."

"Well, yeah, I'm an American." We walked up and down the street, peering into the windows of one wonderful restaurant after another, but none were quite right, one was too dear. I decided to use the word *dear* instead of *expensive* from now on. Oh, look, here's my dear phone bill!

"Basil . . . let's get a torta and go sit in the park. I'm famished, and want to spend time talking with you."

"We're going to have to go downtown. Where I am familiar with the restaurants."

"How about I wait here while you go get the car?"

"I don't like to leave you unescorted in this neighborhood."

"This is a swell neighborhood."

"Please. We will go together and find the car."

Find the car. Of course he didn't remember where he had parked the car. Blocks and blocks. We circled back, out, around, ran into the same cats, the same maids leaning on gates flirting with the mailman. The knife sharpener playing a flute, driving his bike with no hands.

I sank back into the cushioned seat of the car, kicking off my shoes. I took out a pack of cigarettes but he asked me not to smoke in the car. Tears were streaking down both of our faces from the Mexico City smog. I said I thought smoking might form a sort of protective screen.

"Ah, Carlotta, still flirting with danger!"

"Let's go. I'm starving."

But he was taking photos of his children from the glove compartment. I held the pictures in their silver frames. Clear-eyed, determined young people. Lantern-jawed. He was talking about their brilliance, their achievements, their successful careers as physicians. Yes, they saw the son, but Marilyn and her mother didn't get on. Both very headstrong.

"She is quite good with servants," Basil said about his wife. "Never lets them step out of bounds. Were those women your sister's servants?"

"They were. They're more like family now."

We turned the wrong way on a one-way street. Basil backed up, cars and trucks honking at us. On the *periférico* then, speeding along, until there was an accident up ahead and we came to a standstill. Basil turned off the motor and the air-conditioning. I stepped outside for a smoke.

"You'll get run over!"

Not a car was moving for blocks behind us.

We arrived at the Sheraton at four thirty. The dining room was closed. What to do? He had parked the car. We went into a Denny's next door.

"Denny's is where one ends up," I said.

"I'd like a club sandwich and iced tea," I said. "What are you going to have?"

"I don't know. I find food uninteresting."

I was profoundly depressed. I wanted to eat my sandwich and to go home. But I made polite conversation. Yes, they belonged to an English country club. He played golf and cricket, was in a theater group. He had played one of the old ladies in *Arsenic and Old Lace*. Great fun.

"By the way. I bought that house, in Chile, with the pool, off the third hole of the golf course in Santiago. We rent it out, but plan to retire there. Do you know which house I mean?"

"Of course. A lovely house, with wisteria and lilacs. Look under your lilac bushes, you'll find a hundred golf balls. I always sliced my first shot into that yard."

"What are your plans for retirement? For your future?"

"Future?"

"Do you have savings? IRA, that sort of thing?"

I shook my head.

"I have been very concerned about you. Especially that time when you were in the hospital. You *have* knocked about a bit . . . three divorces, four children, so many jobs. And your sons, what do they do? Are you proud of them?"

I was irritable, even though my sandwich had arrived. He had ordered an untoasted cheese sandwich and tea.

"I hate that concept . . . being proud of one's children, taking credit for what they have accomplished. I like my sons. They are loving; they have integrity."

They laugh. They eat a *lot*.

He asked again what they did. A chef, a TV cameraman, a graphics designer, a waiter. They all like what they do.

"It doesn't sound as if any of them are in a position to care for you when you'll need it. Oh, Carlotta, if you had only stayed in Chile. You would have had a serene life. You would still be queen of the country club."

"Serene? I would have died in the revolution." Queen of the country club? Change this conversation, quick.

"Do you and Hilda go to the seashore?" I asked.

"How could anyone, after the coast in Chile? No, there are such throngs of Americans. I find the Mexican Pacific boring."

"Basil, how can you possibly find an ocean boring?"

"What do you find boring?"

"Nothing, actually. I've never been bored."

"But then, you have gone to great lengths not to be bored."

Basil moved his almost uneaten sandwich aside and leaned toward me solicitously.

"Dear Carlotta . . . however will you pick up the pieces of your life?"

"I don't want any of those old pieces. I just go along, try not to do any damage."

"Tell me, what do you feel you have accomplished in your life?"

I couldn't think of a thing.

"I haven't had a drink in three years," I said.

"That's scarcely an accomplishment. That's like saying, 'I haven't murdered my mother.'"

"Well, of course, there is that, too." I smiled.

I had eaten all my triangles of sandwiches and the parsley.

"Could I have some flan and a cappuccino, please?"

It was the only restaurant in the Republic of Mexico that didn't have flan. Jello, sí. "What about you, Basil, what of your ambition to be a poet?"

He shook his head. "I still read poetry, of course. Tell me, what line of poetry do you live by?"

What an interesting question! I was pleased, but perversely unacceptable lines came to mind. Say, sea. Take me! Every woman loves a fascist. I love the look of agony! Because I know it's true.

"Do not go gentle into that good night." I didn't even like Dylan Thomas.

"Still my defiant Carlotta! My line is from Yeats: 'Be secret, and exult.'"

God. I stubbed out my cigarette, finished the instant coffee.

"How about 'miles to go before I sleep'? I'd better get back to Sally's."

Traffic and smog were bad. We inched along. He recited all the deaths of people we had known, the financial and marital failures of all my old boyfriends.

He pulled up at the curb. I said good-bye. Foolishly, I moved to give him a hug. He backed away, into the car door. *Ciao*, I said. Exult!

The house was quiet. Sally was asleep, after her chemo. She stirred fitfully. I made some strong coffee, sat by the canaries, near the fragrance of tuberoses, listening to the man downstairs playing his cello badly.

I crept into bed next to my sister. We both slept until it was dark. Victoria and Mercedes came to find out all about the lunch with Basil.

I could have told them about the lunch. I could have made it a very funny story. How the marigolds grew out and Basil couldn't tell it was the clock of flowers. I could have impersonated him acting one of the old ladies in *Arsenic and Old Lace*. But I lay back against the pillow next to Sally.

"He won't ever call me again."

I cried. Sally and her daughters comforted me. They did not think I was a fool to cry.

Mourning

I love houses, all the things they tell me, so that's one reason I don't mind working as a cleaning woman. It's just like reading a book.

I've been working for Arlene, at Central Reality. Cleaning empty houses mostly, but even empty houses have stories, clues. A love letter stuffed way back in a cupboard, empty whiskey bottles behind the dryer, grocery lists . . . "Please pick up Tide, a package of green linguini and a six pack of Coors. I didn't mean what I said last night."

Lately I've been cleaning houses where somebody has just died. Cleaning and helping to sort things for people to take or to give to Goodwill. Arlene always asks if they have any clothes or books for the Home for Jewish Parents, that's where Sadie, her mother, is. These jobs have been depressing. Either all the relatives want everything, and argue over the smallest things, a pair of ratty old suspenders or a coffee mug. Or none of them want anything to do with anything in the whole house, so I just pack it all up. In both cases the sad part is how little time it takes. Think about it. If you should die . . . I could get rid of all your belongings in two hours max.

Last week I cleaned the house of a very old black mailman. Arlene knew him, said he had been bedridden with diabetes, had died of a heart attack. He had been a mean, rigid old guy, she said, an elder in the church. He was a widower; his wife had died ten years before. His daughter is a friend of Arlene's, a political activist, on the school board in L.A. "She has done a lot for black education and housing; she's one tough lady," Arlene said, so she must be, since that's what people always say about Arlene. The son is a client of Arlene's, and a different story. A district attorney in Seattle, he owns real estate all over Oakland. "I wouldn't say he is actually a slumlord, but . . ."

The son and daughter didn't get to the house until late morning, but I already knew a lot about them, from what Arlene told me, and from clues. The house was silent when I let myself in, that echoing silence of a house where nobody's home, where someone just died. The house itself was in a shabby neighborhood in West Oakland. It looked like a small farmhouse, tidy and pretty, with a porch swing, a well-kept yard with old roses and azaleas. Most of the houses around it had windows boarded up, were sprayed with graffiti. Groups of old winos watched me from sagging porch steps; young crack dealers stood on the corner or sat in cars.

Inside, too, the house seemed far removed from that neighborhood, with lace curtains, polished oak furniture. The old man had spent his time in a big sunroom at the back of the house, in a hospital bed and a wheelchair. There were ferns and African violets crammed on shelves on the windows and four or five bird feeders just outside the glass. A huge new TV and VCR, a compact disc player—presents from his children, I imagined. On the mantel was a wedding picture, he in a tux, his hair slicked back, a pencil-thin mustache. His wife was young and lovely, both were solemn. A photograph of her, old and white-haired, but with a smile, smiling eyes. Solemn the two children's graduation pictures, both handsome, confident, arrogant. The son's wedding picture. A beautiful blond bride in white satin. A picture of the two of them with a baby girl, about a year old. A picture of the daughter with Congressman Ron Dellums. On the bed table was a card that began, "Sorry I was just too tied up to make it to Oakland for Christmas . . ." which could have been from either one of them. The old man's Bible was open to Psalm 104. "The earth shall tremble at the look of him; if he do but touch the hills, they will smoke."

Before they arrived I had cleaned the bedrooms and bathroom upstairs. There wasn't much, but what was in the closets and linen cupboard I stacked in piles on one of the beds. I was cleaning the stairs, turned the vacuum off when they came in. He was friendly, shook my hand; she just nodded and walked up the stairs. They must have come straight from the funeral. He was in a three-piece black suit with a fine gold stripe; she wore a gray cashmere suit, a gray suede jacket. Both of them were tall, strikingly handsome. Her black hair was pulled back into a chignon. She never smiled; he smiled all the time.

I stood behind them as they went through the rooms. He took a carved oval mirror. They didn't want anything else. I asked them if there was anything they could give to the Home for Jewish Parents. She lowered her black eyes at me.

"Do we look Jewish to you?"

He quickly explained to me that people from the Rose of Sharon Baptist Church would be by later to get everything they didn't want. And the medical-supply place for the bed and wheelchair. He said he'd just pay me now, pulled off four twenties from a big stack of bills held by a silver clip. He said after I finished cleaning to lock up the house and leave the key with Arlene.

I was cleaning the kitchen while they were in the sunroom. The son took his parents' wedding picture, his own pictures. She wanted their mother's picture. So did he, but he said, No, go ahead. He took the Bible; she took the picture of her and Ron Dellums. She and I helped him carry the TV and VCR and CD player out to the trunk of his Mercedes.

"God, it's terrible to look at the neighborhood now," he said. She didn't say anything. I don't think she had looked at it. Back inside she sat in the sunroom and looked around.

"I can't picture Daddy watching birds, or taking care of plants," she said.

"Strange, isn't it? But I don't feel I ever knew him at all."

"He's the one who made us work."

"I remember him whipping you when you got a C in math."

"No," she said, "it was a B. A B-plus. Nothing I did was ever good enough for him."

"I know. Still . . . I wish I'd seen him more often. I hate it, how long it was since I came here . . . Yeah, I called him a lot, but . . ."

She interrupted him, telling him not to blame himself, and then they talked about how impossible it would have been for their father to have lived with either of them, how hard it was to get away from their jobs. They tried to make each other feel okay, but you could tell they felt pretty bad.

Me and my big mouth. I wish I would just shut up. What I did was say, "This sunroom is so pleasant. It looks like your father was happy here."

"It does, doesn't it?" the son said, smiling at me, but the daughter glared.

"It's none of your business, whether he was happy or not happy."

"I'm sorry," I said. Sorry I don't slap your mean old mouth. "I could use a drink," the son said. "There's probably nothing in the house."

I showed him the cupboard where there was brandy and some crème de menthe and sherry. I said how about they move into the kitchen and I could go through the cupboards, show them things before I put them into boxes. They moved to the kitchen table. He poured them both big drinks of brandy. They drank and smoked Kools while I went through the cupboards. Neither of them wanted anything, so it all got packed up quickly.

"There are some things in the pantry, though . . ." I knew because I had my eye on them. An old iron—carved wooden handle, made of black cast iron.

"I want that!" they both said. "Did your mother actually iron with that?" I asked the son. "No, she used it to make toasted ham-and-cheese sandwiches. And for corned beef, to press it down."

"I always wondered how people did that . . ." I said, talking away again, but I shut up because she was looking at me that way.

An old beat-up rolling pin, smoothed from wear, silken.

"I want that!" they both said. She actually laughed then. The drink, the heat in the kitchen had softened her hairdo, wisps curled around her face, shiny now. Her lipstick was gone; she looked like the girl in the graduation picture. He took off his coat and vest and tie, rolled up the sleeves of his shirt. She caught me checking out his fine build and shot me that dagger stare.

Just then Western Medical Supply came to get the bed and the wheelchair. I took them to the sunroom, opened the back door. When I got back the brother had poured them both another brandy. He leaned toward her.

"Make peace with us," he said. "Come stay for a weekend, get to know Debbie. And you've never seen Latania. She's beautiful, and she looks just like you. Please."

She was silent. But I could see death working on her. Death is healing, it tells us to forgive, it reminds us that we don't want to die alone.

She nodded. "I'll come," she said.

"Oh, that's great!" He put his hand on hers, but she recoiled, her hand moved, grabbed the table like a rigid claw.

Whoa, you are a cold bitch, I said. Not out loud. Out loud I said, "Now here's something you'll both want, I bet." A heavy old cast-iron waffle maker, the kind you put on top of the stove. My grand-mother Mamie had one. There's nothing like those waffles. Really crisp and brown outside and soft in the center. I put the waffle iron down between them.

She was smiling. "Now this is mine!" He laughed. "You'll have to pay a fortune in overweight luggage."

"I don't care. Do you remember how Mama would make us waffles when we were sick? With real maple syrup?"

"On Valentine's Day she'd make them in the shape of a heart."

"Only they never looked like hearts."

"No, but we'd say 'Mama, they're exactly like hearts!'"

"With strawberries and whipped cream."

There were other things I brought out then, roasting pans and boxes of canning jars that weren't interesting. The last box, on the top shelf, I put on the table.

Aprons. The old-fashioned bib kind. Handmade, embroidered with birds and flowers. Dish towels, embroidered too. All made from flour sacks or gingham from old clothes. Soft and faded, smelling of vanilla and cloves. "This was made from the dress I wore the first day of fourth grade!"

The sister was unfolding each apron and towel and spreading them all out on the table. Oh. Oh, she kept saying. Tears streaked down her cheeks. She gathered up all the aprons and towels and held them to her breast.

"Mama!" she cried. "Dear, dear Mama!"

The brother was crying now too and he went to her. He embraced her, and she let him hold her, rock her. I slipped out of the room and out the back door.

I was still sitting on the steps when a truck pulled up and three men from the Baptist church got out. I took them around to the front door and upstairs, and told them everything that was to go. I helped one man with the things upstairs, and then helped him load what was in the garage, tools and rakes, a lawn mower and a wheelbarrow.

"Well, that's it," one of the men said. The truck backed out and they waved good-bye. I went back inside. The house was silent. The brother and sister had gone. I swept up then and left, locking the doors of the empty house.

Panteón de Dolores

Not "Heavenly Rest" or "Serene Valley." Pantheon of Pain is the name of the cemetery at Chapultepec Park. You can't get away from it in Mexico. Death. Blood. Pain.

Torture is everywhere. In the wrestling matches, Aztec temples, racks of nails in the old convents, bloody thorns on Christ's heads in all the churches. Lord, now all the cookies and candies are made like skulls, since soon it will be the Day of the Dead.

That's the day Mama died, in California. My sister Sally was here, in Mexico City, where she lives. She and her children made an *ofrenda* to our mother.

Ofrendas are fun to make. Offerings to the dead. You make them as pretty as you can. Cascading and brilliant with marigolds and magenta velvets, a flower that looks like brains, and tiny purple *sempiternas*. The main idea about death here is to make it beautiful and festive. Sultry bleeding Christs, the elegance, the ultimate beautiful deadliness of bullfights, elaborately carved tombs, headstones for the graves.

On the *ofrendas* you place everything the dead person might be wishing for. Tobacco, pictures of his family, mangos, lottery tickets, tequila, postcards from Rome. Swords and candles and coffee. Skulls with friends' names on them. Candy skeletons to eat.

On our mother's *ofrenda* my sister's children had put dozens of Ku Klux Klan figures. She hated them for being the children of a

Mexican. Her *ofrenda* had Hershey bars, Jack Daniel's, mystery books, and many, many dollar bills. Sleeping pills and guns and knives, since she was always killing herself. No noose . . . she said she couldn't get the hang of it.

I am in Mexico now. This year we made a lovely *ofrenda*, for my sister Sally, who is dying of cancer.

We had masses of flowers, orange, magenta, purple. Many white votive candles. Statues of saints and angels. Tiny guitars and Paris paperweights. Cancún and Portugal. Chile. All the places she had been. Dozens and dozens of skulls with names and pictures of her children, of all of us who have loved her . . . A picture of Daddy in Idaho, holding her as a baby. Poems from the children who were her students.

Mama, you weren't in the *ofrenda*. We didn't omit you on purpose. We have, in fact, been saying affectionate things about you these past months.

For years, when Sally and I got together we ranted obsessively about how crazy and cruel you were. But these few months . . . well, I guess it is natural when one is dying to sort of sum up what has mattered, what has been beautiful. We have remembered your jokes and your way of looking, never missing a thing. You gave us that. Looking.

Not listening though. You'd give us maybe five minutes, to tell you about something, and then you'd say, "Enough."

I can't figure out why our mother hated Mexicans so much. I mean, well beyond the given prejudice of all her Texan relatives. Dirty, lying, thieving. She hated smells, any smells, and Mexico smells, even above the exhaust fumes. Onions and carnations. Cilantro, piss, cinnamon, burning rubber, rum, and tuberoses. The men smell in Mexico. The whole country smells of sex and soap. That's what terrified you, Mama, you and old D. H. Lawrence too. It's easy to get sex and death mixed up here, since they both keep pulsating away. A two-block stroll wafts sensuality, is fraught with peril.

Although today nobody is supposed to go outside at all, because of the pollution level.

My husband and sons and I lived for many years in Mexico. We were very happy during those years. But we always lived in villages, by the sea or in the mountains. There was such an affectionate ease, a passive sweetness there. Or then, as this was many years ago.

Mexico City now . . . fatalistic, suicidal, corrupt. A pestilential swamp. Oh, but there is a graciousness. There are flashes of such beauty, of kindness and of color, you catch your breath.

I went home two weeks ago, for a week, at Thanksgiving, back to the USA where there is honor and integrity and Lord knows what else, I thought. I got confused. President Bush and Clarence Thomas and antiabortion and AIDS and Duke and crack and homelessness. And everywhere, MTV, cartoons, ads, magazines—just war and sexism and violence. In Mexico, at least a can of cement falls off a scaffold on your head, no Uzis or anything personal.

What I mean is I'm here for an indefinite period. But then what, where will I go?

Mama, you saw ugliness and evil everywhere, in everyone, in each place. Were you crazy or a seer? Either way I can't bear to become like you. I am terrified, I am losing all sense of what is . . . precious, true.

Now I'm feeling like you, critical, nasty. What a dump. You hated places with the same passion you hated people . . . All the mining camps we lived in, the U.S., El Paso, your home, Chile, Peru.

Mullan, Idaho, in the Coeur d'Alene mountains. You hated that mining town the most, because there was actually a little town. "A cliché of a small town." A one-room school, a soda fountain, a post office, a jail. A whorehouse, a church. A little lending library at the general store. Zane Grey and Agatha Christie. There was a town hall, with meetings about blackouts and air raids.

You'd rant about the ignorant tacky Finns all the way home. We would stop for a *Saturday Evening Post* and a big Hershey bar before we climbed up the mountain to the mine, with Daddy holding our hands. Dark because the war just started and the windows in the town were blacked out, but the stars and snow were so bright we could see our way perfectly . . . At home Daddy would read to you until you fell asleep. If it was a really good story you would cry, not because it was sad, just so lovely and everything else in the world was tawdry.

My friend Kentshereve and I would be digging under the lilac bush while you were at the bridge game on Mondays. The three other women would wear housedresses, sometimes even stayed in socks and slippers. It was so cold in Idaho. Often they wore their hair in pin curls and a turban, getting their hair ready for—what? This still is an American custom. You see women everywhere in pink hair rollers. It's some sort of philosophical or fashion statement. Maybe there will be something better, later.

You always dressed carefully. Garter belt. Stockings with seams. A peach satin slip you let show a little on purpose, just so those peasants would know you wore one. A chiffon dress with shoulder pads, a brooch with tiny diamonds. And your coat. I was five years old and even then knew that it was a ratty old coat. Maroon, the pockets stained and frayed, the cuffs stringy. It was a wedding present from your brother Tyler ten years before. It had a fur collar. Oh the poor matted fur, once silver, yellowed now like the peed-on backsides of polar bears in zoos. Kentshereve told me everybody in Mullan laughed at your clothes. "Well, she laughs at all theirs worse, so there."

You'd come teetering up the hill in cheap high heels, your collar turned up around your carefully waved and marcelled bob. A gloved hand grasped the railing of the rickety wooden walk that rose past the mine and the mill. Inside in the living room you'd light the coal stove, kick off your shoes.

You sat in the dark, smoking, sobbing with loneliness and boredom. My mama, Madame Bovary. You read plays. You wished you had been an actress. Noel Coward. *Gaslight.* Anything the Lunts were in, memorizing the lines and saying them out loud while you washed the dishes. "*Oh!* I thought it was your step behind me, Conrad . . . No. Oh, I *thought* it was your step behind me, Conrad . . ."

When Daddy got home, filthy, in heavy miner's boots, a hat with a lamp, he would shower and you'd make cocktails from a little table, with an ice bucket and a seltzer shaker. (This seltzer bottle caused a lot of trouble. Daddy had to remember to buy the cartridges during his rare trips to Spokane. And most visitors resented it. "No, none of that there noisy water. Real water for me.") But that's what they used in plays, and in the *Thin Man* movies.

In *Mildred Pierce* Joan Crawford had a daughter called Sherry, and while the bad guy was spritzing his drink with seltzer he asked Joan Crawford what she wanted to drink.

"I'll take Sherry. Home," she said.

"What a wonderful line!" you said to me as we left the movie theater. "I think I'll change your name to Sherry, so I can use it."

"How about Cold Beer?" I asked. It was my first witticism. Anyway, it was the first time I made you laugh.

The other time was when Earl the delivery boy had brought a box of groceries from the store. I was helping to put them away. Our house was, in fact, a tar-paper shack, just like you said, and the kitchen floor sloped away to the bottom of the room in undulating waves of rotten linoleum and warped boards. I took out three cans of tomato soup and was going to put them in the cupboard but dropped them. They rolled down the floor and crashed against the wall. I looked up, thought you were going to yell, or hit me, but you were laughing. You took some more cans out of the cupboard and sent them rolling down too.

"Here, let's race!" you said. "My canned corn against your peas!"

We were squatting there, laughing, sailing cans down the room crashing them into the others when Daddy came home.

"Stop that this instant! Put those cans away!" There were lots of cans. (You hoarded them, because of the war, which was a bad thing to do, he said.) It took us a long time to get them all back in the cupboard, both giggling, in whispers, and singing "Praise the Lord and Pass the Ammunition" as you handed cans to me on the floor. It was the best time I ever had with you. We had just got them put away when he came to the door and said, "Go to your room." I went. But he meant for you to go to your room too! It didn't take long after that for me to see that when he sent you to your room it was because you had been drinking.

After that, for as long as I knew you, you were mostly in your room. Deerlodge, Montana; Marion, Kentucky; Patagonia, Arizona; Santiago, Chile; Lima, Peru.

Sally and I are in her bedroom now in Mexico, have been here most of the time for the last five months. We go out, sometimes, to the hospital for X-rays and lab tests, to have liquid aspirated from her lungs. Twice we have gone out to the Café Paris for coffee, and once to her friend Elizabeth's for breakfast. But she gets very tired. Even her chemo treatments are done in her room now.

We talk and read, I read out loud to her, people come to visit. The sun hits the plants for a little bit in the afternoon. About half an hour. She says that in February there is a lot of sun. None of the windows face the sky so the light is not direct, actually, but reflected from the wall next door. In the evening when it gets dark I close the curtains.

Sally and her children have lived here for twenty-five years. Sally isn't like our mother at all, in fact almost annoyingly the opposite, in that she sees beauty and goodness everywhere, in everyone. She loves her room, all the souvenirs on the shelves. We'll sit in the living room and she'll say, "That's my favorite corner, with the fern and the mirror." Or another time she'll say, "That's my favorite corner, with the mask and the basket of oranges."

Me, now, all the corners have me stir-crazy.

Sally adores Mexico, with the fervor of a convert. Her husband, her children, her house, everything about her is Mexican. Except her. She's very American, old-fashioned American, wholesome. In a way I am the more Mexican, my nature is dark. I have known death, violence. Most days I don't even notice that period when the room has sunlight in it.

When our father went to war Sally was just a baby. We went by train from Idaho to Texas to live with our grandparents for the Duration. *Duro* = Hard.

One thing that made Mama the way she was was that when she was little their life was very easy and gracious. Her mother and father were from the best Texan families. Grandpa was a wealthy dentist; they had a beautiful home with servants, a nanny for Mama, who spoiled her, as did three older brothers. Then wham bam she got run over by a Western Union boy and was in the hospital almost a year. During that year everything got worse. The Depression, Grandpa's gambling, his drinking. She got out of the hospital to find her world changed. A shabby house down by the smelter, no car, no servants, no room of her own. Her mother, Mamie, working as Grandpa's nurse, no longer playing mah-jongg and bridge. Everything was grim. And scary probably, if Grandpa did to her what he did to both Sally and me. She never said anything about it, but he must have, since she hated him so much, would never let anybody touch her, not even shake hands . . .

The train neared El Paso as the sun came up. It was awesome to see, the space, the wide-open spaces, coming from the dense pine forests. As if the world were uncovered, a lid taken off. Miles and miles of brightness and blue, blue sky. I ran back and forth from windows on each side of the club car that had finally opened, thrilled by this whole new face of the earth.

"It's just the desert," she said. "Deserted. Empty. Arid. And pretty soon we'll be pulling into the hellhole I used to call home."

Sally wanted me to help her get her house on Calle Amores in order. Sort photographs, clothes, and papers, fix shower curtain rods, windowpanes. Except for the front door, none of the doors had doorknobs; you had to use a screwdriver to get in the closets and prop the bathroom door shut with a basket. I called some work-men to come and put in doorknobs. They came and that was okay except they came on a Sunday afternoon while we were having a family dinner and they stayed until about ten at night. What happened was that they put on the doorknobs but didn't tighten any screws, so each doorknob that any of us tried fell off in our hands and then you couldn't open the closet doors at all. Also many screws rolled off and disappeared. I called the men the next day and a few days later they came in the morning, just when my sister had fallen asleep after a bad night. The three of them made so much noise I said forget it, my sister is sick, grave, and you're too loud. Come back another time. I went back into her room but later began to hear some huffing and panting and muffled thuds. They were taking all the doors off the hinges so they could carry them up to the roof to fix them without making any noise.

Am I really just mad because Sally's dying, so get mad at a whole country? The toilet is broken now. They need to take out the en-tire floor.

I miss the moon. I miss solitude.

In Mexico there is never not anyone else there. If you go into your room to read somebody will notice you're by yourself and go keep you company. Sally is never alone. At night I stay until I am sure she is asleep.

There is no guide to death. No one to tell you what to do, how it's going to be.

When we were little our grandmother Mamie took over Sally's care. At night Mama ate and drank and read mysteries in her room. Grandpa ate and drank and listened to the radio in his room. Actually Mama was gone most nights, with Alice Pomeroy and the Parker girls, playing bridge or in Juárez. During the day she went to Beaumont hospital to be a Gray Lady, where she read to blind soldiers and played bridge with maimed ones.

She was fascinated by anything grotesque, just like Grandpa was, and when she got back from the hospital she would call Alice and tell her about all the soldiers' wounds, their war stories, how their wives left when they found out they had no hands or feet.

Sometimes she and Alice went to a USO dance, looking for a husband for Alice. Alice never found a husband, worked at the Popular Dry Goods as a seam ripper until she died.

Byron Merkel worked at the Popular too, in lamps. He was supervisor of lamps. He was still madly in love with Mama after all these years. They had been in the Thespian Club in high school and starred in all the plays. Mama was very small, but still in all the love scenes they had to sit down because he was only five feet two. Otherwise he would have gone on to be a famous actor.

He took her to plays. *Cradle Song. The Glass Menagerie.* Sometimes he'd come over in the evenings and they'd sit on the porch swing. They'd read plays they performed in when they were young. I was always under the porch then in a little nest I had made with an old blanket and a cookie tin with saltines in it. *The Importance of Being Earnest. The Barretts of Wimpole Street.*

He was a teetotaller. I thought that meant he only drank tea, which was all he drank, while she drank Manhattans. That's what they were doing when I heard him tell her he was still madly in

love with her after all these years. He said he knew he couldn't hold
a candle to Ted (Daddy), another strange expression. He was always
saying, "Well, it's a long road to Ho," which I couldn't make out
either. Once, when Mama was complaining about Mexicans, he
said, "Well, give them an inch and they'll take an inch." The trouble with the things he said was he had a deep projecting tenor voice,
so every word seemed weighted with significance, echoed in my
mind. Teetotaller, teetotaller . . .

One night after he had gone home she came in, to the bedroom
where I slept with her. She kept on drinking and crying and scribbling, literally scribbling, in her diary.

"Are you okay?" I finally asked her, and she slapped me.

"I told you to stop saying 'okay'!" Then she said she was sorry
she got mad at me.

"It's that I hate living on Upson Street. All your Daddy ever
writes me about is his ship, and not to call it a boat. And the only
romance in my life is a midget lamp salesman!"

This sounds funny now, but it wasn't then when she was sobbing,
sobbing, as if her heart would break. I patted her and she flinched.
She hated to be touched. So I just watched her by the light of the
streetlamp through the window screen. Just watched her weep.
She was totally alone, like my sister Sally is when she weeps that
way.

So Long

I love to hear Max say hello.

I called him when we were new lovers, adulterers. The phone rang, his secretary answered and I asked for him. Oh, hello, he said. Max? I was faint, dizzy, in the phone booth.

We've been divorced for many years. He is an invalid now, on oxygen, in a wheelchair. When I was living in Oakland he used to call me five or six times a day. He has insomnia: once he called at three a.m. and asked if it was morning yet. Sometimes I'd get annoyed and hang up right away or else I wouldn't answer the phone.

Most of the time we talked about our children, our grandson, or Max's cat. I'd file my nails, sew, watch the A's game while we talked. He's funny, and a good gossip.

I have lived in Mexico City for almost a year now. My sister Sally is very ill. I take care of her house and children, bring her food, give her injections, baths. I read to her, wonderful books. We talk for hours, cry and laugh, get mad at the news, worry about her son out late.

It is uncanny, how close we have become. We have been together all day for so long. We see and hear things the same way, know what the other is going to say . . .

I rarely leave the apartment. None of the windows look out onto the sky, just onto air shafts or the apartments next door. You can see the sky from Sally's bed, but I only see it when I open and close her curtains. I speak Spanish with her and her children, everybody.

Actually Sally and I don't talk that much anymore. It hurts her lung to talk. I read, or sing, or we just lie together in the dark, breathing in unison.

I feel I have vanished. Last week in the Sonora market I was so tall, surrounded by dark Indians, many of them speaking in Nahuatl. Not only was I vanished, I was invisible. I mean for a long time I believed I wasn't there at all.

Of course I have a self here, and a new family, new cats, new jokes. But I keep trying to remember who I was in English.

That's why I'm so glad to hear from Max. He calls a lot, from California. Hello, he says. He tells me about hearing Percy Heath, about protesting the death penalty at San Quentin. Our son Keith made him eggs benedict on Easter Sunday. Nathan's wife, Linda, told Max not to phone her so much. Our grandson Nikko said he was falling asleep in spite of himself.

Max tells me the traffic and weather reports, describes the clothes on the Elsa Klensch show. He asks me about Sally.

In Albuquerque, when we were young, before I met him, I had listened to him play saxophone, watched him race Porsches at Fort Sumter. Everybody knew who he was. He was handsome, rich, exotic. Once I saw him at the airport, saying good-bye to his father. He kissed his father good-bye, with tears in his eyes. I want a man who kisses his father good-bye, I thought.

When you are dying it is natural to look back on your life, to weigh things, to have regrets. I have done this, too, along with my sister these last months. It took a long time for us both to let go of anger and blame. Even our regret and self-recrimination lists get shorter. The lists now are of what we're left with. Friends. Places.

She wishes she were dancing *danzón* with her lover. She wants to see the *parroquia* in Veracruz, palm trees, lanterns in the moonlight, dogs and cats among the dancers' polished shoes. We remember one-room schoolhouses in Arizona, the sky when we skied in the Andes.

She has stopped worrying about her children, what will become of them when she dies. I will probably resume worrying about mine after I leave here, but now we simply drift slowly through the patterns and rhythms of each new day. Some days are full of pain and vomit, others are calm, with a marimba playing far away, the whistle of the *camote* man at night . . .

I don't regret my alcoholism anymore. Before I left California my youngest son, Joel, came to breakfast. The same son I used to steal from, who had told me I wasn't his mother. I cooked cheese blintzes; we drank coffee and read the paper, muttering to each other about Rickey Henderson, George Bush. Then he went to work. He kissed me and said So long, Ma. So long, I said.

All over the world mothers are having breakfast with their sons, seeing them off at the door. Can they know the gratitude I felt, standing there, waving? The reprieve.

I was nineteen when my first husband left me. I married Jude then, a thoughtful man with a dry sense of humor.

He was a good person. He wanted to help me bring up my two baby sons.

Max was our best man. After the wedding, in the backyard, Jude went off to work, where he played piano at Al Monte's bar. My best friend Shirley, the other witness, left almost without speaking. She was very upset about me marrying Jude, thinking I had done it out of desperation.

Max stayed. After the children went to bed we sat around eating wedding cake and drinking champagne. He talked about Spain; I talked about Chile. He told me about the years in Harvard with Jude and Creeley. About playing saxophone when bebop began.

Charlie Parker and Bud Powell, Dizzy Gillespie. Max had been a heroin addict during those bebop days. I didn't know what that meant then, actually. Heroin to me had a nice connotation . . . Jane Eyre, Becky Sharp, Tess.

Jude played at night. He woke late in the afternoon, then he would practice or he and Max would play duets for hours and then we'd have supper. He went off to work. Max would help me do the dishes and put the children to bed.

I couldn't bother Jude at work. When there was a prowler, when the kids got sick, when I got a flat tire it was Max I called. Hello, he said.

Well, anyway, after a year we had an affair. It was intense and passionate, a big mess. Jude wouldn't talk about it. I left him to live by myself with the children. Jude showed up and told me to get into the car. We were going to New York, where Jude would play jazz and we would save our marriage.

We never did discuss Max. We both worked hard in New York. Jude practiced and jammed, played Bronx weddings, strip shows in Jersey until he got into the union. I made children's clothes that even sold at Bloomingdale's. We were happy. New York was wonderful then. Allen Ginsberg and Ed Dorn read at the Y. The Mark Rothko show at MoMA, during the big snowstorm. The light was intense from the snow through the skylights; the paintings pulsated. We heard Bill Evans and Scott LaFaro. John Coltrane on soprano sax. Ornette's first night at the Five Spot.

In the daytime, while Jude slept, the boys and I took the subway all over the city, getting off each day at new stops. We rode ferries, over and over. Once, when Jude was playing at Grossinger's, we camped out in Central Park. That's how nice New York was then, or how dumb I was . . . We lived on Greenwich Street down by the Washington Market, by Fulton Street.

Jude made a red toy box for the boys, hung swings from the pipes in our loft. He was patient and stern with them. At night when he got home we made love. All the anger and sadness and tenderness between us electric in our bodies. It was never spoken out loud.

At night when Jude was at work I read to Ben and Keith, sang them to sleep and then I sewed. I called the Symphony Sid program and asked him to play Charlie Parker and King Pleasure until he told me not to call so often. Summers were very hot and we slept on the roof. Winters were cold and there was no heat after five or on weekends. The boys wore earmuffs and mittens to bed. Steam came out of my mouth as I sang to them.

In Mexico now I sing King Pleasure songs to Sally. "Little Red Top." "Parker's Mood." "Sometimes I'm Happy."

It's pretty horrible when there is nothing else you can do.

In New York when the phone rang at night it was Max.

Hello, he said.

He was racing in Hawaii. He was racing in Wisconsin. He was watching TV, thinking of me. Irises were blooming in New Mexico. Flash floods in arroyos in August. Cottonwoods turned yellow in the fall.

He came to New York often, to hear music, but I never saw him. He would call and tell me all about New York and I would tell him all about New York. Marry me, he said, give me a reason to live. Talk to me, I said, don't hang up.

One night it was bitterly cold, Ben and Keith were sleeping with me, in snowsuits. The shutters banged in the wind, shutters as old as Herman Melville. It was Sunday so there were no cars. Below in the streets the sailmaker passed, in a horse-drawn cart. Clop clop. Sleet hissed cold against the windows and Max called. Hello, he said. I'm right around the corner in a phone booth.

He came with roses, a bottle of brandy, and four tickets to Acapulco. I woke up the boys and we left.

It's not true, what I said about no regrets, although I felt not the slightest regret at the time. This was just one of the many things I did wrong in my life, leaving like that.

The Plaza Hotel was warm. Hot, in fact. Ben and Keith got into the steaming bath with an expression of awe, as if into a Texan baptism. They fell asleep on clean white sheets. In the adjoining room Max and I made love and we talked until morning.

We drank champagne over Illinois. We kissed while the boys slept across from us and clouds billowed outside the window. When we landed, the sky above Acapulco was streaked coral and pink.

The four of us swam and then ate lobster and swam some more. In the morning the sun shone through the wooden shutters making stripes on Max and Ben and Keith. I sat up in bed, looking at them, with happiness.

Max would carry each boy to bed and tuck him in. Kiss him sweet, the way he had kissed his father. Max slept as deeply as they. I thought he must be exhausted from what we were doing, his leaving his wife, taking on a family.

He taught them both to swim and to snorkel. He told them things. He told me things. Just things, about life, people he knew. We interrupted one another telling him things back. We lay on the fine sand on Caleta Beach, warm in the sun. Keith and Ben buried me in the sand. Max's finger tracing my lips. Bursts of color from the sun against my closed sandy eyelids. Desire.

In the evenings we went to a park by the docks where they rented tricycles. Max and I held hands as the boys raced furiously around the park, flashing past pink bougainvillea, red canna lilies. Beyond them ships were being loaded on the docks.

One afternoon my mother and father, chatting away, walked up the gangplank to the S.S. *Stavangerfjord*, a Norwegian ship. My sister had written to me that they were traveling from Tacoma to

Valparaíso. My parents weren't speaking to me then, because of my marriage to Jude. I couldn't call out to them and say, Hi Mama! Hi Daddy! Isn't this a coincidence? This is Max.

But it made me feel good, to know my parents were right there. And now they were at the railings as the ship sailed out to sea. My father was sunburned and wore a floppy white hat. My mother smoked. Ben and Keith just kept riding faster and faster around the cement track, calling to each other, and to us . . . Look at me!

Today there was a big gas explosion in Guadalajara, hundreds of people killed, their homes destroyed. Max called to see if I was all right. I told him how everybody in Mexico thinks it's funny now to go around asking, "Say . . . do you smell gas?"

In Acapulco we made friends at the hotel. Don and Maria, who had a six-year-old daughter, Lourdes. In the evenings the children would color on their terrace until they fell asleep.

We stayed very late, until the moon grew high and pale. Don and Max played chess by the light of a kerosene lantern. Caress of moths. Maria and I lay crosswise on a big hammock, talking softly about silly things like clothes, about our children, love. She and Don had been married only six months. Before she met him she had been very alone. I told her how in the morning I said Max's name before I even opened my eyes. She said her life had been like a dreary record over and over each day and now in a second the record was turned over, music. Max overheard her and he smiled at me. See, *amor*, we're the flip side now.

We had some other friends too. Raúl the diver and his wife, Soledad. One weekend the six of us steamed clams on the terrace of our hotel. All the children had been sent to take naps. But one by one different children would pop up, wanting to watch what was going on. Back to bed! Another would want water, another just plain couldn't sleep. Back to bed. Keith came out and said he saw a giraffe! Now go back to bed, we'll wake you soon. Ben came out and said there were tigers and elephants. Oh for God's sake. But there it was in the street beneath us. A circus parade. We woke all the children then. One of the circus men thought Max was a movie star so they gave us free tickets. We all went to the circus that night. It was magical, but the children fell asleep before the end of the trapeze act.

There was an earthquake in California today. Max called to say that it wasn't his fault and he can't find his cat.

It was the ghostly setting moon that shone upon us as we made love that night. We lay next to each other then under the wooden revolving fan, hot, sticky. Max's hand on my wet hair. Thank you, I whispered, to God, I think . . .

In the mornings when I woke his arms would be around me, his lips against my neck, his hand on my thigh.

One day I woke before the sun came up and he wasn't there. The room was silent. He must be swimming, I thought. I went into the bathroom. Max was sitting on the toilet, cooking something in a blackened spoon. A syringe was on the sink.

"Hello," he said.

"Max, what is that?"

"It's heroin," he said.

That sounds like the end of a story, or the beginning, when really it was just a part of the years that were to come. Times of intense technicolor happiness and times that were sordid and frightening.

We had two more sons, Nathan and Joel. We traveled all over Mexico and the United States in a Beechcraft Bonanza. We lived in Oaxaca, finally settled in a village on the coast of Mexico. We were happy, all of us, for a long time and then it became hard and lonely because he loved heroin much more.

Not detox . . . Max says on the phone . . . Retox, that's what everybody needs. And Just say no? You should say No, thank you. He is joking, he hasn't been on drugs for many years now.

For months Sally and I worked hard trying to analyze our lives, our marriages, our children. She never even drank or smoked like I did.

Her ex-husband is a politician. He stops by almost every day, in a car with two bodyguards, and two escort cars with men in them. Sally is as close to him as I am with Max. So what is marriage anyway? I never figured it out. And now it is death I don't understand.

Not just Sally's death. My country, after Rodney King and the riots. All over the world, the rage and despair.

Sally and I write rebuses to each other so she doesn't hurt her lung talking. Rebus is where you draw pictures instead of words or letters. Violence, for example, is a viola and some ants. Sucks is somebody drinking through a straw. We laugh, quietly, in her room, drawing. Actually, love is not a mystery for me anymore. Max calls and says hello. I tell him that my sister will be dead soon. How are you? he asks.

A Love Affair

It was hard to tend to the front and back offices alone. I had to change dressings, take temperatures and blood pressures, and still try to greet new patients and answer the phones. A big nuisance because to do an EKG or assist in a wound stitching or a Pap smear I'd have to tell the answering service to take calls. The waiting room would be full, with people feeling neglected, and I'd hear the phones ringing ringing.

Most of Dr. B.'s patients were very old. Often the women who got Pap smears were obese, with difficult access, so it took even longer.

I think there was a law that said I had to be present when he was with a female patient. I used to think this was an outdated precaution. Not at all. Amazing how many of those old ladies were in love with him.

I would hand him the speculum and, later, the long stick. After he had the scrapings from the cervix he would smear them on the glass slide I held, which I would then spray with a protective film. I would cover the slide with another one, put it in a box and label it for the lab.

My main job was to get the women's legs high up into the stirrups and their buttocks moved down to the end of the table where they would be even with his eyes. Then I draped a sheet over their knees and was supposed to help the women relax. Chat and make jokes until he came in. That was easy, the chatting part. I knew the patients and they were all pretty nice.

The hard part was when he came in. He was a painfully shy man, with a serious tremor of his hands that occasionally manifested itself. Always when he signed checks or did Pap smears.

He squatted on a stool, eyes level with their vagina, with a light on his forehead. I handed him the (warmed) speculum and, after a few minutes, with the patient gasping and sweating, the long cotton-tipped stick. He held it, waving it like a baton, as he disappeared beneath the sheet, toward the woman. At last his hand emerged with the stick, now a dizzy metronome aimed at my waiting slide. I still drank in those days, so my hand, holding the slide, shook visibly as it tried to meet his. But in a nervous up-and-down tremble. His was back and forth. Slap, at last. This procedure took so long that he often missed important phone calls, and of course the people in the waiting room got very impatient. Once Mr. Larraby even knocked on the door and Dr. B. was so startled he dropped the stick. We had to start all over. He agreed then to hire a part-time receptionist.

If I ever look for another job, I'll ask for an enormous salary. If anyone works for as little as Ruth and I did, something is very suspicious.

Ruth had never had a job and she didn't need a job, which was suspicious enough. She was doing this for fun.

This was so fascinating to me that I asked her to lunch after the interview. Tuna melts at the Pill Hill Café. I liked her right off the bat. She was unlike anybody I had ever met.

Ruth was fifty, married for thirty years to her childhood sweetheart, an accountant. They had two children and three cats. Her hobbies, on the job application, were "cats." So Dr. B. always asked her how her cats were. My hobbies were "reading," so he'd say to me, "On the shores of Itchee Gumee" or "Nevermore, quoth the raven."

Every time there was a new patient he would write a few sentences on the back of the chart. Something he could use for conversation when he entered the exam room. "Thinks Texas is God's country." "Has two toy poodles." "Has five-hundred-dollar-a-day heroin habit." So when he went in to see them he'd say things like "Good morning! Been up to God's country lately?" or "You're out of luck if you think you can get drugs from me."

Over lunch Ruth told me that she had started to feel old and in a rut so she had joined a support group. The Merry Pranksters, or M.P., which really stood for Meno Pause. Ruth always said this like it was two words. The group was dedicated to putting more zip into women's lives. They focused on the members themselves. The last one had been Hannah. The group convinced her to go to Weight Watchers, to Rancho del Sol spa, take bossa nova lessons and then to get liposuction and a face-lift. She looked wonderful but was in two new groups now. One for women who had face-lifts but were still depressed and another for "Women Who Love Too Much." Ruth sighed, "Hannah's always been the kind of woman who has affairs with stevedores."

Stevedores! Ruth used some surprising words, like *heretofore* and *hullabaloo*. Said things like she missed having "That Time of the Month." It always was such a warm and cozy time.

The M.P. group had Ruth take flower arranging, join a theater group, a Trivial Pursuit club, and get a job. She was supposed to have a love affair but she hadn't thought about that yet. She already had zip in her life. She loved flower arranging, and now they were working on making bouquets with weeds and grasses. She had a bit part, nonsinging, in *Oklahoma!*.

I liked having Ruth in the office. We joked a lot with the patients and talked about them as if they were our relatives. She even thought filing was fun, singing, "Abcdefg hi jk lmnop lmnopqrst uvwxyZ!" until I'd say, "Stop, let *me* file."

It was easier now when I was with patients. But, in fact, she did very little work. She studied her Pursuit cards and called her

friends a lot, especially Hannah, who was having an affair with
the dance instructor.

On lunch hour I'd go with Ruth to collect weed bouquets,
scrambling hot and sweaty up the freeway embankment for Queen
Anne's lace and tobacco weed. Rocks in our shoes. She seemed
like an ordinary pretty middle-aged Jewish lady but there was a
wildness and freedom about her. Her shout when she spied a pink
rocket flower in the alley behind the hospital.

She and her husband had grown up together. Their families
were very close, some of the few Jews in a small Iowa town. She
couldn't remember when everybody didn't expect her and Ephraim
to marry. They fell in love for real in high school. She studied home
economics in college and waited for him to graduate in business
and accounting. Of course they had saved themselves for marriage.
They moved into his family home and cared for his invalid mother.
She had come with them to Oakland, was still living with them,
eighty-six years old now.

I never heard Ruth complain, not about the sick old lady or her
children or Ephraim. I was always complaining about my kids or
my ex-husband or a daughter-in-law and especially about Dr. B. He
had me open all his packages in case there were bombs in them.
If a bee or a wasp came in, he went outside until I killed it. These
are just the silly things. He was mean. Especially mean to Ruth,
saying things like "This is what I get for hiring the handicapped?"
He called her "Dyslexia," because she transposed phone numbers.
She did that a lot. About every other day he told me to fire her. I'd
tell him we couldn't. There was no cause. She really helped me
and the patients liked her. She cheered the place up.

"I can't stand cheeriness," he said. "Makes me want to slap the
grin off her face."

She continued to be nice to him. She thought he was like
Heathcliff, or Mr. Rochester in *Jane Eyre*, only little. "Yeah, real
little," I said. But Ruth never heard negative remarks. She believed

that someone, at some time, must have broken Dr. B.'s heart. She brought him kugel and rugelach and hamantaschen, was always thinking of excuses to go into his office. I hadn't figured out that she had chosen him to be the love affair until he came into my office and closed the door.

"You have to fire her! She is actually flirting with me! It is unseemly."

"Well, strange as it may seem, she finds you wildly attractive. I still need her. It's hard to find someone easy to work with. Be patient. Please, sir." The "sir" did it, as usual.

"All right," he sighed.

She was good for me, put zip in my life. Instead of spending my lunch hour brooding and smoking in the alley I'd get dirty and have fun picking bouquets with her. I even started cooking, using some of the hundreds of recipes she xeroxed all day. Baked pearl onions with a dash of brown sugar. She brought in clothes from Schmatta used clothing store and I bought them. A few times when Ephraim was too tired I went with her to the opera.

She was wonderful to go to the opera with, because at intermission she didn't just stand around looking bored like everybody does. She'd lead me around the main foyer so we could admire the clothes and jewels. I wept with her at *La Traviata*. Our favorite scene was the old woman's aria in *The Queen of Spades*.

One day Ruth asked Dr. B. to go to the opera with her. "No! What an inappropriate request!" he said.

"That asshole," I said when he went out the door. All she said was that doctors were just too busy to have love affairs so she guessed it would have to be Julius.

Julius was a retired dentist who had been in the cast of *Oklahoma!*. He was a widower and he was fat. She said fat was good, fat was warm and comfortable.

I asked her if it was because Ephraim was not so interested in sex anymore. *"Au contraire!"* she said. "It's the first thing he thinks of every morning and the last at night. And if he's home in the day he chases me around then too. Really . . ."

I saw Julius at Ephraim's mother's funeral at the Chapel of the Valley. The old woman had died quietly in her sleep.

Ruth and her family were on the steps of the funeral home. Two lovely children, handsome, gracious, comforting their parents, Ruth and Ephraim. Ephraim was darkly handsome. Lean, brooding, soulful. Now he looked like Heathcliff. His sad and dreamy eyes smiled into mine. "Thank you for your kindness to my wife."

"There he is!" Ruth whispered, pointing at red-faced Julius. Gold chains, a too-tight single-breasted blue suit. He must have been chewing Clorets gum, his teeth were green.

"You're crazy!" I whispered back to her.

Ruth had picked the Chapel of the Valley because the undertakers were our favorites. Dr. B.'s patients died often so almost every day some mortician came to get him to sign the death certificate. In black ink, the law required, but Dr. B. persisted in signing them with a blue pen, so the morticians had to drink coffee and hang around until he came back and signed them in black.

I waited in the rear of the chapel, wondering where to sit. Many Hadassah women had come; it was crowded. One of the chapel's morticians appeared next to me. "How lovely you look in gray, Lily," he said. The other one, with a boutonniere, came up the aisle and said in a low mournful voice, "How good of you to come, dear. Do let me find you a nice seat." I followed the two men down the aisle, feeling rather smug, like being known in a restaurant.

It was a beautiful service. The rabbi read the part in the Bible about the good wife being more precious than rubies. Nobody would have thought that about the old woman, I don't think. But I believed the eulogy was about Ruth and so did Ephraim and Julius, the way they were both gazing at her.

On Monday I tried to reason with her. "You are a woman who has everything. Health, looks, humor. A house in the hills.

A cleaning woman. A garbage compactor. Wonderful children. And Ephraim! He is handsome, brilliant, rich. He obviously adores you!"

I told her the group was steering her in the wrong direction. She shouldn't do anything to upset Ephraim. Thank her lucky stars. The M.P. were just jealous. They probably had alcoholic husbands, football-watching husbands, impotent or unfaithful ones. Their children carried beepers, were pierced, bulimic, drugged, tattooed.

"I think you're embarrassed to be so happy, are going to do this so you can share with the M.P.s. I understand. When I was eleven an aunt gave me a diary. All I wrote in it was: 'Went to school, Did homework.' So I started to do bad things in order to have something to write in it."

"It's not going to be a serious affair," she said. "It's just to pep things up."

"How about me having an affair with Ephraim? That would pep me up. You'd be jealous and fall madly in love with him again."

She smiled. An innocent smile, like a child's.

"Ephraim would never do that. He loves me."

I thought she had dropped the affair idea until one Friday she brought in a newspaper.

"I'm going out with Julius tonight. But I'm telling Ephraim that I'm going out with you. Have you seen any of these movies, to tell me about them?"

I told her all about *Ran*, especially when the woman pulls out the dagger, and when the fool weeps. The blue banners in the trees, the red banners in the trees, the white banners in the trees. I was really getting into it, but she said, "Stop!" and asked where we would go after the movie. I took us, them, to Café Roma in Berkeley.

She and Julius went out every Friday. Their romance was good for me. Usually I got home from work, read novels and drank 100-proof vodka until I fell asleep, day in day out. During the Love Affair I began to actually go to string quartets, movies, to hear

Ishiguro or Leslie Scalapino while Ruth and Julius went to the Hungry Tiger and the Rusty Scupper.

They went out for almost two months before they did You Know What. This event was going to occur in Big Sur, on a three-day trip. What to tell Ephraim?

"Oh, that's easy," I said. "You and I will go to a Zen retreat. No phones! Nothing to tell because we're just going to be silent and meditate. We'll sit in the hot springs under the stars. In the lotus position on cliffs overlooking the ocean. Endless waves. Endless."

It was annoying not to be able to go out freely those days, to screen my phone calls. But it worked. Ephraim took the children out to dinner, fed the cats, watered the plants, and missed her. Very very much.

On the Monday after the trip there were three big bouquets of roses in the office. One card said, "To my cherished wife with love." Another was from "Your secret admirer," and one card said, "She Walks in Beauty." Ruth confessed that she had sent that last one to herself. She adored roses. She had hinted to both men that she loved roses, but never dreamed they'd actually send any.

"Get rid of the funeral arrangements right now," Dr. B. said, on his way to the hospital. Earlier he had asked me again to fire her and again I had refused. Why did he dislike her so?

"I told you. She's too cheerful."

"I usually feel the same way about cheerful people. But hers is genuine."

"Christ. That's really depressing."

"Please, give her a chance. Anyway, I have a feeling she's going to be miserable soon."

"I hope so."

Ephraim stopped by to take Ruth to coffee. She had done nothing all morning, had been on the phone to Hannah. I could tell the main reason he had come was to see how she liked the roses. He was very upset about the other ones. She told him one was from a patient called Anna Fedaz, but then just giggled about the secret admirer. Poor guy. I watched jealousy hit him smack in the face, in the heart. Left hook to the gut.

He asked me how I had liked the retreat. I hate to lie, really can't stand lying. Not for moral reasons. It's so hard, figuring it out. Remembering what you have said.

"Well, it was a lovely place. Ruth is very serene and seemed to adapt perfectly to the atmosphere there. I find it hard to meditate. I just worry, or go back over every mistake I ever made in my whole life. But it was, er, centering. Serene. You and Ruth run along now. Have a nice lunch!"

Later I got the scoop. Big Sur had been *the* adventure of Ruth's life. She knew she wouldn't be able to tell the M.P.s about doing You Know What. Oral S. for the first time! Well, yes, she had done Oral S. to Ephraim, but never had it done to *her*. And M-A-R . . . "I know it has a *J* in it somewhere."

"Marijuana?"

"Hush! Well, mostly it made me cough and get nervous. Yes, that was very nice, Oral S. But the way he kept asking, 'Are you ready?' made me imagine we were going somewhere and ruined the mood."

They were going to Mendocino in two weeks. The story was that she and I were going to a writers' workshop and book fair in Petaluma. Robert Haas was to be the writer-in-residence.

One night in the middle of the week, she called and asked if she could come over. Like a fool I expected her, didn't understand that it was a cover, that she had gone to meet Julius. So when Ephraim phoned I could honestly sound cross because she still hadn't arrived, was even crosser the next time. "I'll have her call you the minute she gets here." After a while he called again, this time furious because she was home now and said I had not given her the message.

The next day I told her I wouldn't do this for her anymore. She said that was fine, that they were starting play practice on Monday.

"You and I are in a flower-arranging class on Fridays, at Laney. That's it."

"Well, that's the last one. You've been so lucky he hasn't asked any specifics."

"Of course he wouldn't. He trusts me. But my conscience is clear now. Julius and I don't do You Know What anymore."

"Then what *do* you do? Why go to all this secrecy and trouble to *not* do You Know What anymore?"

"We found out that neither one of us is a swinger type. I like You Know What with Ephraim much more, and Julius isn't that interested. I like the sneaking around part. He likes buying me presents and cooking for me. My favorite thing is to knock on a motel door in Richmond or somewhere and then he opens the door and I rush in. My heart beating away."

"So what do you do then?"

"We play Trivial Pursuit, watch videos. Sometimes we sing. Duets, like 'Bali Hai' or 'Oh, What a Beautiful Morning.' We go for midnight walks in the rain!"

"Walk in the rain on your own time!" Dr. B. shouted. We hadn't noticed him come in.

He was serious. He stood there while she packed up all her *Bon Appétit* magazines and Trivial Pursuit cards and her knitting. He told me to write her a check for two weeks' pay, plus what we owed her.

After Dr. B. left she called Julius, told him to meet her at Denny's right away.

"My career is ruined!" she sobbed.

She hugged me good-bye and left. I moved out to her desk, where I could see the waiting room.

Ephraim came in the door. He walked slowly toward me and shook my hand. "Lily," he said, in his deep enveloping voice. He told me that Ruth was supposed to have met him at the Pill Hill Café for lunch, but she never showed up. I told him that Dr. B.

had fired her, for no reason. She probably had completely forgotten lunch, had gone home. Or shopping, maybe.

Ephraim continued to stand there.

"She can find much better jobs. I'm the office manager, and of course I'll give her a good recommendation. I'll really miss her."

He stood there, looking at me.

"And she will miss you." He leaned in the little window above my desk.

"This is for the best, my dear. I want you to know that I understand. Believe me, I feel for you."

"What?"

"There are many things I don't share with her as you do. Literature, Buddhism, the opera. Ruth is a very easy woman to love."

"What are you saying?"

He held my hand then, looked deep into my eyes as his soft brown ones filled with tears.

"I miss my wife. Please, Lily. Let her go."

Tears began to slide down my cheeks. I felt really sad. Our hands were a warm wet little pile on the ledge.

"Don't worry," I said. "Ruth loves only you, Ephraim."

Let Me See You Smile

It's true, the grave is more powerful than a lover's eyes. An open grave, with all its magnets. And I say this to you, you who when you smile make me think of the beginning of the world.

—Vicente Huidobro, Altazor

Jesse threw me for a loop. And I take pride in my ability to size people up. Before I joined Grillig's firm, I was a public defender for so long I had learned to assess a client or a juror almost at first glance.

I was unprepared too because my secretary didn't announce him over the intercom and he had no appointment. Elena just led him into my office.

"Jesse is here to see you, Mr. Cohen."

Elena introduced him with an air of importance, using only his first name. He was so handsome, entered the room with such authority, I thought he must be some one-name rock star I hadn't heard of.

He wore cowboy boots and black jeans, a black silk shirt. He had long hair, a strong craggy face. About thirty was my first guess, but when he shook my hand there was an indescribable sweetness in his smile, an openness in his hazel eyes that was innocent and childlike. His raspy low voice confused me even more.

He spoke as if he were explaining patiently to a young inexperienced person. Me.

He said he had inherited ten thousand dollars and wanted to use it to hire me. The woman he lived with was in trouble, he said, and she was going to trial in two months. Ten counts against her.

I hated to tell him how far his money would go with me.

"Doesn't she have a court-appointed attorney?" I asked.

"She did, but the asshole quit. He thought she was guilty and a bad person, a pervert."

"What makes you think I won't feel the same way?" I asked.

"You won't. She says you are the best civil liberties lawyer in town. The deal is she doesn't know I'm here. I want you to let her think you're volunteering to do this. For the principle of the thing. This is my only condition."

I tried to interrupt here, to say, "Forget it, son." Tell him firmly that I wasn't going to do it. No way could he afford me. I didn't want to touch this case. I couldn't believe this poor kid was willing to give all his money away. I already hated the woman. Damn right she was guilty and a bad person!

He said that the problem was the police report, which the judge and jury would read. They would preconvict her because it was distorted and full of lies. He thought I could get her off by showing that his arrest was false, that the report of hers was libelous, the cop she hit was brutal, the arresting officer was psychotic, evidence had definitely been planted. He was convinced that I could discover that they had made other false arrests and had histories of brutality.

He had more to say about how I should handle this case. I can't explain why I didn't blow up, tell him to get lost. He argued passionately and well. He should have been a lawyer.

I didn't just like him. I even began to see that spending his entire inheritance was a necessary rite of passage. A heroic, noble gesture.

It was as if Jesse were from another age, another planet. He even said at some point that the woman called him "The Man Who Fell to Earth." This made me feel better about her somehow.

I told Elena to cancel a meeting and an appointment. He spoke all morning, simply and clearly, about their relationship, about her arrest.

I am a defense attorney. I'm cynical. I am a material person, a greedy man. I told him I would take the case for nothing.

"No. Thank you," he said. "Just please tell her that you're doing it for no charge. But it's my fault she got into this trouble and I want to pay for it. What will it be? Five thousand? More?"

"Two thousand," I said.

"I know that's too low. How about three?"

"Deal," I said.

He took off one of his boots and counted off thirty warm hundred-dollar bills, fanned them out on my desk like cards. We shook hands.

"Thanks for doing this, Mr. Cohen."

"Sure. Call me Jon."

He settled back down and filled me in.

He and his friend Joe were dropouts, had run away from New Mexico last year. Jesse played the guitar, wanted to play in San Francisco. On his eighteenth birthday he was to inherit money from an old woman in Nebraska (another heartbreaking story). He had planned to go to London, where he had been asked to join a band. An English group had played in Albuquerque, liked his songs and guitar playing. He and Joe had no place to stay when they got to the Bay Area, so he looked up Ben, who had been his best friend in junior high. Ben's mother didn't know they were runaways. She said it was okay for them to stay awhile in the garage. Later she found out and called their parents, calmed the parents down, told them they were doing fine.

It had all worked out. He and Joe did yard work and hauling, other odd jobs. Jesse played with other musicians, was writing songs. They got along great with Ben and with his mother, Carlotta. She appreciated how much time Jesse spent with her youngest kid Saul, taking him to ball games, fishing, climbing at Tilden. She taught school and worked hard, was glad too for help with laundry and carrying groceries and dishes. Anyway, he said, it was a good arrangement for everybody.

"I had met Maggie about three years before. They called her to our junior high in Albuquerque. Somebody had put acid in Ben's milk at lunch. He freaked out, didn't know what was happening. She came to get him. They let me and Joe go with her, in case he got violent. I thought she was going to take him to a hospital, but she drove us all down by the river. The four of us sat in the rushes, watching red-winged blackbirds, calming him down and actually helping him have a pretty cool trip. Maggie and I got along fine, talking about birds and the river. I usually don't talk much but with her there is always a lot I need to say."

I turned a recorder on at this point.

"So we stayed a month at their house in Berkeley, then another month. At night we'd all sit around the fire talking, telling jokes. Joe had a girlfriend by then and so did Ben so they'd go out. Ben was still a senior and he sold his jewelry and rock star photos on Telegraph, so I didn't see him much. Weekends I'd go to the marina or the beach with Saul and Maggie."

"Excuse me. You said her name was Carlotta. Who's Maggie?"

"I call her Maggie. At nights she'd grade papers and I'd play my guitar. We talked all night sometimes, our whole life stories, laughing, crying. She and I are both alcoholics, which is bad if you look at it one way, but good if you look at how it helped us say things to each other that we had never told anybody before. Our childhoods were scary and bad in exactly the same way, but like negatives of each other's. When we got together her kids freaked out, her friends said it was sick, incestuous. We are incestuous but in a weird way. It's like we are twins. The same person. She writes stories. She does the same thing in her stories that I do in my music. Anyway, every day we knew each other more deeply, so that when we finally ended up in bed it was as if we had already been inside each other. We were lovers for two months before I was supposed to leave. The idea was to get my money in Albuquerque on December 28, when I turned eighteen, and then go to London. She was making me go, said I needed the experience and we needed to split.

"I didn't want to go to London. I may be young but I know what she and I have together is galaxies beyond regular people. We know each other in our souls, all the bad and the good. We have a kindness to each other."

He told me then the story of going to the airport with her and Joe. Joe's belt knife and zippers had turned on the alarm at security, all three were strip-searched and Jesse missed the plane. He was hollering about his guitar and music being on the plane, got put into handcuffs, was being beaten by the police when Maggie came in.

"We all got arrested. It's in the report," he said. "The newspaper headline was 'Lutheran Schoolteacher, Hell's Angels in Airport Brawl.'"

"Are you a Hell's Angel?"

"Of course not. But the report says I am. Joe looks like one, wishes he was. He must have bought ten copies of that paper. Anyway, she and Joe went to jail in Redwood City. I spent a night in juvenile hall and then they sent me to New Mexico. Maggie phoned me on my birthday and told me everything was fine. She didn't say a word about any trial, and she didn't tell me she had been evicted and fired, that her ex-husband was taking her kids to Mexico. But Joe did, even though she told him not to. So I came back here."

"How did she feel about that?"

"She was furious. Said I had to leave and go to London. That I needed to learn and to grow. And she was believing all the shit about her being bad because I was seventeen when we got together. I seduced her. Nobody seems to get that part, except her. I'm not your typical teenager."

"True," I said.

"But anyway, we are together now. She agreed not to decide anything until after the trial. Not to look for a job or a place. What I'm hoping is by that time she'll go away with me."

He handed me the police report. "The best thing is for you to read this and then we'll talk. Come over for dinner. Friday okay? After you've read this. Maybe you can find out something about the cop. Both cops. Come early," he said, "when you get off work. We live just down the street."

Nothing applied anymore. I couldn't say it was inappropriate. That I had plans. That my wife might mind.

"Sure, I'll be there at six." The address he gave me was one of the worst blocks in town.

It was a beautiful Christmas. Sweet presents for each other, a great dinner. Keith invited Karen, one of my students. I guess it's childish, but it made me feel good for him to see how much she looked up to me. Ben's girlfriend Megan made mince pies. Both of them helped me with dinner and it was fun. Our friend Larry came. Big fire, nice old-fashioned day.

Nathan and Keith were so glad Jesse was leaving that they were really nice to him, even gave him presents. Jesse had made gifts for everyone. It was warm and festive, except then in the kitchen Jesse whispered, "Hey, Maggie, whatcha gonna do when I'm gone?" and I thought my heart would break. He gave me a ring with a star and a moon. By coincidence we each gave the other a silver flask. We thought it was great. Nathan said, "Ma, that's so disgusting," but I didn't hear him then.

Jesse's plane was leaving at six. Joe wanted to come along. I drove us to the airport in the rain. "The Joker" and "Jumpin' Jack Flash" on the radio. Joe was sipping from a can of beer and Jesse and I from a pint of Beam. I never gave it a thought, that I was contributing to their delinquency. They were drinking when I met them. They bought liquor, never got carded. The truth was I was so much in denial about my own drinking I wasn't likely to worry about theirs.

When we got inside the airport, Jesse stopped and said, "Christ. You two will never find the car." We laughed, not realizing it would be true.

We weren't exactly drunk, but we were high and excited. I was trying not to show how desperate I was about him leaving.

I realize now how much attention we must have attracted. All of us very tall. Joe, a dark Laguna Indian with long black braids, in motorcycle leather, a knife on his belt. Big boots, zippers and chains. Jesse in black, with his duffel bag and guitar. Jesse. He was otherworldly. I couldn't even glance up at him, his jaw, his teeth, his golden eyes, flowing long hair. I would weep if I looked at him. I was dressed up for Christmas in a black velvet pantsuit, Navajo jewelry. Whatever it was, the combination of us, plus all the buzzers that Joe's metal set off going through security . . . they saw us as a security risk, took us into separate rooms and searched us. They went through my underwear, my purse, ran their fingers through my hair, between my toes. Everywhere. When I got out of there I couldn't see Jesse, so I ran to the departure gate. Jesse's flight had left. He was yelling at the agent that his guitar was on the plane, his music was on the plane. I had to go to the bathroom. When I came out no one was at the ticket counter. The plane had gone. I asked somebody if the tall young man in black had made the plane. The man nodded toward a door with no sign on it. I went in.

The room was full of security guards and city police. It was sharp with the smell of sweat. Two guards were restraining Joe, who was handcuffed. Two policemen held Jesse and another was beating him on the head with a foot-long flashlight. A sheet of blood covered Jesse's face and soaked his shirt. He was screaming with pain. I walked completely unnoticed across the room. All of them were watching the policeman beating Jesse, as if they were looking at a fight on TV. I grabbed the flashlight and hit the cop on the head with it. He fell with a thud. "Oh Jesus, he's dead," another one said.

Jesse and I were handcuffed and then taken through the airport and down to a small police station in the basement. We sat next to each other, our hands fastened behind us to the chairs. Jesse's eyes were stuck shut with blood. He couldn't see and the wound on his scalp continued to bleed. I begged them to clean it or bandage it. To wash his eyes. They'll clean you up at Redwood City Jail, the guard said.

"Fuck, Randy, the dude's a juvenile! Somebody's got to take him over the bridge!"

"A juvenile? This bitch is in big trouble. I ain't taking him. My shift's almost over."

He came over to me. "You know the peace officer you hit? They have him in Intensive Care. He might die."

"Please. Could you wash his eyes?"

"Fuck his eyes."

"Lean down a little, Jesse."

I licked the blood off of his eyes. It took a long time; the blood was thick and caked, stuck in his lashes. I had to keep spitting. With the rust around them his eyes glowed a honey amber.

"Hey, Maggie, let me see your smile."

We kissed. The guard pulled my head away and slapped me. "Filthy bitch!" he said. Just then there was a lot of yelling and Joe got thrown in with us. They had arrested him for using obscene language in front of women and children. He had been angry when they wouldn't tell him anything about us.

"This one is old enough for Redwood City."

Since his arms were cuffed behind him, he couldn't hug us, so he kissed us both. Far as I remember he had never kissed either of us on the lips before. He said later it was because our mouths were so bloody it made him feel sad. The police called me a pervert again, seducing young boys.

I was disgusted by then. I didn't get it yet, didn't understand the way everyone would see me. I had no idea that my charges were adding up. One of the policemen read them to me from the counter across the room. "Drunk in public, interfering with arrest, assaulting a police officer, assault with a deadly weapon, attempted murder, resisting arrest. Lewd and lascivious behavior, sexual acts upon a minor (licking his eyes), contributing to the delinquency of minors, possession of marijuana."

"Hey, no way!" Joe said.

"Don't say anything," Jesse whispered. "This will work for us. Must have been planted. We had all just been searched, right?"

"Shit yeah," Joe said. "Plus we would have smoked it if we had it."

They took Jesse away. They put Joe and me in the back of a squad car. We drove miles and miles to the Redwood City jail. All I could think of was that Jesse was gone. I figured they would send him to Albuquerque and then he'd go to London.

Two nasty butch cops gave me a vaginal and rectal exam, a cold shower. They washed my hair with lye soap, getting it in my eyes. They left me without a towel or a comb. All they gave me to wear was a short short gown and some tennis shoes. I had a black eye and a swollen lip, from when they hit me after they took the flashlight away. The cop who took me downstairs had kept twisting the cuffs so there were open bloody cuts on both wrists, like stupid suicides.

They didn't let me have my cigarettes. The two whores and one wino with me let me have their last wet drags at least. Nobody slept or spoke. I shook all night from cold, from needing a drink.

In the morning we went in a bus to the courthouse. I talked through a window, by phone, to a fat red lawyer who read the report to me. The report was distorted and false all the way through.

"Advised of three suspicious characters in airport lobby. Woman with two Hell's Angels, one Indian. All armed and potentially dangerous." I kept telling him that things said in the report were total lies. The lawyer ignored me, just kept asking me if I was fucking the kid.

"Yes!" I finally said. "But that's just about the only thing I'm not charged with."

"You would have been if I had written it. Statutory rape."

I was so tired I got the giggles, which made him madder. Statutory rape. I get visions of Pygmalion or some Italian raping the Pietà.

"You're a sicko," he said. "You are charged with performing sexual acts upon a minor in public."

I told him I was trying to get the blood off Jesse's eyes so he could see.

"You actually licked it off?" he sneered.

I can imagine what hell prison must be. I could really understand how prisoners just learn to be worse people. I wanted to kill him. I asked him what was going to happen. He said I'd be arraigned and a court date would be set. I'd come in, plead innocent, hope that when we went to court we got a judge who was halfway lenient. Getting a jury in this town is a problem too. Far-right, religious people out here, hard on drugs, sex crimes. Hell's Angels were Satan to them and marijuana, forget it.

"I didn't have marijuana," I said. "The cop put it there."

"Sure he did. To thank you for sucking his dick?"

"So, are you going to defend me or prosecute me?"

"I'm your appointed defense lawyer. See you in court."

Joe was in court too, chained to a string of other men in orange. He didn't look at me. I was black and blue, my hair curled wild around my face and the shift barely covered my underpants. Later Joe actually admitted I looked so sleazy he had pretended he didn't know me. We both got assigned court dates in January. When his case got to court the judge just laughed and dropped the charges.

I had called home. It was hard enough telling Ben where I was. I was too ashamed to ask anyone to post bail, so I waited another day for them to let me out on my own recognizance. Stupidly I got that by having them call the principal where I taught. She was a woman who liked me, respected me. I still had no idea how people were going to judge me. It baffles me now how blind I was, but now I'm sober.

The police told me that Joe needed me to put up bond for him, so when I got out I went to a bondsman. It must not have been much, since I wrote him a check.

We figured out how to get to the airport. But it's like seeing Mount Everest. It just looked close. We walked in the rain, freezing cold, miles and miles. It took us most of the day. We laughed a lot, even after we tried to take a shortcut through a dog kennel. Climbing a fence with Dobermans barking and snarling beneath us. Abbott and Costello. No one would pick us up when we got to the freeway. Not true, some guy in a truck finally did, but we were almost there, waved him on.

This was the worst part of the entire situation. I'm serious. Trying to find the damn car. We went all the way around every vast level, up and up and then back down around and around then back up around and around until we both were crying. Just bawling away from being so tired and hungry and cold. An elderly black man saw us, and we didn't scare him even though we were soaked through and crying like fools. He didn't even mind us getting mud and water in his spotless old Hudson car. He drove up and down and around over and over saying that the good Lord would help us, surely. And when we found the car we all said, "Praise the Lord." When we got out he said to us, "God bless you." "God bless you and thank you," Joe and I said in unison, like a response in church.

"That dude is a fucking angel."

"He really is one," I said.

"Yeah, that's what I just said. A for-real angel."

There was more than half a pint of Jim Beam in the glove compartment. We sat there with the heater on and the windows steamed up, eating Cheerios and croutons from the bag for feeding ducks and finishing the bottle of whiskey.

"I'll admit it," he said. "Nothing ever tasted so good."

We were quiet all the way home in the rain. He drove. I kept wiping the steam off the windows. I asked him not to tell my kids or Jesse about all the charges or about the cop. It was a disturbing-the-peace problem, okay? Cool, he said. We didn't speak after that. I didn't feel guilty or ashamed, didn't worry about the trouble I was in or what I was going to do. I thought about Jesse being gone.

I tried to call Cheryl before I went to Jesse's, but she hung up on me, tried again but the machine was on. I was going to drive but worried about parking in their neighborhood. I was worried about walking in their neighborhood too. I guess it says something that I left my Porsche in the office garage, walked the seven or eight blocks to their apartment.

The downstairs door was graffitied plywood behind metal bars. They buzzed me into a dusty marble foyer, lit from a star-shaped skylight four stories up. It was still a beautiful tile-and-marble building, with a sweep of stairs, faded mirrors in art deco frames.

Someone slept against an urn; figures with their faces averted passed me on the stairs, all vaguely familiar from the courthouse or jail.

By the time I got to their apartment I was out of breath, sickened by smells of urine, cheap wine, stale oil, dust. Carlotta opened the door. "Come in," she smiled. I stepped into their technicolor world that smelled of corn bread and red chili, limes and cilantro and her perfume. The room had high ceilings, tall windows. There were oriental rugs on the polished wood floors. Huge ferns, banana plants, birds of paradise. The only furniture in this room was a bed with red satin sheets. Outside in the late sun was the golden dome of the Abyssinian Baptist Church, a grove of tall, old palm trees, the curve of the BART train. The view was like a vista in Tangiers. She let me absorb this for a minute, then she shook my hand.

"Thank you for helping us, Mr. Cohen. Eventually I'll be able to pay you."

"Don't worry about that. I'm glad to do it," I said, "especially now that I've read the report. It's an obvious distortion."

Carlotta was tall and tanned, in a soft white jersey dress. She looked around thirty, had what my mother used to call bearing. She was even more of a surprise than the apartment, than Jesse, well maybe not Jesse. I could see how the combination of them would be disturbing. I kept staring at her. She was a lovely woman. I don't mean pretty, although she was. Gracious. If we did end up going to trial, she would look terrific in court.

This would turn out to be only my first visit. I came back every Friday after that, walking, no, rushing from my office to their place. It was as if I had taken some drink, like Alice, or was in a Woody Allen movie. Not where the actor climbs down from the screen. I climbed up into it.

That first evening she led me into the other room, which had a fine Bokhara carpet, some saddlebags, a table set for three, with flowers and candles. "Angie" was playing on the stereo. These tall windows had bamboo blinds and the slight wind made shadows like banners on the walls.

Jesse called hello from the kitchen, came out to shake my hand. He was in jeans and a white T-shirt. They both glowed with color, had been at the estuary all day.

"How do you like our place? I painted it. Check out the kitchen. Baby-shit yellow, nice, no?"

"It is fantastic, this apartment!"

"And you like her. I knew you would." He handed me a gin and tonic.

"How did you . . . ?"

"I asked your secretary. I'm the cook tonight. You probably have questions to ask Maggie while I finish up."

She led me to the "terrace," a space outside the windows, above the fire escape, big enough for two milk crates. I did have dozens of questions. The report said she claimed to be a teacher. She told me about losing her job at a Lutheran high school, about being evicted. She was frank. She said the neighbors had been complaining for a long time, because there were so many of them living there, because of loud music. This had just been the last straw. She was glad her ex-husband took the three youngest to Mexico.

"I'm completely mixed up, messed up, right now," she said. It was hard to believe her because of her beautiful calm voice.

She briefly told me what happened at the airport, taking more blame for it than Jesse had given her. "As far as the charges, I am guilty of them, except the marijuana, they planted that. But the way they *describe* it is sick. Like Joe *did* kiss us both, but from friendship. I don't have any sex ring with young boys. What was sick and wrong was how the cop was beating Jesse, and how others stood there watching it. Any normal person would have done what I did. Although, thank God, the cop didn't die."

I asked her what she was going to do after the trial. She looked panicked, whispered what Jesse had told me in the office, that they had decided not to deal with it until the trial.

"But I can get it together. Get myself together then." She said she spoke Spanish, thought about applying at hospitals for jobs, or as a court translator. She had worked for almost a year on a trial in New Mexico, had good references. I knew the case, and the judge and lawyer she had worked with. Famous case . . . an addict who shot a narc five times in the back and got off with manslaughter. We talked about that brilliant defense for a while, and I told her where to write about court translating.

Jesse came out with some guacamole and chips, a fresh drink for me, beers for them. She slid to the ground and he sat. She leaned back against his knees. He held her throat with one fine long-fingered hand, drank his beer with the other.

I will never forget it, the way he held her throat. The two of them were never flirtatious or coy, never made erotic or even demonstrative gestures, but their closeness was electric. He held her throat. It wasn't a possessive gesture; they were fused.

"Of course, Maggie can get a dozen jobs. And she can find a house and her kids can all come home. Thing is they are better off without her. Sure they miss her and she misses them. She was a good mother. She raised them right, gave them character and values, a sense of who they are. They are confident and honest. They laugh a lot. Now they are with their daddy, who is very rich. He can send them to Andover and Harvard, where he went. Rest of the time they can sail and fish and scuba dive. If they come back to her, I'll have to leave. And if I leave, she'll drink. She won't be able to stop and that will be a terrible thing."

"What will you do if you leave?"

"Me? Die."

The setting sun was in her brilliant blue eyes. Tears filled her eyes, caught in the lashes and didn't fall, reflected the green palms so that it looked like she was wearing turquoise goggles.

"Don't cry, Maggie," he said. He tilted her head back and drank the tears.

"How could you tell she was crying?" I asked.

"He always knows," she said. "At night, in the dark when I'm facing away from him, I can smile and he'll say, 'What's so funny?'"

"She's the same. She can be out cold. Snoring. And I'll grin. Her eyes will pop open and she'll be smiling back at me."

We had dinner then. A fantastic meal. We talked about everything but the trial. I can't remember how I got started on stories about my Russian grandmother, dozens of stories about her. I hadn't laughed so hard in years. Taught them the word *shonda*. What a *shonda*!

Carlotta cleared the table. The candles were halfway down. She came back with coffee and flan. As we were finishing, she said, "Jon, may I call you Counselor?"

"God, no," Jesse said. "That sounds like junior high. He'll ask me where my anger comes from. Let's call him Barrister. Barrister, have you given some thought to this lady's plight?"

"I have, my good man. Let me get my briefcase and I'll show you just where we stand."

I said yes to a cognac. They both were drinking whiskey and water now. I was excited. I wanted to be matter-of-fact, but I was too pleased. I went through the document and compared it with a three-page list of untrue, misleading, libelous, or slanderous statements from the report. "Lewd," "wanton behavior," "lascivious manner," "threatening," "menacing," "armed and dangerous." Pages of statements that could prejudice a judge and jury against my client, which in fact had given me a distorted idea of her even after talking with Jesse.

I had a copy from airport security saying that she and her clothing and bag had been thoroughly searched and no drugs or weapons had been found.

"The best part, though, is that you were right, Jesse. Both these guys have long lists of serious violations. Suspensions for improper

use of force, beating suspects. Two separate investigations for killing unarmed suspects. Many, many complaints of brutality, exces-
sive force, false arrest, and manufacturing evidence. And this is
only after a few days' research! We do know that both these cops
have had serious suspensions, were demoted, sent from beats in
the city to South San Francisco. We will insist upon Internal
Affairs investigations of the arresting officers, threaten to sue the
San Francisco Police Department."

"So, let's not just threaten them, let's do it," Jesse said.

I would get to learn that drink gave him courage but it made her
more fragile. She shook her head. "I couldn't go through with it."

"Bad idea, Jesse," I said. "But it is a good way to handle the case."

The court date wasn't until the end of June. Although my aides
continued to get more evidence against the policemen, there
wasn't much we needed to discuss. If the case wasn't dismissed,
then we'd have to postpone the trial and, well, pray. But I still went
over to the Telegraph apartment every Friday. It made my wife,
Cheryl, furious and jealous. Except for handball games, this was
the first time I ever went anywhere without her. She didn't understand why she couldn't come too. And I couldn't explain, not even
to myself. Once she even accused me of having an affair.

It was like an affair. It was unpredictable and exciting. Fridays
I would wait all day until I could go over there. I was in love with
all of them. Sometimes Jesse, Joe, and Carlotta's son Ben and I
would play poker or pool. Jesse taught me to be a good poker player,
and a good pool player. It made me feel childishly cool to go with
them into downtown pool halls and not be afraid. Joe's mere presence made us all safe anywhere.

"He's like having a pit bull, only cheaper to feed," Jesse said.

"He's good for other things," Ben said. "He can open bottles with
his teeth. He's the best laugher there is." That was true. He rarely
spoke, but caught humor immediately.

Sometimes we walked with Ben in downtown Oakland while
he took photographs. Carlotta got us to make frames with our

hands, look at things as if through a lens. I told Ben it had changed my way of seeing.

What Joe liked to do was to sneak into photographs. When the contacts were printed, there he'd be sitting on a stoop with some winos or looking lost in a doorway, arguing with a Chinese butcher about a duck.

One Friday, Ben brought a Minolta, told me he'd sell it to me for fifty dollars. Sure. I was delighted. Later I noticed that he gave the money to Joe, which made me wonder.

"Play with it before you get any film. Just walk around at first, looking through it. Half the time I don't have any film in my camera."

The first photographs I took were at a store only a few blocks from my office. It sells one-shoes for a dollar each. One side of the room has piles of old left shoes, the right side has right shoes. Old men. Poor young men. The old shoe seller in a rocking chair putting the money in a Quaker Oats box.

That first roll of film made me happier than anything in a long time, even a good trial. When I showed them the prints, they all high-fived me. Carlotta hugged me.

Ben and I went out together several times, early in the morning, in Chinatown, the warehouse district. It was a good way to get to know someone. I'd be focusing on little kids in school uniforms, he'd be taking an old man's hands. I told him I felt uncomfortable taking people, that it seemed intrusive, rude.

"Mom and Jesse helped me with this. They always talk to everybody, and people talk back. If I can't get a picture without the person seeing me now I'll just talk to them, come right out and ask, 'Do you mind if I take your picture?' Most of the time they say, 'Of course I mind, asshole.' But sometimes they don't mind."

A few times we talked about Carlotta and Jesse. Since they all got along so well, I was surprised by his anger.

"Well, sure I'm mad. Part of it is childish. They're so tight I feel left out and jealous, like I lost my mother and my best friend. But another part of me thinks it's good. I never saw either one of them happy before. But they're feeding each other's destructive side, the part that hates themselves. He hasn't played, she hasn't written since they moved to Telegraph. They're going through his money like water, drinking it mostly."

"I never get the feeling that they are drunk," I said.

"That's because you've never seen them sober. And they don't really start drinking until we've gone. Then they career around town, chasing fire trucks, doing God knows what. Once they got into the U.S. Mail depot and were shot at. At least they're nice drunks. They are incredibly sweet to each other. She never was mean to us kids, never hit us. She loves us. That's why I can't understand why she's not getting my brothers back."

Another time, on Telegraph, he showed me the words to a song Jesse had written. It was fine. Mature, ironic, tender. Reminded me of Dylan, Tom Waits, and Johnny Cash mixed together. Ben also handed me an *Atlantic Monthly* with a story of hers in it. I had read the story a few months before, had thought it was great. "You two wrote these fine things?" They both shrugged.

What Ben said had made sense, but I didn't see any self-hatred or destructiveness. Being with them seemed to bring out a positive side of me, a corny side.

Carlotta and I were alone on the terrace. I asked her why being there made me feel so good. "Is it simply because they are all young?"

She laughed. "None of them are young. Ben was never young. I was never young. You probably were an old child too, and you like us because you can act out. It is heaven to play, isn't it? You like coming here because the rest of your life vanishes. You never mention your wife, so there must be troubles there. Your job must be troubles. Jesse gives everybody permission to be themselves and to think about themselves. That it's okay to be selfish.

"Being with Jesse is sort of a meditation. Like sitting zazen, or being in a sensory deprivation tank. The past and future disappear. Problems and decisions disappear. Time disappears and the present acquires an exquisite color and exists within a frame of only now this second, exactly like the frames we make with our hands."

I saw she was drunk, but still I knew what she meant, knew she was right.

For a while, Jesse and Maggie slept every night on a different roof downtown. I couldn't imagine why they did this, so they took me to one. First we found the old metal fire escape, and Jesse jumped high up and pulled it down. Once we were up the stairs and onto the ladder, he pulled the stairs up after us. Then we climbed, high. It was eerie and magical looking out onto the estuary, the bay. There was still a faint pink sunset beyond the Golden Gate Bridge. Downtown Oakland was silent and deserted. "On weekends, it's just like *On the Beach* down here," Jesse said.

I was awed by the silence, by the sense of being the only ones there, the city beneath us, the sky all around. I was not sure where we were until Jesse called me over to a far ledge. "Look." I looked, and then I got it. It was my office, on the fifteenth floor of the Leyman Building, a few floors above us. Only a few windows away was Brillig's. The small tortoise-shaded light was on. Brillig sat at his big desk with his jacket and tie off, his feet on a hassock. He was reading. Montaigne probably, because the book was bound in leather and he was smiling.

"This isn't a nice thing to do," Carlotta said. "Let's go."

"Usually you love to look at people in windows."

"Yes, but if you know who they are it is not imagining but spying."

Going back down the fire escape I thought that this typical argument was why I liked them. Their arguments were never petty.

Once I arrived when Joe and Jesse were still out fishing. Ben was there. Maggie had been crying. She handed me a letter from her fifteen-year-old, Nathan. A sweet letter, telling her what they all were doing, saying that they wanted to come home.

"So, what do you think?" I asked Ben when she went to wash her face.

"I wish they'd get rid of the idea that it's Jesse or the kids. If she got a job and a house, stopped drinking, if he'd come by once in a while, they'd see it could be okay. It *could* be okay. Trouble is they're both scared that if the other one sobers up, they'll leave."

"Will she stop drinking if he leaves?"

"God no. I hate to think about that."

Ben and Joe went to a ball game that night. Joe always referred to them as the "fuckin' A's."

"*Midnight Cowboy*'s on TV. Want to come watch it?" Jesse asked. I said, sure, I loved that film. I thought they meant to go to a bar, forgetting about his age. No, they meant the Greyhound bus station, where we sat in adjoining seats, each with a little TV set we put quarters in. During the commercials Carlotta got more quarters, popcorn. Afterward we went to a Chinese restaurant. But it was closing. "Yes, we always arrive when it's closing. That's when they order takeout pizza." How they had originally found this out I can't imagine. They introduced me to the waiter and we gave him money. Then we sat around a big table with the waiters and chefs and dishwashers, eating pizzas and drinking Cokes. The lights were off; we ate by candlelight. They were all speaking Chinese, nodding to us as they passed around different kinds of pizza. I felt somehow that I was in a real Chinese restaurant.

The next night Cheryl and I were meeting friends for dinner in Jack London Square. It was a balmy night, the top was down on the Porsche. We had had a good day, made love, lazed around in bed. As we got near the restaurant, Cheryl and I were laughing, in a good mood. We got stopped by one of the freight trains that invariably crawled through the Square. This one went on and on. I heard a shout.

"Counselor! Jon! Hey, Barrister!" Jesse and Carlotta were waving to me from a boxcar, blowing kisses.

"Don't tell me," Cheryl said. "That must be Peter Pan and his ma." She said, "Jon's personal Bonnie and Clyde."

"Shut up."

I had never said that to her before. She stared straight ahead, as if she hadn't heard me. We went to the elegant restaurant with our elegant, articulate liberal friends. The food was excellent, the wines perfect. We talked about films and politics and law. Cheryl was charming; I was witty. Something terrible had happened between us.

Cheryl and I are divorced now. I think our marriage began to end because of those Friday nights, not because she began having an affair. She was furious because I never took her to meet them. I'm not sure why I didn't want to, whether I was afraid she would dislike them, or they would dislike her. Something else . . . some part of me that I was ashamed to let her see.

Jesse and Carlotta had already forgotten the boxcar when I next saw them.

"Maggie's hopeless. We could learn how to do it. We could travel all over the USA. But every time we start clickety clacking along, she gets hysterical. We've only got as far as Richmond and Fremont."

"No, once to Stockton. Far. It's terrifying, Jon. Although lovely too, and you do feel free, like it's your own personal train. Problem is nothing scares Jesse. What if we ended up in North Dakota in a blizzard and they locked us in? There we'd be. Frozen."

"Maggie, you can't be worrying so much. Look what you do to yourself! Got your shorts in a knot about some snowstorm in South Dakota."

"North Dakota."

"Jon, tell her not to worry so much."

"Everything is going to work out, Carlotta," I said. But I was frightened too.

•

We checked out the watchman at the marina. At seven thirty he was always at the other end of the piers. We'd toss our gear over and then climb the fence, down by the water where it wasn't wired for an alarm. It took us a few times before we found our perfect boat, *La Cigale*. A beautiful big sailboat with a teak deck. Low in the water. We'd spread out our sleeping bag, turn the radio on low, eat sandwiches and drink beer. Sip whiskey later. It was cool and smelled like the ocean. A few times the fog lifted and we saw stars. The best part was when the huge Japanese ships filled with cars came up the estuary. Like moving skyscrapers, all lit up. Ghost ships gliding past not making a sound. The waves they made were so big they were silent, rolling, not splashing. There were never more than one or two figures on any of the decks. Men alone, smoking, looking out at the city with no expression at all.

Mexican tankers were just the opposite. We could hear the music, smell the smoky engines before we saw the rusty ships. The whole crew would be hanging off the sides, waving to girls on terraces of restaurants. The sailors were all laughing or smoking or eating. I couldn't help it, once I called out *Bienvenidos!* to them, and the watchman heard me. He came over and shone his flashlight at us.

"I seen you two here a coupla times. Figured you weren't hurtin' nobody, and weren't stealing, but you could get me in a mess of trouble."

Jesse motioned for him to come down. He even said, "Welcome aboard." We gave him a sandwich and a beer and told him if we got caught, we'd be sure to show there was no way he would have seen us. His name was Solly. He came every night then, for dinner at eight, and then he'd go on his rounds. He'd wake us early in the morning, before light, just as the birds were starting to whirr above the water.

Sweet spring nights. We made love, drank, talked. What did we talk about so much? Sometimes we'd talk all night long. Once we talked about the bad things from when we were little. Even

acted them out with each other. It was sexy, scary. We never did it
again. Our conversations were about people, mostly, the ones we
met walking around town. Solly. I loved hearing him and Jesse tell
about farmwork. Solly was from Grundy Center, Iowa, had been
stationed at Treasure Island when he was in the navy.

Jesse never read books, but words people said made him happy.
A black lady who told us she was as old as salt and pepper. Solly
saying he up and left his wife when she started gettin' darty-eyed
and scissor-billed.

Jesse made everybody feel important. He wasn't kind. *Kind* is a
word like *charity*; it implies an effort. Like that bumper sticker about
random acts of kindness. It should mean how someone always is,
not an act he chooses to do. Jesse had a compassionate curiosity
about everyone. All my life I have felt that I didn't really exist at
all. He saw me. I. He saw who I was. In spite of all the dangerous
things we did, being with him was the only time I was ever safe.

The dumbest dangerous thing we did was swim out to the island in Lake Merritt. We put all our gear—change of clothes, food,
whiskey, cigarettes—in plastic and swam out to it. Farther than it
looks. The water was really cold, stinking foul dirty, and we stank
too, even when we changed clothes.

The park is beautiful during the day, rolling hills and old oak
trees, the rose garden. At night it throbbed with fear and mean-
ness. Horrible sounds came magnified to us across the water. Angry fucking and fighting, bottles breaking. People retching and
screaming. Women getting slapped. The police and grunts, blows.
The now familiar sound of police flashlights. Lap lap the waves
against our little wooded island, but we shivered and drank until
it quieted down enough for us to dare swim for shore. The water
must have been really polluted, we were both sick for days.

Ben showed up one afternoon. I was alone. Joe and Jesse had
gone to play pool. Ben grabbed me by the hair and took me to the
bathroom.

"Look at your drunk self! Who are you? What about my brothers? Dad and his girl are on cocaine. Maybe with you they'd die in a car wreck or you'd burn the house down, but at least they wouldn't think drinking was glamorous. They need you. I need you. I need not to hate you." He was sobbing.

All I could do was what I had done a million times before. Say over and over, "I'm sorry."

But when I told Jesse we had to stop, he said okay. Why not smoking too, while we were at it. We told the guys we were going backpacking near Big Sur. We drove down the hairpin Highway 1 above the water. There was a moon and the foam of the ocean was neon white. Jesse drove with the lights off, which was terrifying and the start of our fighting. After we got there and up in the woods it began to rain. It rained and rained and we fought more, something about ramen noodles. It was cold but we both had bad shakes on top of that. We only lasted one night. We drove home and got drunk, tapered off before trying again.

This time was better. We went to Point Reyes. It was clear and warm. We watched the ocean for hours, quiet. We hiked in the woods, ran on the beach, told each other how great pomegranates tasted. We had been there about three days when we were awakened by weird grunts. Thrashing toward us in the foggy woods were these creatures, like aliens with oblong heads, making guttural sounds, weird laughs. They walked stiff-legged and with a rocking gait. "Good morning. Sorry to disturb you," a man said. The group turned out to be severely retarded teenagers. Their elongated heads were actually rolled-up sleeping bags on top of their packs. "Christ, I need a smoke," Jesse said. It was good to get home to Telegraph. We still didn't drink.

"Amazing how much time drinking took up, no, Maggie?"

We went to movies. Saw *Badlands* three times. Neither of us could sleep. We made love day and night, as if we were furious at each other, sliding off the silk sheets onto the floor, sweating and spent.

One night Jesse came into the bathroom when I was reading a letter from Nathan. He said they had to come home. Jesse and I fought all night. Really fought, hitting and kicking and scratching until we ended up sobbing in a heap. We ended up getting really drunk for days, the craziest we ever got. Finally I was so poisoned with alcohol that a drink didn't work, didn't make me stop shaking. I was terrified, panicked. I believed that I was not capable of stopping, of ever taking care of myself, much less my children.

We were crazy, made each other crazier. We decided neither of us was fit to live. He'd never make it as a musician, had already blown it. I had failed as a mother. We were hopeless alcoholics. We couldn't live together. Neither one of us was fit for this world. So we would just die. It is awkward to write this. It sounds so selfish and melodramatic. When we said it, it was a horrible bleak truth.

In the morning we got in the car, headed for San Clemente. I'd arrive at my parents' house on Wednesday. On Thursday I'd go to the beach and swim out to sea. This way it would be an accident and my parents could deal with my body. Jesse would drive back and hang himself on Friday, so Jon could find him.

We had to taper off drinking just to make the trip. We called Jon, Joe, and Ben, to let them know we were going away, would see them next Friday. We took a slow trip down. It was a wonderful trip. Swimming in the ocean. Carmel and Hearst's Castle. Newport Beach.

Newport Beach was so great. The motel lady knocked on our door and said to me, "I forgot to give your husband the towels."

We were watching *Big Valley* when Jesse said, "What do you think? Shall we get married or kill ourselves?"

We were close to my parents' house when we got into a ridiculous fight. He wanted to see Richard Nixon's house before he dropped me off. I said that I didn't want one of the last acts in my lifetime to be seeing Nixon's house.

"Well, fuck off, get out here then."

I told myself that if he said he loved me I wouldn't get out, but he just said, "Let me see your smile, Maggie." I got out, got my suitcase from the backseat. I couldn't smile. He drove off.

My mother was a witch; she knew everything. I hadn't told them about Jesse. I had told them I had been laid off at school, the kids were in Mexico, that I was job hunting. But I had only been there for an hour when she said, "So, you planning to commit suicide, or what?"

I told them I was depressed about finding a job, that I missed my sons. I had thought a visit with them would be a good idea. But it just made me feel that I was procrastinating. I'd better go back in the morning. They were pretty sympathetic. We all were drinking a lot that evening.

The next morning my father drove me to John Wayne Airport and bought me a ticket for Oakland. He kept saying that I should be a receptionist in a doctor's office, where I'd get benefits.

I was on the MacArthur bus headed for Telegraph about the time I was supposed to be drowning. I ran the blocks from Fortieth Street home, terrified now that Jesse had died already.

He wasn't home. There were lilac tulips everywhere. In vases and cans and bowls. All over the apartment, the bathroom, the kitchen. On the table was a note, "You can't leave me, Maggie."

He came up behind me, turned me around against the stove. He held me and pulled up my skirt and pulled down my underpants, entered me and came. We spent the whole morning on the kitchen floor. Otis Redding and Jimi Hendrix. "When a Man Loves a Woman." Jesse made us his favorite sandwich. Chicken on Wonder Bread with mayonnaise. No salt. It's an awful sandwich. My legs were shaking from making love, my face sore from smiling.

We took a shower and got dressed, spent the night up on our own roof. We didn't talk. All he said was "It's much worse now." I nodded into his chest.

Jon arrived the next night, then Joe and Ben. Ben was pleased that we weren't drinking. We hadn't decided not to, just hadn't. Of course they all asked about the tulips.

"Place needed some fucking color," Jesse said.

We decided to get Flint's Barbeque and go to the Berkeley Marina.

"I wish we could take them to our boat," I said.

"I have a boat," Jon said. "Let's go out on my boat."

His boat was smaller than *La Cigale*, but it was still nice. We went out, using the engine, went all around the bay in the sunset. It was beautiful, the cities, the bridge, the spray. We went back to the pier and had dinner on deck. Solly walked past, looked scared when he saw us. We introduced him to Jon, told him he had taken us out on the water.

Solly grinned, "Boy, you two must have loved that. A boat ride!"

Joe and Ben were laughing. They had loved it, being out in the bay, the smell and freedom of it. They were talking about getting a boat and living on it. Planning it all out.

"What's the matter with you guys?" Joe asked us. It was true. The three of us were quiet, just sitting there.

"I'm depressed," Jon said. "I've had this boat for a year, and this is the third time I've been out on it. Never have sailed the damn thing. My priorities are all out of whack. My life is a mess."

"I'm . . ." Jesse shook his head, didn't finish. I knew he was sad for the same reason I was. This was a real boat.

Jesse said he didn't want to go to court. I told Carlotta I would be by for her really early. It was the time of gas rationing, so you never knew how long the lines would be. I picked her up on the corner by Sears. Jesse was with her, looking pale, hungover.

"Hey, man. Don't worry. It'll be fine," I said. He nodded.

She put a scarf over her hair. She was clear-eyed and apparently calm, wearing a dusty-rose dress, patent leather pumps, a little bag.

"Jackie O goes to court! The dress is perfect," I said.

They kissed good-bye.

"I hate that dress," he said. "When you get back I get to burn it." They stood looking at each other.

"Come on, get in the car. You're not going to jail, Carlotta, I promise."

We did have a long wait for gas. We talked about everything but the trial. We talked about Boston. The Grolier Book Shop. Lochober's restaurant. Truro and the dunes. Cheryl and I had met in Provincetown. I told her Cheryl was having an affair. That I didn't know what I felt. About the affair, about our marriage. Carlotta put her hand over mine, on the gearshift.

"I'm so sorry, Jon," she said. "The hardest part is not knowing how you feel. Once you do, well, then, everything will be clear to you. I guess."

"Thanks a lot." I smiled.

Both the policemen were in the courtroom. She sat across from them in the spectator section. I spoke with the prosecutor and the judge and we went to his chambers. The two of them looked hard at her before we went in.

It went like clockwork. I had page after page of documentation about the police, the paperwork from the security check that did not find marijuana. The judge got the idea about the police report even before I really got into it.

"Yes, yes, so what do you propose?"

"We propose to sue the San Francisco Police Department unless all charges are dismissed." He thought about it, but not for long.

"I think it appropriate to dismiss the charges."

The prosecutor had seen it coming, but I could tell he hated facing the policemen.

We got back into the courtroom, where the judge said that because of a lawsuit pending against the San Francisco Police

Department he felt it appropriate to drop all charges against Carlotta Moran. If the policemen had had flashlights, they would have bludgeoned Carlotta to death right there in the courtroom. She couldn't resist an angelic smile.

I felt let down. It had been so quick. And I had expected her to be happier, more relieved. If the other lawyer had handled the case, she'd be locked up now. I even said this to her, fishing for compliments.

"Hey, how about a little elation, er, gratitude?"

"Jon, forgive me. Of course I'm elated. Of course we're grateful. And I know what you charge. We really owe you thousands and thousands of dollars. More than that was that we got to know you, and you liked us. And we love you now." She gave me a warm hug then, a big smile.

I was ashamed, told her to forget the money, that it had gone beyond a case. We got into the car.

"Jon, I need a drink. We both need breakfast."

I stopped and bought her a half-pint of Jim Beam. She took some big gulps before we got to Denny's.

"What a morning. We could be in Cleveland. Look around us." Denny's in Redwood City was like being in the heartland of America.

I realized that she was trying hard to show me she was happy. She asked me to tell her everything that happened, what I said, what the judge said. On the way home, she asked me about other cases, what were my favorites. I didn't understand what was going on until we were on the Bay Bridge and I saw the tears. When we got off the bridge, I pulled over and stopped, gave her my handkerchief. She fixed her face in the mirror, looked at me with a rictus of a smile.

"So, I guess the party's over now," I said. I put the car top up just in time. It started to rain hard as we drove on toward Oakland.

"What are you going to do?"

"What do you advise, Counselor?"

"Don't be sarcastic, Carlotta. It's not like you."

"I'm very serious. What would you do?"

I shook my head. I thought about her face, reading Nathan's letter. I remembered Jesse holding her throat.

"Is it clear to you? What you are going to do?"

"Yes," she whispered, "it's clear."

He was waiting on the corner by Sears. Soaking wet.

"Stop! There he is!"

She got out. He came over, asked how it went.

"Piece of cake. It was great."

He reached in and shook my hand. "Thank you, Jon."

I turned the corner and pulled over to the curb, watched them walk away in the drenching rain, each of them deliberately stomping in puddles, bumping gently into each other.

Mama

"Mama knew everything," my sister Sally said. "She was a witch. Even now that she's dead I get scared she can see me."

"Me too. If I'm doing something really lame, that's when I worry. The pitiful part is that when I do something right I'll hope she can. 'Hey Mama, check it out.' What if the dead just hang out looking at us all, laughing their heads off? God, Sally, that sounds like something she'd say. What if I am just like her?"

Our mother wondered what chairs would look like if our knees bent the other way. What if Christ had been electrocuted? Instead of crosses on chains, everybody'd be running around wearing chairs around their necks.

"She told me, 'Whatever you do, don't breed,'" Sally said. "And if I were dumb enough to ever marry, be sure he was rich and adored me. 'Never, ever marry for love. If you love a man you'll want to be with him, please him, do things for him. You'll ask him things like "Where have you been?" or "What are you thinking about?" or "Do you love me?" So he'll beat you up. Or go out for cigarettes and never come back.'"

"She hated the word *love*. She said it the way people say the word *slut*."

"She hated children. I met her once at an airport when all four of my kids were little. She yelled 'Call them off!' as if they were a pack of Dobermans."

"I don't know if she disowned me because I married a Mexican or because he was Catholic."

"She blamed the Catholic church for people having so many babies. She said popes had started the rumor that love made people happy."

"Love makes you miserable," our mama said. "You soak your pillow crying yourself to sleep, you steam up phone booths with your tears, your sobs make the dog holler, you smoke two cigarettes at once."

"Did Daddy make you miserable?" I asked her.

"Who, him? He couldn't make anybody miserable."

But I used Mama's advice to save my own son's marriage. Coco, his wife, called me, crying away. Ken wanted to move out for a few months. He needed his space. Coco adored him; she was desperate. I found myself giving her advice in Mama's voice. Literally, with her Texan twang, with a sneer. "Jes' you give that fool a little old taste of his own med'cine." I told her never to ask him back. "Don't call him. Send yourself flowers with mysterious cards. Teach his African gray parrot to say, 'Hello, Joe!'" I advised her to stock up on men, handsome, debonair men. Pay them if necessary, just to hang out at their place. Take them to Chez Panisse for lunch. Be sure different men were sitting around whenever Ken was likely to show up, to get clothes or visit his bird. Coco kept calling me. Yes she was doing what I told her, but he still hadn't come home. She didn't sound so miserable though.

Finally one day Ken called me. "Yo, Mom, get this . . . Coco is such a sleaze. I go to get some CDs at our apartment, right? And here is this jock. In a purple Lycra bicycle suit, probably sweaty, lying on my bed, watching Oprah on my TV, feeding my bird."

What can I say? Ken and Coco have lived happily ever after. Just recently I was visiting them and the phone rang. Coco answered it, talked for a while, laughing occasionally. When she hung up Ken asked, "Who was that?" Coco smiled, "Oh, just some guy I met at the gym."

•

"Mama ruined my favorite movie," I told Sally. "*The Song of Berna-dette*. I was going to school at St. Joseph's then and planned to be a nun or, preferably, a saint. You were only about three years old then. I saw that movie three times. Finally she agreed to come with me. She laughed all through it. She said the beautiful lady wasn't the Virgin Mary. 'It's Dorothy Lamour, for God's sake.' For weeks she made fun of the Immaculate Conception. 'Get me a cup of coffee, will you? I can't get up. I'm the Immaculate Conception.' Or, on the phone to her friend Alice Pomeroy, she'd say, 'Hi, it's me, the sweaty conception.' Or, 'Hi, this is the two-second conception.'"

"She was witty. You have to admit it. Like when she'd give panhandlers a nickel and say, 'Excuse me, young man, but what are your dreams and aspirations?' Or when a cabdriver was surly she'd say, 'You seem rather thoughtful and introspective today.'"

"No, even her humor was scary. Through the years her suicide notes, always written to me, were usually jokes. When she slit her wrists she signed it Bloody Mary. When she overdosed she wrote that she had tried a noose but couldn't get the hang of it. Her last letter to me wasn't funny. It said that she knew I would never forgive her. That she could not forgive me for the wreck I had made of my life."

"She never wrote me a suicide note."

"I don't believe it. Sally, you're actually jealous because I got all the suicide notes?"

"Well, yes. I am."

When our father died Sally had flown from Mexico City to California. She went to Mama's house and knocked on the door. Mama looked at her through the window but she wouldn't let her in. She had disowned Sally years and years before.

"I miss Daddy," Sally called to her through the glass. "I am dying of cancer. I need you now, Mama!" Our mother just closed the venetian blinds and ignored the banging banging on her door.

Sally would sob, replaying this scene and other sadder scenes over and over. Finally she was very sick and ready to die. She had stopped worrying about her children. She was serene, so lovely and sweet. Still, once in a while, rage grabbed her, not letting her go, denying her peace.

So every night then I began to tell Sally stories, like telling fairy tales.

I told her funny stories about our mother. How once she tried and tried to open a bag of Granny Goose potato chips, then gave up. "Life is just too damn hard," she said and tossed the bag over her shoulder.

I told her how Mama hadn't spoken to her brother Fortunatus for thirty years. Finally he asked her to lunch at the Top of the Mark, to bury the hatchet. "In his pompous ol' head!" Mama said. She got him though. He forced her to have pheasant under glass and when it came she said to the waiter, "Hey, boy, got any ketchup?"

Most of all I told Sally stories about how our mother once was. Before she drank, before she harmed us. Once upon a time.

"Mama is standing at the railing of the ship to Juneau. She's going to meet Ed, her new husband. On her way to a new life. It is 1930. She has left the Depression behind, Grandpa behind. All the sordid poverty and pain of Texas is gone. The ship is gliding, close to land, on a clear day. She is looking at the navy-blue water and the green pines on the shore of this wild clean new country. There are icebergs and gulls.

"The main thing to remember is how tiny she was, only five foot four. She just *seemed* huge to us. So young, nineteen. She was very beautiful, dark and thin. On the deck of the ship she sways against the wind. She is frail. She shivers with cold and excitement. Smoking. The fur collar pulled up around her heart-shaped face, her jet-black hair.

"Uncle Guyler and Uncle John had bought Mama that coat for a wedding gift. She was still wearing it six years later, so I got to know it. Burying my face in the matted nicotine fur. Not while she was wearing it. She couldn't bear to be touched. If you got too close she'd put her hand up as if to ward off a blow.

"On the deck of the ship she feels pretty and grown-up. She had made friends on the voyage. She had been witty, charming. The captain flirted with her. He poured her more gin that gave her vertigo and made her laugh out loud when he whispered, 'You're breaking my heart, you dusky beauty!'

"When the ship got into the harbor of Juneau her blue eyes filled with tears. No, I never once saw her cry either. It was sort of like Scarlett in *Gone With the Wind*. She swore to herself. No one is ever going to hurt me again.

"She knew that Ed was a good man, solid and kind. The first time she let him bring her home, to Upson Avenue, she had been ashamed. It was shabby; Uncle John and Grandpa were drunk. She was afraid Ed wouldn't ask her out again. But he held her in his arms and said, 'I am going to protect you.'

"Alaska was as wonderful as she had dreamed. They went in ski-planes into the wilderness and landed on frozen lakes, skied in the silence and saw elk and polar bears and wolves. They camped in the woods in summer and fished for salmon, saw grizzlies and mountain goats! They made friends; she was in a theater group and played the medium in *Blithe Spirit*. There were cast parties and potlucks and then Ed said she couldn't be in the theater anymore because she drank too much, acted in a manner that was beneath her. Then I was born. He had to go to Nome for a few months and she was alone with a new baby. When he got back he found her drunk, stumbling around with me in her arms. 'He ripped you from my breast,' she told me. He completely took over my care, fed me from a bottle. An Eskimo woman came in to watch me while he was at work. He told Mama she was weak and bad, like all the Moynihans. He protected her from herself from then on, didn't let her drive or have any money. All she could

do was walk to the library and read plays and mysteries and
Zane Grey.

"When the war came you were born and we went to live in
Texas. Daddy was a lieutenant on an ammunition ship, off Japan.
Mama hated being back home. She was out most of the time, drinking more and more. Mamie stopped working at Grandpa's office so
that she could take care of you. She moved your crib into her room;
she played with you and sang to you and rocked you to sleep. She
didn't let anybody near you, not even me.

"It was terrible for me, with Mama, and with Grandpa. Or alone,
most of the time. I got in trouble at school, ran away from one
school, was expelled from two others. Once I didn't speak for six
months. Mama called me the Bad Seed. All her rage came down
on me. It wasn't until I grew up that I realized she and Grandpa
probably didn't even remember what they did. God sends drunks
blackouts because if they knew what they had done they would
surely die of shame.

"After Daddy got back from the war we lived in Arizona and
they were happy together. They planted roses and gave you a puppy
called Sam and she was sober. But already she didn't know how to
be with you and me. We thought she hated us, but she was only
afraid of us. She felt it was we who had abandoned her, that we
hated her. She protected herself by mocking us and sneering, by
hurting us so we couldn't hurt her first.

"It seemed that moving to Chile would be a dream come true
for Mama. She loved elegance and beautiful things, always wished
they knew 'the right people.' Daddy had a prestigious job. We were
wealthy now, with a lovely house and many servants, and there
were dinners and parties with all the right people. She went out
some at first but she was simply too scared. Her hair was wrong,
her clothes were wrong. She bought expensive imitation antique
furniture and bad paintings. She was terrified of the servants. She
had a few friends that she trusted; ironically enough she played

poker with Jesuit priests, but most of the time she stayed in her
room. And Daddy kept her there.

"'At first he was my keeper, then he was my jailer,' she said. He
thought he was helping her, but year after year he rationed drinks
to her and hid her, and never ever got her any help. We never went
near her, nobody did. She'd fly into rages, cruel, irrational. We
thought nothing we did was good enough for her. And she did hate
to see us do well, to grow and accomplish things. We were young
and pretty and had a future. Do you see? How hard it was for her,
Sally?"

"Yes. It was like that. Poor pitiful Mama. You know, I'm like her
now. I get mad at everyone because they are working, living. Sometimes I hate you because you're not dying. Isn't that awful?"

"No, because you can tell me this. And I can tell you I'm glad it's
not me that is dying. But Mama never had a soul to tell anything
to. That day, on the ship, coming into port, she thought she would.
Mama believed Ed would be there always. She thought she was
coming home."

"Tell me about her again. On the boat. When she had tears in
her eyes."

"Okay. She tosses her cigarette into the water. You can hear it
hiss, as the waves are calm near the shore. The engines of the boat
turn off with a shudder. Silently then, in the sound of the buoys
and the gulls and the mournful long whistle of the boat they glide
toward the berth in the harbor, banging softly against the tires on
the dock. Mama smoothes down her collar and her hair. Smiling,
she looks out at the crowd, searching for her husband. She has
never before known such happiness."

Sally is crying softly. "*Pobrecita. Pobrecita*," she says. "If only I
could have been able to speak to her. If I had let her know how
much I loved her."

Me . . . I have no mercy.

Carmen

Outside every drugstore in town there were dozens of old cars with kids fighting in the backseat. I would see their mothers inside Payless and Walgreens and Lee's, but we didn't greet each other. Even women I knew . . . we acted like we didn't. We waited in line while the others bought terpin hydrate with codeine cough syrup and signed for it in a large awkward ledger. Sometimes we wrote our right names, sometimes made the names up. I could tell that, like me, they didn't know which was worse to do. Sometimes I'd see the same women at four or five drugstores a day. Other wives or mothers of addicts. The pharmacists shared our complicity, never acting like they knew us from before. Except once a young one at Fourth Street Drugs called me back to the counter. I was terrified. I thought he was going to report me. He was really shy and blushed when he apologized for interfering in my affairs. He said he knew I was pregnant and he was worried about me buying so much cough syrup. It had a high alcohol content, he said, and it could be easy for me to become an alcoholic without realizing it. I didn't say that it wasn't for me. I said thanks, but I began to cry as I turned and ran out of the store, crying because I wanted Noodles to be clean when the baby came. "How come you're crying, Mama? Mama's crying!" Willie and Vincent were jumping around the backseat. "Sit down!" I reached around and whacked Willie on the head. "Sit down. I'm crying because I'm tired and you guys won't be still."

There had been a big bust in town and a bigger one in Culiacán, so there was no heroin in Albuquerque. Noodles at first had told me he would taper off on the cough syrup and stay clean, so he'd be clean when the baby came in two months. I knew he couldn't. He'd never been so strung out before and now he had hurt his back at a construction job. At least he had disability.

He was on his knees, talking, had crawled to get the phone. I know, I know, I've been to the meetings. I'm sick too, an enabler, a co-addict. All I can say is I felt love, pity, tenderness for him. He was so thin, so sick. I would do anything for him not to hurt this way. I knelt down and put my arms around him. He hung up the phone.

"Fuck, Mona, they've busted Beto," he said. He kissed me and held me, called the kids over and hugged them. "Hey, you guys, give your old man a hand, be my crutches to the bathroom." When the boys left I went in and shut the door. He was shaking so bad I had to pour the cough syrup into his mouth. The smell made me retch. His sweat, his shit, the whole trailer smelled of rotten oranges from the syrup.

I fixed dinner for the boys and they watched *Man from U.N.C.L.E.* on TV. All the kids in school wore Levi's and T-shirts except Willie. In third grade, and he wore black pants and a white shirt. His hair was combed like the blond guy on TV. The boys had bunk beds in a tiny room, Noodles and I slept in the other bedroom. I already had a bassinet at the foot of our bed, diapers and baby clothes in every spare nook. We owned two acres in Corrales, near the clear ditch, in a grove of cottonwoods. At first we had plans to start building our adobe house, plant vegetables, but just after we got the land Noodles got strung out again. Most of the time he was still working construction, but nothing had happened about the house and now winter was coming.

I made a cup of cocoa and went out on the step. "Noodles, come see!" But he didn't answer. I heard the twist of another syrup cap. There was a gaudy splendid sunset. The vast Sandia Mountains were a deep pink, the rocks on the foothills red. Yellow cottonwoods blazed on the riverbank. A peach-colored moon was already rising. What's the matter with me? I was crying again. I hate to see anything lovely by myself. Then he was there, kissing my neck and putting his arms around me.

"You know they are called the Sandias because they are shaped like watermelons." "No," I said, "it's because of the color." We had that argument on our first date, have repeated it a hundred times. He laughed and kissed me, sweet. He was fine now. That's the lousy thing about drugs, I thought. They work. We sat there watching nighthawks sweep across the field.

"Noodles, don't have any more terps. I'll stash the rest of the bottles, give it to you just when you get sick. Okay?"

"Okay." He wasn't hearing me. "Beto was going to score in Juárez, from La Nacha. Mel is down there. He'll test it. He can't bring it. He can't cross the border. I need you to go. You are the perfect person to do it. You're Anglo, pregnant, sweet-looking. You look like a nice lady."

I am a nice lady, I thought.

"You'll fly to El Paso, take a cab over the border, and then fly back. No problem."

I remembered waiting in the car outside the building where La Nacha lived, being afraid in that neighborhood.

"I'm the worst person to go. I can't leave the kids. I can't go to jail, Noodles."

"You won't go to jail. That's the point. Connie'll keep the kids. She knows you have family in El Paso. There could be an emergency. The kids would love to go to Connie's."

"What if narcs stop me, ask me what I'm doing there?"

"We still have Laura's ID. It looks like you, maybe not so pretty but you're both gueras with blue eyes. You'll have a ratty piece of paper with 'Lupe Vega' scrawled on it and an address next door to Nacha's. Say you're looking for your maid, she hasn't shown, she owes you money, something like that. Just act dumb, have them help you look for her."

I finally agreed to go. He said Mel would be there and to watch him try it out. "You'll know if it's good." Yes, I knew the look of a good rush. "Whatever you do, don't leave Mel alone in the room. You leave alone, though, not even with Mel. Have your own cab come back for you in an hour. Don't let them call you a cab."

I got ready to go, called Connie and told her my uncle Gabe had died in El Paso, could she keep the kids for the night, maybe another day. Noodles gave me a thick envelope with money in it, taped closed. I packed a bag for the boys. They were happy to go. Connie's six kids were like cousins. When I took them to the door Connie shooed them inside, came out onto the porch and hugged me. Her black hair was up in tin rollers, like a kabuki headdress. She wore cutoffs and a T-shirt, looked about fourteen.

"You don't ever have to lie to me, Mona," she said.

"Did you ever do this?"

"Yeah, lots of times. Not after I had children. You won't do it again, I'll bet. Take care. I'll pray for you."

It was still hot in El Paso. I walked across the sinking soft tarmac from the plane, smelling the dirt and sage I remembered from childhood. I told the cabdriver to take me to the bridge, but first drive around the alligator pond.

"Alligators? Them old alligators died off years ago. Still want to see the plaza?"

"Sure," I said. I leaned back and watched the neighborhoods flash by. There were changes but as a kid I had skated over this whole city so many times that it seemed I knew every old house and tree. The baby was kicking and stretching. "You like my old hometown?"

"What's that?" the cabdriver asked.

"Sorry, I was talking to my baby."

He laughed. "Did he answer?"

I crossed the bridge. I was still happy just with the smells of woodfires and caliche dirt, chili, and the whiff of sulfur from the smelter. My friend Hope and I used to love to give smart answers when the border guards asked our nationality. Transylvanian, Mozambican.

"USA," I said. Nobody seemed to notice me. Just in case, I didn't take any of the cabs by the border but walked some more blocks. I ate some *dulce de membrillo*. Even as a kid I didn't like it, but liked the idea that it came in a little balsa box and you used the lid for a spoon. I looked at all the silver jewelry and shell ashtrays and Don Quijotes until I made myself get into a cab and hand him the piece of paper with Lupe's name and the wrong address. "*Cuanto?*"

"Twenty dollars."

"Ten."

"*Bueno.*" Then I could no longer pretend I wasn't scared. He drove fast for a long time. I recognized the deserted street and the stucco building. He stopped a few doors down. In broken Spanish I asked him to be back in an hour. For twenty dollars. "Okay. *Una hora.*"

It was hard climbing the stairs to the fourth floor. I was big with the baby and my legs were swollen and sore. I caught my breath in sobs at each landing. My knees and hands were shaking. I knocked on the door of number 43, Mel opened it and I stumbled in.

"Hey, sweetheart, what's happening?"

"Water, please." I sat on a dirty vinyl sofa. He brought me a Diet Coke, wiped the top with his shirt, smiled. He was dirty, handsome, moved like a cheetah. A legend by now, escaping from jails, jumping bond. Armed and dangerous. He brought me a chair to put my feet up on, rubbed my ankles.

"Where is La Nacha?" The woman was never referred to just as Nacha. "The Nacha," whatever that meant. She came in, dressed in a black man's suit and a white shirt. She sat at a chair behind a desk. I couldn't tell if she was a male transvestite or a woman trying to look like a man. She was dark, almost black, with a Mayan face, red-black lipstick and nail polish, dark glasses. Her hair was short, slick. She held a stubby hand out to Mel without looking at me. I handed him the money. I saw her count the money.

That's when I got afraid, really afraid. I had thought I was getting drugs for Noodles. All I cared about was him not being sick. I had thought there was maybe a big wad of tens, twenties in the packet. There were thousands of dollars in La Nacha's hand. He hadn't just sent me to get shit for him. I was making a big, dangerous score. If they caught me it would be as a dealer, not a user. Who would take care of the boys? I hated Noodles.

Mel saw that I was shaking. I think I even gagged. He fished around in his pockets, came up with a blue pill. I shook my head. The baby.

"Oh, for Christ's sake. It's just a Valium. You'll mess that baby up worse if you don't take it. Take it. Get it together! You hear me?"

I nodded. His scorn shook me. I was calm even before the pill worked.

"Noodles told you I was going to test the shit. If it's good I'll say so and you just take the balloon and leave. You know where to put it?" I knew but would never do that. What if it broke and got to the baby?

He was a devil, could read my mind. "If you don't put it there I will. It's not going to break. Your baby is all wrapped up in a drug-proof bag, safe against every evil of the outside world. Once he's born, sugar, hey, that's another story."

Mel watched as La Nacha weighed the packet and nodded as she handed it to him. She had never looked at me. I watched Mel shoot up. Put cottons and water into a spoon, sprinkle a pinch of brown heroin into it, cook it. Tie up, hit a vein in his hand, blood backing up then plunge and the tie falling off as his face instantly stretched back. He was in a wind tunnel. Ghosts were flying him into another world. I had to pee, I had to throw up. "Where's the bathroom?" La Nacha motioned to the door. I found the bathroom down the hall by the smell. When I got back I remembered that I wasn't supposed to leave Mel alone. He was smiling. He handed me the condom, rolled up into a ball.

"Here you go, precious, you have a good trip. Go on now, put it away like a good girl." I turned around and acted like I was shoving it inside myself but it was just inside my too-tight underpants. Outside, in the dark of the hall I moved it to my bra.

I took the steps slowly, like a drunk. It was dark, filthy.

At the second landing I heard the door open downstairs, noises from the street. Two young boys ran up the stairs. *"Fíjate no más!"* One of them pinned me to the wall, the other got my purse. Nothing was in it but loose bills, makeup. Everything else was in a pocket inside my jacket. He hit me.

"Let's fuck her," the other one said.

"How? You need a dick four feet long."

"Turn her around, *bato*."

Just as he hit me again a door opened and an old man came running down the stairs with a knife. The boys turned and ran back outside. "Are you well?" the man asked in English.

I nodded. I asked him to go with me. "I hope there is a taxi outside."

"You wait here. If it's there I'll have him use the horn three times."

Your mother did teach you to be a lady, I thought when I wondered about the etiquette. Should I offer him money? I didn't. His toothless smile was sweet as he opened the taxi door for me.

"Adiós."

•

I was nauseated on the little twin-engine plane to Albuquerque. I smelled like sweat and the couch and the pee-stained wall. I asked for an extra sandwich and nuts and milk.

"Eatin' for two now!" the Texan across from me grinned.

I drove from the airport home. I'd get the boys after I had a shower. As I drove down the dirt road toward our trailer I could see Noodles in his pea jacket, pacing and smoking outside.

He looked desperate, didn't even come to greet me. I followed him inside.

He sat at the edge of the bed. On the table his outfit was ready and waiting. "Let me see it." I handed him the balloon. He opened the cupboard above the bed and put it on the tiny scale. He turned and slapped me hard across the face. He had never hit me before. I sat there, numb, next to him. "You left Mel alone with it. Didn't you. Didn't you."

"There is enough there to have put me away for a long time," I said.

"I told you not to leave him. What am I going to do now?"

"Call the police," I said, and he slapped me again. This one I didn't even feel. I got a strong contraction. Braxton-Hicks, I thought to myself. Whoever was Braxton-Hicks? I sat there, sweating, stinking of Juárez, and watched him pour the contents of the rubber into a film canister. He shook some onto the cottons in his spoon. I knew with a sick certainty that always if there were a choice between me and the boys or drugs, he'd go for the drugs.

Hot water gushed down my legs onto the carpet. "Noodles! My water is breaking! I have to go to the hospital." But by then he had fixed. The spoon made a clink onto the table, his rubber tube fell from his arm. He leaned back against the pillow. "At least it's good shit," he whispered. I got another contraction. Strong. I tore off the

filthy dress and sponged myself, put on a white *huipil*. Another
contraction. I called 911. Noodles had nodded out. Should I leave
him a note? Maybe he'd call the hospital when he woke. No. He
would not think of me at all.

First thing he'd do, he'd shoot up what was left in the cottons,
have another little taste. I tasted copper in my mouth. I slapped
his face but he didn't move.

I opened the can of heroin, holding it with a Kleenex. I poured
a large amount into the spoon. I added a little water, then closed
his beautiful hand around the can. There was another bad contraction. Blood and mucus were sliding down my legs. I put a
sweater on, got my Medi-Cal card, and went outside to wait for
the ambulance.

They took me straight to the delivery room. "The baby's
coming!" I said. The nurse took my Medi-Cal card, asked questions: phone, husband's name, how many live births, what was
my due date.

She examined me. "You're totally dilated, the head is right
here."

Pains were coming one after another. She ran to get a doctor.
While she was gone the baby was born, a little girl. Carmen. I
leaned down and picked her up. I laid her, warm and steaming, on
my stomach. We were alone in the quiet room. Then they came
and wheeled us careening into the big lights. Somebody cut the
cord and I heard the baby cry. An even worse pain as the placenta
came out and then they were putting a mask over my face. "What
are you doing? She is born!"

"The doctor is coming. You need an episiotomy." They tied my
hands down.

"Where is my baby? Where is she?" The nurse left the room.
I was strapped to the sides of the bed. A doctor came in. "Please
untie me." He did and was so gentle I became frightened. "What
is it?"

"She was born too early," he said, "weighed only a few pounds. She didn't live. I'm sorry." He patted my arm, awkwardly, like patting a pillow. He was looking at my chart. "Is this your home number? Shall I call your husband?"

"No," I said. "Nobody's home."

Silence

I started out quiet, living in mountain mining towns, moving too often to make a friend. I'd find me a tree or a room in an old deserted mill, to sit in silence.

My mother was usually reading or sleeping so I spoke mostly with my father. As soon as he got in the door or when he took me up into the mountains or down dark into the mines, I was talking nonstop.

Then he went overseas and we were in El Paso, Texas, where I went to Vilas school. In third grade I read well but I didn't even know addition. Heavy brace on my crooked back. I was tall but still childlike. A changeling in this city, as if I'd been reared in the woods by mountain goats. I kept peeing in my pants, splashing until I refused to go to school or even speak to the principal.

My mother's old high school teacher got me in as a scholarship student at the exclusive Radford School for Girls, two bus rides across El Paso. I still had all of the above problems but now I was also dressed like a ragamuffin. I lived in the slums and there was something particularly unacceptable about my hair.

I haven't talked much about this school. I don't mind telling people awful things if I can make them funny. It was never funny. Once at recess I took a drink from a garden hose and the teacher grabbed it from me, told me I was common.

But the library. Every day we got to spend an hour in it, free to look at any book, at every book, to sit down and read, or go through the card catalogue. When there were fifteen minutes left the librarian let us know, so we could check out a book. The librarian was so, don't laugh, soft-spoken. Not just quiet but nice. She'd tell you, "This is where biographies are," and then explain what a biography was.

"Here are reference books. If there is ever anything you want to know, you just ask me and we'll find the answer in a book."

This was a wonderful thing to hear and I believed her.

Then Miss Brick's purse got stolen from beneath her desk. She said that it must have been me who took it. I was sent to Lucinda de Leftwitch Templin's office. Lucinda de said she knew I didn't come from a privileged home like most of her girls, and that this might be difficult for me sometimes. She understood, she said, but really she was saying, "Where's the purse?"

I left. Didn't even go back to get the bus money or lunch in my cubby. Took off across town, all the long way, all the long day. My mother met me on the porch with a switch. They had called to say I had stolen the purse and then run away. She didn't even ask me if I stole it. "Little thief, humiliating me," whack, "brat, ungrateful," whack. Lucinda de called her the next day to tell her a janitor had stolen the purse but my mother didn't even apologize to me. She just said, "Bitch," after she hung up.

That's how I ended up in St. Joseph's, which I loved. But those kids hated me too, for all of the above reasons but now worse for new reasons, one being that Sister Cecilia always called on me and I got stars and Saint pictures and was the pet! pet! until I stopped raising my hand.

Uncle John took off for Nacogdoches, which left me alone with my mother and Grandpa. Uncle John always used to eat with me, or drink while I ate. He talked to me while I helped him repair furniture, took me to movies and let me hold his slimy glass eye. It was terrible when he was gone. Grandpa and Mamie (my grandma) were at his dentist office all day and then when they got home Mamie kept my little sister safe away in the kitchen or in Mamie's room. My mother was out, being a gray lady at the army hospital or playing bridge. Grandpa was out at the Elks or who knows. The house was scary and empty without John and I'd have to hide from Grandpa and Mama when either of them was drunk. Home was bad and school was bad.

I decided not to talk. I just sort of gave it up. It lasted so long Sister Cecilia tried to pray with me in the cloakroom. She meant well and was just touching me in sympathy, praying. I got scared and pushed her and she fell down and I got expelled.

That's when I met Hope.

School was almost over so I would stay home and go back to Vilas in the fall. I still wasn't talking, even when my mother poured a whole pitcher of iced tea over my head or twisted as she pinched me so the pinches looked like stars, the Big Dipper, Little Dipper, the Lyre up and down my arms.

I played jacks on the concrete above the steps, wishing that the Syrian kid next door would ask me over. She played on their concrete porch. She was small and thin but seemed old. Not grown-up or mature but like an old woman-child. Long shiny black hair with bangs hanging down over her eyes. In order to see she had to tip her head back. She looked like a baby baboon. In a nice way, I mean. A little face and huge black eyes. All of the six Haddad kids looked emaciated but the adults were huge, two or three hundred pounds.

I knew she noticed me too because if I was doing cherries in the basket so was she. Or shooting stars, except she didn't ever drop a jack, even with twelves. For weeks our balls and jacks made a nice bop bop crash bop bop crash rhythm until finally she did come over to the fence. She must have heard my mother yelling at me because she said,

"You talk yet?"

I shook my head.

"Good. Talking to me won't count."

I hopped the fence. That night I was so happy I had a friend that when I went to bed I called out, "Good night!"

We had played jacks for hours that day and then she taught me mumblety-peg. Dangerous games with a knife. Triple flips into the grass, and the scariest was one hand flat on the ground, stabbing between each finger. Faster faster faster blood. I don't think we spoke at all. We rarely did, all summer long. All I remember are her first and last words.

I have never had a friend again like Hope, my onliest true friend. I gradually became a part of the Haddad family. I believe that if this had not happened I would have grown up to be not just neurotic, alcoholic, and insecure, but seriously disturbed. Wacko.

The six children and the father spoke English. The mother, grandma, and five or six other old women spoke only Arabic. Looking back, it seems like I went through sort of an orientation. The children watched as I learned to run, really run, to vault the fence, not climb it. I became expert with the knife, tops, and marbles. I learned cusswords and gestures in English, Spanish, and Arabic. For the grandma I washed dishes, watered, raked the sand in the backyard, beat rugs with a woven-cane beater, helped the old women roll out bread on the Ping-Pong tables in the basement. Lazy afternoons washing bloody menstrual rags in a tub in the backyard with Hope and Shahala, her older sister. This seemed not disgusting but magic, like a mysterious rite. In the mornings I stood in line with the other girls to get my ears washed and my hair braided, to get kibbe on fresh hot bread. The women hollered at me, "*Hjadda-dinah!*" Kissed me and slapped me as if I belonged there. Mr. Haddad let me and Hope sit on couches and drive around town in the bed of his Haddad's Beautiful Furniture truck.

I learned to steal. Pomegranates and figs from blind old Guca's yard, Blue Waltz perfume, Tangee lipstick from Kress's, licorice and sodas from the Sunshine Grocery. Stores delivered then, and one day the Sunshine delivery boy was bringing groceries to both our houses just as Hope and I were getting home, eating banana Popsicles. Our mothers were both outside.

"Your kids stole them Popsicles!" he said.

My mother slapped me whack whack. "Get inside, you criminal lying cheating brat!" But Mrs. Haddad said, "You lousy liar! *Hjaddadinah! Tlajhama!* Don't you talk bad about my kids! I'm not going to your store no more!"

And she never did, taking a bus all the way to Mesa to shop, knowing full well that Hope had stolen the Popsicle. This made sense to me. I didn't just want my mother to believe me when I was innocent, which she never did, but to stand up for me when I was guilty.

When we got skates Hope and I covered El Paso, skated over the whole town. We went to movies, letting the other in by the fire exit door. *The Spanish Main, Till the End of Time.* Chopin bleeding all over the piano keys. We saw *Mildred Pierce* six times and *The Beast with Five Fingers* ten.

The best time we had was the cards. Anytime we could, we hung out around her brother Sammy, who was seventeen. He and his friends were handsome and tough and wild. I have told you about Sammy and the cards. We sold chances for musical vanity boxes. We brought him the money and he gave us a cut. That's how we got the skates.

We sold chances everywhere. Hotels and the train station, the USO, Juárez. But even neighborhoods were magic. You walk down a street, past houses and yards, and sometimes in the evening you can see people eating or sitting around and it's a lovely glimpse of how people live. Hope and I went inside hundreds of houses. Seven years old, both funny-looking in different ways, people liked us and were kind to us. "Come in. Have some lemonade." We saw four Siamese cats who used the real toilet and even flushed it. We saw parrots and one five-hundred-pound person who had not been out of the house for twenty years. But even more we liked all the pretty things: paintings and china shepherdesses, mirrors, cuckoo clocks and grandfather clocks, quilts and rugs of many colors. We liked sitting in Mexican kitchens full of canaries, drinking real orange juice and eating pan dulce. Hope was so smart, she learned Spanish just from listening around the neighborhood, so she could talk to the old women.

We glowed when Sammy praised us, hugged us. He made us bologna sandwiches and let us sit near them on the grass. We told them all about the people we met. Rich ones, poor ones, Chinese ones, black ones until the conductor made us leave the colored waiting room at the station. Only one bad person, the man with the dogs. He didn't do anything or say anything bad, just scared us to death with his pale smirky face.

When Sammy bought the old car, Hope figured it out right away. That nobody was going to get any vanity box.

She leaped in a fury over the fence into my yard, howling, hair flying like an Indian warrior in the movies. She opened her knife and made big gashes in our index fingers, held them dripping together.

"I will never ever speak to Sammy again," she said. "Say it!"

"I will never ever speak to Sammy again," I said.

I exaggerate a lot and I get fiction and reality mixed up, but I don't actually ever lie. I wasn't lying when I made that vow. I knew he had used us, lied to us, and cheated all those people. I was never going to speak to him.

A few weeks later I was climbing the hill up Upson, near the hospital. Hot. (See, I'm trying to justify what happened. It was always hot.) Sammy pulled up in the old blue open car, the car Hope and I had worked to pay for. It is true too that coming from mountain towns and except for some taxis I had rarely been in a car.

"Come for a ride."

Some words drive me crazy. Lately every newspaper article has a benchmark or a watershed or an icon in it. At least one of these applies to that moment in my life.

I was a little girl; I don't believe it was an actual sexual attraction. But I was awed by his physical beauty, his magnetism. Whatever the excuse . . . Well, so okay, there is no excuse for what I did. I spoke to him. I got into the car.

It was wonderful, riding in the open car. The wind cooled us off as we sped around the Plaza, past the Wigwam theater, the Del Norte, the Popular Dry Goods Company, then up Mesa toward Upson. I was going to ask him to let me out a few blocks before home just as I saw Hope in a fig tree on the vacant lot where Upson and Randolph came together.

Hope screamed. Sat up in the tree shaking her fist at me, cursing in Syrian. Maybe everything that has happened to me since was a result of this curse. Makes sense.

I got out of the car, sick at heart, shaking, climbed the stairs to our house like an old person, fell onto the porch swing.

I knew that it was the end of my friendship and I knew I was wrong.

Each day was endless. Hope walked past me as if I were invisible, played on the other side of the fence as if our yard did not exist. She and her sisters spoke only Syrian now. Loud if they were outside. I understood a lot of the bad things they said. Hope played jacks alone on the porch for hours, wailing Arabic songs, beautiful; her harsh plaintive voice made me weep for missing her.

Except for Sammy, none of the Haddads would speak to me. Her mother spat at me and shook her fist. Sammy would call to me from the car, away from our house. Tell me he was sorry. He tried to be nice, saying he knew that she was really still my friend and please don't be sad. That he understood why I couldn't talk to him, to please forgive him. I turned away so I couldn't see him when he spoke.

I have never been so lonely in my life. Benchmark lonely. The days were endless, the sound of her ball relentless hour after hour on the concrete, the swish of her knife into the grass, glint of the blade.

There weren't any other children in our neighborhood. For weeks we played alone. She perfected knife tricks on their grass. I colored and read, lying on the porch swing.

She left for good just before school started. Sammy and her father carried her bed and bed table and a chair down to the huge furniture truck. Hope climbed in back, sat up in the bed so she could see out. She didn't look at me. She looked tiny in the huge truck. I watched until she disappeared. Sammy called to me from the fence, told me that she had gone to Odessa, Texas, to live with some relatives. I say Odessa, Texas, because once someone said, "This is Olga; she's from Odessa." And I thought, so? Turned out it was in the Ukraine. I thought the only Odessa was where Hope went.

School started and it wasn't so bad. I didn't care about being always alone or laughed at. My back brace was getting too small and my back hurt. Good, I thought, it's what I deserve.

Uncle John came back. Five minutes in the door he said to my mother, "Her brace is too small!"

I was so glad to see him. He fixed me a bowl of puffed wheat with milk, about six spoons of sugar, and at least three tablespoons of vanilla. He sat across from me at the kitchen table, drinking bourbon while I ate. I told him about my friend Hope, about everything. I even told him about the school troubles. I had almost forgotten them. He grunted or said, "Hot damn!" while I talked and he understood everything, especially about Hope.

He never said things like "Don't worry, it will all work out." In fact, once Mamie said, "Things could be worse."

"Worse?" he said. "Things could be a heckuva lot better!" He was an alcoholic too, but drink just made him sweeter, not like them. Or he'd take off, to Mexico or Nacogdoches or Carlsbad, to jail sometimes, I realize now.

He was handsome, dark like Grandpa, with only one blue eye since Grandpa shot out the other one. His glass eye was green. I know that it is true that Grandpa shot him, but how it happened has about ten different versions. When Uncle John was home he slept in the shed out back, near where he had made my room on the back porch.

Uncle John wore a cowboy hat and boots and was like a brave movie cowboy part of the time, at others just a pitiful crying bum.

"Sick again," Mamie would sigh about them.

"Drunk, Mamie," I'd say.

I tried to hide when Grandpa was drunk because he would catch me and rock me. He was doing it once in the big rocker, holding me tight, the chair bouncing off the ground inches from the red-hot stove, his thing jabbing jabbing my behind. He was singing, "Old Tin Pan with a Hole in the Bottom." Loud. Panting and grunting. Only a few feet away Mamie sat, reading the Bible while I screamed, "Mamie! Help me!" Uncle John showed up, drunk and dusty. He grabbed me away from Grandpa, pulled the old man up by his shirt. He said he'd kill him with his bare hands next time. Then he slammed shut Mamie's Bible.

"Read it over, Ma. You got it wrong, the part about turning the other cheek. That don't mean when somebody hurts a child."

She was crying, said he'd like to break her heart.

While I was finishing the cereal he asked me if Grandpa had been bothering me. I said no. I told him that he had done it to Sally, once, that I saw.

"Little Sally? What did you do?"

"Nothing." I had done nothing. I had watched with a mixture of feelings: fear, sex, jealousy, anger. John came around, pulled up a chair and shook me, hard. He was furious.

"That was rotten! You hear me? Where was Mamie?"

"Watering. Sally had been asleep, but she woke up."

"When I'm gone you're the only one here with any sense. You have to protect her. Do you hear me?"

I nodded, ashamed. But I was more ashamed of how I had felt when it happened. He figured it out somehow. He always understood all the things you didn't even get straight in your head, much less say.

"You think Sally has it pretty good. You're jealous of her because Mamie pays her so much attention. So even if this was a bad thing he was doing at least it used to be your bad thing, right? Honey, sure you're jealous of her. She's treated swell. But remember how mad you got at Mamie? How you begged her to help you? Answer me!"

"I remember."

"Well, you were as bad as Mamie. Worse! Silence can be wicked, plumb wicked. Anything else you done wrong, 'sides from betraying your sister and a friend?"

"I stole. Candy and . . ."

"I mean hurting people."

"No."

He said he was going to stick around awhile, get me straightened out, get his Antique Repair Shop going before winter.

I worked for him weekends and after school in the shed and the backyard. Sanding, sanding or rubbing wood with a rag soaked in linseed oil and turpentine. His friends Tino and Sam came sometimes to help him with caning, reupholstering, refinishing. If my mother or Grandpa came home they left the back way, because Tino was Mexican and Sam was colored. Mamie liked them, though, and always brought out brownies or oatmeal cookies if she was there.

Once Tino brought a Mexican woman, Mecha, almost a girl, really pretty, with rings and earrings, painted eyelids and long nails, a shiny green dress. She didn't speak English but pantomimed could she help me paint a kitchen stool. I nodded, sure. Uncle John told me to hurry up, paint fast before the paint ran out, and I guess Tino told Mecha the same thing in Spanish. We were furiously slapping the brushes around the rungs and up the legs, fast as we could while the three men held their sides, laughing at us. The two of us figured it out at about the same time, and we both began laughing too. Mamie came out to see what the fuss was. She called Uncle John over to her. She was really mad about the woman, said it was wicked to have her here. John nodded and scratched his head. When Mamie went in, he came over and after a while said, "Well, let's call it a day."

While we cleaned the brushes, he explained that the woman was a whore, that Mamie figured that out by the way she was dressed and painted. He ended up explaining a lot of things that had bothered me. I understood more about my parents and Grandpa and movies and dogs. He forgot to tell me that whores charged money, so I was still confused about whores.

"Mecha was nice. I hate Mamie," I said.

"Don't say that word! Anyhow you don't hate her. You're mad because she doesn't like you. She sees you out wandering the streets, hanging out with Syrians and Uncle John. She figures you're a lost cause, a born Moynihan. You want her to love you, that's all. Anytime you think you hate somebody, what you do is pray for them. Try it, you'll see. And while you're busy praying for her, you might try helping her once in a while. Give her some kinda reason to like a surly brat like you."

On weekends sometimes he'd take me to the dog track in Juárez, or to gambling games around town. I loved the races and was good at picking winners. The only time I liked going to card games was when he played with railroad men, in a caboose at the train yards. I climbed the ladder to the roof and watched all the trains coming in and going out, switching, coupling. It got to be that most of the card games were in the back of Chinese laundries. I'd sit in the front reading for hours while somewhere in back he played poker. The heat and the smell of cleaning solvent mixed with singed wool and sweat was nauseating. A few times he left out the back way and forgot me, so that only when the laundryman came to close up did he find me asleep in the chair. I'd have to go home, far, in the dark, and most of the time nobody would be there. Mamie took Sally to choir practice and to the Eastern Star and to make bandages for servicemen.

About once a month we'd go to a barbershop. A different one each time. He'd ask for a shave and a haircut. I'd sit on a chair reading *Argosy* while the barber cut his hair, just waiting for the shave part. Uncle John would be tilted way back in the chair and just as the barber was finishing the shave he'd ask, "Say, do you happen to have any eyedrops?" which they always did. The barber would stand over him and put drops in his eyes. The green glass eye would start spinning around and the barber would scream bloody murder. Then everybody'd laugh.

If only I had understood him half as much as he always understood me, I could have found out how he hurt, why he worked so hard to get laughs. He did make everybody laugh. We ate in cafés all over Juárez and El Paso that were like people's houses. Just a lot of tables in one room of a regular house, with good food. Everybody knew him and the waitresses always laughed when he asked if it was warmed-over coffee.

"Oh, no!"

"Well, how'd you get it so hot?"

I could usually tell just how drunk he was, and if it was a lot I'd make some excuse and walk or ride the trolley home. One day though, I had been sleeping in the cab of the truck, woke after he got in and started off. We were on Rim Road going faster faster. He had a bottle between his thighs, was driving with his elbows as he counted the money he held in a fan over the steering wheel.

"Slow down!"

"I'm in the money, honey!"

"Slow down! Hold on to the wheel!"

The truck thumped, shuddered high up and then thumped down. Money flew all over the cab. I looked out the back window. A little boy was standing in the street, his arm bleeding. A collie was lying next to him, really bloody, trying to get up.

"Stop. Stop the truck. We have to go back. Uncle John!"

"I can't!"

"Slow down. You have to turn around!" I was sobbing hysterically.

At home he reached across and opened my door. "You go on in."

I don't know if I stopped speaking to him. He never came home. Not that night, not for days, weeks, months. I prayed for him.

The war ended and my father came home. We moved to South America.

Uncle John ended up on skid row in Los Angeles, a really hopeless wino. Then he met Dora, who played trumpet in the Salvation Army band. She had him go into the shelter and have some soup and she talked to him. She said later that he made her laugh. They fell in love and were married and he never drank again. When I was older I went to visit them in Los Angeles. She was working as a riveter at Lockheed and he had an antique repair shop in his garage. They were maybe the sweetest two people I ever knew, sweet together, I mean. We went to Forest Lawn and the La Brea tar pits and the Grotto restaurant. Mostly I helped Uncle John in the shop, sanding furniture, polishing with the turpentine and linseed oil rag. We talked about life, told jokes. Neither of us ever mentioned El Paso. Of course by this time I had realized all the reasons why he couldn't stop the truck, because by this time I was an alcoholic.

Mijito

I want to go home. When *mijito* Jesus falls asleep I think about home, my mamacita and my brothers and sisters. I try to remember all the trees and all the people in the village. I try to remember me because I was different then, before *tantas cosas que han pasado*. I had no idea. I didn't know television or *drogas* or fear. I have been afraid since the minute I left the trip and the van and the men and running and even when Manolo met me I got more afraid because he wasn't the same. I knew he loved me and when he held me it was like by the river, but he was changed, with fear in his gentle eyes. All of the United States was scary coming to Oakland. Cars in front of us, behind us, cars going the other way cars cars cars for sale and stores and stores and more cars. Even in our little room in Oakland where I'd wait for him the room was full of noise, not just the television but cars and buses and sirens and helicopters, men fighting and shooting and people yelling. The *mayates* frighten me and they stand in groups all down the street so I was afraid to go outside. Manolo was so strange I was afraid he didn't want to marry me but he said, "Don't be crazy, I love you *mi vida*." I was happy but then he said, "Anyway you need to be legal so you can get welfare and food stamps." We got married right away and that same day he took me to the welfare. I was sad. I wanted to maybe go to a park or have some wine, a little *luna de miel* party.

We lived in the Flamingo Motel on MacArthur. I was lonely. He was gone most of the time. He got mad at me for being so scared but he forgot how different it was here. We didn't have inside bathrooms or lights at home. Even the television frightened me; it seemed so real. I wished we had a little house or room that I could make pretty and where I could cook for him. He would come with Kentucky Fry or Taco Bell or hamburgers. We ate breakfast every day in a little café and that was nice like in Mexico.

One day there was a banging on the door. I didn't want to open it. The man said he was Ramón, Manolo's uncle. He said Manolo was in jail. He was going to take me to talk to him. He made me pack up all my things and get in the car. I kept asking him, "Why? What happened? What did he do?"

"*No me jodes! Cállate,*" he told me. "*Mira,* I don't know. He'll tell you. All I know is you'll be staying with us until he goes to court."

We went into a big building and then in an elevator to the top floor. I had never been in an elevator. He talked to some police and then one took me through a door to a chair in front of a window. He pointed to a phone. Manolo came and sat down on the other side. He was thin and unshaven and his eyes were full of fear. He was shaking and pale. All he was wearing was some orange night-clothes. We sat there, looking at each other. He picked up a phone and pointed to me to pick up mine. It was my first telephone call. It didn't sound like him but I could see him talking. I was so afraid. I can't remember everything, except that he said he loved me and he was sorry. He said he would let Ramón know when he'd go to court. He hoped he'd come home to me then. But if he didn't, to wait for him, my husband. Ramón and Lupe were *buena gente,* they would take care of me until he got out. They needed to take me to the welfare to change my address. "Don't forget. I'm sorry," he said in English. I had to think how you said it in Spanish. *Lo siento.* I feel it.

If only I had known. I should have told him I'd love him and wait for him always, that I loved him with all of my heart. I should have told him about our baby. But I was so worried and too frightened to talk into the phone so I just looked at him until the two policemen took him away.

In the car I asked Ramón what had happened, where did they take him? I kept asking him until he stopped his car and said how did he know, to shut up. My check and food stamps would go to them for feeding me and I'd need to take care of their kids. As soon as I could I had to get my own place and move out. I told him I was three months pregnant and he said, "Fuck a duck." That's the first English I said out loud. "Fuck a duck."

Dr. Fritz should be here soon, so at least I can get some of these patients into rooms. He should have been here two hours ago, but as usual he added another surgery. He knows he has office hours Wednesdays. The waiting room is packed, babies screaming, children fighting. Karma and I'll be lucky to get out of here by seven. She's the office supervisor, what a job. The place is steamy and hot, reeking of dirty diapers and sweat, wet clothes. It's raining of course, and most of these mothers have taken long bus rides to get here.

When I go out there I sort of cross my eyes, and when I call the patient's name I smile at the mother or grandmother or foster care mom but I look at a third eye in their forehead. I learned this in Emergency. It's the only way to work here, especially with all the crack babies and AIDS and cancer babies. Or the ones who will never grow up. If you look the parent in the eyes you will share it, confirm it, all the fear and exhaustion and pain. On the other hand once you get to know them, sometimes that's all you can do, look into their eyes with the hope or sorrow you can't express.

The first two are post-ops. I set out gloves and suture removers, gauze and tape, tell the mothers to undress the babies. It won't be long. In the waiting room I call Jesus Romero.

A teenage mother walks toward me, her infant wrapped in a rebozo like in Mexico. The girl looks cowed, terrified. *"No inglés,"* she says.

In Spanish I tell her to take off everything but his diaper, ask her what is the matter.

She says, "*Pobre mijito*, he cries and cries all the time, he never stops."

I weigh him, ask her his birth weight. Seven pounds. He is three months old, should be bigger by now.

"Did you take him for his shots?"

Yes, she went to La Clinica a few days ago. They said he has a hernia. She didn't know babies needed shots. They gave him one and told her to come back next month but to come here right away.

Her name is Amelia. She is seventeen, had come from Michoacán to marry her sweetheart but now he is in Soledad prison. She lives with an uncle and aunt. She has no money to go back home. They don't want her here and don't like the baby because he cries all the time.

"Do you breast-feed him?"

"Yes, but I don't think my milk is good. He wakes up and cries and cries."

She holds him like a potato sack. The expression on her face says, "Where does this sack go?" It occurs to me that she has nobody to tell her anything at all.

"Do you know to change breasts? Start off each time with a different breast and let him drink a long time, then put him on the other breast for a while. But be sure and change. This way he gets more milk and your breasts make more milk. He may be falling asleep because he's tired, not full. He also is probably crying because of the hernia. The doctor is very good. He'll fix your baby."

She seems to feel better. Hard to tell, she has what doctors call a "flat affect."

"I have to go to the other patients. I'll be back when the doctor comes." She nods, resigned. She has that hopeless look you see on battered women. God forgive me, because I am a woman too, but when I see women with that look I want to slap them.

Dr. Fritz has come, is in the first room. No matter how long he makes the mothers wait, no matter how mad Karma and I get, when he is with a child we all forgive him. He is a healer. The best surgeon, he does more surgeries than the others combined. Of course they all say he is obsessive and egomaniacal. They can't say he is not a fine surgeon though. He is famous, actually, was the doctor who risked his life to save the boy after the big earthquake.

The first two patients go quickly. I tell him there is a pre-op with no English in room 3, that I'd be right in. I clean the rooms and put more patients in. When I get to room 3 he is holding the baby, showing Amelia how to push the hernia in. The baby is smiling at him.

"Have Pat put him on the surgery schedule. Explain the pre-op and fasting carefully. Tell her to call if she can't push it in when it pops out." He hands her back the baby. "*Muy bonito*," he says.

"Ask her how Jesus got the bruises on his arms. The ones you should have made note of." He points to the marks on the underside of the baby's arms.

"I'm sorry," I say to him. When I ask her she looks frightened and surprised. "*No sé.*"

"She doesn't know."

"What do you think?"

"Seems to me that she's . . ."

"I can't believe you're going to say what I think you are. I have calls to return. I'll be in room one in ten minutes. I'll need some dilators, an eight and a ten."

He was right. I was going to say that she seemed a victim herself, and yes, I know what victims often do. I explain to her how important the surgery is, and the pre-op the day before. To call if the baby was sick or had a bad diaper rash. No milk three hours before the surgery. I get Pat to come set up a date with her and go over the instructions again.

I forget about her then until at least a month has gone by when for some reason it occurs to me she never brought the baby for a post-op. I asked Pat when the surgery was.

"Jesus Romero? That man is such a retard. No-show for the first surgery. Didn't bother to call. I call her and she says she couldn't get a ride. O-kay. So I tell her we'll have a same-day pre-op, to come in really early for an exam and blood work, but that she has got to come. And hallelujah, she shows. But guess what?"

"She feeds the baby a half hour before surgery."

"You got it. Fritz will be out of town so next slot I have is a month away."

It was very bad living with them. I couldn't wait until Manolo and I would be together. I gave them my check and food stamps. They gave me just a little money for things for me. I took care of Tina and Willie, but they didn't speak Spanish, didn't pay me any attention. Lupe hated having me there and Ramón was nice except when he got drunk he was always grabbing me or poking at me from behind. I was more afraid of Lupe than him so when I wasn't working in the house, I just stayed in my little corner in the kitchen.

"What are you doing there for hours and hours?" Lupe asked me.

"Thinking. About Manolo. About my *pueblo*."

"Start thinking about moving out of here."

Ramón had to work on the court day so Lupe took me. She could be nice sometimes. In the court we sat in the front. I almost didn't know him when he came in, handcuffed and with chains tying his legs together. Such a cruel thing to do to Manolo, who is a sweet man. He stood under the judge and then the judge said something and two polices took him away. He looked back at me, but I didn't know him with that face of anger. My Manolo. On the way home Lupe said it didn't look good. She didn't understand the charges either but it wasn't just possession of drugs, because they would've sent him to Santa Rita. Eight years in Soledad prison is bad.

"Eight years? *Cómo que* eight years!"

"Don't you go lose it now. I'll put you out right here in the street. I'm serious."

Lupe told me I had to go to the clinica because I was pregnant. I didn't know she meant I should have an *aborto*. "No," I told the lady doctor, "no, I want my baby, *mijito*. His daddy is gone, my baby is all I have." She was nice at first but then she got mad, said I was just a child I couldn't work, how could I care for him? That I was selfish, *porfiada*. "It's a sin," I told her. "I won't do it. I want my baby." She threw her notebook down on the table.

"*Válgame diós.* At least come in for checkups before the baby is born."

She gave me a card with the day and time to come but I never went back. The months went by slow. I kept waiting to hear from Manolo. Willie and Tina just watched the tele and were no trouble. I had the baby at Lupe's house. She helped but Ramón hit her when he got home and hit me too. He said bad enough I showed up. Now a kid too.

I try to keep out of their way. We have our little corner in the kitchen. Little Jesus is beautiful and he looks like Manolo. I got pretty things for him at the Goodwill and at Payless. I still don't know what Manolo did to go to jail or when we will hear from him. When I asked Ramón he said, "Kiss Manolo good-bye. See if you can get some work."

I watch Lupe's kids while she works and keep their house clean. I do all the wash in the laundromat downstairs. But I get so tired. Jesus cries and cries *no importa* what I do. Lupe told me I had to take him to the clinica. The buses scare me. The *mayates* grab at me and scare me. I think they're going to take him from me.

In the clinica they got mad at me again, said I should have had prenatal care, that he needed shots and was too small. He was seven pounds I said, my uncle weighed him. "Well, he's only eight now." They gave him a shot, said I had to come back. The doctor said Jesus had a hernia, which could be dangerous. He had to see a surgeon. A woman there gave me a map and wrote down the bus and BART train to get to the surgeon's office, told me where to stand even to get the bus and BART back. She called and made me an appointment.

Lupe had taken me, she was outside in the car with the kids when I got in. I told her what they said and then I began to cry. She stopped the car and shook me.

"You're a woman now! Face it. We'll give you some time till Jesus is okay, then you're going to have to figure out your own life. The apartment is too small. Ramón and I are dead tired and your kid cries day and night, or you do, worse. We're sick of it."

"I'm trying to help out," I said.

"Yeah, thanks a lot."

We were all up early the day I took him to the surgeon's. Lupe had to take the kids to day care. It's free and they like it better than staying home with just me so they were happy. But Lupe was mad because she had to drive so far to child care and now Ramón had to take the subway. It was scary, the bus, and then the BART and then another bus. I was too nervous to eat so I was hungry and dizzy from being frightened. But then I saw the big sign like they told me and I knew it was the right place. We had to wait so long. I left home at six in the morning and the doctor didn't see Jesus until three. I was so hungry. They explained everything real clear and the nurse told me about feeding him different to make more milk. The doctor was nice with Jesus and said he was *bonito* but he thought I hurt him, showed her blue spots on his arms. I didn't see the spots before. It's true. I hurt my baby, *mijito*. It was me who made them last night when he cried and cried. I had him under the blankets with me. I held him tight, "Hush hush stop crying, stop it stop it." I never grabbed him like that before. He didn't cry any less or any more.

Two weeks went past. I marked the days on the calendar. I told Lupe I had to go to the pre-op one day and for the surgery the next day.

"No way, José," Lupe said. The car was in the shop. She couldn't take her Willie and Tina to child care. So I didn't go.

Ramón stayed home. He was drinking beer and watching an A's game. The kids were taking a nap and I was feeding Jesus in the kitchen. "Come on in and watch the game, *prima*," he said so I went in. Jesus was still drinking but I had him covered with a blanket. Ramón got up for more beer. He hadn't seemed drunk until he got up but then he was falling around, then he was on the floor by the sofa. He pulled the blanket down and my T-shirt up. "Gimme some of that *chichi*," he said and was sucking on my other breast. I shoved him away and he hit the table but Jesus fell too and the table scratched his shoulder. There was blood running down his little arm. I was washing it with a paper towel and the phone rang.

It was Pat the lady from surgery real mad because I didn't call and didn't go. "I'm sorry," I told her in English.

She said there was a cancellation tomorrow. I could get the pre-op on the same day if I for sure took him real early. Seven in the morning. She was mad at me. She said he could get real sick and die, that if I kept missing surgeries the state could take him away from me. "Do you understand this?"

I said yes, but I didn't believe they could take my baby away from me.

"Are you coming tomorrow?" she asked.

"Yes," I said. I told Ramón that the next day I had to take Jesus for surgery, could he watch Tina and Willie.

"So I suck your tit you think you get something back? Yeah, I'll be here. I'm out of work anyways. Don't get any ideas about telling

Lupe nothing. Your ass would be out of here in five minutes. Which would be fine with me, but as long as it's here I mean to get me some."

He took me in the bathroom then, with Jesus in the living room crying on the floor and the kids hitting on the door. He bent me over the sink and banged and banged into me but he was so drunk it didn't last long. He slid to the floor passed out. I went out. I told the kids that he was sick. I was shaking so bad I had to sit down, rocked *mijito* Jesus and watched cartoons with the kids. I didn't know what to do. I said an Ave Maria but it seemed like there was so much noise everywhere how could a prayer ever get heard?

When Lupe got home he came out. I could tell the way he looked at me he knew he had done something bad but he didn't remember what. He said he was going out. She said terrific.

She opened the refrigerator. "Asshole drank all the beer. Go to the Seven-Eleven, Amelia, will you? Oh Christ, you can't even buy beer. What good are you? Have you even looked for a job or a place?"

I told her I had been watching the kids, how could I go anywhere? I said tomorrow was Jesus's surgery.

"Well, as soon as you can, you get started. They have ads for jobs and houses on billboards in groceries, the pharmacy."

"I can't read."

"They have ads in Spanish."

"I can't read Spanish *tampoco*."

"Fuck a duck."

I said it too. "Fuck a duck." It made her laugh, at least. Oh how I miss my pueblo, where the laughter is soft like breezes.

"Okay, Amelia. Tomorrow I'll look for you, I'll call around. Do me a favor and watch the kids now. I need a drink. I'll be at the Jalisco."

She must have run into Ramón, they came back together really late. There was only beans and Kool-Aid for the kids and me to eat. No bread, no flour for tortillas. Jesus was fast asleep in our corner in the kitchen but the minute I lay down he started to cry. I fed him. I could tell he was getting more now but after he slept awhile he was crying again. I tried to give him a pacifier but he just pushed it out. I was doing it again, holding him so tight whispering, "Hush hush," but then I stopped when I realized that I was hurting him but also I didn't want the doctor to see blue marks. The shoulder was bad enough all scraped and bruised, *pobrecito*. I prayed again to our mother Mary to help me, please to tell me what to do.

It was dark when I left the next morning. I found people who helped me get the right bus and BART and another bus. At the hospital they showed me where to go. They took blood from Jesus's arm. A doctor examined him but he didn't speak Spanish. I don't know what he was writing down. I know he wrote about the shoulder because he measured it with his thumb and then wrote. He looked at me with a question. "Children's push," I said in English and he nodded. They told me the surgery would be at eleven so I had fed him at eight. But hours and hours went by until it was one o'clock. Jesus was screaming. We were in a space with a bed and a chair. I was sitting in the chair but then the bed looked so good I got on it and held him to me. My breasts were dripping with milk. It's like they heard him crying. I couldn't bear it and I thought just a few seconds of milk wouldn't hurt.

Dr. Fritz was yelling at me. I took Jesus off my breast but he shook his head and nodded at me to go on ahead and feed him. A Latina nurse came in then to say they couldn't do the surgery now. She said they had a big waiting list and I had screwed them over twice. "You call Pat, get another date. Go on now, go home. Call her tomorrow. That child needs the surgery, you hear me?"

In my whole life at home nobody ever got mad at me.

When I stood up I must have fainted. The nurse was sitting by me when I woke up.

"I ordered you a big lunch. You must be hungry. Did you eat today?"

"No," I said. She fixed pillows behind me and a table over my lap. She held Jesus while I ate. I ate like an animal. Everything, soup, crackers, salad, juice, milk, meat, potatoes, carrots, bread, salad, pie; it was good.

"You need to eat well every day while you're nursing the baby," she said. "Will you be all right, going home?"

I nodded. Yes. I felt so good, the food was so good.

"Come on, now. Get ready to go. Here are some diapers for him. My shift was over an hour ago and I need to lock up."

Pat has a hard job. Our office of six surgeons is in Children's Hospital in Oakland. Every day each surgeon has a packed schedule. Also every day some get canceled, others put in their place and several emergencies added as well. One of our doctors is on call every day for the emergency room. All kinds of traumas, chopped-off fingers, aspirated peanuts, gunshot wounds, appendixes, burns, so there can be six or eight surprise surgeries a day.

Almost all of the patients are Medi-Cal and many are illegal aliens and don't even have that, so none of our doctors are in this for the money. It's an exhausting job for the office staff too. I work ten-hour days a lot. The surgeons are all different and for different reasons can be a pain in the butt sometimes. But even though we complain we respect them, are proud of them too, and we get a sense that we help. It is a rewarding job, not like working in a regular office. It has for sure changed the way I see things.

I have always been a cynical person. When I first started working here I thought it was a huge waste of taxpayers' money to do ten, twelve surgeries on crack babies with weird anomalies just so they could be alive and disabled after a year spent in a hospital, then moved from one foster home to another. So many without mothers, much less fathers. Most of the foster parents are really great but some are scary. So many children who are disabled or with brain damage, patients who will never be more than a few years old. Many patients with Down's syndrome. I thought that I could never keep a child like that.

Now I open the door to the waiting room and Toby who is all distorted and shaky, Toby who can't talk, is there. Toby who pees and shits into bags, who eats through a hole in his stomach. Toby comes to hug me, laughing, arms open. It's as if these kids are the result of a glitch God made answering prayers. All those mothers who don't want their children to grow up, who pray that their child will love them forever. Those answered prayers got sent down as Tobys.

For sure Tobys can crack up a marriage or a family, but when they don't it seems to have the reverse effect. It brings out the deepest good and bad feelings and the strengths and dignity that otherwise a man and a woman would never have seen in themselves or the other. It seems to me that each joy is savored more, that commitment has a deeper dimension. I don't think I'm romanticizing either. I study them hard, because I saw those qualities and they surprised me. I've seen several couples divorce. It seemed inevitable. There was the martyr parent or the slacking parent, the blamer, the why-me or the guilty one, the drinker or the crier. I've seen siblings act out from resentment, cause even more havoc and anger and guilt. But much more often I have seen the marriage and the family grow closer, better. Everybody learns to deal, has to help, has to be honest and say it sucks. Everybody has to laugh, everybody has to feel grateful when whatever else the child can't do he can kiss the hand that brushes his hair.

I don't like Diane Arbus. When I was a kid in Texas there were freak shows and even then I hated the way people would point at the freaks and laugh at them. But I was fascinated too. I loved the man with no arms who typed with his toes. But it wasn't the no arms that I liked. It was that he really wrote, all day. He was seriously writing something, liking what he was writing.

I admit it is pretty fascinating when the women bring in Jay for a pre-op with Dr. Rook. Everything is bizarre. They are midgets. They look like sisters, maybe they are, they are very tiny and plump with rosy cheeks and curly hair, turned-up noses and big smiles. They are lovers, stroke each other and kiss and fondle with no embarrassment. They had adopted Jay, a dwarf baby, with multiple, serious problems. Their social worker, who is, well, gigantic, has come with them, to carry him and his little oxygen tank and diaper bag. The mothers each carry a stool, like a milking stool, and sit on the little stools in the exam rooms talking about Jay and how much better he is, he can focus now, recognizes them. Dr. Rook is going to do a gastrostomy on him so he can be fed by a tube through an opening in his stomach.

He is an alert but calm baby, not especially small but with a huge deformed head. The women love to talk about him, willingly tell us how they carry him between them, how they bathe him and care for him. Pretty soon he'd need a helmet when he crawled because their furniture was only a foot or so high. They had named him Jay because it was close to joy, and he brought them so much joy.

I am going out the door to get some paper tape. He is allergic to tape. Look back and see the two mothers on tiptoes looking up at Jay, who is on his stomach on the exam table. He is smiling at them, they at him. The social worker and Dr. Rook are smiling at each other.

"That is the sweetest thing I ever saw," I say to Karma.

"Poor things. They're happy now. But he may only have a few more years, if that," she says.

"Worth it. Even if they had today and no more. It's still worth all the pain later. Karma, their tears will be sweet." I surprised myself saying this, but I meant it. I was learning about the labor of love.

Dr. Rook's husband calls her patients river babies, which makes her furious. He said that's what people used to call such babies in Mississippi. He is a surgeon with us too. He somehow manages to get almost all the surgeries with real insurance like Blue Cross. Dr. Rook gets most of the disabled or totally non-functioning children, but not just because she is a good surgeon. She listens to the families, cares about them, so she gets a lot of referrals.

Today there is one after another. The children are mostly older and heavy. Dead weight. I have to lift them, then hold them down while she removes the old button and puts in a new one. Most of them can't cry. You can tell it must really hurt but there are just tears falling sideways into their ears and this awful unworldly creaking, like a rusty gate, from deep inside.

The last patient is so cool. Not the patient, but what she does. A pretty red-faced newborn girl with six fingers on each hand. People always joke when babies are born about making sure it has five fingers and five toes. It's more common than I thought. Usually the doctors schedule them for an in-and-out surgery. This baby is only a few days old. Dr. Rook asks me for Xylocaine and a needle and some catgut. She deadens the area around the finger and then she ties a tight knot at the base of each extra little finger. She gives them some liquid Tylenol in case the baby seems to be hurting later, tells them not to touch it, that pretty soon, like a navel, the finger would turn black and fall off. She said her father had been a doctor in a small town in Alabama, that she had watched him do that.

Once, Dr. Kelly had seen a little boy who had six fingers on each hand. His parents really wanted the surgery but the child didn't. He was six or seven years old, a cute kid.

"No! I want them! They're mine! I want to keep them!"

I thought old Dr. Kelly might reason with the boy, but instead he told the parents that it seemed to him the child wanted to continue having this distinction.

"Why not?" he said. The parents couldn't believe he was saying this. He told the parents that if the boy changed his mind then they could do it. Of course, the younger the better.

"I like how he sticks up for his rights. Put her there, son," and he shook the kid's hand. They left, the parents furious, cursing at him, the child grinning.

Will he always feel this way? What if he plays the piano? Will it be too late if or when he changes his mind? Why not six fingers? They are weird anyway and so are toes, hair, ears. I wish we had tails, myself.

I am daydreaming about having a tail or leaves instead of hair, cleaning and restocking the exam rooms for the night when I hear a banging on the door. Dr. Rook had gone and I was the only one there. I unlock the door and let in Amelia and Jesus. She is crying, shivering as she speaks. His hernia is out and she can't push it in.

I get my coat, turn on the alarms and lock the door, walk with her down the block to the emergency room. I go in to be sure she gets registered. Dr. McGee is on call. Good.

"Dr. McGee is a sweet old doctor. He'll take care of your Jesus. They'll probably operate on him tonight. Don't forget to call to bring the baby to the office. In about a week. Call us. *Oye*, for God's sake, don't feed him."

It was crowded on the subway and the bus but I wasn't afraid. Jesus was sleeping. It seemed like the Virgin Mary answered me. She told me to take my next welfare check and go home to Mexico. The *curandera* would take care of my baby and my *mamacita* would know how to stop him from crying. I would feed him bananas and papayas. Not mangos because sometimes mangos give babies stomachaches. I wondered when babies got teeth.

Lupe was watching a telenovela when I got home. Her kids were asleep in the bedroom.

"Did he get the surgery?"

"No. Something happened."

"Yeah, I'll bet. What dumb thing did you do? Huh?"

I put him down in our corner without waking him up. Lupe came into the kitchen.

"I found a place for you. You can stay there at least until you find your own place. You can get your next check here and then tell Welfare your new address. Do you hear me."

"Yes. I want my check money. I'm going home."

"You're crazy. First place, this month's money is spent. Whatever you have is the last of it. *Estas loca?* It wouldn't get you even halfway to Michoacán. Look, girl, you're here. Find a job in a restaurant, someplace they'll let you stay in the back. Meet some guys, go out, have some fun. You're young, you're pretty, would be if you fixed yourself up. You're as good as single. You're learning English fast. You can't just give up."

"I want to go home."

"Fuck a duck," she said and she went back to the tele.

I was still sitting there when Ramón came in the back door. I guess he didn't see her on the sofa. He started grabbing my breasts and kissing my neck. "Sugar, I want some sugar!"

"*Ya estuvo,*" she said. To Ramón she said, "Go soak your head, you stinking fat pig," and shoved him out of the room. To me she just said, "You're out of here. Get all your shit together. Here's a plastic bag."

I put everything in my *bolsa* and the bag, picked up Jesus.

"Go on, take him and get in the car. I'll bring the things."

It looked just like a boarded-up old store but there was a sign, and a cross over the door. It was dark but she banged on the door. An old Anglo man came out. He shook his head and said something in English but she talked louder, pushed me and Jesus through the door and took off.

He turned on a flashlight. He tried to talk to me but I shook my head. No English. He was probably saying they didn't have enough beds. The room was full of cots with women on them, a few children. It smelled bad, like wine and vomit and pee. Bad, dirty. He brought me some blankets and pointed to a corner, same size as my kitchen corner. "Thank you," I said.

It was horrible. The minute I lay down, Jesus woke up. He wouldn't stop crying. I made sort of a tent to keep the sound in, but some of the women were cussing and saying, "Shaddup shaddup." They were mostly old white wino women but some young black ones who were shoving me and pushing me. One little one was slapping me with tiny hands like quick hornets.

"Stopit!" I screamed. "Stopit! Stopit!"

The man came out with the flashlight and led me through the room into a kitchen and a new corner. "*Mis bolsas!*" I said. He understood and went back in and brought my bags. "I'm sorry," I said in English. Jesus nursed and fell asleep, but I leaned against the wall and waited for morning. I am learning English, I thought. I went over all the English I knew. Court, Kentucky Fry, hamburger, good-bye, greaser, nigger, asshole, ho, Pampers, How much? Fuck a duck, children, hospital, stopit, shaddup, hello, I'm sorry, *General Hospital, All My Children*, inguinal hernia, pre-op, post-op, *Geraldo*, food stamps, money, car, crack, pólis, *Miami Vice*, José Canseco, homeless, real pretty, No way, José, Excuse me, I'm sorry, please, please, stopit, shaddup, shaddup, I'm sorry. Holy Mary mother of God pray for us.

Just before light the man and an old woman came in and started to boil water for oatmeal. She let me help her, pointed to sugar and napkins to put in the middle of the lined-up tables.

We all had oatmeal and milk for breakfast. The women looked really bad off, crazy or drunk some of them. Homeless and dirty.

We all waited in line to take a shower, by the time it was Jesus and me the water was cold and just one little towel. Then me and Jesus were homeless too. During the day the space was a nursery for children. We could come back at night for soup and a bed. The man was nice. He let me leave my *bolsa* there so I just took some diapers. I spent the day walking around Eastmont Mall. I went to a park but then I was scared because men came up to me. I walked and walked and the baby was heavy. The second day the little one who had been slapping me showed me or somehow I understood her that you can ride all day on the buses, getting transfers. So I did that because he was too heavy and this way I could sit down and look around or sleep when Jesus did because at night I didn't sleep. One day I saw where La Clinica was. I decided the next day I'd go there and find somebody there to help me. So I felt better.

The next day though, Jesus started to cry in a different way, like barking. I looked at his hernia and it was pooched way out and hard. I got on the bus right away but still it was long, the bus then BART then another bus. I thought the doctor's was closed but the nurse was there, she took us to the hospital. We waited a long time but they finally took him to surgery. They said they'd keep him for the night, put me on a cot next to a little box for him. They gave me a ticket to go and eat in the cafeteria. I got a sandwich and a Coke and ice cream, some cookies and fruit for later but I fell asleep it was so good not to be on the floor. When I woke the nurse was there. Jesus was all clean and wrapped in a blue blanket.

"He's hungry!" she smiled. "We didn't wake you when he got out of surgery. Everything went fine."

"Thank you." Oh, thank God! He was fine! While I fed him I cried and prayed.

"No reason to cry now," she said. She had brought me a tray with coffee and juice and cereal.

Dr. Fritz came in, not the doctor that did the surgery, the first doctor. He looked at Jesus and nodded, smiled at me, looked over his chart. He lifted the baby's shirt. There was still a scrape and a bruise on his shoulder. The nurse asked me about it. I told her it had been the kids where I was staying, that I didn't live there no more.

"He wants you to know that if he sees any more bruises he is going to call CPS. Those are people who might take your baby, or maybe they will just want you to talk to somebody."

I nodded. I wanted to tell her that I needed to talk to somebody.

We have had some busy days. Both Dr. Adeiko and Dr. McGee were on vacation so the other doctors were really busy. Several Gypsy patients, which always means the whole family, cousins, uncles, everybody comes. It always makes me laugh (not really laugh, since he doesn't like any joking or unprofessional behavior), because one thing Dr. Fritz always does when he comes into the room is politely greet the parent, "Good morning." Or if it's both, he'll nod at each and say, "Good morning. Good morning." And with Gypsy families I suffer not laughing when he squeezes into the room and says, "Good morning. Good morning. Good morning. Good morning. Good morning," etc. He and Dr. Wilson seem to get a lot of hypospadias babies, which is when male babies have holes on the side of their penises, sometimes several so that when they pee it's like a sprinkler. Anyway, one Gypsy baby called Rocky Stereo had it but Dr. Fritz fixed it. The whole family, about a dozen adults and some children, had come for the post-op and were all shaking his hand. "Thank you. Thank you. Thank you. Thank you." Worse than his good mornings! It was sweet and funny and I started to say something later, but he glared. He never discusses patients. None of them do, actually. Except Dr. Rook, but only rarely.

I don't even know the original diagnosis for Reina. She is four-teen now. She comes in with her mother, two sisters, and a brother. They push her in a huge stroller-wheelchair her father made. The sisters are twelve and fifteen, the boy is eight, all beautiful children, lively and funny. When I get in the room they have her propped on the exam table. She is naked. Except for the feeding button her body is flawless, satin smooth. Her breasts have grown. You can't see the hooflike growth she has instead of teeth, her exquisite lips are parted and bright red. Emerald green eyes with long black lashes. Her sisters have given her a shaggy punk cut, a ruby stud in her nose, painted a butterfly tattoo on her thigh. Elena is polishing her toenails while Tony arranges her arms be-hind her head. He is the strongest, the one who helps me hold her upper torso while her sisters hold her legs. But right now she lies there like Manet's *Olympia*, breathtakingly pure and lovely. Dr. Rook stops short like I did, just to look at her. "God, she is beautiful," she says.

"When did she start to menstruate?" she asks.

I hadn't noticed the Tampax string among the jet-black silken hairs. The mother says it is her first time. Without irony she says,

"She is a woman now."

She is in danger now, I think.

"Okay, hold her down," Dr. Rook says. The mother grabs her waist, the girls her legs, Tony and I hold her arms. She fights vio-lently against us but Dr. Rook at last gets the old button out and puts in a new one.

She was the last patient of the day. I'm cleaning the room, put-ting fresh paper on the table when Dr. Rook comes back in. She says, "I'm so grateful for my Nicholas."

I smile and say, "And I for my Nicholas." She's talking about her six-month-old baby, I'm talking about my six-year-old grandson.

"Good night," we say and then she goes over to the hospital.

I go home and make a sandwich, turn on an A's game. Dave Stewart pitching against Nolan Ryan. It has gone into ten innings when the phone rings. Dr. Fritz. He's at the ER, wants me to come. "What is it?"

"Amelia, remember her? There are people who can speak Spanish, but I want you to talk to her."

Amelia was in the doctor's room at the ER. She had been sedated, stared even more blankly than usual. And the baby? He leads me to a bed behind a curtain.

Jesus is dead. His neck was broken. There are bruises on his arms. The police are on the way, but Dr. Fritz wants me to talk to her calmly first, see if I can find out what happened.

"Amelia? Remember me?"

"Sí. Cómo no? How are you? Can I see him, mijito Jesus?"

"In a minute. First I need for you to tell me what happened."

It took a while to figure out that she had been riding around on buses in the daytime, spending the nights in a homeless shelter. When she got there tonight two of the younger women took all her money from where she had it pinned inside her clothes. They hit her and kicked her, then left. The man who runs the place didn't understand Spanish and didn't know what she was saying. He kept telling her to be quiet, put his fingers up to his mouth to tell her to be quiet, to keep the baby quiet. Then later the women came back. They were drunk and it was dark and other people were trying to sleep, but Jesus kept crying. Amelia had no money at all now and didn't know what to do. She couldn't think. The two women came. One slapped her and the other one took Jesus, but Amelia grabbed him back. The man came and the women went to lie down. Jesus kept crying.

"I couldn't think about what to do. I shook him to make him be quiet so I could think about what to do."

I held her tiny hands in mine. "Was he crying when you shook him?"

"Yes."

"Then what happened?"

"Then he stopped crying."

"Amelia. Do you know that Jesus is dead?"

"Yes, I know. *Lo sé*." And then in English she said, "Fuck a duck. I'm sorry."

502

502 was the clue for 1-Across in this morning's *Times*. Easy. That's the police code for Driving While Intoxicated, so I wrote in DWI. Wrong. I guess all those Connecticut commuters knew you were supposed to put in Roman numerals. I had a few moments of panic, as I always do when memories of my drinking days come up. But since I moved to Boulder I have learned to do deep breathing and meditation, which never fail to calm me.

I'm glad I got sober before I moved to Boulder. This is the first place I ever lived that didn't have a liquor store on every corner. They don't even sell alcohol in Safeway here and of course never on Sundays. They just have a few liquor stores mostly on the outskirts of town, so if you're some poor wino with the shakes and it's snowing, Lord have mercy. The liquor stores are gigantic Target-size nightmares. You could die from DTs just trying to find the Jim Beam aisle.

The best town is Albuquerque, where the liquor stores have drive-through windows, so you don't even have to get out of your pajamas. They don't sell on Sundays either though. So if I didn't plan ahead there was always the problem of who in the world could I drop in on who wouldn't offer a wine cooler.

Even though I had been sober for years before I moved here I had trouble at first. Whenever I looked in the rearview mirror I'd go "Oh no," but it was just the ski racks everybody has on their cars. I have never actually even seen a police car in pursuit or seen anyone being arrested. I have seen policemen in shorts at the mall, eating Ben & Jerry's frozen yogurt, and a SWAT team in a pickup truck. Six men in camouflage with big tranquilizer rifles, chasing a baby bear down the middle of Mapleton.

This must be the healthiest town in the country. There is no drinking at frat parties or football games. No one smokes or eats red meat or glazed doughnuts. You can walk alone at night, leave your doors unlocked. There are no gangs here and no racism. There aren't many races, actually.

That dumb 502. All these memories came flooding into my head, in spite of the breathing. The first day of my job at U——, the Safeway problem, the incident at San Anselmo, the scene with A——.

Everything is fine now. I love my job and the people I work with. I have good friends. I live in a beautiful apartment just beneath Mount Sanitas. Today a western tanager sat on a branch in my backyard. My cat Cosmo was asleep in the sun so he didn't chase it. I am deeply grateful for my life today.

So God forgive me if I confess that once in a while I get a diabolical urge to, well, mess it all up. I can't believe I'd even have this thought, after all those years of misery. Officer Wong either taking me to jail or to detox.

The Polite One, we all called Wong. We called all the other ones pigs, which would never have applied to Officer Wong, who was very nice, really. Methodical and formal. There were never any of the usual physical interchanges between you and him like with the others. He never slammed you against the car or twisted the cuffs into your wrist. You stood there for hours as he painstakingly wrote up his ticket and read you your rights. When he cuffed you he said, "Permit me," and "Watch your head" when you got into the car.

He was diligent and honest, an exceptional member of the Oakland police force. We were lucky to have him in our neighborhood.

I am really sorry now about that one incident. One of the steps of AA is to make amends with people you have wronged. I think I have made most of the amends I could. I owe Officer Wong one. I wronged Wong for sure.

Back then I lived in Oakland, in that big turquoise apartment on the corner of Alcatraz and Telegraph. Right above Alcatel Liquors, just down from the White Horse, across the street from the 7-Eleven. Good location.

The 7-Eleven was sort of a gathering place for old winos. Although, unlike them, I went to work every day, they ran into me in liquor stores on weekends. Lines at the Black and White that opened at six a.m. Late-night haggling with the Pakistani sadist who worked at the 7-Eleven.

They were all friendly with me. "How ya been, Miss Lu?" Sometimes they asked me for money, which I always gave them, and several times when I had lost my job, I asked them. The group of them changed as they went to jails, hospitals, death. The regulars were Ace, Mo, Little Ripple, and The Champ. These four old black guys would spend their mornings at the 7-Eleven and their afternoons snoozing or drinking in a faded aqua Chevrolet Corvair parked in Ace's yard. His wife Clara wouldn't let them smoke or drink in the house. Winter and summer, rain or shine, the four would be in that car. Sleeping like little kids on car trips, heads on folded hands, or looking straight ahead as if they were on a Sunday drive, commenting on everybody who drove or walked by, passing around a bottle of port.

When I'd come up the street from the bus stop I'd holler out, "How's it going?" "Jes' fine!" Mo would say. "I got my wine!" And Ace would say, "I feel so well, got my muscatel!" They'd ask about my boss, that fool Dr. B.

"Just quit that ol' job! Get yourself on SSI where you belong! You come sit with us, sister, pass the time in comfort, don't need no job!"

Once Mo said I didn't look so good, maybe I needed detox.

"Detox?" The Champ scoffed. "Never detox. Retox! That's the ticket!"

The Champ was short and fat, wore a shiny blue suit, a clean white shirt, and a porkpie hat. He had a gold watch with a chain and he always had a cigar. The other three all wore plaid shirts, overalls, and A's baseball hats.

One Friday I didn't go to work. I must have been drinking the night before. I don't know where I had gone in the morning, but I remember coming back and that I had a bottle of Jim Beam. I parked my car behind a van across the street from my building. I went upstairs and fell asleep. I woke to loud knocking on my door.

"Open your door, Ms. Moran. This is Officer Wong."

I stashed the bottle in the bookcase and opened the door. "Hello, Officer Wong. How can I help you?"

"Do you own a Mazda 626?"

"You know I do, sir."

"Where is that car, Ms. Moran?"

"Well, it's not in here."

"Where did you park the vehicle?"

"Up across from the church." I couldn't remember.

"Think again."

"I can't remember."

"Look out the window. What do you see?"

"Nothing. The 7-Eleven. Telephones. Gas tanks."

"Any parking places?"

"Yeah. Amazing. Two of them! Oh. I parked it there, behind a van."

"You left the car in neutral, without the parking brake on. When the van left, your vehicle followed it down Alcatraz during rush-hour traffic, proceeded to cross into the other lane, narrowly missing cars, and sped down the sidewalk, almost harming a man, his wife, and a baby in a stroller."

"Well. Then what?"

"I'm taking you to see then what. Come along."

"I'll be right out. I want to wash my face."

"I'll stay right here."

"Please. Some privacy, sir. Wait outside the door."

I took a big drink of whiskey. Brushed my teeth and combed my hair.

We walked silently down the street. Two long blocks. Damn.

"If you think about it, it's pretty miraculous that my Mazda didn't hit anything or hurt anybody. Don't you think so, Officer Wong? A miracle!"

"Well, it did hit something. It is a miracle that none of the gentlemen were in the car at the time. They got out to watch your Mazda coming down the street."

My car was nuzzled into the right fender of the Chevy Corvair. The four men were standing there, shaking their heads. Champ puffed on his cigar.

"Thank the Lord you wasn't in it, sister," Mo said. "First thing I did, I opened the door and said, 'Where she be?'"

There was a big dent in the fender and the door of the Chevrolet. My car had a broken bumper and headlight, broken turn-signal light.

Ace was still shaking his head. "Hope you got insurance, Miz Lucille. I got me one classic car here what has some serious damage."

"Don't worry, Ace. I got insurance. You bring me an estimate as soon as you can."

The Champ spoke to the others quietly. They tried not to smile but it didn't work. Ace said, "Just sittin' here minding our own business and look what happens! Praise the Lord!"

Officer Wong was writing down my license plate numbers and Ace's license plate numbers.

"Does that car have a motor in it?" he asked Ace.

"This here car is a museum piece. Vintage model. Don't need no motor."

"Well, guess I'll try to back out of here without running into anybody," I said.

"Not so fast, Ms. Moran," Officer Wong said. "I need to write up a citation."

"A citation? Shame on you, Officer!"

"You can't be writing this lady no ticket. She was asleep at the time of the incident!"

The old guys were crowding around him, making him nervous.

"Well," he sputtered, "she's guilty of reckless . . . reckless . . ."

"Can't be reckless driving. She wasn't driving the car!"

He was trying to think. They were muttering and grumbling. "Shame. Shameful. Innocent taxpayers. Poor thing, on her own and all."

"I definitely smell alcohol," Officer Wong said.

"That's me!" all four of them said at once, exhaling.

"No sir," Champ said. "If you ain't doing the D you can't get the DWI!"

"That's the truth!"

"Sure enough."

Officer Wong looked at us with a very discouraged expression. The police radio began squawking. He quickly put his pad into his pocket, turned, and hurried to the squad car, took off with lights and siren.

The insurance check came very soon, sent to me but written out to Horatio Turner. The four men were sitting in the car when I handed the check to Ace. Fifteen hundred dollars.

That afternoon was the only time I sat inside the old car. I had to slide in after The Champ since the other door wouldn't open. Little Ripple, who was little, sat on my other side. They were all drinking Gallo Port but brought me a big Colt 45. They toasted me. "Here's to our lady Lucille!" That's how I was known in the neighborhood after that.

The sad part was that this happened in early spring. Officer Wong still had spring and summer on that same beat. Every day he had to pass by the guys in the Chevrolet Corvair, smiling and waving.

Of course I had other encounters with Officer Wong after that one, not pleasant at all.

Here It Is Saturday

The ride from city to county jail goes along the top of the hills above the bay. The avenue is lined with trees and that last morning it was foggy, like an old Chinese painting. Just the sound of the tires and the wipers. Our leg chains made the sound of oriental instruments and the prisoners in orange jumpsuits swayed together like Tibetan monks. You laugh. Well, so did I. I knew I was the only white guy on the bus and that all these dudes weren't the Dalai Lama. But it was beautiful. Maybe I laughed because I felt silly, seeing it that way. Karate Kid heard me laugh. Old Chaz has a wet brain now for sure. Most of the men going to jail now are just kids for crack. They don't hassle me, think I'm just an old hippy.

The first view of the prison is awesome. After a long climb you come upon a valley in the hills. The land used to be the summer estate of a millionaire called Spreckles. The fields around the county jail are like the grounds of a French castle. That day there were a hundred Japanese plum trees in bloom. Flowering quince. Later on there were fields of daffodils, then iris.

In front of the jail is a meadow where there is a herd of buffalo. About sixty buffalo. Already there were six new calves. For some reason all the sick buffalo in the U.S. get sent here. Veterinarians treat them and study them. You can tell when dudes on the bus are doing their first time because they all freak out. "Whoa! What the fuck! Do they feed us buffalo? Check them mothers out."

The prison and the women's jail, the auto shop and the green-houses. No people, no other houses, so it seems as if you're suddenly in an ancient prairie lit by sunbeams in the mist. The Bluebird bus always frightens the buffalo even though it comes once a week. They break into a gallop, stampede off toward the green hills. Like a tourist on safari I was hoping I'd get a view of the fields.

The bus unloaded us into the basement holding cell where we waited to get processed. A long wait and still another butt search. "Chaz, don't be laughin' now," Karate Kid said. He told me CD was here, had been violated. Jail talk is like Spanish. The cup breaks itself. You don't violate your parole. The police violate you.

Sunnyvale gang shot the Chink. I hadn't heard that. I knew CD loved his brother Chink, a big-time dealer in the Mission. "Heavy," I said.

"No shit. Everybody gone by the time the police come except CD be sittin' there holding the Chink's head. All they had on him was violation. Six months. He'll do three maybe. Then he'll get the motherfuckers."

I lucked out and got the third tier (but no view), a cell with only two surly kids and Karate, who I know from the street. Only three other white guys on the tier, so I was glad Karate was with me. The cells were meant for two people. Usually there are six men in them; we'd get two more in a week. The Kid would spend his time lifting weights and practicing kicks and lunges, whatever he does.

When we got here Mac was the deputy in charge. He's always laying AA rap on me. He knows I like to write though, brought me a yellow pad and a pen. Said he saw I was in for B and E and bur-glary, would be staying awhile. "Maybe this time you'll do a fourth step, Chaz." That's when you admit all your wrongs.

"Better bring me about ten more tablets," I told him.

Anything you can say about prison is a cliché. Humiliation. The waiting, the brutality, the stench, the food, the endlessness. No way to describe the incessant earsplitting noise.

•

For two days I had bad shakes. One night I must have had a seizure, or else fifty guys beat me up in my sleep. Split my lip, broke
some teeth, black and blue all over. Tried to make sick bay but
none of the guards would go for it.

"You don't ever have to go through this again," Mac said.

At least they let me stay on my bunk. CD was on another tier
but during exercise I could see him down in the yard, smoking
with other dudes, listening while they laughed. Most of the time
he walked around alone.

Weird how some people have power. Meanest mothers out
there deferred to him, just by how they stood back when he passed
by. He's not huge like his brother, but has the same strength and
cool. They had a Chinese mother and black father. CD has one
long pigtail down his back. He is an unworldly color, like an old
sepia photograph, black tea with milk.

Sometimes he reminds me of a Masai warrior, other times a
Buddha or a Mayan god. He'd stand there not moving, not blinking an eye, for half an hour. He has the calm indifference of a god.
I probably sound like a nut or a fag. Anyway, he has this effect on
everybody.

I met him in County when he'd just turned eighteen. It was our
first time in jail. I turned CD on to books. The first time he fell in
love with words was Stephen Crane's *The Open Boat*. Every week
the guy from the library would come and we'd give him back our
books and get more. Latinos have an elaborate sign language they
use in here. Me and CD started speaking in book. *Crime and
Punishment*, *The Stranger*, Elmore Leonard. I was in one other
time when he was and by then he was turning me on to different
writers.

Out on the street I'd run into him sometimes. He'd always give
me money, which was awkward, but I was out there panhandling,

so I never said no. We'd sit on a bus stop bench and talk. CD's read more than I have by now. He's twenty-two. I'm thirty-two but people always figure I'm a lot older. I feel around sixteen. I've been drunk since then, so a lot has passed me by. I missed Watergate, thank God. I still talk like a hippy, say things like "groovy" and "what a trip."

Willie Clampton woke me by banging on my bars when the tier got back from the yard. "Yo, Chaz, what's happening? CD says welcome home."

"Say, how you been, Willie?"

"Cool. Couple more *Soul Train*s I'm gone. You dudes got to sign up for writing class. They got righteous classes now. Music, pottery, drama, painting. They even let them over from the women's jail. Say, Kid, Dixie's in the class. Word."

"No way. What's Dixie doing in County?"

Karate Kid used to pimp Dixie. She ran her own feminist operation now, girls and coke to big-time lawyers, county supervisors. Whatever she was in for she'd be out soon. She was about forty but still looked fine. On the street you'd take her for a Neiman Marcus buyer. She never copped to knowing me but always gave me five or ten bucks and a big grin. "Now, young man, you use this to get a nice nourishing breakfast."

"So what you write?"

"Stories, rap, poems. Check out my poem:

Police cars rolling back to back
They don't care
'cause it's black on black

and

Two wet sugars
for one cigarette
Big score."

Karate and I laughed. "Go ahead on, motherfuckers, laugh. Dig this."

Damned if he didn't recite a sonnet by Shakespeare. Willie. His deep voice above the insanity of jail noise.

"'Shall I compare thee to a summer's day? Thou art more lovely and more temperate . . .'

"Teacher's white, old. Old as my gramma, but she's cool. Ferragamo boots. First day she came in wearing Coco perfume. She couldn't believe I knew it. Now she wears different ones. I know them all. Opium, Ysatis, Joy. Only one I missed was Fleurs de Rocaille."

Sounded like he said it perfectly. Karate and me laughed our heads off about him and his Fleurs de Rocaille.

Actually one sound you hear a lot in jail is laughter.

This is not your normal jail. I've been in normal jails, Santa Rita, Vacaville. A miracle I'm still alive. County #3 has been on *60 Minutes* for how progressive it is. Computer training, mechanics, printing. A famous horticulture school. We supply the greens for Chez Panisse, Stars, other restaurants. This is where I got my G.E.D.

The head of the jail, Bingham, is something else. He's an ex-con, for one thing. Murdered his father. Did serious time for it. When he got out he went to law school, decided to change the prison system. He understands jail.

Nowadays he'd have walked, got self-defense for being abused. Hell, I could get off Murder One easy, just tell a jury about my ma. Stories about my father, I could be the fuckin' Zodiac.

They're going to build a new jail, next to this one. Bingham says this jail is the same as the street. Same power structure, attitudes, brutality, drugs. The new jail will change all this. You won't want to come back to it, he says. Face it, part of you likes to get back in here, get some rest.

Signed up for the class just to see CD. Mrs. Bevins said that CD had told her about me.

"That ol' wino? Bet you heard plenty about me. I'm the Karate Kid. I'll be makin' you smile. Put some pep in your step. Glide in your stride."

A writer called Jerome Washington wrote about this kind of Uncle Tomming. Talking jive to whites. Things like "I be's so rich I had money in bof my shoes." True, we love it. The teacher was laughing. "Just ignore him," Dixie said. "He's incorrigible."

"No way, mama. Encourage me all you want."

Mrs. Bevins had me and Karate fill out a questionnaire while they read their work out loud. I thought the questions would be about our education and police record, but they were things like "Describe your ideal room," "You are a stump. Describe yourself as a stump."

We were scribbling away, but I was listening to Marcus read a story. Marcus is a brutal guy, Indian, a serious felon. He wrote a good story, though, about a little kid watching his dad get beat up by some rednecks. It was called, "How I Became a Cherokee."

"This is a fine story," she said.

"The story is fucked. It was fucked when I first read it someplace. I never knew my father. I figured this was the kind of bullshit you want from us. Bet you come all over yourself how you help us unfortunate victims of society get in touch with our feelings."

"I don't give a rat's ass about your feelings. I'm here to teach writing. Matter of fact you can lie and still tell the truth. This story is good, and it rings true, wherever it came from."

She was backing to the door while she spoke. "I hate victims," she said. "For sure I don't want to be yours." She opened the door, told the guards to take Marcus up to the tier.

"If this class goes right what we will be doing is trusting each other with our lives," she said. She told me and Karate that the assignment had been to write about pain. "Read your story, please, CD."

When he finished reading the story, Mrs. Bevins and I smiled at each other. CD smiled too. First time ever I saw him really smile, little white teeth. The story was about a young man and a girl looking in the window of a junk store in North Beach. They're talking about the stuff, an old picture of a bride, some little shoes, an embroidered pillow.

The way he described the girl, her thin wrists, the blue vein on her forehead, her beauty and innocence, it broke your heart. Kim was crying. She's a young Tenderloin whore, mean little bitch.

"Yeah, it's cool, but it ain't pain," Willie said.

"I felt pain," Kim said.

"Me too," Dixie said. "I'd kill to have somebody see me that way."

Everybody was arguing, saying it was about happiness, not pain.

"It's about love," Daron said.

"Love, no way. Dude doesn't even touch her."

Mrs. Bevins said to notice all the mementos of dead people. "The sunset is reflected in the glass. All the images are about the fragility of life and love. Those tiny wrists. The pain is in the awareness that the happiness won't last."

"Yeah," Willie said, "except in this story he be engrafting her new."

"Say wha', nigger?"

"That's from Shakespeare, blood. It's what art does. It freezes his happiness. CD can have it back any old time, just reading that story."

"Yeah, but he can't be fuckin' it."

"You've got it perfectly, Willie. I swear this class understands better than any class I ever taught," she said. On another day she said that there was little difference between the criminal mind and the mind of the poet. "It is a matter of improving upon reality, making our own truth. You have an eye for detail. Two minutes in a room you have everything and everybody scoped out. You all can smell a lie."

The classes were four hours long. We talked while we wrote, in between reading our work, listening to things she read. Talked to ourselves, to her, to one another. Shabazz said it reminded him of Sunday school when he was a kid, coloring pictures of Jesus and talking away real soft just like here. Shabazz is a religious fanatic, in for beating his wife and kids. His poems were a cross between rap and Song of Solomon.

The writing class changed my friendship with Karate Kid. We wrote every night in our cell and read our stories to each other, took turns reading out loud. Baldwin's "Sonny's Blues." Chekhov's "Sleepy."

I stopped being self-conscious after the first day, reading aloud "My Stump." My stump was the only one left in a burned-out forest. It was black and dead and, when the wind blew, bits of charcoal crumbled and fell away.

"What have we got here?" she asked.

"Clinical depression," Daron said.

"We got us one burnt-out hippy," Willie said. Dixie laughed, "I see a very poor body image." "The writing is good," CD said. "I really felt how bleak and hopeless everything is."

"True," Mrs. Bevins said. "People are always saying 'tell the truth' when you write. Actually it is hard to lie. The assignment seems silly . . . a stump. But this is deeply felt. I see an alcoholic who is sick and tired. This stump is how I would have described myself before I stopped drinking."

"How long were you sober before you felt different?" I asked her. She said it worked the other way around. First I had to think I wasn't hopeless, then I could stop.

"Whoa," Daron said, "if I want to hear this shit I'll sign up for AA meetings."

"Sorry," she said. "Do me a favor, though. Don't answer this out loud. Each of you. Ask yourself if the last time, or times, you were arrested, whatever it was for—were you high on drugs or alcohol at the time?" Silence. Busted. We all laughed. Dwight said, "You know that group MADD, Mothers Against Drunk Drivers? We got our own group, DAM. Drunks Against Mothers."

Willie left a couple of weeks after I got there. We were sorry to see him go. Two of the women got in a fight so there was only Dixie, Kim, and Casey left, and six guys. Seven when Vee de la Rangee took Willie's place. Puny, pimply ugly transvestite with blond permanent, black roots. He wore a plastic bread fastener for a nose ring, about twenty along each ear. Daron and Dwight looked like they might kill him. He said he had written some poems. "Read us one."

It was a lush violent fantasy about the drag-heroin world. After he read no one said anything. Finally CD said, "That's some powerful shit. Let's hear some more." Like CD gave everybody permission to accept this guy. Vee took off from there and by the next class he was at home. You could see how much it meant to him, to be heard. Hell, I felt that way too. Once I even had the nerve to write about when my dog died. I didn't even care if they laughed, but nobody laughed.

Kim didn't write that much. A lot of remorse poems about the child that got taken away from her. Dixie wrote sardonic things to the theme of "Vice Is So Nice." Casey was fantastic. She wrote about heroin addiction. Really got to me. Most of the guys in here sold crack but either didn't use it that much or were too young to know what years and years of voluntarily returning to hell can do to you. Mrs. Bevins knew. She didn't talk that much about it, but enough to make it seem pretty cool that she had stopped.

We all wrote some good things. "That's great!" Mrs. Bevins said to Karate once. "You get better every week."

"No lie? So, Teach, am I as good as CD?"

"Writing isn't a contest. All you do is your own work better and better."

"But CD's your favorite."

"I don't have a pet. I have four sons. I have a different feeling for each one. It's the same with you guys."

"But you don't be telling us to go to school, get a scholarship. You're always getting on him to change his life."

"She does that with all of us," I said, "except Dixie. She's subtle though. Who knows, I might sober up. Anyway, CD is the best. We all know that. First day I got here I saw him down in the yard. You know what I thought? I thought he looked like a god."

"I don't know about god," Dixie said. "But he has star quality. Right, Mrs. Bevins?"

"Give me a break," CD said.

Mrs. Bevins smiled. "Okay. I'll cop. I think every teacher sees this sometimes. It's not simply intelligence or talent. It's a nobility of spirit. A quality which could make him great at whatever he wanted to do."

We were quiet then. I think we all agreed with her. But we felt sorry for her. We knew what it was he wanted to do, was going to do.

We got back to work then, choosing pieces for our magazine. She was going to have it typeset and then the jail printshop would print it.

She and Dixie were laughing. They both loved to gossip. Now they were rating some of the deputies. "He's the kind leaves his socks on," Dixie said. "Right. And flosses before."

"We need more prose. Let's try this assignment for next week, see what you come up with." She handed out a list of titles from Raymond Chandler's notebook. We all had to choose one. I took *We All Liked Al.* Casey liked *Too Late for Smiling.* CD liked *Here It Is Saturday.* "In fact," he said, "I think we should call our magazine that."

"We can't," Kim said. "We promised Willie we were going to use his title, *Through a Cat's Eye.*"

"Okay, so what I want is two or three pages leading up to a dead body. Don't show us the actual body. Don't tell us there's going to be a body. End the story with us knowing there is going to be a dead body. Got it?"

"Got it."

"Time to go, gentlemen," the guard said, opening the door. "Come here, Vee." She blasted him with perfume before sending him back up. The homosexual tier was pretty miserable. Half of it was old senile winos, the rest were gays.

I wrote a great story. It came out in the magazine and I still read it over and over. It was about Al, my best friend. He's dead now. Only she said I didn't do the assignment right because I told about me and the landlady finding Al's body.

Kim and Casey wrote the same horrible story. Kim's was about her old man beating her, Casey's about a sadistic john. You knew that they would end up murdering the guys. Dixie wrote a fine story about a woman in solitary. She has an asthma attack really bad but no one can hear her. The terror and pitch-black darkness. Then there is an earthquake. The end.

You can't imagine what it is like to be in prison during an earthquake.

CD wrote about his brother. Most of CD's stories had been about him when they were little. The years they were lost to each other in different foster homes. How they found each other by chance, in Reno. This story took place in the Sunnyvale district. He read it in a quiet voice. None of us moved. It was about the afternoon and evening leading up to the Chink's death. The details about the meeting of two gangs. It ended with Uzi fire and CD turning the corner.

The hairs were standing up on my arm. Mrs. Bevins was pale. Nobody had told her CD's brother was dead. There wasn't a word about his brother in the story. That's how good it was. The story was so shimmering and taut there could only be one end to it. The room was silent until finally Shabazz said, "Amen." The guard opened the door. "Time to go, gentlemen." The other guards waited for the women while we filed out.

CD was set to get out of jail two days after the last day of class. The magazines would be out the last day and there was going to

be a big party. An art exhibit and music by the prisoners. Casey,
CD, and Shabazz were going to read. Everybody would get copies
of *Through a Cat's Eye.*

We had been excited about the magazine but none of us had
known how it would feel. To see our work in print. "Where is CD?"
she asked. We didn't know. She gave each of us twenty copies. We
read our pieces out loud, applauding one another. Then we just sat
there, reading our own work over and over to ourselves.

The class was short because of the party. A mess of deputies
came in and opened the doors between our room and the art
class. We helped set up tables for the food. Stacks of our magazines looked beautiful. Green on the purple paper tablecloth. Guys
from horticulture brought in big bouquets of flowers. Student
paintings were on the walls, sculptures on stands. One band was
setting up.

First one band played, then came our reading and then the other
band. The reading went fine and the music was great. Kitchen
dudes brought in food and soft drinks and everybody got in line.
There were dozens of guards but they all seemed to be having a
good time too. Even Bingham was there. Everybody was there
except CD.

She was talking with Bingham. He is so cool. I saw him nod
and call a guard over. I knew Bingham had said to let her go up on
the tier.

She wasn't gone long, even after all the stairs and six locked
steel gates. She sat down, looking sick. I took her a can of Pepsi.

"Did you talk with him?"

She shook her head. "He was lying under a blanket, wouldn't
answer me. I slid the magazines through the bars. It's horrible up
there, Chaz. His window is broken, rain coming through it. The
stink. The cells are so small and dark."

"Hey, it's heaven up there now. Nobody's there. Imagine those
cells with six dudes in them."

"Five minutes, gentlemen!"

Dixie and Kim and Casey hugged her good-bye. None of us guys said good-bye. I couldn't even look at her. I heard her say, "Take care, Chaz."

I just realized that I'm doing that last assignment again. And I'm still doing it wrong, mentioning the body, telling you that they killed CD the day he got out of County.

B.F. and Me

I liked him right away, just talking to him on the phone. Raspy, easygoing voice with a smile and sex in it, you know what I mean. How is it that we read people by their voices anyway? The phone company information lady is officious and patronizing and she isn't even a real person. And the guy at the cable company who says our business means a lot to them and they want to please us, you can hear the sneer in his tone.

I used to be a switchboard operator in a hospital, spent all day talking to different doctors that I never saw. We all had favorites and ones that we couldn't stand. None of us had ever seen Dr. Wright but his voice was so smooth and cool we were in love with him. If we had to page him we'd each put a dollar down on the board, would race to answer calls and be the one to get his, win the money and say, "Hell-oh there, Dr. Wright. ICU is paging you, sir." Never did see Dr. Wright in real life but when I got a job working in Emergency I got to know all the other doctors I had talked to on the phone. I soon learned that they were just as we imagined them. The best physicians were the ones who were prompt to answer, clear and polite, the worst were those who used to yell at us and say things like "Do they hire the handicapped at the switchboard?" They were the ones who let the ER see their patients, who had the Medicaid patients sent to County. Amazing how the ones with sexy voices were just as sexy in real life. But no, I can't describe how people get the quality into their voice of just waking up or of wanting to go to bed. Check out Tom Hanks's voice. Forget it. Okay, now Harvey Keitel's. And if you don't think Harvey is sexy just close your eyes.

Now I have a really nice voice. I'm a strong woman, mean even, but everyone thinks I'm really gentle because of my voice. I sound young even though I'm seventy years old. Guys at the Pottery Barn flirt with me. "Hey. I'll bet you're really gonna enjoy lying on this rug." Stuff like that.

I've been trying to get somebody to lay tiles in my bathroom. People who put ads in the paper for odd jobs, painting, etc., they don't really want to work. They all are pretty booked up right now or a machine answers with Metallica in the background and they don't return your call. After six tries B.F. was the only one who said he'd come over. He answered the phone, Yeah, this is B.F., so I said, Hey this is L.B. And he laughed, real slow. I told him I had a floor job and he said he was my man. He could come anytime. I figured he was a smart-aleck in his twenties, good-looking, with tattoos and spiky hair, a pickup truck and a dog.

He didn't show on the day he said he would but he called the next day, said something had come up, could he make it that afternoon. Sure. Later that day I saw the pickup, heard him banging on my door, but it took me a while to get there. I've got bad arthritis and also I get tangled up in my oxygen hose. Hold your horses! I yelled.

B.F. was holding on to the wall and to the banister, gasping and coughing after he climbed the three steps. He was an enormous man, tall, very fat and very old. Even when he was still outside, catching his breath, I could smell him. Tobacco and dirty wool, rank alcoholic sweat. He had bloodshot baby-blue eyes that smiled. I liked him right away.

He said he could probably use some of that air of mine. I told him he should get him a tank but he said he was afraid he'd blow himself up smoking. He came on in and headed for the bathroom. It's not like I needed to show him where it was. I live in a trailer and there aren't too many places it could be. But he just stomped off shaking the place as he walked. I watched him measure for a while then went to sit in the kitchen. I could still smell him. The pong of him was madeleine-like for me, bringing back Grandpa and Uncle John, for starters.

Bad smells can be nice. A faint odor of skunk in the woods. Horse manure at the races. One of the best parts about the tigers in zoos is the feral stench. At bullfights I always liked to sit high up, in order to see it all, like at the opera, but if you sit next to the *barrera* you can smell the bull.

B.F. was exotic to me simply because he was so dirty. I live in Boulder, where there is no dirt. No dirty people. Even all the runners look like they just got out of the shower. I wondered where he drank, because I have also never seen a dirty bar in Boulder. He seemed the kind of man who liked to talk when he drank.

He was talking to himself in the bathroom, groaning and panting as he got down on the floor to measure the linen closet. When he heaved himself back up, with a God DAMN, I swear the whole house swayed back and forth. He came out, told me I needed forty-four square feet. Can you believe it? I said. I bought forty-six! Well, you got a good eye. Two good eyes. He grinned with brown false teeth.

"You can't walk on it for seventy-two hours," he said.

"That's crazy. I never heard of such a thing."

"Well, it's a fact. The tiles need to set."

"My whole life I never heard anybody say, 'We went to a motel while the tile set.' Or 'Can I stay at your place until my tile sets?' Never once heard this mentioned."

"That's because most people who have tile laid have two bathrooms."

"So what do people do who have one?"

"Keep the carpet."

The carpet was in when I bought the trailer. Orange shag, stained.

"I can't stand that carpet."

"Don't blame you. All I'm saying is you have to stay off the tiles for seventy-two hours."

"I can't do that. I take Lasix for my heart. I'm in there twenty times a day."

"Well then you just go ahead on in there. But if the tiles shift don't you be saying it was my fault, because I lay a good tile."

We settled on a price for the job and he said he'd come on Friday morning. He was obviously sore after bending down. Gasping for air, he limped out of the house, stopping to lean on the kitchen counter and then on the stove in the living room. I followed him to the door, making the same rest stops. At the foot of the stairs he lit up a cigarette and smiled up at me. Glad to meet you. His dog waited patiently in the truck.

He never came on Friday. He didn't call, so I tried his number on Sunday. No answer. I found the newspaper page with all the other numbers. None of them answered either. I imagined a western barroom filled with tile-setters, all holding bottles or cards or glasses, their heads lying asleep on the table.

He called yesterday. I said hello and he said, "How you been, L.B.?"

"Swell, B.F. Wondering if I'd ever see you again."

"How about I stop by tomorrow?"

"Sounds good to me."

"Around ten?"

"Sure," I said. "Any time."

Wait a Minute

Sighs, the rhythms of our heartbeats, contractions of childbirth, orgasms, all flow into time just as pendulum clocks placed next to one another soon beat in unison. Fireflies in a tree flash on and off as one. The sun comes up and it goes down. The moon waxes and wanes and usually the morning paper hits the porch at six thirty-five.

Time stops when someone dies. Of course it stops for them, maybe, but for the mourners time runs amok. Death comes too soon. It forgets the tides, the days growing longer and shorter, the moon. It rips up the calendar. You aren't at your desk or on the subway or fixing dinner for the children. You're reading *People* in a surgery waiting room, or shivering outside on a balcony smoking all night long. You stare into space, sitting in your childhood bedroom with the globe on the desk. Persia, the Belgian Congo. The bad part is that when you return to your ordinary life all the routines, the marks of the day, seem like senseless lies. All is suspect, a trick to lull us, rock us back into the placid relentlessness of time.

When someone has a terminal disease, the soothing churn of time is shattered. Too fast, no time, I love you, have to finish this, tell him that. Wait a minute! I want to explain. Where is Toby, anyway? Or time turns sadistically slow. Death just hangs around while you wait for it to be night and then wait for it to be morning. Every day you've said good-bye a little. Oh just get it over with, for God's sake. You keep looking at the Arrival and Departure board. Nights are endless because you wake at the softest cough or sob, then lie awake listening to her breathe so softly, like a child. Afternoons at the bedside you know the time by the passage of sunlight, now on the Virgin of Guadalupe, now on the charcoal nude, the mirror, the carved jewelry box, dazzle on the bottle of Fracas. The *camote* man whistles in the street below and then you help your sister into the *sala* to watch Mexico City news and then U.S. news with Peter Jennings. Her cats sit on her lap. She has oxygen but still their fur makes it hard to breathe. "No! Don't take them away. Wait a minute."

Every evening after the news, Sally would cry. Weep. It probably wasn't for long but in the time warp of her illness it went on and on, painful and hoarse. I can't even remember if at first my niece Mercedes and I cried with her. I don't think so. Neither of us are criers. But we would hold her and kiss her, sing to her. We tried joking, "Maybe we should watch Tom Brokaw instead." We made her *aguas* and teas and cocoa. I can't remember when she stopped crying, soon before her death, but when she did stop it was truly horrible, the silence, and it lasted a long time.

When she cried sometimes she'd say things like "Sorry, it must be the chemo. It's sort of a reflex. Don't pay any attention." But other times she would beg us to cry with her.

"I can't, *mi Argentina*," Mercedes would say. "But my heart is crying. Since we know it is going to happen we automatically harden ourselves." This was kind of her to say. The weeping simply drove me crazy.

Once while she was crying, Sally said, "I'll never see donkeys again!" which struck us as hilariously funny. She became furious, smashed her cup and plates, our glasses and ashtray against the wall. She kicked over the table, screaming at us. Cold calculating bitches. Not a shred of compassion or pity.

"One *pinche* tear. You don't even look sad." She was smiling by now. "You're like police matrons. 'Drink this. Here's a tissue. Throw up in the basin.'"

At night I would get her ready for bed, give her pills, an injection. I'd kiss her and tuck her in. "Good night. I love you, my sister, *mi cisterna*." I slept in a little room, a closet, next to her, could hear her through the plywood wall, reading, humming, writing. Sometimes she would cry then and those were the worst times, because she tried to muffle these silent sad weepings with her pillow.

At first I would go in and try to comfort her, but that seemed to make her cry more, become more anxious. The sleeping medicine would turn around and wake her up, get her agitated and nauseous. So I would just call out to her, "Sally. Dear Sal *y pimienta*, Salsa, don't be sad." Things like that.

"Remember in Chile how Rosa put hot bricks in our beds?"

"I'd forgotten!"

"Want me to find you a brick?"

"No, *mi vida*, I'm falling asleep."

She had had a mastectomy and radiation and then for five years she was fine. Really fine. Radiant and beautiful, wildly happy with a kind man, Andrés. She and I became friends, for the first time since our hard childhood. It had felt like falling in love, the discovery of each other, how much we shared. We went to the Yucatán and to New York together. I'd go to Mexico or she would come up to Oakland. When our mother died, we spent a week in Zihuatanejo, where we talked all day and all night. We exorcised our parents and our own rivalries and I think we both grew up.

I was in Oakland when she called. The cancer was in her lungs now. Everywhere. There was no time left. *Apúrate.* Come right now!

It took me three days to quit my job, pack up, and move out. On the plane to Mexico City, I thought about how death shreds time. My ordinary life had vanished. Therapy, laps at the Y. What about lunch on Friday? Gloria's party, dentist tomorrow, laundry, pick up books at Moe's, cleaning, out of cat food, babysit grandsons Saturday, order gauze and gastrostomy buttons at work, write to August, talk to Josee, bake some scones, C.J. coming over. Even eerier was a year later clerks in the grocery or bookstore or friends I ran into on the street had not noticed that I had been gone at all.

I called Pedro, her oncologist, from the airport in Mexico, wanting to know what to expect. It had sounded like a matter of weeks or a month. "*Ni modo*," he said. "We'll continue chemo. It could be six months, a year, perhaps more."

"If you had just told me, 'I want you to come now,' I would have come," I said to her later that night.

"No, you wouldn't!" she laughed. "You are a realist. You know I have servants to do everything, and nurses, doctors, friends. You'd think I didn't need you yet. But I want you now, to help me get everything in order. I want you to cook so Alicia and Sergio will eat here. I want you to read to me and take care of me. Now is when I'm alone and scared. I need you now."

We all have mental scrapbooks. Stills. Snapshots of people we love at different times. This one is Sally in deep green running clothes, cross-legged on her bed. Skin luminescent, her green eyes limned with tears as she spoke to me. No guile or self-pity. I embraced her, grateful for her trust in me.

In Texas, when I was eight and she was three, I hated her, envied her with a violent hissing in my heart. Our grandma let me run wild, at the mercy of the other adults, but she guarded little Sally, brushed her hair and made tarts just for her, rocked her to sleep and sang "Way Down in Missoura." But I have snapshots of her even then, smiling, offering me a mud pie with an undeniable sweetness that she never lost.

In Mexico City the first months passed in a flash, like in old movies when the calendars flip up the days. Speeded-up Charlie

Chaplin carpenters pounded in the kitchen, plumbers banged in the bathroom. Men came to fix all the doorknobs and broken windows, sand the floors. Mirna, Belen and I tore into the storeroom, the *topanco*, the closets, the bookcases and drawers. We tossed out shoes and hats, dog collars, Nehru jackets. Mercedes and Alicia and I brought out all Sally's clothes and jewelry, labeled them to give to different friends.

Lazy sweet afternoons on Sally's floor, sorting photographs, reading letters, poems, gossiping, telling stories. The phone and doorbell rang all day. I screened the calls and visitors, was the one who cut them short if she was tired, or didn't if she was happy, like with Gustavo always.

When someone is first diagnosed with a fatal illness, they are deluged with calls and letters and visits. But as the months go by and the time turns into hard time, fewer people come. That's when the illness is growing and time is slow and loud. You heard the clocks and the church bells and vomiting and each raspy breath.

Sally's ex-husband Miguel and Andrés came every day, but at different times. Only once did the visits coincide. I was surprised by how the ex-husband was automatically deferred to. He had remarried long ago, but there still was his pride to consider. Andrés had been in Sally's room only a few minutes. I brought him in a coffee and pan dulce. Just as I set it on the table, Mirna came in to say, "The señor is coming!"

"Quick, into your room!" Sally said. Andrés rushed into my room, carrying his coffee and pan dulce. I had just shut him in when Miguel arrived.

"Coffee! I need coffee!" he said, so I went into my room, took the coffee and pan dulce from Andrés, and carried them in to Miguel. Andrés disappeared.

I got very weak, and had trouble walking. We thought it was *estress* (no word in Spanish for stress), but finally I fainted on the street and was taken to an emergency room. I was critically anemic from a bleeding esophageal hernia. I was there several days for blood transfusions.

I felt much stronger when I got back, but my illness had frightened Sally. Death reminded us it was still there. Time got speeded up again. I'd think she was asleep and would get up to go to bed.

"Don't go!"

"I'm just going to the bathroom, be right back." At night if she choked or coughed, I'd wake up, go in to check on her.

She was on oxygen now and rarely got out of bed. I bathed her in her room, gave her injections for pain and nausea. She drank some broth, ate crackers sometimes. Crushed ice. I put ice in a towel and smashed it smashed it smashed it against the concrete wall. Mercedes lay with her and I lay on the floor, reading to them. I'd stop when they seemed to be asleep, but they'd both say, "Don't stop!"

Bueno. "I defy anyone to say that our Becky, who has certainly some vices, has not been presented to the public in a perfectly genteel and inoffensive manner . . ."

Pedro aspirated her lung, but it still became more and more difficult for her to breathe. I decided we should really clean her room. Mercedes stayed with her in the living room while Mirna and Belen and I swept and dusted, washed the walls and windows and floors. I moved her bed so that it lay horizontally beneath the window; now she could see the sky. Belen put clean ironed sheets and soft blankets on the bed and we carried her back in. She leaned back on her pillow, the springtime sun full on her face.

"*El sol,*" Sally said. "I can feel it."

I sat against the other wall and watched her look out her window. Airplane. Birds. Jet trail. Sunset!

Much later I kissed her good night and went to my little room. The humidifier on her oxygen tank bubbled like a fountain. I waited to hear the breathing that meant she slept. Her mattress creaked. She gasped, and then moaned, breathing heavily. I listened and waited and then I heard the clink clink of curtain rings above her bed.

"Sally? Salamander, what are you doing?"

"I'm looking at the sky!"

Near her I looked out my own little window.

"*Oye*, sister . . ."

"Yes," I said.

"I can hear you. You are crying for me!"

It has been seven years since you died. Of course what I'll say next is that time has flown by. I got old. All of a sudden, *de repente*. I walk with difficulty. I even drool. I leave the door unlocked in case I die in my sleep, but it's more likely I'll go endlessly on until I get put away someplace. I am already dotty. I parked my car around the corner because there was someone in my usual spot. Later when I saw the empty spot I wondered where I had gone. It's not so strange that I talk to my cat but I feel silly because he is totally deaf.

But there's never enough time. "Real time," like the prisoners I used to teach would say, explaining how it just seemed that they had all the time in the world. The time wasn't ever theirs.

I teach in a pretty, *fresa*, mountain town now. The same Rocky Mountains Daddy used to mine, but a far cry from Butte or Coeur d'Alene. I'm lucky though. I have good friends here. I live in the foothills where deer walk dainty and modest past my window. I saw skunks mating in the moonlight; their jagged cries were like oriental instruments.

I miss my sons and their families. I see them maybe once a year and that's always great, but I'm no longer really a part of their lives. Or of your children's either. Although Mercedes and Enrique came here to get married!

So many others have gone. I used to think it was funny when someone said, "I lost my husband." But that is how it feels. Someone is missing. Paul, Aunt Chata, Buddy. I understand how people believe in ghosts or have séances to call the dead. I go for months without thinking of anyone but the living, and then Buddy will come with a joke, or there you vividly are, evoked by a tango or an *agua de sandia*. If only you could speak to me. You're as bad as my deaf cat.

You last arrived a few days after the blizzard. Ice and snow still covered the ground, but we had a fluke of a warm day. Squirrels and magpies were chattering and sparrows and finches sang on the bare trees. I opened all the doors and curtains. I drank tea at the kitchen table feeling the sun on my back. Wasps came out of the nest on the front porch, floated sleepily through my house, buzzing in drowsy circles all around the kitchen. Just at this time the smoke alarm battery went dead, so it began to chirp like a summer cricket. The sun touched the teapot and the flour jar, the silver vase of stock.

A lazy illumination, like a Mexican afternoon in your room. I could see the sun in your face.

Homing

I have never seen the crows leave the tree in the morning but every evening about a half an hour before dark, they start flying in from all over town. There may be regular herders who swoop around in the sky for blocks calling for the others to come home, or perhaps each one circles around gathering stragglers before it pops into the tree. I've watched enough, you'd think I could tell by now. But I only see crows, dozens of crows, flying in from every direction from far away and five or six circling like over O'Hare, calling calling, and then in a split second suddenly it is silent and no crows are to be seen. The tree looks like an ordinary maple tree. No way you'd know there were so many birds in there.

I happened to be on my front porch when I first saw them. I had been downtown and was on my portable oxygen tank, sitting on the porch swing to look at the evening light. Usually I sit out on the back porch where my regular hose reaches. Sometimes I watch the news at that time or fix dinner. What I mean is I could easily have no idea that that particular maple tree is filled with crows at sundown.

Do they all leave together then for still another tree to sleep in, higher up on Mount Sanitas? Maybe, because I'm up early, sitting at the window facing the foothills, and I have never seen them come out of the tree. I see deer though, going up into the hills of

Mount Sanitas and Dakota Ridge, and the rising sun glowing pink against the rocks. If there is snow and it is very cold, there is alpenglow, when the ice crystals turn the color of the morning into stained glass pink, neon coral.

Of course it is winter now. The tree is bare and there are no crows. I'm just thinking about the crows. It's hard for me to walk so the few blocks uphill would be too much for me. I could drive, I suppose, like Buster Keaton having his chauffeur drive him across the street. But I think it would be too dark then to see the birds inside the tree.

I don't know why I even brought this up. Magpies flash now blue, green against the snow. They have a similar bossy shriek. Of course I could get a book or call somebody and find out about the nesting habits of crows. But what bothers me is that I only accidentally noticed them. What else have I missed? How many times in my life have I been, so to speak, on the back porch, not the front porch? What would have been said to me that I failed to hear? What love might there have been that I didn't feel?

These are pointless questions. The only reason I have lived so long is that I let go of my past. Shut the door on grief on regret on remorse. If I let them in, just one self-indulgent crack, whap, the door will fling open gales of pain ripping through my heart blinding my eyes with shame breaking cups and bottles knocking down jars shattering windows stumbling bloody on spilled sugar and broken glass terrified gagging until with a final shudder and sob I shut the heavy door. Pick up the pieces one more time.

Maybe this is not so dangerous a thing to do, to let the past in with the preface "What if?" What if I had spoken with Paul before he left? What if I had asked for help? What if I had married H? Sitting here, looking out the window toward the tree where now there are no branches or crows, the answers to each "what if" are strangely reassuring. They could not have happened, this what if, that what if. Everything good or bad that has occurred in my life has been predictable and inevitable, especially the choices and actions that have made sure I am now utterly alone.

But what if I were to go way back, to before we moved to South América? What if Dr. Mock had said I couldn't leave Arizona for a year, that I needed extensive therapy and adjustments to my brace, possibly surgery for my scoliosis? I would have joined my family the following year. What if I had lived with the Wilsons in Patagonia, went weekly to the orthopedist's in Tucson, reading *Emma* or *Jane Eyre* on the hot bus ride?

The Wilsons had five children, all of them old enough to work at the General Store or the Sweet Shop the Wilsons owned. I worked before and after school at the Sweet Shop with Dot, and shared the attic room with her. Dot was seventeen, the oldest child. Woman, really. She looked like a woman in the movies the way she put on pancake makeup and blotted her lipstick, blew smoke out of her nose. We slept together on the hay mattress covered with old quilts. I learned not to bother her, to lie quiet, thrilled by her smells. She tamed her curly red hair with Wildroot oil, smeared Noxzema on her face at night, and always put Tweed on her wrists and behind her ears. She smelled of cigarettes and sweat and Mum deodorant and what I later would learn was sex. We both smelled like old grease because we cooked hamburgers and fries at the Sweet Shop until it closed at ten. We walked home across the main street and the train tracks quickly past the Frontier saloon and down the street to her folks' house. The Wilson house was the prettiest in town. A big two-story white house with a picket fence and a garden and a lawn. Most of the houses in Patagonia were small and ugly. Transient mining town houses painted that weird train station mining camp butterscotch brown. Most of the people worked up the mountain at the Trench and Flux mines where my father had been superintendent. Now he was an ore buyer in Chile, Peru, and Bolivia. He hadn't wanted to go, didn't want to leave the mines, working down in the mines.

My mother had convinced him to go, everybody had. It was a big opportunity and we would be very rich.

He paid the Wilsons for my room and board, but they all decided it would be good for my character for me to work just like the other kids. We all worked hard, too, especially Dot and me, because we worked so late and then got up at five a.m. We opened up for the three buses of miners going from Nogales to the Trench. The buses arrived within fifteen minutes of one another; the miners had just enough time for one or two coffees and some doughnuts. They'd thank us and wave on their way out, *Hasta luego!* We'd finish washing up, make ourselves sandwiches for lunch. Mrs. Wilson got there to take over and we'd go to school. I was still in the grade school up on the hill. Dot was a junior.

When we got home at night she'd sneak back out to see her boyfriend, Sextus. He lived on a ranch in Sonoita, had left school to help his dad. I don't know what time she got back in. I was asleep the minute my head was on my pillow. The minute I hit the hay! I loved the idea of a hay mattress like in *Heidi*. The hay felt good and smelled good. It always seemed like I had just closed my eyes when Dot was shaking me to wake up. She would already have washed or showered and dressed, and while I did she brushed her hair into a pageboy and made up her face. "What are you staring at? Fix up the bed if you got nothing else to do." She really didn't like me, but I didn't like her back so I didn't care. On the way to the Sweet Shop, she'd tell me over and over I better keep quiet about her seeing Sextus, her daddy would kill her. Everybody in town knew about her and Sextus already or I would have told somebody, not her folks, but somebody, just because she was so mean. She was just mean on principle. She figured she should hate this kid they put up in her own room. The truth was we got along well otherwise, grinning and laughing, good teamwork, slicing onions, making sodas, flipping burgers. Both of us fast and efficient, both of us enjoyed people, the kind Mexican miners mostly, who joked and teased us in the mornings. After school, kids from school and town people came in, for sodas or sundaes, to play the jukebox and the pinball machine. We served hamburgers, chili dogs, grilled cheese. We had tuna and egg salad and potato salad and coleslaw Mrs. Wilson made. The most popular dish though was the chili Willie Torres's mother brought over every afternoon. Red chili in the winter, pork and green chilis in summer. Stacks of flour tortillas we'd warm on the grill.

One reason Dot and I worked so hard and so fast was we had an unspoken agreement that after we did all the dishes and cleaned the grill, she'd go out back with Sextus and I'd handle the few pie and coffee orders between nine and ten. Mostly I did homework with Willie Torres.

Willie worked until nine at the assayer's office next door. We had been in the same grade together at school and I had made friends with him there. On Saturday mornings I'd come down with my dad in the pickup to get groceries and mail for the four or five families that lived on the mountain by the Trench mine. After he did all the buying and loading, Daddy would stop by Mr. Wise's Assay Office. They'd drink coffee and talk about ore, mines, veins? I'm sorry, I didn't pay attention. I know it was about minerals. Willie was a different person in the office. He was shy at school, had come from Mexico when he was eight, so even though he was smarter than Mrs. Boosinger, he had trouble reading and writing sometimes. His first valentine to me was "Be my sweat-hart." Nobody made fun of him though, like they did of me and my back brace, yelling, "Timber!" when I came in because I was so tall. He was tall too, had an Indian face, high cheekbones and dark eyes. His clothes were clean but shabby and too small, his straight black hair long and raggedy, cut by his mother. When I read *Wuthering Heights*, Heathcliff looked like Willie, wild and brave.

In the Assay Office he seemed to know everything. He was going to be a geologist when he grew up. He showed me how to

spot gold and fool's gold and silver. That first day my father asked
what we were talking about. I showed him what I had learned.
"This is copper. Quartz. Lead. Zinc."

"Wonderful!" he said, really pleased. During the drive home I
got a geological lecture on the land all the way up to the mine.

On other Saturdays Willie showed me more rocks. "This is
mica. This rock is shale, this is limestone." He explained mining
maps to me. We'd paw through boxes filled with fossils. He and
Mr. Wise went out looking for them. "Hey, this one! Look at this
leaf!" I didn't realize I loved Willie since our closeness was so quiet,
had nothing to do with the love girls talked about all the time, not
like romance or crushes or ooh Jeeny loves Marvin.

In the Sweet Shop we'd close the blinds, sit at the counter doing
our homework for that last hour, eating hot fudge sundaes. He
could trip the jukebox to keep playing "Slow Boat to China," "Cry,"
and "Texarkana Baby" over and over. He was good at arithmetic
and algebra and I was good with words so we helped each other. We
leaned against each other, our legs hooked around the stools. He
even hooked his elbow onto the part of my back brace that stuck
out and I didn't mind. Usually if I saw that anybody even noticed
the brace under my clothes I'd feel sick with embarrassment.

More than anything else we shared being sleepy. We never
said, "Gee, I'm sleepy. Aren't you sleepy?" We were just tired together, leaned yawning together at the Sweet Shop. Yawned and
smiled across the room at school.

His father was killed in a cave-in at the Flux mine. My father
had been trying to get it shut down ever since we got to Arizona.
That was his job for years, checking on mines to see if the veins
were running out or if they were unsafe. They called him "Shut-
'em-down Brown." I waited in the pickup truck when he went to
tell Willie's mother. This was before I knew Willie. My father
cried all the way home from town, which frightened me. It was
Willie who later told me my father had fought to get pensions for

the miners and their families, how much that helped his mother. She had five other children, did washing and cooking for people.

Willie was up as early as I was, chopping wood, getting his brothers and sisters breakfast. Civics class was the worst, impossible to stay awake, to be interested. It came at three o'clock. One endless hour. In the winter the woodstove steamed up the windows and our cheeks would be blazing red. Mrs. Boosinger blazed under her two purple spots of rouge. In summer with the windows open and flies buzzing around, bees humming and the clock ticking so drowsy so hot, she'd be talking talking about the First Amendment and whap! bang her ruler on the table. "Wake up! Wake up! You two jellyfish have no backbone! Sit up! Open your eyes. Jellyfish!" She once thought I was asleep but I was only resting my eyes. She said, "Lulu, who is the secretary of state?"

"Acheson, ma'am." That surprised her.

"Willie, who is the secretary of agriculture?"

"Topeka and Santa Fe?"

I think we both were drunk with sleepiness. Every time she'd whack us on the head with the civics book we'd laugh harder. She sent him to the hall and me to the cloakroom, found us both curled up fast asleep after class.

A few times Sextus climbed up to Dot's room. I'd hear him whisper, "The kid asleep?"

"Out like a light." And it was true. No matter how hard I tried to stay awake to watch what they did, I'd fall asleep.

A weird thing happened to me this week. I could see these small quick crows flying just past my left eye. I'd turn but they would be gone. And when I closed my eyes, lights would flash past like motorcycles on the highway zooming by. I thought I was hallucinating or had cancer of the eye, but the doctor said they were floaters, that lots of people get them.

"How can there be lights in the dark?" I asked, as confused as I used to be about the refrigerator. He said that my eye told the brain there was light so my brain believed it. Please don't laugh. This merely exacerbated the crow situation. It brought up the tree falling in the forest all over again too. Maybe my eyes just told my brain about crows in the maple tree.

One Sunday morning I woke up and Sextus was sleeping on the other side of Dot. I might have been more interested if they had been a more attractive couple. He had a buzz cut and pimples, white eyebrows and a huge Adam's apple. He was a champion roper and barrel rider though, and his hog had won three years in a row at 4-H. Dot was homely, just plain homely. All the paint she put on didn't even make her look cheap, it only accentuated her little brown eyes and big mouth that prominent eyeteeth kept open in a permanent semi-snarl. I shook her gently and pointed to Sextus. "Oh Jesus wept," she said and woke him up. He was out the window, down the cottonwood and gone in seconds. Dot pinned me against the hay, made me swear not to say a word. "Hey, Dot, I haven't so far, have I?"

"You do, I'll tell on you and the Mexkin." I was shaken, she sounded like my mother.

It was nice not worrying about my mother. I was a nicer person now. Not surly or sullen. Polite and helpful. I didn't spill or break or drop things like at home. I never wanted to leave. Mr. and Mrs. Wilson kept saying I was a sweet girl, a good worker, and how they felt I was one of the family. We had family dinners on Sundays. Dot and I worked until noon while they went to church, then we closed up, went home, and helped make dinner. Mr. Wilson said grace. The boys poked each other and laughed, talked about basketball, and we all talked about, well, I don't remember. Maybe we didn't actually talk much, but it was friendly. We said, "Please pass the butter." "Gravy?" My favorite part was that I had my own napkin and napkin ring that went on the sideboard with everyone else's.

On Saturdays I got a ride to Nogales and then a bus to Tucson.
The doctors put me in a medieval painful traction for hours, until
I couldn't take it anymore. They measured me, checked for nerve
damage by sticking pins in me, hitting my legs and feet with ham-
mers. They adjusted the brace and the lift on my shoe. It looked
like they were coming to a decision. Different doctors squinted at
my X-rays. The famous one they had been waiting for said my verte-
brae were too close to my spinal cord. Surgery could cause paralysis,
shock to all the organs that had compensated for the curvature. It
would be expensive, not just the surgery, but during recovery I
would have to lie immobile on my stomach for five months. I was
glad they didn't seem to want surgery. I was sure that if they straightened my spine I would be eight feet tall. But I didn't want them to
stop checking me; I didn't want to go to Chile. They let me have
one of the X-rays that showed a silver heart Willie gave me. My
S-shaped spine, my heart in the wrong place and his heart right in
the center. Willie put it up in a little window in the back of the
Assay Office.

Some Saturday nights there were barn dances, way out in El-
gin or Sonoita. In barns. Everybody from miles and miles would go,
old people, young people, babies, dogs. Guests from dude ranches.
All of the women brought things to eat. Fried chicken and potato
salad, cakes and pies and punch. The men would go out in bunches
and hang around their pickups, drinking. Some women too, my
mother always did. High school kids got drunk and threw up, got
caught necking. Old ladies danced with each other and children.
Everybody danced. Two-step mostly, but some slow dances and
jitterbug. Some square dances and Mexican dances like *La Varso-
viana*. In English it's "Put your little foot, put your little foot right
there," and you skip skip and whirl around. They played everything
from "Night and Day" to "Detour, There's a Muddy Road Ahead,"
"Jalisco no te Rajes" to "Do the Hucklebuck." Different bands every
time but with the same kind of mix. Where did those ragtag won-

derful musicians come from? *Pachuco* horn and guiro players, big-hatted country guitarists, bebop drummers, piano players that looked like Fred Astaire. The closest I ever heard anything come to those little bands was at the Five Spot in the late fifties. Ornette Coleman's "Ramblin'." Everybody raving how new and far-out he was. Sounded Tex-Mex to me, like a good Sonoita hoedown.

The staid pioneer-type housewives got all dressed up for the dances. Toni permanents and rouge, high heels. The men were leathery hardworking ranchers or miners, brought up in the Depression. Serious God-fearing workers. I loved to see the faces of the miners. The men I'd see coming off a shift dirty and drawn now red-faced and carefree, belting out an "Ah-hah, San Antone!" or an "*Aí, Aí, Aí,*" because not only did everybody dance, everybody sang and hollered too. At intervals Mr. and Mrs. Wilson would slow down to pant, "Have you seen Dot?"

Willie's mom went to the dances with a group of friends. She danced every dance, always in a pretty dress, her hair up, her crucifix flying. She was beautiful and young. Ladylike too. She didn't dance close on slow dances or go out to the pickups. No, I didn't notice that. But all the Patagonia women did and mentioned it in her favor. They also said she wouldn't be a widow for long. When I asked Willie why he never came, he said he didn't know how to dance and besides he had to watch the kids. But other children go, why couldn't they come. No, he said. His mother needed to have fun, get away from them sometimes.

"Well, how 'bout you?"

"I don't care that much. I'm not being unselfish. I want my ma to find another husband as much as she does," he said.

If diamond drillers were in town the dances really livened up. I don't know if there still are diamond drillers, but in those mining days they were a special breed. Always two of them roaring into the camp ninety miles an hour in a cloud of dust. Their cars were not pickups or regular sedans but sleek two-seaters with glossy paint that shined through the dust. The men didn't wear denim or khakis like the ranchers or miners. Maybe they did when they went down in the mines, but traveling or at dances they wore dark suits and silky shirts and ties. Their hair was long, combed in a pompadour, with long sideburns, a mustache sometimes. Even though I saw them only at western mines, their license plates usually were from Tennessee or Alabama or West Virginia. They never stayed long, a week at the most. They got paid more than brain surgeons, my father said. They were the ones who opened a good vein or found one, I think. I do know they were important and their jobs were dangerous. They looked dangerous and, I know now, sexy. Cool and arrogant, they had the aura of matadors, bank robbers, relief pitchers. Every woman, old ones, young ones, at the barn dances wanted to dance with a diamond driller. I did. The drillers always wanted to dance with Willie's mother. Somebody's wife or sister who had had too much to drink invariably ended up outside with one of them and then there was a bloody fight, with all the men streaming out of the barn. The fights always ended with somebody shooting a gun off in the air and the drillers high-tailing off into the night, the wounded gallants returning to the dance with a swollen jaw or a blackening eye. The band would play something like "You Two-Timed Me One Time Too Often."

One Sunday afternoon Mr. Wise drove me and Willie up to the mine, to see our old house. I got homesick then, smelling my daddy's Mr. Lincoln roses, walking around under the old oaks. Rocky crags all around and views out into the valleys and to Mount Baldy. The hawks and jays were there and the ticky-tick drum cymbal sound of the pulleys in the mill. I missed my family and tried not to cry, but I cried anyway. Mr. Wise gave me a hug, said not to worry, I'd probably be going to join them once school was out. I looked at Willie. He jerked his head at me to look at the doe and fawns that gazed at us, only a few feet away. "They don't want you to go," he said.

So I probably would have gone to South America. But then there was a terrible earthquake in Chile, a national disaster, and my family was killed. I went on living in Patagonia, Arizona, with the Wilsons. After high school I got a scholarship to the University of Arizona where I studied journalism. Willie got a scholarship too, and had a double major in geology and art. We were married after graduation. Willie got a job at the Trench and I worked for the *Nogales Star* until our first son, Silver, was born. We lived in Mrs. Boosinger's beautiful old adobe house (she had died by then) up in the mountains, in an apple orchard near Harshaw.

I know it sounds pretty corny, but Willie and I lived happily ever after.

What if that had happened, the earthquake? I know what. This is the problem with "what ifs." Sooner or later you hit a snag. I wouldn't have been able to stay in Patagonia. I'd have ended up in Amarillo, Texas. Flat space and silos and sky and tumbleweeds, not a mountain in sight. Living with Uncle David and Aunt Harriet and my great-grandmother Grey. They would have thought of me as a problem. A cross to bear. There would be a lot of what they would call "acting out," and the counselor would refer to as cries for help. After my release from the juvenile detention center it would not be long before I would elope with a diamond driller who was passing through town, headed for Montana, and, can you believe it? My life would have ended up exactly as it has now, under the limestone rocks of Dakota Ridge, with crows.

A Note on Lucia Berlin

THE WRITING

Lucia Berlin (1936–2004, pronunciation: Lu-see-a) published seventy-six short stories during her lifetime. Most, but not all, were collected in three volumes from Black Sparrow Press: *Homesick* (1991), *So Long* (1993), and *Where I Live Now* (1999). These gathered from previous collections of 1980, 1984, and 1987, and presented newer work.

Early publication commenced when she was twenty-four, in Saul Bellow's journal *The Noble Savage* and in *The New Strand*. Later stories appeared in the *Atlantic Monthly*, *New American Writing*, and countless smaller magazines. *Homesick* won an American Book Award.

Berlin worked brilliantly but sporadically throughout the 1960s, 1970s, and most of the 1980s. By the late '80s, her four sons were grown and she had overcome a lifelong problem with alcoholism (her accounts of its horrors, its drunk tanks and DTs and occasional hilarity, occupy a particular corner of her work). Thereafter she remained productive up to the time of her early death.

THE LIFE

Berlin was born Lucia Brown in Alaska in 1936. Her father was in the mining industry and her earliest years were spent in the mining camps and towns of Idaho, Kentucky, and Montana.

In 1941, Berlin's father went off to the war, and her mother moved Lucia and her younger sister to El Paso, where their grandfather was a prominent, but besotted, dentist.

Soon after the war, Berlin's father moved the family to Santiago, Chile, and she embarked on what would become twenty-five years of a rather flamboyant existence. In Santiago, she attended cotillions and balls, had her first cigarette lit by Prince Aly Khan, finished school, and served as the default hostess for her father's society gatherings. Most evenings, her mother retired early with a bottle.

By the age of ten, Lucia had scoliosis, a painful spinal condition that became lifelong and often necessitated a steel brace.

In 1955 she enrolled at the University of New Mexico. By now fluent in Spanish, she studied with the novelist Ramon Sender. She soon married and had two sons. By the birth of the second, her sculptor husband was gone. Berlin completed her degree and, still in Albuquerque, met the poet Edward Dorn, a key figure in her life. She also met Dorn's teacher from Black Mountain College, the writer Robert Creeley, and two of his Harvard classmates, Race Newton and Buddy Berlin, both jazz musicians. And she began to write.

Newton, a pianist, married Berlin in 1958. (Her earliest stories appeared under the name Lucia Newton.) The next year, they and the children moved to a loft in New York. Race worked steadily and the couple became friends with their neighbors Denise Levertov and Mitchell Goodman, as well as other poets and artists including John Altoon, Diane di Prima, and Amiri Baraka (then LeRoi Jones).

In 1960, Berlin and her sons left Newton and New York, and traveled with their friend Buddy Berlin to Mexico, where he became her third husband. Buddy was charismatic and affluent, but he also proved to be an addict. During the years 1961–68, two more sons were born.

By 1968, the Berlins were divorced and Lucia was working on a master's degree at the University of New Mexico. She was employed as a substitute teacher. She never remarried.

The years 1971–94 were spent in Berkeley and Oakland, California. Berlin worked as a high school teacher, switchboard operator, hospital ward clerk, cleaning woman, and physician's assistant while writing, raising her four sons, drinking, and finally, prevailing over her alcoholism. She spent much of 1991 and 1992 in Mexico City, where her sister was dying of cancer. Her mother had died in 1986, a probable suicide.

In 1994, Edward Dorn brought Berlin to the University of Colorado, and she spent the next six years in Boulder as a visiting writer and, ultimately, associate professor. She became a remarkably popular and beloved teacher, and in just her second year, won the university's award for teaching excellence.

During the Boulder years she thrived in a close community that included Dorn and his wife, Jennie, Anselm Hollo, and her old pal Bobbie Louise Hawkins. The poet Kenward Elmslie became, like the prose writer Stephen Emerson, a fast friend.

Her health failing (the scoliosis had led to a punctured lung, and by the mid-1990s she was never without an oxygen tank), she retired in 2000 and the next year moved to Los Angeles at the encouragement of her sons, several of whom were there. She fought a successful battle against cancer, but died in 2004, in Marina del Rey.

2 1982 02944 20

Acknowledgments

Throughout the several years that have gone into this book, support, enthusiasm, and effort have come from many quarters, and despite an inherent sadness, the process has often brought actual joy. Would that Lucia could know.

Profuse thanks to the publishers of previous volumes, including several who can no longer accept them. Michael Myers and Holbrook Teter (Zephyrus Image), Eileen and Bob Callahan (Turtle Island), Michael Wolfe (Tombouctou), Alastair Johnston (Poltroon), and John Martin and David Godine (Black Sparrow) make up the honor roll. All who could cooperated generously.

The writers Barry Gifford and Michael Wolfe spearheaded the effort behind the collection at hand. They, together with Jenny Dorn, Jeff Berlin, Gayle Davies, Katherine Fausset, Emily Bell, and Lydia Davis, were unstinting and expert in their work on behalf of the book. At FSG, an exemplary and wide-ranging team joined Emily, contributing with élan and commitment. I think you all know how grateful Lucia would be. Please know that I am as well.

—S.E.